3/23

How I'll Kill You

How I'll Kill You

REN DeSTEFANO

BERKLEY
NEW YORK

BERKLEY
An imprint of Penguin Random House LLC
penguinrandomhouse.com

Library of Congress Cataloging-in-Publication Data

Names: DeStefano, Ren, author.
Title: How I'll kill you / Ren DeStefano.
Other titles: How I will kill you
Description: New York : Berkley, [2023]
Identifiers: LCCN 2022026266 (print) | LCCN 2022026267 (ebook) |
ISBN 9780593438305 (hardcover) | ISBN 9780593438329 (ebook)
Subjects: LCGFT: Thrillers (Fiction) | Novels.
Classification: LCC PS3604.E7644 H69 2023 (print) |
LCC PS3604.E7644 (ebook) | DDC 813/.6--dc23/eng/20220702
LC record available at https://lccn.loc.gov/2022026266
LC ebook record available at https://lccn.loc.gov/2022026267

Printed in the United States of America
1st Printing

Interior art: Map © Viktor Shumatov / Shutterstock
Book design by Alison Cnockaert

For S.T., who is nothing at all like the siblings in this book

. . . and, when the time comes to let it go . . . let it go.

—MARY OLIVER

How I'll Kill You

1

"WHAT ABOUT THAT ONE?"

My sister whispers into the phone, as though anyone but me can hear her. She's excited, and I feel my own heart starting to race at the prospect of what's about to come. I've only helped identify the mark before. I've never picked one for myself.

I'm sitting alone in a booth at the roadside diner, cradling a luke-warm cup of black coffee. It's Saturday and there's a lunch rush. Forks and plates and laughter all around me. A little girl keeps turning in her booth to smile at me. She holds up the drawing she's made on her paper place mat and I flash her a thumbs-up. She giggles and turns back to her family.

"Which?" I ask. My Bluetooth headset is hidden by my hair. When I look through the window, I catch my faded reflection. Dark curls. Small-rimmed glasses with slender frames. They're cheap readers I bought in a gas station six states back, and even though they're the lightest corrective lenses I could find, my vision is still blurry when I look through them. Beggars can't be choosers. We were limited to places that wouldn't have surveillance cameras, which meant only stopping for gas in the middle of nowhere.

I don't look like myself. It took an hour to curl my wavy hair, the curling iron charged in the car's cigarette lighter. I burned my neck twice, and I can feel the sore starting to rub against the collar of my blouse.

My identical sister is watching from the silver car in the parking lot. Even with these lenses, I see everything, and so does she. No one draws a breath near us that we don't know about.

From where she's parked, my sister watches me. Every mirror in the car is adjusted just so. I chose a seat by the only window with broken blinds.

"Red jacket at the bar," she says.

I know who she means. Red Jacket has been sitting there since I ordered my first refill. He touches the straw in his half-empty glass of ice water and scrolls through his phone. It's been a good ten minutes and he hasn't ordered anything. I shake my head. No good. He's waiting for someone. Probably a date. He doesn't have a wedding band. Wives are messy but girlfriends are even messier. Worse yet—siblings. The best mark is someone who is utterly and completely alone.

Maybe this diner was a bad idea. I've been in Rainwood for less than two days, and already I can see that it's a family town. This place is crawling with kids. Everyone is dressed like they're going to church.

The bell rings as a new patron opens the door, and I raise my eyes over the rims of my glasses.

He enters the diner shrouded in a beam of afternoon Arizona sun. For a moment I think he's looking at me, but then I realize he's eyeing the motorcycle in the parking lot through my window. His? No. He's got car keys in his hand. No helmet, and his hair is neatly trimmed and combed. He keeps it short, but I can see that it would be curly if he let it go. Thick chestnut waves are just starting to form, likely soon to be cut short.

He's got a square jaw, cheeks flushed by the waxing summer heat. Muscles and a blue button-up shirt. His eyes are bright and brown, lit up like there's a sun behind them. All of him glowing.

I imagine what he will be like: He has a mom who loves him. He calls her on Sundays. He crouches down to pet dogs when they strain on the owner's leash to sniff his shoes. He drives with the windows down and the sun beating hard on his skin, and he sings along and knows all the words. Our eyes will meet from across the room at a dinner party and he'll wink at me before turning back to his conversation.

There's a girl somewhere out there who broke his heart. He still feels it, a little knife twisting deep in his chest when he's reminded of her. But he'll never let on. He won't tell me about his past for a long, long time. After spending the day together, we'll sit in comfortable silence and he'll feel vulnerable, and he'll take a deep breath and say, *Can we talk?*

Moments yet to come flick through my head like shutter clicks from an antique camera, and I realize that he has always been in me.

An old doo-wop song is playing softly, barely audible amid the din, and at once it's as though a church choir is humming it just for us.

He doesn't see me because he isn't supposed to. Not yet. I am just a tiny little planet in a black, black galaxy, surrounded by debris and dead stars. But I see him, and that's all that matters.

I stare down at my coffee. The neon light swims like a wobbly moon on the dark surface. I can feel my sister watching me, waiting for me to speak.

I say, "I found him."

There are about a thousand ways I could do it. Slice a box cutter through his jugular or slip antifreeze into his coffee so it happens slow. I don't know how I'll kill him yet, but I know that, for him, I'll come up with something special.

I leave cash on the table for my coffee and a tip, and nobody notices me when I slip outside to meet Moody in the car.

Moody and I have always been especially close. Before the first murder, we talked about it. We composed stories in our heads and then shared them with each other, adding to each other's ideas with new details. *"Yeah, yeah, I like that!"* and *"I bet it would smell like . . ."* They were just fantasies. Our first fantasized victim was the counselor at Moody's group home, a wiry man with red hair who never smiled. He told Moody that he was tired of her bullshit and that was why she could never find a permanent placement.

"I'd slash his throat," Moody had snarled at me. She wrote about it with red pen in a peace-sign journal, and I added to it with my thin purple Sharpie, until over the weeks we had composed a little novel in rainbow colors of all the ways he would die. Next, a man I saw on the news who left his dog tied to a fence to die in the Texas heat. And then Moody's foster father. When we were first separated at age five, I went to live with a family in a blue house with rosebushes out front, and Moody was sent to a couple who collected foster children for the state checks. Her foster father spent all day in a recliner that gave him a full view of the kitchen, and he'd shoot his BB gun at her whenever she tried to open the fridge between meals.

Those fantasies and that shared journal bonded us through years in which we were utterly powerless. They connected us so that we never felt alone.

Now we're driving through endless desert. Already I love the landscape, bare and open and honest. Just dirt and sky. I bet it never rains here when monsoon season is over, and the dry ground is ever-shifting, and the wind will blow away my tracks. I could walk for hours across that yawning brown earth; I could splatter it with blood and fat drops of sweat. The heavy, fragrant kind of sweat that comes only when you've really exhausted yourself and your muscles burn. When you've earned it. And by morning that ground would all be clean again, as though I'd never existed at all.

We're a good five miles out from the diner before my sister looks at me. We are completely identical, right down to the curls she worked into her own hair after I'd finished with the curling iron this morning. We do this in case one of us needs to pretend to be the other in a pinch. She's wearing oversize sunglasses that hide most of her face and she takes a deep breath. Gratified. Tasting the air. Committing this day to her memory so that we'll be able to share it forever. Years from now, we'll huddle up and whisper and giggle about that day at the diner when I found my first mark. We'll live inside it like a snow globe: The cacti in the distance. The lizard running across the road, narrowly avoiding our tire. The mark's license plate and his green Buick gleaming hot in the parking lot.

My sister didn't see the mark's eyes, though. That part is just for me. That otherworldly deep brown that was practically glowing. *Look at me*, I'd thought, even though I knew he couldn't. It would ruin everything if he'd noticed me.

Those eyes. I feel warm at the memory, lines of nerves shooting electric up and down my legs.

My sister says, "I'm proud of you."

She breaks me out of my daydream, but still I smile, feeling like a little girl. Her approval means everything to me. Even though we're the same age, I've always felt like I was the youngest. More naïve than

I should be. Unlike my sister Moody, who wears her body with confidence. She is sweet first, and then before you realize you've fallen for her, she is sharp and deadly. I would pity the men she's left in her wake if their hearts had meant anything to me.

"You did that all on your own." Her fingers flex and tighten on the steering wheel. "You showed great instincts, Sissy."

"Sissy" is what she's called me since we were babies, and it's as real a name as any I've ever been called, but it's a secret that we don't share with outsiders. Town after town, I adopt whatever name is on the IDs we are able to make up. Now that we're in Arizona, I'll be Jade Johnson. Johnson is one of the three most common names in the state. Google "Jade Johnson" and you'll get a thousand results. Makes it easy to fake an identity and disappear before things get hairy.

"I just *felt* him, Moody," I say. "It's like we talked about." I'm breathless. Butterflies fill up my chest and spread their wings. "He walked into the room and I could see everything that was about to happen."

Moody laughs. "All right, but you know that's only half of it." She nods to the open road. "We've been driving for a while. See anything that stands out yet?"

I force myself to be alert. I look at the paper map laid out in my lap. It came with the car and I don't think it was ever unfolded before I opened it. But we can't use a smartphone for this part. We left it back at the apartment, so if anything happens, I can say I was home.

"Pull over here at the ten-mile marker," I say.

"You sure?" Moody raises her eyebrows over her glasses. "It's really out in the open. You'll have to drag him a long way."

"No, I won't," I say, proud of how sure I sound.

She veers over. There's nobody around. We're miles out from anything, but I know that this won't be true for long. I've done my research. This land will be cluttered in a year. Modular homes, made to order, on brand-new roads carved like black snakes into the desert. People will be born here. Raise their children here. But right now, for just a little while longer, it's nothing but me and Moody and the lizards.

I climb out of the car. The door slams as Moody gets out behind me. She stands beside me, and together we look up at the massive white sign.

COMING SOON: RAINWOOD EAST SUBDIVISION

I feel Moody's smile. "You clever bitch," she says, and wraps her arms around my shoulders.

This day is wonderful and warm. I feel like I've just been kissed. I feel like I've just burst through the ribbon at the finish line of a triathlon.

"Walk me through it," Moody says, letting go of me.

"I drove by yesterday while you were still asleep," I say. I point to the cranes in the distance. Beams are neatly piled. A cement mixer stands idle. "I'll have to keep a close eye on the papers and see how the development is coming along. They'll do the roads first. I could bury him where they pour the asphalt."

"What are the risks?" Moody asks, challenging me.

"Before they pour the asphalt, they'll excavate the soil," I say. "Anything soft, like pebbles or loose dirt, will be packed down. I'll have to bury him before they do that, but so deep they never reach him when they start to excavate."

"What if they pave right after?" Moody asks.

"They won't," I say. "Once the asphalt is poured, it has to be compacted right away. For something so big as a subdivision, it'll take all day. They'll excavate and do the prep the day before."

I wait for Moody to give me a hypothetical challenge, but she crouches low, hiding herself behind the front tire on the passenger side. A second later, I see the red pickup truck slow to a stop on the opposite side of the road.

The driver rolls down his window. He's old enough to be my father, with a full head of silver hair, a white wifebeater, and arms like tree trunks. "Afternoon, honey," he says. "Did you get yourself a flat tire?"

He hands me the explanation so that I don't have to come up with one myself. I gnaw pensively on my lip. "I think I hit a nail," I say. "But it's fine. I called my dad."

I'm twenty-five, but I look much younger. If I fidget and raise my shoulders shyly, I'm still in high school. I've got finals coming up, a boyfriend who kisses me clumsily, but I'm too innocent to sleep with him until we're married. I know nothing about life, and I see all older men like they're father figures.

I fall easily into these roles because I have to play them all the time. The man buys it a little too much. He gives me an endearing smile that makes my stomach lurch. He is ruining my perfect day with his sweaty, flushed face. He puts his truck in park, turns off the ignition.

Fuck.

"Get rid of him," Moody hisses at my ankles. My eyes flit to her for just a second. *I'm trying.*

"I bet I can get you up and running before he gets here," the man says. He's huge. Probably muscular back in his prime, but flabby now, with a round gut that hangs over his faded jeans. "Which tire?"

"The front driver's side," I say, sprinting around the car and away from Moody's furious eyes. I pop the trunk, panic setting in. *Stupid*, I tell myself. Stopping here was so stupid. I just had to make Moody pull over so I could gloat about my great idea, and now we've been seen.

Deep breath. I can get us through this. He's just going to put the spare tire on and then preen about what a hero he is. Then he'll get back in his filthy truck and go home to his wife. He won't remember my face, some awkward teenage damsel in distress that he can fantasize about later. He won't remember the details. In his imagination, he'll have saved me. The reality won't leave any impression at all.

I survey the trunk. It's just the spare tire, a wrench, and a tire iron, everything shiny and clean because this car is right off the used lot.

"This tire doesn't look too bad," the man says, kicking it with the tip of his boot. "You sure it just doesn't need a little air?"

"That's probably it," I say. "I don't know much about cars. But my dad will know."

Always say your dad is on the way, even if you've never met your dad. They don't have to know that. Always say there is some man who is older and bigger and protective, every man's nightmare.

But this one doesn't seem deterred at all, and I wonder if I'm reading him all wrong. He doesn't want to fuck me. He has a daughter my age. He goes to church and earns an honest living fixing things. I glance to his truck for a sign—a crucifix hanging from the rearview mirror, a concealed-carry bumper sticker, anything else to tell me who he is—but there's nothing.

He kneels down beside the car and studies the tire, his bushy brow furrowed as he tries to find a flat that isn't there.

Moody crawls in silence and I watch her shadow move toward me from the other side of the car. I don't even hear her breathe.

"I probably just imagined it," I say. *Please just go.* I try to will him to stand up and walk over to his truck and drive away. "I'll put air in it at the gas station. I know how to do that."

But he won't let it go. Why won't he let it go? Men. I wish it had been a woman driving that truck. Women are cautious and paranoid and smart. They see a damsel in distress and they say a little prayer if they acknowledge her at all, but they keep going. Women know that this world is dangerous and there's no such thing as innocent. Maybe a 120-pound woman in a blue tank top and cutoff shorts on the side of the road isn't dangerous at all. But maybe she is.

Moody is losing patience. Behind the man, I see her advancing toward the trunk. She's crouched low like a jungle cat on the hunt. She grabs the tire iron, meeting the sudden anger in my gaze with a fire of her own.

Moody would say that I'm naïve and that this presents a risk for our operation. But I'm the one she calls to clean the messes she makes. I shake my head at her just slightly while the man isn't looking.

"What?" the man says, and I think that, by some miracle, he's found something wrong with the tire. We really did go over a nail. But when I look at him, I realize he heard the sound of Moody's shoe against the loose gravel. She hides behind the open trunk, but he can see her shadow on the ground when he peers under the car. "Is someone else there?" he asks.

I close my eyes for a second. It's as close as I ever come to saying a prayer. The tire iron is three-quarters of an inch and it weighs two pounds, about as much as a baseball bat. I played softball with my foster siblings, and I think of that now as my sister thunders toward him. There's a sickening crack. The man lets out a groan and goes still. Blood streams out from his temple.

Moody stands triumphant in the gleaming sun. After only a half second of revelry, she gets to work. She grabs the man's wrists like it's the only thing to do. When I don't move, she looks up with fire in her eyes.

"You didn't have to do that," I cry, surprising even myself with my outrage. "I was handling it."

"You were taking too long," Moody says, an edge accentuating her words now. "He saw both of us. This was the only way."

"You took it too far, Moody." I'm glaring at her, defiant as she waits for me to help her clean the mess she's made for us. "He was only going to put the spare tire on the car."

"And what happens in a few months when your boyfriend goes missing and he has a sudden revelation about a pair of identical twins driving a silver Honda?"

"He won't—"

"Psychic, are we?" She tugs uselessly at his arms, waiting for me to regain myself and help her.

"We don't have to kill him!" I burst out. I don't know what's gotten into me. This man is nothing. A stranger. An obstacle who compromises our safety if we leave him here.

"Let's at least get him into the trunk before you turn this into an existential crisis," Moody says. "If anyone drives by and sees this, it's over." *Over.* That word is loaded. We'll be arrested. It won't turn into much. We'll say he attacked us and it was self-defense, and they'll probably let us go after a day or two. But they'll find out our real names, the legal ones we never use. We'll be fingerprinted and in the system forever. That means if a fingerprint is ever left at the scene of our next kill, we'll be found out. Our clean streak irrevocably ended.

I grab the man's ankles. His boots are caked with mud, and I wonder where he managed to find mud out in the desert. He's heavy, but malleable. He folds into the trunk like a picnic chair. I toss the tire iron in beside him and slam the door shut.

"Did you get any blood on you?" Moody asks.

"No," I say. The only blood is a collection of droplets that fell onto the road. I grab the water bottle from the cup holder and dump it out, and the red washes away, rolling down onto the dirt and disappearing.

"What about the truck?" I ask.

"We didn't touch it. Leave it." Moody gets into the driver's side and waves impatiently for me to follow.

As we drive off, I look back at the red pickup truck in the mirror, getting smaller until it's gone from view.

It shouldn't matter to me, but I hope he was an awful man.

2

HERE IS WHAT'S SUPPOSED TO HAPPEN: NOW THAT I'VE identified my mark, I spend a day following him, learning who he is so that I'll know how to play the part. I'll meet him in some spontaneous, unexpected way. Smile shyly, wrap my hair around my finger. I'll make him love me, whether this takes days or weeks, until he's helpless in my palm. And then I'll kill him.

I've never dealt the killing blow, but I'm the reason we never get caught. I know how to hide a body until it's safe to dispose of it. The number one mistake is trying to make sure the body disappears entirely. People set fires or submerge their victims in acid, bleach every inch of the crime scene and throw their rubber gloves in a dumpster five miles away, thinking this makes them clever. But bones don't burn, acid isn't the eraser you'd think it is—besides which, it's impossible to handle—and rubber gloves are a suspicious purchase to make right when your spouse goes missing.

The body is going to be found. That's almost inevitable. Make your peace with this, and plan for where you'll be when that happens. Hot weather accelerates decomposition; wildlife eats at the flesh and scatters the bones.

People have families who look for them, and small towns like Rainwood, Arizona, don't see a lot of people disappear, so while the police may not have the resources, they'll have the time. The key is to make sure the body has no ties to you and that you're gone when it emerges. It's as simple as that.

Right now, I should be following my mark. Getting to know his habits, making sure there isn't a girlfriend or a wife or a nettling mother.

Please don't let there be a woman in his life. This would mean I have to pick someone else. Someone who won't get wary of me. A daughter or a niece would be worse. Little girls are more insightful than the most hardened detectives, and they're too young yet to be anything but honest.

Instead of learning about my mark, I'm here, on a roped-off trail of the Skyline Hiking Hill, because Moody couldn't just let me handle things. This trail is less popular than some of the ones on surrounding desert mountains. Not as scenic, and with paths too narrow and rocky for runners. The Serpent's Trail is closed off because a twelve-year-old boy fell to his death three months ago. And judging by the physique of the man Moody clubbed with that tire iron, nobody will come looking for him on any hiking trails.

As it is, Moody and I worked up a sweat carrying him up the narrow channel in the pitch black. We had to wait until nightfall, leaving him in the trunk as we drove for hours. I had hoped the heat would do the job of killing him so we wouldn't have to; it's a wonder he survived, and a shame for him. Moody walked with a flashlight pinned between her lips, the only thing saving us from stepping into the abyss.

Now Moody is gone and I wait for her to come back. Just the man and me. I didn't want to, but I had to hit him with the tire iron when he started moaning. "It's better if you're not conscious," I'd said by way of apology.

I don't have the flashlight. Moody took it for her descent. Things are chirping in the wilderness. An owl coos gently and flutters skyward.

The man is still breathing, and I can just see his white wifebeater rising and falling in the frail moonlight. I gnaw my lip, bearing down so hard I taste copper. I'm trying to resist letting my imagination paint another picture, the way I do when I stare at strangers for too long. It will do no good to think about who he is, because whatever that might be, he won't be it for much longer.

Instead, I think of my mark. Right now he's home, I tell myself. He's got a condo, I imagine, with cream-colored walls because he doesn't have anyone in his life to teach him about color schemes. I can see more hues. I look at a plain wall and see what sorts of shades would depict which sorts of moods. He's still blank, probably little more than a recliner and a large-screen TV. It's a Saturday night, and he's home. In his shower, standing in the roils of steam, alone.

He doesn't even lock his door, unconcerned as he is. If I knew where he lived, I could walk right in. Tiptoe across the living room floor, follow the sound of the water down the hallway until I find the room that radiates the warmth of the steam. Pull back the curtain with a *whoosh* and a clatter of the plastic shower rings, and see him. Rivers going down the hills of his muscles. Hair rumpled and wet. All of him.

His eyes would go wide with shock, but I wouldn't hurt him. No garrote, no knife. Not this time. Not yet. Nothing but me.

The crunch of pebbles under someone's shoes shocks me back to the present. "Sissy?" someone whispers.

A flashlight clicks on and meets me squarely in the eye. Moody is standing before me, sweat darkening her shirt from armpit to hip. We keep in good shape, but neither of us is used to this terrain.

A figure emerges from behind her, slender, hair drawn back, and identical to Moody and me. Iris.

"You couldn't have picked someplace more level?" Iris complains, even though she's not even out of breath.

As though in answer, the man coughs and opens his eyes. I move to stand beside my sisters, and I watch as his expression juggles between delirious and astonished. He's seeing triple.

"Well, this is a special moment for you," Iris tells him, and I dread the enjoyment she's taking from this, though I don't say as much. "Not many people get to see all three of us at once. Unfortunately, it means you're going to have to die."

The man digs his heels into the dirt and tries to propel himself away from us. His gaze cuts to me, as though he can somehow tell us apart and he realizes I'm the one he pulled over to help; I'm the one who tried to spare him. He looks right into me, and for a second I can't move. "Help," he whispers. He doesn't shout it. He knows there's no one but the coyotes and owls to hear. "Help. Please." The words aren't for my sisters, or for the bright stars burning through the velvet sky. They're for me.

I can only stare back at him. *Who are you? Who is out there missing you?*

I'm sorry. I mouth the words to him and then look over sharply to make sure Iris and Moody haven't seen, but they aren't paying me any mind. Iris waves the flashlight around slowly, tracing the cliffside. "Not many places to dig," she says, and stomps her foot against the ground. "The earth is hard as rocks."

I take comfort in my sister's familiar practical calm. When it comes to murder, Iris is unsentimental, analytical, as though we've convened on this hiking trail to assemble a new bookshelf.

"Nobody comes here," Moody says. "Trail's closed. I can see why now. Almost broke our necks."

"There's a lot of brush in the hillside," I say, capturing their attention. My sisters are more experienced than me. Last month, when it was Iris's turn, she strangled her lover with a garrote fashioned from her lace bra. That's her favorite method, standing behind them and clenching her fingers and her teeth until she feels them leave. She kills them in intimate places—the bedroom, the car after they've just had sex at a scenic overlook, and never when Moody or I am nearby. One of my sisters is out in public to be an alibi, while I'm waiting for the cue to come and clean up.

I'm the one who keeps us from getting caught. I never miss a detail, not a single drop of blood or a pair of headlights on the road behind us when there's a body in the trunk. I've just never been the one to *do* it.

With this one, I didn't have much time to plan. Since this is the desert, I hadn't planned on a water burial anyway. We've only been in Rainwood for a day and a half. I'm still learning where the rivers and landfills are. I can't have a search history on any of our devices, so I've been limited to travel brochures and paper maps. Real estate listings are also a good source, as the listing agents will mention any notable landmarks within a few miles of their properties.

"He only has a head injury," I say. "Could have gotten that hitting his head during a fall."

"How long before they find him, you think?" Moody asks.

"It'll be a few weeks," I say. "He has a wedding ring. Someone will be looking. But not here."

"Seems like a place kids would come to drink," Iris challenges my logic.

"They won't go down this incline," I say. "No footholds. Nothing but trees and brush. They'll keep to the trails."

Iris considers this, and after a moment she nods. "Okay. So we just roll him."

"We get on our knees and roll him," I say. "No kicking. Shoe prints."

"Who's doing it?" Moody asks. She looks at me, and my heart thuds in my chest. *Not me.* This isn't how my first time is supposed to go, with this man who is meaningless, whose story I don't know. I am thinking of my mark from the diner again, how beautiful he is, out there waiting for me to come to him. He's supposed to be my first. Serendipity. I've already decided I'll kill him in a way that forces us to look into each other's eyes.

Iris knows what I'm thinking. She reaches around her head to wind her ponytail into a bun. "It's really time you pulled your weight, Sis," she tells me. "You're long overdue."

"Hey." Moody stands between us, shielding me from Iris's impenetrable stare. "It's her first kill. She deserves for it to be special."

"Does she?" Iris's calm breaks just slightly. She is exhausted from days of driving, recovering from her latest kill while listening to Moody and me prattle on excitedly about my upcoming first. "Then, would you care to explain why you've gotten us into this situation? Sis should be out there learning about her mark right now."

"He saw both of us," Moody counters. "What was I supposed to do?"

Not bash him with a tire iron, I think but don't say. *Let him go home to whoever is missing him. Let the pages that will soon print his missing posters be used for something else.*

Iris glares at me where I stand behind Moody's shoulder. She's gauging me, trying to figure out how I let this happen. Moody has an itchy trigger finger, but I'm a voice of reason, and she usually listens to me.

"In any case, here we are," I say. "We have to deal with it." Taking sides with either of my sisters won't play well—even if I do hate Moody for putting us in this mess. I want to be following my target right now, watching his silhouette through the blinds as he moves around his bedroom. I want to be imagining how he smells and what it will be like to touch him, and whether to bury him in one piece.

Iris is still looking at me when she tells Moody in a harsh whisper, "We aren't supposed to kill people just because they inconvenience us. Lovers only. We talk it over. We plan."

"It was an emergency," Moody says, stubborn as ever. She seems pleased with herself. She did this to protect us, and she wants us to thank her for it. Now it's my turn to step between them before this turns into a fight. Our victim is writhing in the darkness, moaning with terror in his eyes as we talk of killing him.

"Iris." My voice is gentle. I meet her eyes. They're beady, the green of them practically gone in the darkness. *Please,* I'm telling her. Please don't make this more complicated, more awful, than it already is. My sisters have six kills between them, three apiece. The last time I tried to find a victim of my own, I panicked, ruined everything, and Iris had to save me. Iris is right to be irritated, but I can't let this kill fall to me. The first kill is special. You can't get that back.

For me, and only me, Iris softens just enough to see reason. She points the flashlight at Moody accusingly. "Fine," Iris says. "I'll take this one. But this can't happen again."

"Yes, ma'am." Moody's sarcasm flirts a precarious line and I shove her, which only makes her giggle.

Still, Iris doesn't seem bothered as she saunters over to the man, flashlight in her teeth. He looks up at her, wild-eyed, like she's an angel that has just swooped down from the skies in a swirl of hellfire. The sound he makes is pitched and small, like a mewling little boy. When people know they're going to die, they become children again. They shrink back down to when they were still aware of how helpless they truly are. Back when there were monsters in closets and skeletal hands reaching out at them from under their beds.

This man hasn't been a little boy in a long, long time. But all 250 pounds of him is quivering now, and tears make his eyes shine. He looks up at Iris, and he doesn't plead with her the way he tried with me. Iris has a way about her, and when you look at her, you know that you're already dead.

"It'll only hurt a bit," she says. "And then it'll be just like going to sleep." She uses both hands to suffocate him. One on his mouth and one on his nose. She straddles his chest, and he bucks with a lot of strength, given how concussed he is. He grabs at her arms, but he doesn't have the strength left to pry her off of him.

Suffocation is one of the slowest ways to die. If you have practiced lungs, like a diver or an athlete, your lung capacity is better. You can hold your breath for minutes.

This man isn't a diver. It takes little more than a minute for his limbs to fall slack. Iris holds on for another minute just to be sure. We can't have him gasping anew after we leave and clawing his way back through the brush to identify us.

Once Iris is satisfied that he's dead, she stands, and it's my turn. I wield the tire iron again as I kneel beside him. He's still and waxen, his eyes closed. I probe my fingers inside his mouth, still wet and warm. I rap the iron carefully against his front teeth. They're spaced apart, but pearly and clean.

The front teeth come out easily, only chipping a little. But those little bits won't be enough to hold against his dental records, so I let them crumble away down his throat. It's an arduous process, pulling teeth, but I let it take however long it has to. He took care of his teeth; no crowns or fillings, which is an unexpected but appreciated thing. He's not wearing any buttons or a belt—nothing but his wedding band to wipe my fingerprints off of, but still, I'm careful about where I touch him. If we're lucky, the coyotes and crows and bugs will eat away at anything identifiable before he's found.

It's better to work without gloves. Gloves leave fibers. Traces of latex, microscopic strands of cotton or plastic or rubber—all of which is more damning than DNA. But fingerprints will be long gone once the skin starts to rot.

When it's done, we push him over the ledge and he rolls down the embankment. He barrels between trees and shrubs until he's out of sight and the snapping of branches ceases.

I try to stop it, but my imagination flares up, bright as the stars in the cloudless sky.

He has a wife at home, twirling her wedding ring as she texts him for the thirtieth time. We checked his pockets for a phone so that we wouldn't be tracked, but he isn't carrying one. He's left it in the truck, the screen lighting up and going black again with each unanswered message. She wonders if he's left her, if this is a punishment for a fight they've had or a callous remark she made in passing. *Can't you do the damn laundry for once?*

Now that it's dark and she's started to worry, she sees all the good he's done. Raising their children, making sure the oil is always changed in all the cars on time, giving her a good-natured smile as he falls into an exhausted heap on the couch beside her in the evenings.

Please just come home, she is typing out, and then whispering, and then praying the words.

I stand at the edge of the hiking trail for several minutes, listening for any sign of life.

There is nothing, not even a breeze.

3

IF NOT FOR MY SISTERS AND THE TRAGIC CIRCUMSTANCES
of our upbringing, I would be living an empty life and bound for
heartbreak.

It started when we were nineteen.

Iris called me, frantic, in the middle of the night. She had her own
apartment above a laundromat in downtown Clovis. She was so proud
of that place—all five hundred square feet of it. She kept it tidy and
burned incense at all hours to hide the smell from the dumpster in
the alley outside her bedroom window. At night, there was the persistent throb of the bar across the street, the music loud enough to
rattle the porcelain angel figurines on the shelves. They'd come with
the place, and Iris had decided they made her living room look
homey—a word she'd never used before, because we'd never had a
home.

"Just come," she'd sobbed, and then hung up. All my calls went straight to voicemail. I sped the whole way over there, sure that some-one had just climbed up the fire escape to murder her. But what I found was a different sort of violence.

Blood, deep and dark, pooled on her thrift store rug and splattered across the angel figurines.

She'd been sleeping with her old high school guidance counselor—a forty-something married father of two. He strung her along for months, promising to leave his wife. He broke her heart a hundred times, and then Iris plunged a kebab skewer through his.

"You watch all of those crime shows," Moody said, emerging from the kitchen with a bottle of bleach she'd found under the sink. "Help us make this go away."

We moved with a practical calm, the three of us, and when it was through, Iris's ill-fated lover was resting in six garbage bags, wound tightly with duct tape. If it were only one of us, or even two, I'm sure we would have been caught. We would have missed a detail. But we were a perfect team, the three of us.

After a lifetime of being torn apart, we were finally together, fi-nally able to help one another in all the ways we never could when we were being jostled helplessly by the foster system. All those years of loneliness, of wanting, of being kept apart, had brought us to this desperate moment. Knee-deep in the water of the San Joaquin River in the velvet black night, we weighted the pieces of the man with rocks, and a promise started to form. In the coming days, it slowly became obvious what we needed to do.

We wouldn't deprive ourselves of love, but our hearts would be weapons. We would love the men we found completely and without inhibition, put a lifetime into our brief time together. Live out every fantasy we desired. And then we would kill them.

There would never be another lover to break one of us. We would break all of them first.

WHEN I STEP OUTSIDE in the morning, I'm officially Jade Johnson.

My sisters are making themselves scarce in our one-bedroom condo. The shades are drawn, the TV playing in the living room at all hours, so nobody will think it strange if they hear multiple voices talking when Jade Johnson lives there alone.

Last time, in Texas, we were twins. Iris was the one stalking her mark, lurking in all the corners of his life and waiting for the kill, while Moody and I took turns being her twin.

This time, it's all me.

My first Arizona morning is bold and audacious, a bright halo of gold ringed by shades and shades of blue. It stares me down like a wicked unblinking eye. It knows who I am and what I'm here for, and the sky will keep my secret, but it wants me to know nonetheless that it sees.

I won't be here for long. I've just got a boy to hunt. That's all.

"Hey, stranger." A voice jolts me just as I've touched the handle of the car door. I look up and see a woman about my age standing on the balcony of the condo next to mine. A trail of smoke coils around her. She stretches her arms out, tapping the ashes from her cigarette so they flutter away. "You must be the quietest neighbor we've ever had. Didn't even know anyone had moved in until I saw you come out."

Had she been standing there this whole time? I didn't hear her. I'd looked but hadn't seen anyone when I came outside.

She watches me like she's never seen another soul before and I'm the most riveting thing on the planet. Her elbow rests on the railing,

25

her skin catching a scrap of gold as sunlight stretches around the condo complex. I can see how she eluded me. There's a small privacy wall beside her front door, just wide enough to hide her slender form by a hair.

"Hi," I say, flashing all my teeth when I wave. She's going to be a problem if I don't address it; I know this is the truth because she's a planner. She didn't light that cigarette until after I'd walked right past her because she knew I'd smell it.

Over the years, my neighbors have been all the seven sins. But whatever their shortcomings, I always knew when they were around.

"Sorry about the ashes everywhere," she says, and takes a slow drag. The smoke tumbles out clumsily around her words. "The last neighbor complained. I'm trying to quit, but, you know."

She isn't trying to quit. That's a thing that people say whenever their habits are out in the open. It's a test, whether or not she realizes it, to gauge if she can trust me, or whether I'm going to give her shit about the thing she loves. And she must love it, if she's doing it at seven o'clock in the morning on a Sunday when she could be sleeping instead.

"I don't mind," I say.

She nods to the guitar case I've just hoisted into the back seat. "You in a band?"

"Something like that," I say. "See you later."

Shit. I turn the key in the ignition. I back out of my assigned spot slowly, checking all the mirrors. *Shit. Shit.*

I glance in my mirror one last time before I turn out onto the street. She isn't looking at me anymore. She sits in one of two white plastic chairs in the tiny space, one leg crossed lazily over the other. I saw a wedding band on her finger, wedged against a modest engagement ring. Although all the units here come with two parking spaces, there is only one car parked diagonally across both her spaces. Young and broke. They'd have to be if they're living here.

Forget about her. I can't have anyone else in my head. Right now, I need to concentrate.

It's Sunday and I've got lost time to make up for. We came to Rainwood just before the weekend because it's a church town. Three-quarters of this state is religious and the foremost faith is Protestant. Thank foster care for my prowess when it comes to Jesus. I can say I went to Sunday school and I don't even have to lie. I always got the religious ones. Moody and Iris were taken in largely by a revolving door of heathens. They can tell you everything about changing diapers or hiding weapons, waking up before your lecherous foster brother peels back the covers and elbowing him in the nose. We pool our skills where we can.

My mark is a churchgoing man. *On the Cross Bible Chapel* was printed in chipped letters on a steel cross dangling from his keychain. I saw it when he left his keys on the counter and went to use the restroom. He's trusting enough to leave his possessions; that's good. He isn't the suspicious, wary type. After confirming his burial place with Moody, I should have spent yesterday tailing him, learning his habits. I could have run into him at the Safeway, apologizing profusely when my cart rammed into his. I had a perfect vision of how I wanted it to go, with my hair in a messy bun, a pink lace bra sticking out from around my tank top as though I'd tried to hide it but the straps had a mind of their own. I wanted to chew Bubble Yum. When women smell like candy, it drives men insane. I wanted to look up at him and bite my lip and let something flash in my eyes.

But instead, I was up on the hiking trail chiseling the teeth out of the man who wanted to help me with my tire.

Always have a backup plan. If there's one reliable thing about every Protestant church, it's that they love music. Not those weepy elegies the Catholics howl out like ancient monks, but worship rock, with amplifiers and drums. I'll just have to hope my mark is devout enough to attend every Sunday.

I arrive early and park in the commuter lot across the street. Just in case there's a camera, I get out and check my tires with the pressure gauge I keep in the glove box. I act frazzled, like I barely know what I'm doing.

I'm wearing a floral dress that comes down past my knees. It's strapless and fitted, and in the right setting it might even be sexy. But when I pair it with this white cardigan I look like my foster mother. She'd kneel before me in the church parking lot, lick her thumbs and brush them across my cheeks, fuss with my uncooperative little-girl hair, and beg me to act like an angel through the service. No chewing the gum I find under the pews and blowing bubbles, no provoking my foster brothers by daring them to burp for a dollar.

I would have done as she asked, if only she didn't keep promising to adopt me. I couldn't bear the guilt of letting her take me and not my sisters. As it was, I hated myself for wishing I could stay there forever.

Service starts at eight o'clock and it's only seven thirty. I climb back into the driver's side and watch as cars of the faithful file in. Families come out of most of them, and this makes me worry. My mark didn't have a wedding ring, and when I watched him in the diner, he ordered a short stack and home fries and nobody came to join him. But that doesn't mean he's alone in life.

Iris and Moody had to start over when their marks weren't right before. Iris was unbothered, but Moody skulked around our hotel room for days and I knew she was devastated.

I have an irrational thought. If my mark isn't the one, I'll make him the one. I'll drive his girlfriend away. I'll get him to hate his mother, turn him against his protective sister. I'll make him love me. However I have to do it, I will.

My heart gallops when I see his green Buick file in between two minivans. Even from here, I recognize his profile.

Mine. The word surrounds me, coiling around my form like my neighbor's cigarette smoke. He's mine. I press on the gas, so flustered that I forget to pull the car into gear first. It rumbles and roars at me. I take a breath. My stomach is fluttering.

Some distant part of me understands that I need to keep cool. Grip the wheel. Deep breath. By the time I find a parking spot, he's well out of his car. He's wearing black dress pants and a gray button-up that comes to his elbows. No tie. He doesn't overthink it. He's comfortable in his body, easy. He works out just enough to get those muscles, but not so much that he lives at the gym. He's lean, not veiny. Elegant but solid and with big hands. He juggles his keys in one fist and stuffs them into his pocket as he walks.

The metal double doors are wide open. People convene there and talk and hug and shake hands. He's no different. A woman opens her arms wide, standing on tiptoes to kiss him on the cheek.

I feel sick. She's petite like a sparrow, with a delicate face and angelic blond curls. She puts her hand on his chest and laughs at something he says.

I imagine her lying on the hiking trail with the same terror in her eyes as the man from last night. Her mouth, with its bright pink lipstick, open in an astonished O as I systematically relieve her of her teeth.

But if I wanted to kill her, I'd have to take her on as a lover. That's the rule, and I only have room in my heart for one kill at a time.

My mark keeps moving, and the little sparrow greets the next visitors with the same hug and welcoming kiss. She's gone by the time I work up the nerve to get out of the car. I'm wearing black suede flats and they make hard sounds against the sidewalk. I decided not to wear heels. I'm already tall, and men like to be taller.

I'm greeted by a woman who reminds me, for the second time today, of my foster mother Elaine. Every church has one or five Elaines. Salt-and-pepper hair, cheery smile, chomping at the bit to save the shit out of your soul. They're just so excited that you're here, and can't you feel the spirit? Isn't this a beautiful day?

Truth be told, I don't hate the affection. Elaine tried so desperately to love me. I was deposited onto her doorstep at five years old, still feeling like a jagged broken piece of a greater whole without my identical sisters. One of her sons was a year younger than me, the other a year older.

I stood sobbing in the middle of a stranger's driveway. "It'll be okay," Elaine had said. "My boys will teach you how to shoot hoops. We have a real river in the yard, and if you catch a frog, I'll even let you keep it for a day or two. How's that?"

My foster family gave me a taste of what a normal life would have been like. They tried; they really did. They even let my sisters come over and visit. But when I saw Moody and Iris six months into my foster placement, their sadness became my own. I didn't want to be happy if they weren't.

As we played in the yard, we came upon a dead field mouse, mutilated by the blades of the lawn mower. "Put it in that lady's bed," Moody had told me, and because I loved my sister, I did it to make her happy. I pretended to hate my foster family as much as she did. I never told my sisters how much it pained me to carry that mangled carcass by the tail and set it on Elaine's floral bedspread. I never told them the shame I felt later when I heard Elaine scream in disgust.

This Elaine is named Jeannie. She holds a paper coffee cup with the stirrer sticking out, and she asks me who I'm here with. I give her my rehearsed story: I drove down because my great-aunt recently passed away and left me with a small bit of money. I'm just here for a few months to get her affairs in order, but I'm lost if I don't go to church on Sundays. So, here I am, if you'll have me.

Casually, I work in that I love to sing.

The key to a believable story is to keep it simple. Avoid unnecessary details, and don't answer questions you haven't been asked. Weave in true things that are quick and easy to prove.

Jeannie wraps an arm around my shoulders and says, "She sings!" getting the attention of two women chatting beside a table of quartered bagels and coffee jugs. "Oh, say you're not busy after the service. We'd love to hear you."

I hunch my shoulders shyly. "I have my guitar in the car."

Jeannie looks at me like I've just answered all her prayers. I haven't talked to my mark yet; I saw him file into the chapel area while I was giving Jeannie the life story of Jade Johnson. But I can feel his nearness, the way the air starts to shift and the sky gets heavy before a summer rain.

When Jeannie starts to chat with the two other women, I slip away and enter the chapel room. It's bright and cheerful, with a vaulted ceiling, white walls, and a worn blue carpet. It smells like baby powder, perfume, and fresh laundry. Parents shush their fidgeting children, and the wooden pews creak out a chorus as bodies settle into them.

My mark is standing up at the podium, adjusting the mic stand for a nervous-looking teenage boy in a tuxedo. Amplifiers and speakers rest on either side of the modest stage.

It's all so perfect, I could believe I'm dreaming. There's a serendipity to your first kill. It's just like falling in love, but more romantic because it's permanent.

He loves music, or at least knows how to get the sound system set up. I watch from a pew in the middle of the room and wonder who this boy is to him. A nephew? Son? Brother? But a moment later, the boy's parents come up to whisper something encouraging, and my mark sprints back to his seat. They're nothing to each other.

Five more teenagers take up the stage, among whom are a stick-thin boy at the drums and a girl sitting daintily with her violin. The service begins with their rendition of "Amazing Grace." The boy sings a high soprano, and it's flawless, especially given that it comes from a boy with a sheen of grease on his face.

I sit through a sermon about the dire importance of hoisting one's burden onto God's shoulders, and by the fourth hymn, I'm so anxious that I'm buzzing. I've been staring at the back of his head for forty-five minutes, memorizing the lines that the light makes in his golden brown hair, imagining the stylist's fingers running through and through those curls, shearing them just before they grow unruly.

He was always beautiful, I think. A little boy with heavy lashes and dark pink lips. Tall and athletic in his teen years. And now, somewhere squarely in his twenties, bearing the cool charisma of someone who has always been comfortable in his skin. He takes care of his body—even his nails are trimmed and clean.

How is he alone? Sitting between a dozing grandma and a family of four, seemingly unattached to any of them. All it will take is for one girl to look at him and see how ripe he is, like a blushing apple that will fall from the branch at a touch, with no resistance.

When the service ends, he pulls his phone out of his pocket and taps twice at something on the screen before shoving it back in with the cross keychain and the ring with three different keys on it. Car, home, mailbox.

I wait for half the congregation to be gone. I pretend to be interested in something on my phone, even though there's not much to it. It's brand-new, with only the numbers of the car rental place and Apple tech support. I haven't even downloaded any games yet. I need to know who my mark is before I know who Jade Johnson is.

Jeannie is the one who hands him to me, God fucking bless her. She stands at the door that leads to a small kitchen with another cup of coffee in hand. "Jade! I hope you can still stay. I want Edison to hear you sing."

Edison.

Edison.

The name fills me with rivers. I know it belongs to him even before he's the one to turn around in the pew and look at me. His eyes find mine, and he feels it. Feels me. I know he does. He's been waiting for me in this sea of meaningless faces that drift between the pews. I'm the one who's going to love him the way that they can't.

When he smiles, I see all his perfect teeth. Years of braces to make that even smile. Just a bit of stubble on his chin, little flecks that wink like dark stars in the sky of his face. He stands—not all the way, just enough—and extends his arm out to mine. A tuft of hair falls forward to have a better look at me.

I rise like it's nothing, like the world hasn't just crested into a wave with us at the summit, and let him shake my hand.

His skin is rough, cool, and he hooks his thumb over the back of my palm. It sweeps back and forth just slightly, and goddamn it, just like that I'm wet. My stomach is ice-cold. My face is clammy and numb.

"Hi," he says, and his voice is deeper than I'd expected, but still cadenced and mellow.

"Hi." My armpits are hot and damp. "I'm Jade."

"Jade," he says, and I hate that name because it isn't mine, but it's one of the first words he'll ever say to me. "It's great to meet you. Let's see what you've got."

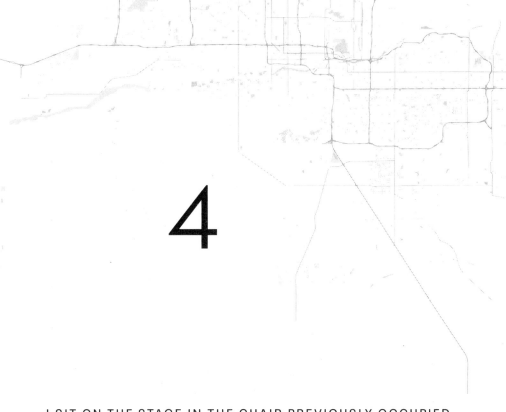

4

I SIT ON THE STAGE IN THE CHAIR PREVIOUSLY OCCUPIED by the girl with the violin, and I pluck at my guitar strings to test the tension, even though I know they're perfect. Down, up, down on the top strings, up, down, up on the bottom ones. "Ave Maria" teases us in those simple notes, and in the corner of my vision I see him smile.

He sits in the front pew, his fists clasped between his opened legs. I let him think I'm fumbling to find the music, though I know it like my own soul. I play those chords over and over, and then I start to sing.

It's like there's someone else living inside me when I sing. This high soprano comes out, knowing all the inflections to "Ave Maria," sounding so unlike the voice I use to speak.

I first heard this song on one of Elaine's Christian CDs that she played while she drove us to our extracurriculars in her minivan. My foster brothers were fighting over whose turn it was with the Game

Boy Advance. One of them threw the Mario Kart cartridge into the front seat so neither of them would have it, and the other let out a keening wail. Elaine turned up the volume.

I was seven, and I'd never heard a song in another language before. I didn't know what any of the words meant, or why my eyes filled up with tears. I swiped them away, angry with myself. But I could feel the whole world in that song. All the tsunamis washing away cities on the news, and monsoon seasons, and the children in those *700 Club* segments with distended bellies and emaciated faces. I could see my sisters: Iris pressed to the rear window of the car with her face all wet, and Moody biting down on the ear of her stuffed pink bunny so she wouldn't scream as we were all separated.

When I finish singing, I feel exposed, the guitar unable to hide my nakedness. *Did you hear it?* I ask Edison with my silence. *My life story. I've just told you.* I've just taken him deep down into the part of myself that frightens me.

Suddenly, looking at him takes effort, and I worry that I'll see rejection in his eyes. I make myself face him. He blinks at me, leaning back in the pew, and when he finally speaks, he says, "Wow."

A piece of hair slips over my shoulder, and I use the guitar pick to tuck it back.

In the rear of the room, a group of women has stopped cleaning up the snacks to watch me.

"You have a gift, honey," Jeannie says, pressing her hand against her heart.

Precious few things are given to us in this life. True love and money and a bit of attention are hard to come by. I didn't even have a mother. If there's something that was given to you for nothing, you'd better take it and use it any chance you get. It may be your only way to survive.

Jeannie senses what exists between Edison and me. She looks between us, smiling, her eyebrows raised. She's an excellent wingman, telling him my little story about what brings me to Rainwood.

"How long have you been here?" Edison asks as I lay my guitar back into its case. His voice is perfect. He's considerate, not too loud, aware that we're in a church and that I've just shared something intimate with him. He's patient, and I'm glad I didn't run into him at the Safeway. He doesn't want a girl who smells like candy and flutters her lashes at him. He's sensitive. He observes me with care; he holds this moment we've just shared in both hands and inspects all the shades and cracks of it.

"Only a couple of days," I say. "Haven't learned where anything is yet."

"Where are you staying?"

"A rental off West Rock Road," I say. My chest is cold and then hot.

"You know what's good to eat around here is Still's," Jeannie says. I'd managed to completely forget that she was still here. She gives me a good-natured wink before she turns and grabs the trash can to finish cleaning up. I've known her for an hour, but already she's bestowing something precious on me. *Here you go,* she's saying. *You need each other. Don't hurt him.*

When Edison first goes missing, nobody will know that he's dead but me. Hope is that powerful thing that bonds communities like these. I'll come to the church, frantic that he didn't meet me for breakfast and his car's not at his place. I'll still be hearing his final breath in my head, a lone chord of a secret song, and I'll see that violent flash of life in his eyes. He'll be the most alive in that final moment because he'll know that it's his last.

Jeannie will comfort me. As the days pass, she and the congregation will help me comb through the desert for him. When I'm exhausted and weak and my limbs are rubbery with grief, I'll drop on the side of the road and sob. Jeannie will hold me and we'll love him together. We'll remember him, and in some very dark place she isn't yet ready to face, Jeannie will know, like I will, that he's gone.

Edison smiles at me, scratching uncertainly at the back of his head. "Still's is only good if you like a lot of grease after your Sunday service."

The girls he's dated have all been vegetarians, petite like the little sparrow who kissed him at the door. They've gone running with him and done anything he wanted in bed, and as confident as he is, he struggled to keep up with their energy. He hid his vices—greasy food, an occasional beer—to be the perfect man for them. He's tired of competing.

"I'm starving," I say. "Give me all the grease."

He laughs and it's fucking music. "Where's your car?" he says. "You can follow me out."

MOODY AND I PASSED Still's on our way into town yesterday. Moody thought it was a consignment shop until I pointed out the patio tables folded against the wall. It's a small square building in the middle of nowhere, and the parking lot is full. In small towns, everyone pools together in places like this.

Edison pulls into a space and I get the one right beside him. He looks over and smiles at me, and we're in on some sly little secret. I know where we are, but I'll pretend that I'm lost without him to guide me through this desert. We're two miles from the diner and three miles from the subdivision where Edison will be buried.

"Hi," I say when I step out of the car, and I marvel that I'm speaking to him. I'm using such an ordinary word to greet him, when just hours ago he was the world's greatest mystery to me. Now he smiles and lets me walk beside him as we navigate the crowd.

It defies physics that so many people are able to fit into this small space. I wish Jeannie had suggested something less crowded.

A mother hurries past us, corralling three small children in the perimeter of her outstretched arms. Edison takes my elbow and gently pulls me out of the way. My legs ache with longing, and I pretend to observe something on my shoe so that he doesn't see the goofy smile overtaking my face.

When it's our turn at the front of the line, he asks me what I want, and I shrug. I am easygoing and whatever he needs me to be. "You pick," I say. "I trust you."

As promised, the food is pure grease. By the time we find a patio table outside, the oil from the fries has made the paper plate translucent.

It's gotten hotter now that the sun is higher in the sky. I shrug out of my cardigan and drape it across the back of the chair. He doesn't look at my shoulders. He's polite, not distant, but cautious in the way that people are around strangers.

When we have sex, it'll be like a confession. We'll breathe hard and stumble across the room and knock over the nightstand while we're clawing at our clothes. He'll throw me on the bed. He'll grab my wrists and hold them up over my head, and his eyes will be dark and animal. I'll say his name over and over. He'll know and I'll know that this is how it has to be, that we have been waiting all this time to find each other.

Killing him will be just the same. I'll make it slow, but it will never be slow enough, because if I had my way, it would last forever. The dark depth in those beautiful eyes when he looks at me and sees what I am. His hands digging into my skin. The life and the desperation and the pleading. "I'm not Jade Johnson," I'll say. "I'm Sissy." After months of hiding my name, it'll be a relief to say, and I'll make him say it too. I'll ask him if he loves me, and he'll say he does because he'll do anything when I'm the one who decides how long he gets to breathe.

"How is it?" he asks me when I bite into the cheeseburger. Its juice is running down my wrist and I suck it up without bothering with the flimsy napkins.

"Oh my God, amazing," I say with my mouth full.

He laughs. We sit below the patio speakers, and Israel Kamaka-wiwoʻole's "Somewhere Over the Rainbow / What a Wonderful World" medley is playing, barely audible over all the chatter.

"Did you know this song almost never happened?" I say. "IZ called the recording studio in the middle of the night because he had the idea for it. Most recording engineers would hang up on anyone trying to record a song that late, but he was so polite that the engineer got out of bed to do it for him."

Edison chews pensively for a moment and then dabs neatly at the corners of his mouth with his napkin. His lips are smooth, not a hint that they've ever been chapped a day in his life.

"Really?" he says.

"I think he was in poor health when he recorded it," I say. "If you listen closely at the beginning, you can hear how hard he's breathing."

Edison sets down his burger and leans back. He's scrutinizing me, his eyes narrowed. His expression is so playful, like we're sitting over a game of chess and he's waiting to see how I'll best him. "I never knew who sang this," he says. "I just think of it as that song they played on every TV drama in the nineties."

"It definitely fit that style," I say. "It has *slow-death-scene montage* written all over it."

Edison laughs, a sound that's so loud and uninhibited it startles me. My stomach flips. He has me, and he doesn't have a damn clue. *Smile back*, I remind myself. He'll think I'm weird if I just stare at him, though I could stare at him like a daft schoolgirl all day. "You've got your own way of observing things," he tells me. "Don't you?"

I press my lips together, suddenly too self-aware. "I tend to over-think things sometimes."

He shakes his head. "No," he says. "You just really see them."

I study his face. Is he nervous? His smile is a little wider than it was back at the church, and his pupils are dilated, lips parted.

"Anyway, I like the original version from *The Wizard of Oz* best," he says.

Of course he does. He loves old movies whose actors are long dead. He's chivalrous and romantic, and he'll say *It's a Wonderful Life* still holds up in today's world. He goes on. "I heard a rumor that they shot the first part of that movie in black and white, and then Technicolor was invented during filming, so they shot the rest of it in color."

I force myself to eat a handful of fries. If I don't eat, he'll think I hate the food, when really, it's just that I'm too excited and my stomach is all in knots. "I've never seen it," I say.

"*The Wizard of Oz*?" He raises his eyebrows. "That doesn't seem possible."

I love *The Wizard of Oz*. The book too.

"Honest." I trace an X across my heart.

Tell me it's your favorite movie. Tell me we have to watch it together.

He wears his smile like a favorite shirt, and I know that he uses it to mask something.

"It's a classic, Jade," he says. "You should really remedy that."

Yesterday, I liked that name. I chose it partly because of how common it is, but partly because I've always had a thing for greens. But now I envy this nonexistent Jade Johnson like she's a windswept lover on the front of a tawdry romance novel. Jade will get the man. Jade will have her happy ending. It will be Jade whom Edison murmurs for in bed, and whose name he writes on the card when we spend our only Christmas together.

I could have given him my real name. The legal one I never use. But it was too risky. It's been seven years since my sisters or I have been called by the names that were given to us by the state. Those cold syllables are meaningless and dead, like costumes hanging in a closet with no one to wear them.

"I guess I should," I say. No invite. Not yet. That's okay. We can play this slow. For him, I've got all the time in the world.

He asks me where I'm from, and the answers I give him are mostly true. I was born in California. I have two sisters. I'm the baby. I say this because it implies that I have parents, when in truth I've never met them. Whoever my mother is, either she doesn't want to be found or she's dead. She pushed my sisters and me out into the world—in which order, we'll never know—and when we were just days old, someone found the three of us crammed into a single stroller at a rest stop, wrapped in clean towels and with our umbilical cords tied off with plain white shoelaces.

We were all over the news in 1999. Triplets don't get left out in the scorching sun every day. Our mother could have been the mistress of a corrupt politician, or a scared teenage girl. She could have watched us on the news, our photos taking up three identical squares in the evening segments, as she hid all the signs that she had ever been pregnant and crammed back into her jeans. Or she could have planned to love us as we grew inside her, but then someone stole us away and cut her throat, and as the world searched for the mother of the triplets

Doe, she was decomposing in a landfill somewhere, her corpse none the wiser.

I want to tell this to Edison, I realize. But he wouldn't be able to love me if I tore away this mask. No one but my sisters would.

For Edison, I ease into Jade. I let her wear my skin.

I steal a picture of him, holding my phone under the table. But even at this awkward angle, he's beautiful, the sun catching the sharp edges of his cheeks and making the brown of his eyes glimmer— candied amber in the Arizona sun. I'll have to show him to my sisters for their final approval. We never settle on a kill unless we've all agreed, and I'm the only one who's gotten a good look at him.

I'm not worried that they'll reject him. Iris isn't particular. She'll say that he's passable. Moody will say that he looks strong but that she's confident I can take him down on my own. They're so desperate for me to follow through with a kill that they'll all but put the knife in my hands.

A sharp pain jars me from my thoughts. I look down to see a jagged splinter boring into my index finger, and I curse before I can stop myself.

"Did the table get you?" Edison says, and I look up to see sympathy in his eyes. He holds out his hand. "Let me see."

Careful, Sissy, I tell myself, because I am all too eager to comply. I offer my wounded finger to him tentatively, as though I'm cautious rather than intrigued. "Hold still," he says, and without questioning it, I do. I watch as he carefully works the splinter from my skin with such precision that I don't feel a thing.

Blood wells up at the wound, dark and contained to its tiny sphere. Edison brings my finger to his lips, and my mind goes hazy with shock when I feel the warm softness of his mouth.

He does this like it's natural, like he hasn't just caused the whole world to stop just for us. I'm inside him. My blood on his tongue.

"There," he says. "All better." He licks his lip, and I know that he can still taste me there.

He looks at me, and I think I see a challenge in that face of his. A question. A dare.

Who are you really? his eyes say. I want to answer. I want to tell him the truth, even though it would ruin everything if he knew.

5

IN THE MORNING, UNFAMILIAR VOICES OUTSIDE WAKE ME.
I open my eyes to a bedroom with peach walls, a bed, and a dresser
left behind by the previous occupants.

Having sisters like Iris and Moody means that I'm always home.
We grew up like bits of debris drifting, helpless, on the surface of
some deep sea. I'm told we were quiet babies. Not the sort to fuss or
throw fits. Iris nearly starved to death that first month. She had mal-
absorption, and nobody knew she was suffering because she didn't
even cry. She just took it like a stoic on a hunger strike. She was nearly
lifeless by the time someone thought to call an ambulance. There's a
photo of her from then, the world's tiniest queen on a throne of tubes
and wires, staring icily up at her subjects.

It's because of our peculiar quiet that our early foster families kept
all three of us. Give us some formula, change the diapers, cash the

checks from the state. Leave us in our playpen to rot all day. Who's to know? We won't tell.

But as we got older, this was no longer the case. The state has a hard enough time keeping two orphaned siblings in the same home, much less triplets. Between the ages of five and eighteen, my sisters and I drifted between group homes and foster homes, hardened anew at each reunion by the things we'd experienced while we were apart. Fate brought us together arbitrarily and then separated us just as easily. My sharpest memories are of their fingers being pried from mine, either by the force with which we were torn away, or by the impatient heavy hand of whoever was tasked with transporting us.

All our conversations were whispers as we crept into the same bed at night for protection, or screams through car windows and across parking lots.

Now where one goes, we all go. Always.

Because Jade Johnson is supposed to be living alone, we rented a one-bedroom condo. It's three levels: a bedroom and modest bathroom on the top floor, a living room and dining room and even tinier bathroom on the main, and a laundry room at the bottom, with a door through which we can slip away without being seen, because no neighboring windows overlook it.

We share the queen-size bed, and I spent last night wedged between Moody and the wall. I was up late, lying on my back, holding my phone over my head and smiling in the glow of the screen as Edison and I talked about movies and the perfect music to listen to when you've had a bad day.

Moody is still asleep, limbs sprawled, her dark hair tangled across her face. Iris is missing, ever the early riser, and I can hear the soft murmur of the TV downstairs. That isn't what woke me, though. Someone is chattering outside. I move to the window and peel back the blinds. My neighbor—the woman with the cigarette—is standing on her balcony and talking to a man with fair skin and neatly combed blond hair. He's so groomed it's almost unreal, like a billboard ad for custom suits.

He talks in a soft hum that I can't hear, but whatever he says makes her smile at him. Before he turns for the stairs, she grabs his collar in both hands and reels him in for a kiss.

They're a beautiful couple. Two little cake toppers standing upon layers of buttercream frosting. Life in this shitty complex is an adventure for them. He's dressed for the job he wants—a pressed tailored suit, silk tie—and one day he's going to buy them a house.

I wonder what it's like to have a forever with someone. I've never looked at anyone and seen the future, not even my own face in the mirror.

I'll have to befriend the woman next door. There's always a little bit of social networking involved when my sisters have targeted their marks, but it's a delicate balance. I'll keep an eye on her. If she works during the day, it will make things much easier. But if she's home, that means she'll pop up as unexpectedly as she did yesterday, and my sisters and I will have to stay vigilant.

Once her husband is gone, she emerges from the house with a trash bag. It's large and unwieldly, but she carries it over her shoulder like it weighs nothing. She paces across the parking lot and tosses it into the blue dumpster meant for recycling. The loud slap of each step in her bright yellow flip-flops echoes in the empty space. She lights a cigarette as she sashays up the stairs and falls into a patio chair. Black tank top, no bra, short hair still rumpled in the back. Her husband took the car. She's got nowhere to be.

Her eyes flit up to my window and I back away, though I'm sure she wouldn't be able to see me.

As I make my way downstairs, I hear the whir of the blender. Iris sets two glasses down on the counter, having anticipated my arrival.

"You were up late texting him," she says as I slide onto a barstool.

I set the phone on the counter and check my messages again. Nothing new in the past eight hours.

I force myself to drink the smoothie Iris pours out, even though I secretly hate them. In Texas, when we were playing the role of twins, two of us could leave the motel at the same time. There were breakfast options. Scrambled eggs, gigantic slabs of buttered toast, and bacon for days. But here we're sharing the role of Jade Johnson, and that means the blinds are always drawn and we'll have to be careful about how we come and go. It also means buying a modest amount of groceries.

"How is it?" Iris asks, and it takes me a moment to realize that she's talking about Edison, not the smoothie.

"Still new," I say. "I'm going to start slow. He seems like he can get skittish on me."

"Given any thought to how you're going to do it?" She moves around the kitchen, inspecting the cabinets and drawers. The condo came furnished, and it hasn't been updated since the 1980s.

"No," I say. A lie. Iris crouches down to rummage through the mostly empty cabinet where we've stashed canned goods, muttering about honey for her tea.

"Jade is going to the store," she says. By the way she says it, I know she means she's going to be the one to go.

"I'll go," I say. "Get me a list. See if Moody wants—"

"I need to get out of this fucking apartment, Sis." She whirls to face me, and I see the irritation written all across her face.

We're identical right down to the way we shape our eyebrows, but even the other kids in the group homes always knew which one of us was Iris. There's an intensity about her, like she's just stopped in to escape something she's running from. Back then, she always wore long sleeves, even in the summer, and hid a box cutter at her wrist.

"Anything special I need to know about Jade?" she asks.

I don't want Iris to be Jade, I realize. Jade is mine. Jade is the one who holds on to the only smartphone we bought, and after Edison is dead, the phone will be purged and then destroyed. But for now, the phone and Edison are both alive and well and filled with his thoughts. After he fell asleep last night, I read his texts over again, pretending they were new. I committed them to memory as best as I could, because in six short months I'll have to delete them. Edison will only be alive in my head.

"Iris." I try to match her determination and fail. "I'll go to the store. This is my thing."

She stares at me for a long time. I gulp down the last of the smoothie but don't take my eyes off her.

"Okay, Sissy, I wasn't going to say this." She reaches across the counter and puts her hand over mine. We're both wearing maroon nail polish. "You should have been able to make that kill Saturday night. With that man on the hiking trail."

This wounds me, and I guard myself before she can see the betrayal in my eyes. "You told Moody she was wrong to put us into that position."

"She was wrong," Iris says. "It was a stupid, hasty move and I laid into her about it. But it doesn't change the fact that it was your turn."

"He wasn't my kill," I say.

"That's what you said about the last one too." She squeezes my hand. "You panicked."

She should be directing this lecture at Moody, not me. As though Moody has never flubbed a murder before. When it was her first time, in Montana three years ago, she cried. She was sobbing and blotchy when I showed up, and she threw her blood-smeared arms around me. I had to pry her off so that I could get to work. It didn't help that she'd tried something ambitious—lacing his coffee with his prescription Ambien and then slitting his wrists in the bathtub. A suicide would make cleanup someone else's problem. She thought this made her a genius.

Instead, her lover vomited everything up in the tub and fought her off, managing to slice her hand with the kitchen knife she'd used on his wrists. He was determined to live, and they struggled around the bathroom like it was a WWE rink, blood smeared all in the tile grout and the towels. Eventually he lost enough blood that he collapsed. I spent all night crawling on the floor with a bottle of peroxide and a toothbrush, getting rid of every last drop.

And Iris wants to talk about who panicked. If it weren't for me, we'd all be serving life in a women's correctional facility.

The phone blips and my heart responds with a rapid flutter. Iris grabs it before I can see what the message says. She grins.

"Iris."

"I can be Jade," Iris says, and presses her hand to her chest like a heartsick war widow. She starts to type and I hear the click of each letter she presses. "Dearest Edison, last night I thought of you as I touched myself—"

I scramble around the counter and she holds the phone over her head, cackling. She tries to run for it, and I hook my arms around her waist. She's still typing as she staggers for the doorway.

"Iris!"

"It's just the grocery store, Sissy. Don't be a baby."

I kick at the backs of her knees, and she buckles. The phone flies into the living room, mostly empty aside for a hideous floral couch and a flat-screen TV that murmurs softly. I go down with Iris when she falls, and in a whirl she flips me onto my back. Her eyes are dark, jaw clenched. Her fists close around my fingers, crushing the bones, and I cry out.

We don't say anything. We only stare.

I draw my knee up and thrust it into Iris's stomach. Her eyes flash as I knock the wind out of her. She grapples at my shirt. I grab my phone from the carpet and scramble to my feet. I'm barely upright before Iris bull-rushes me onto the couch. I fall facedown onto the cushions, and she pins my hands behind my back, crushing me with her weight until I don't even have the air to tell her that I can't breathe.

Panic flares up and I struggle, all my other instincts gone. A feeble croak comes out of me and my vision tunnels.

Iris leans down. She's calm and collected now that she's gained the upper hand. "What are you going to do, little sister?" she says. "If your boyfriend fights back and I'm not there to save you, how will you get out of it?"

The world goes blurry and dark, and I fight to hang on to the words. My arms have gone numb. My legs feel miles away.

Think, I order myself. When I try to roll out from under her, she only jabs her knee more into my spine. With all the strength I have, I bend my knees, cross my ankles, and kick her with as much force as I can manage. My heels land into her flesh with a satisfying whack. She eases up just long enough for me to tumble out onto the floor.

I land on my hands and knees, gasping. Iris grabs me by the forearm and I try to get away, but she only hauls me to my feet.

We're both breathing hard. She's slightly hunched because I hit her lower back full force. Her eyes are dark and stony. After a few seconds, she grabs my face in her hands and kisses my forehead.

"I love you," she pants. "You know that, yeah?"

I want to punch her. I hate her. But all that fire and venom coil themselves around my soul, and the truth is that she means so much to me that I'd die if anything happened to her. Iris and Moody both.

I nod, still wheezing. "Yeah."

Sharks are murderous before they're born. The biggest embryo develops eyes and teeth before its siblings and hunts them one by one, filling the womb up with blood. Sharks are born knowing what death looks like. And what survival looks like.

When the egg split into three, Iris got the teeth, and I got the keen eye. Moody got the hunter's instinct. Warily we orbited one another in the darkness, but somehow we knew even then that we needed one another. The world was going to be our enemy, and we wouldn't survive unless it was together.

Iris hands me the phone as the feeling slowly comes back to my fingertips. "Go to the store, Jade," she says. "Don't forget the goddamn raw honey."

I glance down at the screen, not letting on that my heart is still pounding as I check my messages. Edison still hasn't replied since last night. This morning's text was an automated message from the phone company to let me know my bill is due. Iris's message is still typed and unsent in the text field.

She gives me a playful wink when I look up at her, and I meet her with a blank expression. I can read anyone, but Iris is the only one who can read me back.

6

THE NEIGHBOR IS STILL OUTSIDE WHEN I STEP OUT ONTO
the porch. The smell of menthol cigarettes and some manufactured
sugary scent lingers warmly in the morning air.

She's staring down at her phone, but she looks up when she
hears me.

"Hey," I say.

The strap of her flip-flop dangles from one toe as her leg bobs
gently up and down, draped across her knee. "Hi," she says, not quite
as cheery as she was yesterday. "Sorry if our music kept you up last
night. These walls can be pretty thin."

"I didn't hear anything," I lie. I fell asleep to the persistent throb
of some unidentifiable song. But I don't mind. Growing up in the
foster system, you almost don't know what quiet even sounds like.

I start down the stairs, but she says, "Wait. Are you going through
town?"

I turn to face her, but I don't answer the question. Not until I know what she wants.

"Because I really need to go to the ATM, and Tim took the car."

"I'm just going to Safeway," I tell her. "I'm not sure if that counts as 'through town.'" I give her my best contrite shrug. I'm just a lost, timid, shy thing in someone else's state. "I don't know where every-thing is yet."

Her eyes widen and her face lights up, and it's so charming that it almost knocks me back. She hasn't been ugly a day in her life. I can tell, because she doesn't care that her hair is a disaster and bits of burgundy lipstick are cracked and clinging to her mouth from the day before. She's friendly to me because the world has been good to her, the way it often is to the pretty ones. She was popular in high school, nice to everyone. If anyone was ever mean to her, she wouldn't have noticed. She would have spun around in the hallway, smiling with all her teeth, and asked them to repeat themselves because she didn't quite hear them. And they would have been instantly shamed into silence.

I've only known her for a handful of minutes, and already I can feel a pull to find out what she wants—what small thing I can do for her. Offer her a lighter because hers is out of fluid, or retrieve some-thing she's dropped through the slats of the deck.

"That's perfect. They have an ATM right by the door!" She's al-ready sprinting inside, and she's back out a moment later with a pink leather purse hanging on her shoulder. It's designer, not a knockoff. The stitches around the zipper are perfect, and that's the best way to tell. It must have cost at least two months' rent.

This sets an alarm bell off for me. It's clear that Tim is the only one who works, while she is left to languish at home all day without a car or anything to do but watch the neighbors.

Not your problem, Sissy, I have to remind myself. I'm not here to insert myself into my neighbors' marriage. I am only here to utilize her to my advantage however I might need to. But I can't shake the sense that something isn't right.

"Your car is that silver one, right?" she says.

I don't know anything about mothers, but the ones in books always told their daughters not to get into cars with strangers. I guess they meant men. The shadowy, strange ones who try to snatch you off the sidewalk. If I had a daughter, I would tell her the truth, which is that the whole world is bad and you had better learn how to use anything at your disposal as a weapon.

Two days ago, there was a man in the trunk on his way to certain death. After we got rid of him, I combed through the wool lining with a flashlight. I didn't find any blood, but I took a pair of craft scissors and shaved some of the fibers that looked a little discolored anyway. Never use the flashlight on your phone. All that data gets stored. There was a teenage girl on the news who was found dead in the woods. Her boyfriend had utilized his phone's flashlight for three hours the night she went missing, and that was enough to put him away.

Now the car is clean. There's a water bottle, mostly empty, in the cup holder, and a green pine tree air freshener. I'm thinking about getting a crystal cross from the Christian bookstore I saw in town. Crystals fill every space with pale little rainbows.

"I'm Dara." The neighbor clips on her seat belt and gives me a coy smile. "Probably should have opened with that."

Already, she interests me. Getting to know her routines and earn her trust won't be a chore, I can tell. I've never had a female friend, apart from my sisters. Not even the pretend kind, like Dara will have to be.

"Jade," I say, and put the car in reverse. "You might have to show me where Safeway is. I got lost last time."

On the way to the store, she asks where I'm from and what brings me here. I give her the same story, and as I do, I listen for my phone. It's almost nine, and it's a Monday. Edison would be at work by now. He doesn't have read receipts on his phone, and I'll have to remedy that when I get my hands on it. Just a quick adjustment in the settings that he won't notice on his end, but it will make all the difference for me.

Dara asks if she can roll down her window. The AC is too much and she likes the fresh air. I tell her sure. I'm easy—I can just go with it. Inside, my stomach is hot and anxious. Why hasn't he texted back? I played everything perfectly. I asked questions, but not too many, and I answered all of his. *What do you do for work? Oh, that sounds like a great way to meet people. Me? I want to be a musician. I'm thinking about setting up a YouTube but I'm afraid of putting myself out there, you know?*

My phone pings. Dara checks her own phone to see if it's for her, but it's not, and she squints as the sunlight hits her face.

I have to force myself not to speed. I let Dara guide me through streets I am already familiar with, and I pretend that I'm interested in what she says. I should be paying attention, studying her, but all I can think about is that one lone text. It has to be from Edison. My sisters have burner phones, and my smartphone number isn't programmed into them. We bought three identical flip phones, calling cards, no internet, paid in cash and for emergencies only.

The burner phones were a source of contention. The less technology, the better. But Iris insisted. She is also the one who insisted I do this mission alone, and I know she's right. At twenty-five, unlike both my sisters, I've never dealt the fatal blow and I'm still a virgin. I've hidden behind the cleanup and the research, and if Iris hadn't been so damn demanding, it would be her turn again, not mine.

If I didn't kill Edison, I wouldn't be able to have him at all. That's the rule. Sex is only for men we murder. No distractions. If I hadn't been on the hunt in that diner, I wouldn't have even seen him because I wouldn't have been looking. The world and all its patrons have a muted sheen to me, like a city overtaken by early-morning fog. I'm never here for long, and no one matters beyond what I can make them do for me. Not even Dara—sweet, benevolent creature that she is. We'll never be real friends. I'll come in for wine and we'll gossip about the neighbors, and I'll get her to trust me. But she's just like the frogs I caught in Elaine's pond and put in little jars with wax paper and a rubber band on the top. I can't keep her.

If Dara knew what I really am, she would be thankful for that.

We make it to the Safeway and split up at the door. She heads for the ATM by the bottle return and tells me to take my time. She'll find me when she's done.

I grab a cart, smiling sweetly at the teenage boy who has just finished rolling them in from the parking lot. As soon as I'm behind the cereal aisle, I slip my phone out of my purse.

The aurora borealis burns brightly in its twist of rainbow colors against the night sky, and superimposed over that is a text from Edison:

You shouldn't give up on your dream, Jade.

Edison is the type who falls over himself to help people—I saw that at the church, the way he patiently fielded requests to repair a leaking pipe in the church basement and a running toilet at someone's grandmother's nursing home. If he tries to set up an online presence for my music, I'll have to come up with a creative way to say no without arousing suspicion or wounding him.

But none of that matters right now because he replied. He's still here with me.

I move through the store in a haze that's almost manic, biting my lip, throwing random boxes and bags into the cart.

It's too soon to reply. Give it ten minutes. *I'm busy, Edison, and my life doesn't revolve around you.*

Bruises are starting to form around my wrists. Little nebulas of pink and purple and blue, courtesy of Iris. I fight the anger that flares up. Iris and her temper, Iris and her moods. When we were kids, she would sneak up on Moody and me. Lock us in closets, hook an elbow around our necks, always getting us when we were absolutely alone. Walking home from the store or sleeping. She would demand that we fight back and she wouldn't relent until we got in a good punch. Once, I jammed a hairpin up her nose to stop her strangling me. It was the only thing I had and I really thought I was going to die.

She fell back, hemorrhaging blood through her nostril, and there was pride burning in her eyes when she looked at me.

Without Iris, life would be a lot more peaceful, or Moody and I wouldn't have survived this long. I'm not sure which.

From where I'm standing, I have a clear view down the aisle and between two cashiers at Dara. She extracts a huge wad of cash from the ATM, and then she holds it in one hand and stares at it.

It must be at least a thousand dollars. More than I would expect anyone from our apartment complex to just have at their disposal. After about a minute, she grabs an envelope from the service desk and stashes her money inside. She unzips a compartment inside her purse—notably *not* her wallet—and tucks it away.

Well. Miss Girl Next Door is full of surprises.

She meets me in the produce section and she helps me figure out which avocados are ripe enough to eat.

"So, you're a musician," she says. "What types of music?"

"I'm not any good," I tell her with a self-deprecating laugh. I perfected this laugh in group homes and tested it thoroughly on my foster parents. It makes boys melt, but it puts girls at ease. "I just sing in church."

"I bet you are good," she counters. "I wish I were able to sing. Or do anything, really. I can't even keep a job."

While she's distracted by the bin of tomatoes, I sneak a glance at her. I mistook her bubbly presence for confidence, but that was wrong. There's a mask that keeps slipping, and I can't quite figure her out.

She bumps her shoulder against mine, cigarettes and sweet shampoo flooding my senses. "Look," she whispers. I follow her gaze and see an elderly man in a motorized scooter. He eases a can off of the shelf and slips it into the pocket of his oversize cardigan.

"Poor thing," she says. From her frown, she really does pity him.

There's a wad of cash in her purse. She could go full Mother Teresa if she wanted to help him. But she only goes back to the tomatoes.

The man drives up the aisle. He picks up a bag of pretzels, considers it, and puts it back. As he does, he hooks his sleeve under a toothbrush hanging on an end display and it slips into his sweater.

"I've been there," I say.

"Yeah?" Dara looks at me, and I don't know what to make of her expression. Searching, but cautious.

Befriending her is a necessity, but it will also be a risk.

"Not a lot of money in singing," I say. "And a girl's gotta eat."

She gives me a closed-mouth smile, and it warms her eyes. Obscure as she is, I know I've just scored a point.

At the checkout line, I pull out my phone again.

As the cashier counts out my change, I think about what to say.

Thanks with a smiley face? Bland. He'll think I'm not interested.

You're so sweet? Generic. He'll think I'm too pure.

Maybe we can do a duet sometime? God, just kill me.

I can clean a man's blood from the tiles. I can ease the plastic bag from his lifeless face and soak it to remove the DNA and then use it the next morning to hold my flowers at the farmer's market. I can cut off his limbs while I'm fully naked so that I won't have to do the laundry, and bury all the pieces. But figuring out what to say to a man you're trying to seduce is its own brand of frustrating.

When we get to the parking lot, Dara sidles up against me again. To anyone walking past, we'd be best friends, even lovers, the way she carries herself as though she's known me forever. "So," she teases, "what's their name?"

"Whose?" I try to feign ignorance as I load the bags into the trunk, but she only laughs.

"I saw the way you were looking at your phone," she says. My cheeks burn. If Moody were here, she'd call me a helpless virgin and kick me in the shin.

I look at Dara again and I consider. She's married, and nobody plays music that loudly in the middle of the night because they're sleeping. She knows about love. Knows about passion.

You're Jade, I remind myself. *Sissy may be an idiot at love, but Jade is as seasoned as you want.* I slip into the role like I'm sinking into a warm bath, and the calm slowly washes through me.

"I've historically made bad choices, romance-wise," I say. "This one is still new. I just don't want to screw it up."

She gasps, hands on her hips. "Name!" she whispers playfully.

"Edison." I hand this to her like a precious breakable heirloom. "I met him at church."

I load the last bag, and Dara closes the trunk door with a slam. "A churchman, huh?" she says. "The choirboy kind, or the son-of-a-preacher-man kind?"

"A little bit of both," I guess. "We just started talking and we're at that awkward part where everything I say makes me sound like a dumb schoolgirl."

There's a mischievous gleam in her eye. "Go get your guitar out of the back seat. We're going to make this man love you."

Dara records a clip of me singing the first stanza of "Stairway to Heaven" while I pluck at the chords on my guitar.

"Trust me," she says. "He'll go wild. This song is magic. It makes people think about how lonely they are."

She holds my phone between us, and we both watch the clip play back. My voice sounds out, soft and slow, with just a touch of a rasp.

"What if he doesn't like Led Zeppelin?" I say.

"Everyone likes Led Zeppelin," she says. "More importantly, men like a woman who likes Led Zeppelin. Send it."

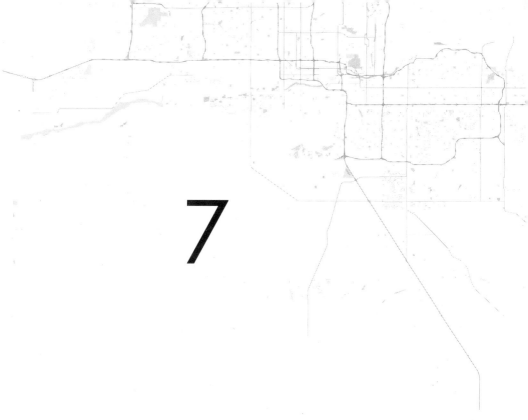

7

DARA'S INSTINCTS ARE RIGHT. AFTER I TEXTED EDISON that song, he asked me if I'd like to go hiking. Just the two of us alone in the middle of nowhere.

There are parts of the Arizona desert that are an unfinished painting. Rocks, gravel, and sky without so much as a cloud. Like the artist stopped here, afraid of making a single mistake. Edison, though, is not as simple as the landscape. As we trudge up the hiking trail, breathing hard in the dry late-morning heat, I smell the fragrant sweat of him. The cotton of his shirt, the sharp, sweet cologne in his deodorant. I can't identify it, but I'd bet the packaging is all black, marketed for men and offering the promise of mystery.

Sweat beads the back of his neck, and I wonder what his skin tastes like. He already knows the taste of me—my skin, my blood.

I've fallen a pace behind him and he turns to make sure I'm all right. I shake the daze out of my head and give him a smile. He thinks

I'm tired, that maybe I can't keep up. That's good. I want him to feel stronger than me. In control.

"Here's as good a place as any to stop," he says.

I nod, breathless. Not because of the heat or the hike, but because of his nearness. The way the air changes around him.

I slip out of my backpack and sit on the flat top of a boulder that's big enough for the both of us to have our makeshift picnic. I don't talk, not even to ask him what he's packed us for lunch. Instead, I listen to the hard and steady gulps he takes from his bottle, the plastic crunching in his palm. His stomach gurgles as the water rushes in. When I kill him, there's no need to make a mess. Not like Moody, who treats her kills like a low-budget slasher flick. No, when I kill Edison, I think I'll find a pretty way to do it. Just a sharp purple line across his throat, or a ring of mood-ring blue around his mouth where I've smothered him, his eyes dark and open, their whites gleaming in the moonlight.

Still, I think about cutting him open. Finding the chambers of his heart. Observing his stomach and whatever contents are left there. The parts of himself so deep that even he has never seen them.

When I look up, his eyes are on me. The depth of his gaze disarms me, and a moment later, he blinks it away. I wasn't meant to see his interest. His intrigue. I smile coyly like a church girl with a crush, but I don't say anything. I rambled about music during our first date at Still's, and I sent him my cover of "Stairway to Heaven," and now it's his turn to talk. He unpacks our little picnic in silence, though. He doesn't want to waste time with pleasantries or insult me with small talk. He's trying to find the right words—something that will be worthy of me.

My sisters have never had this problem. Iris, confident and regal, can transform herself into anything that attracts her victim. She can giggle like a lovesick teenager or wield her sexuality like a lingerie model. Moody has an eye for chaos. She finds the men who will fall hard and fast for her, and they spend most of their time with their tongue in her mouth. And if either of them were here right now, they'd lose patience with Edison. They'd tell me to find someone who finds me irresistible. Someone who doesn't waste my time with all this caution.

Patience, I tell them, and myself. He's the one. I can feel it. I'll coax it out of him.

He looks at me when I stand. "Where are you going?"

"I dropped my hair clip," I say, taking a few cautious steps down the trail.

I glance up at him as he abandons his task and rises to join me, and I catch his perplexed expression. There is no hair clip. My hair is pulled into a simple ponytail, perfect for hiking. It's long enough to fit into the hair tie without the help of any clips, but I've worked a couple of strands loose. He's noticed.

"What does it look like?" he asks. He doesn't believe me. He knows something is up, but just as he noticed the way I wore my hair, he observes me now with curiosity. He second-guesses himself.

"Gold," I say. "With little rhinestones."

He's close to me now, his head bowed as he looks at the nondescript pebbles and dust at our feet. So close that I can feel his warmth, different from that of the rising morning air. He's so alive in this barren place. His smell fills me and I can taste it.

We're close to the edge of the trail; if I let myself fall over the edge, I'll go rolling down a steep incline and my fall will eventually be broken by some dying shrubs or possibly a cactus. I'll sprain something for sure, possibly even break a bone. I think of Moody slashing furiously at the jugular of her last lover, all those months of passion coming to an ugly head. I think of Iris, cool and calm, but with rope burns cutting into her palms, the only proof that she lets herself get lost in the heat of her kills.

I kick at the crumbling edge of the trail, and I let myself topple backward. Best to find out right away if he's the type to pick me up and dust me off, or if he's vigilant enough to save me before I hit the ground. It will help me plan my next moves. The shriek I make isn't an act—even though this was deliberate, some part of me is still afraid to let go. Survival instincts. I feel the open air, the absolute nothingness all around me, and I brace myself for the crash.

Fingers coil around my forearm, grasping me down to the bone. And then I'm reeled back to earth. I feel him before I feel my own feet on the ground. I open my eyes and I'm staring at the sharp angles of his throat and jaw. His open mouth. He's grasping both of my arms as though I nearly just teetered off into a bottomless abyss, rather than a little hill.

When I bring my gaze up to his, his brown eyes have gone all dark. Worry? Desire? No, something else. Something that's been there all along and that doesn't have words, but I understand it, because I have it inside me too.

Breathless, I can't help but smile. Today's mission was to make him speak to me so that I could learn more about him. But all this time, I haven't needed words at all. Neither of us do.

He raises one hand and tucks the loose hair out of my face, his touch cautious and slow. I feel the calluses of his fingers, his palm. He works those hands. The tendons within them connect to all his muscles and flesh, all of him taut and carefully constructed.

"Edison," I say, at the exact moment he says, "Jade."

His heart and mine are beating in a hard tandem gallop. His hand trails down the side of my face, and my breath catches when his thumb traces my lip. He takes his time exploring the length of it, where the skin turns soft and damp the closer he gets to my tongue. It would be so easy for me to open my mouth and taste him, but I don't move, afraid to break this fragile line he's casting me.

He's like me. If I suspected it before, I know it now. It's about the space between the words. What he does, not what he says. Most of the time when I say anything at all, it's an act—I'm playing a part to run point for my sisters, and now, to reel in my first kill. He's playing a part too. The dutiful churchgoing man whose smiles are congenial, but whose real self is hard-won.

This is him, now, touching me. This is me, not Jade, looking back at him. It's reckless and stupid to let him see what's really there. He might realize the monster I am if we stay in this place for too long, but I can't look away.

"You're all right," he tells me, a rasp to his low voice. It's a command. *I've got you*, he's saying. *Nothing will ever happen to you while I'm here.*

It's the overpowering desire that snaps me back to my senses. I can't lose control—not ever, and especially not now, so early into our relationship, when the slightest mistake could scare him away and ruin everything. So I smile at him, easing back into my mask. "I'm so clumsy," I say, Jade once more.

He smiles too. Relief as he slips back into his own act. Back to the facade he wears for the world. We sit to have our little picnic, abandoning the fictional hair clip. But the fear still hangs between us. Not the fear that I might have slipped and tumbled off the hiking trail, but that we're both still falling down something much steeper, and that we'll never catch ourselves; we'll never stop; it's already too late.

———

I THINK ABOUT THE moment Edison grabbed me. How I could feel the tension in all his muscles. The intense look on his face.

He's lost someone. He'll never let it happen again. Who was it? An old lover? A sibling? A friend? He's vigilant. Like my sisters. Like me.

Moody holds my head in her lap as we watch *Wheel of Fortune*. She was irritated when I came home from today's picnic with Edison without much to report. *What did you talk about? Nothing. Well—what did he say? Not much.* Admittedly, I've held back on the details. I told my sisters that Edison packed peanut butter sandwiches for us—I could have made us something, but it was a test. I wanted to find out what kind of a bachelor he was. Not the kind who can cook, but more important, not a man of excess. I can do something with this knowledge.

"Boring," Iris had said. I didn't tell them about my stunt falling over the hiking trail, even though they would have gone wild over it and called me a genius. But they would get nervous if I told them about the raw look on his face when he held me, and that I felt something change between us. The perfect victim is just smart enough to be interesting, but not too clever. He shouldn't see the real me, and I shouldn't be trying to show it to him.

Iris thinks I should just find someone else. She saw the picture of him that I snuck during our first date, taken from under the table with part of his face obscured by the umbrella stand. "There are a million more like that in towns like these," she said.

But there isn't another Edison. I think of him and I feel sick. Last night, I lay awake and thought about the sparrow from church kissing him. She'd come over with a homemade cobbler and say she just wanted to check in. He would invite her inside.

I grab my phone and stare at the message screen. He hasn't sent me anything since we parted ways earlier this afternoon. "I'm going to text him," I say.

"There's something wrong with him." Iris is knitting a scarf with the same baby blue yarn she used to garrote a man she dated back in Idaho. "Reasonably attractive, single, and not trying to get into the sack with someone as beautiful as you? Someone fucked that man's head up."

Moody rakes her fingers through my hair. "She might be right, Sis." Her approach wields more compassion than that of Iris, to whom one man is the same as the next.

I can't argue when they're on the same side against me. They didn't feel what I felt today. I didn't tell them what his touch did to me in the church. Besides that, I can't argue when I can barely explain it myself.

"He's the one," I say. I've been quiet all evening, wondering just what the hell is wrong with me. Wondering why I can't tell my sisters the truth. He's just a man, and practically a stranger. If I blow our cover, if I screw this up, it's not just my own safety I'm jeopardizing, but my sisters' as well.

But I can't help myself. That moment is mine, and I'm still working out my next move.

It will be fine, Sissy. Nothing will go wrong. You've cleaned up everyone's messes for all these years.

The show goes to commercial, and Iris looks at Moody and then at me. "I pushed you into this," she says. "It's not too late to change it up. It can be Moody's turn. You can run the cleanup."

I sit up. "You don't think I can do this," I say. "You both still think of me as your baby sister."

"Sis—" Moody is already starting with that mollifying tone of hers, but this time, I won't listen to it.

"No," I interrupt her. "I don't have the luxury of just diving head-first into a kill like the two of you, because there isn't someone else to clean up after me if I make a mistake. *I* have to clean up. I'm more than just the janitor, you know. This is my kill and I'm going to do it my own way."

Before I can tell whether that's shock or pride on Iris's face, I breeze past both of them. I storm up the stairs and into the bedroom.

I start a new text to Edison: Hey . . . How's your night going?

Whoosh. Sent.

The three dots appear, disappear, appear, disappear. Then they stop entirely. The TV hums softly downstairs, and music thrums in through the wall we share with Dara and Tim.

I type again: You okay?

I restrain myself. Sending this is the dumbest possible move. It reeks of desperation, and if this is going to work, I have to stay in control. When Moody first started, she chased more than one man away in the early stages by being too clingy. The goal is to make him want you and think it's his own idea.

What happened? I thought I had you. Don't you know how beautiful it will be when we look into each other's eyes for the last time? I've already dreamed of how I'll do it.

The phone rings and I'm so startled that I drop it. EDISON CHURCH in bold white letters. For a horrible moment I worry that I actually typed out what was in my head, but of course I didn't. He would have called the police before he ever called me after reading something like that.

"Hello?" I answer.

On the other end of the line, across town, through the still, warm evening he sighs. "Hey, Jade."

He sounds exhausted, like he's just come off a long day.

"Hi." I elongate the syllable and make my voice extra soft. Being tired, I understand. I'm patient, compassionate. "How are you?"

"Is it too late to be calling?" he asks.

Wheel of Fortune is down to the final bonus round. The befuddled contestant throws out her desperate guesses. "It's only seven thirty."

"Do you have to be up early?" he asks.

"What's going on?" I say. If I answer his questions, I won't be able to steer the conversation, and I need to know what I'm dealing with. "You sound—a little out of it."

"Can you come over?"

"Edison, I—"

"Forget it," he says. "I'm sorry. I'm so sorry. I don't know why I said that."

He doesn't sound right. His voice doesn't have that cool reserve it had during our first date. Almost sleepy now, and at the cusp of some emotional edge, like he's holding something back. I think of the sparrow bringing him cobbler. All the beautiful church ladies who smiled at him. His eyes glinting amber in the sun when he sat across from me and told me I had my own way of seeing things.

He is mine, and right now, he needs me.

"I'll be right there," I say. "What's the address?"

I hurry down the stairs, and Moody and Iris look up when I reach for the doorknob. "Where are you going?" Moody asks.

I turn and look at them. Moody, whose faith in me is shaken by our sister, and Iris, who has to be in charge of everything, even though she doesn't know shit about DNA because she's just good at the fun parts.

When I step outside, there's nothing they can do to stop me without blowing our cover, and this brings me profound satisfaction. I was three ounces smaller than my sisters when we were weighed at the hospital after being found, and for this, I've forever been labeled the baby. Being the youngest sibling is like being a kite in a tailwind, always tugged along by their whims and only worth the entertainment I can bring when it suits them. Sometimes Moody will give me a little slack, but only until Iris sinks her teeth into that soft little heart of hers and changes her mind.

They don't deserve an explanation, and I don't give them one. Let them spend the night conspiring about how green I am, how I'm not ready and I'm going to mess this up. I'll show them what I can do.

When I turn onto Edison's street, his house is the first on the left. It's a one-story Spanish mission with a clay roof, 764 in black numerals by the door.

This is a surprise, and I'm intrigued. I was positive Edison lived in an apartment. Single, twenty-nine years old, with a car that's old enough to legally vote. But the house is on a nice grid—a people-who-have-their-shit-together neighborhood. The kind of place that has a watch committee and an annual Christmas cookie swap. Edison is working on a contractor's income, not salaried, which means he's either making bank building houses or he's good at saving his money.

The front yard is loose gravel, not a shred of grass in the entire suburb. I park beside his car and peer over the wall that borders the backyard. There's the skeleton of a swing set, minus the actual swings, and not so much as a hedge. This could mean anything, I tell myself. Swings are hard to transport and the previous owner left it behind. Besides which, children need more than a broken swing set to entertain themselves, and the yard looks like it hasn't been used in a long time. The lawn chairs are all stacked against the side of the house, and there's a patio umbrella lying in the dirt with no table to hold it. A glazed ceramic toad sits watchfully by the back door.

My man is full of mystery. Whatever Edison has to tell me, I'll meet him with compassion. On the phone, he had the voice of someone who needs to make a confession. If he's wrong for me, I'll make adjustments. I'll fit into whatever path he's on and I'll make it work.

It would be something if he's lured me out here, alone after sundown, because he wants to murder me. It would drastically shorten our relationship; still, I would welcome it. We would wrestle around the living room, knocking the pictures from the wall and stumbling over furniture. I'd scream, let him think he'd won, and trip and land on my back on the kitchen tiles. He would crawl over me, and when he saw the loving smile on my face, he would be so taken aback that he wouldn't realize I'd jammed my box cutter into his kidney until he saw his blood pouring out onto my shirt. I would kiss him, hold him, tell him that I wished he weren't so impatient—I would have liked for him to be my first.

He comes to the door before I've had a chance to ring the bell, and he looks so different from the man I saw this afternoon that I could almost believe I'm at the wrong house. His stubble has filled in, and his eyes are bleary, their sparkle dulled but not entirely squelched. His smile wavers and then turns into a pensive line, like guests assembling around a buffet table after a funeral.

"Edison?" I instantly wish I'd brought cookies. I should have baked something and had it wrapped in plastic in a decorative dish and ready to go. But I hadn't expected him to look so sad.

He watches me through the screen door but doesn't move to let me in.

"I have to tell you something," he says. He pauses, runs his hand through his hair. The curls wrap around his fingers like they're desperate to be touched. From where I'm standing, I can smell the alcohol, and my stomach sinks.

No. Oh no.

This man—this beautiful man who was put before me in that diner—is broken. He's drowning in pain, and it's so unlike me to have missed it, but all the signs were there. The warm smile on Jeannie's face when she pushed us together on Sunday. The lost look in his eyes when I sang.

"Edison." At my dulcet tone, his eyes fill with tears. Not a single one spills, though, and he musters up his bravado.

"I thought I was ready for this, but I'm not," he says.

"Ready for what?" I ask.

"For someone like you." He shakes his head. "It's been a year, and I just—can't."

Open the door. Tell me everything. Let me save you.

It's as though he reads my mind, because he stands aside to let me in. I step inside his house and I'm surrounded by his world. High ceilings, immaculate hardwood floors, black leather couches surrounding an ornate marble fireplace that's been remodeled into a bookshelf. Paperback novels are squeezed against DIY handbooks, a Spanish-to-English dictionary, and a half dozen albums from one of those services that turns your Instagram photos into a book.

That shelf is the only indication that anyone actually lives here. The rest of the place is immaculate enough to have been staged by a real estate agent—other than the three bottles of Jack Daniel's on the coffee table in varying degrees of emptiness. There's a lone shot glass among them, shimmering with amber droplets.

He walks to the couch like a man defeated and falls into the leather recliner. "How much time do you have?"

I walk into the kitchen. As I pour a glass of water for him at the sink, I count ten plants—hanging from the ceiling, resting on the counter, and a three-foot lemon tree on the bay window. I return a minute later with a glass of ice water and a damp dish towel. When I bring him these things, he looks up at me like I'm a guardian angel.

"I've got all night," I say softly. I sit on the edge of the coffee table, obscuring his view of the bottles so that he can see only me. "Here." I fold the damp towel and drape it around the back of his neck so that it will cool his flushed skin.

He takes a tentative sip of the water and stares down at the ice cubes. "Her name was Sheila," he says. "We were both in recovery. She was five years sober and I was almost three."

Romance novels on the shelves. The lace-trimmed decorative hand towel draped over the oven handle. Sheila.

"Her car broke down on the interstate. It's a dead zone on that stretch, and she must have been walking to find some reception. Some kids were speeding, not paying attention, and they veered right into the shoulder and—" His voice chokes off, but he makes himself say it. "Killed her."

I put my hand over his. He's shaking. "Oh, Edison. I'm so sorry."

"I stayed sober through all of it," he goes on. "Every second of the day, it felt like someone from that church was coming by to check on me. AA meetings and Bible study, week after week, fifty-two weeks in a fucking year."

I smile at this hint of the real Edison. He's in there, and I'm slowly coaxing him toward me. The Edison that only comes out when he's alone. Not so polished and sweet and eager to please. Not smiling from across a picnic table or sending me polite texts. I squeeze his hand, and he brings it to his cheek, letting me feel the rough stubble. I smell the Jack and the tears, and he's giving it all to me, only me. Not the shining church girls or motherly Jeannie, or any of his perfect neighbors in their Spanish-style houses.

I'm in his world, in his mind, up against his skin.

"Last week was the first anniversary of her death," he says. "I thought I'd gotten through it, but—four years of sobriety, gone."

"It's all right," I say.

"No." He shakes his head. "I fucked up."

He's still holding on to my hand, and I bring two fingers to his lips. They're warm and impossibly soft. Through the drunken sheen in his eyes, he gives me the most desperate look. He's mine, he's telling me. He's trusting me with all the little pieces, broken and whole.

"Everyone fucks up," I say. "I do it all the time."

He laughs through his nostrils, and his breath on my skin sends chills roiling through my blood. He's around me, in me.

"No," he says. "You're perfect."

He sets the water down, and his hand is still cold from the ice when he brings it to my cheek. His knuckles are rough, his touch light, his palm almost broad enough to eclipse the side of my face. "You're so beautiful," he tells me. "You're the most beautiful thing I've ever seen." His eyes are dark and full. I breathe in his scent and it fills me up and makes my skin go hot.

Before I can exhale, he's holding my face and he's kissing me. At my gasp, his fingers rake through my hair, giving it the lightest tug as he draws me closer.

He pushes forward, fingers raining down my arms, my hips, the small of my back. He sets my nerves on fire and I breathe hard against his open mouth. Jack Daniel's and salt and a smell like suntan oil and warm sand.

I let him push me back against the couch, his hands eclipsing mine up over my head. My body rises against him when he trails kisses up my neck and behind my ear.

"I want you," he rasps, a hungry sound that reminds me of the first time I heard him speak. Deep and smooth. He's been waiting to show me this side of himself, and I realize now that this is what I felt that day at the diner. All those moments flashing through my head. His life, his energy, flooding me with so much force that for a second I couldn't breathe.

A cry comes out of me because I want him too. I've always wanted him. As my sisters cycled through lovers, I watched and waited for the one who would call to me. But state after state, all I saw was gray, all the voices blurred to a meaningless thrum.

Edison is all color, an explosion of gasps and kisses. He can't keep his hands off me, and my skin flares to life wherever his open palms land. I make another sound, and his mouth captures it in a kiss.

One day, this will have to end. I'll wring the last breaths out of him, and I'll do it without my sisters because I don't want them to see how deeply I'll mourn him. I'll do all my crying before I set about disposing of his remains. I'll move on, and he will always be with me wherever I go.

But for now, he's alive and I'm alive. I sweep my hands under his shirt, feeling the solid muscle that ripples in the dunes of his skin.

"Edison," I whisper. I want him to look at me. I want to see his eyes. But he buries his face into the curl of my throat as he fumbles with the button of my denim shorts.

I ease back, and when he still won't look up, I grab his wrists to stop him. He notices immediately and murmurs, "What is it? What's wrong?"

I keep my voice gentle. "Look at me."

At last, he does. That pitiful look is still in his eyes. He's mourning the woman tucked away in those photo albums, and he's drunk. If we do this now, he'll hate himself in the morning when he sobers up. He'll think he betrayed his dead love, and he won't want to see me again, because no matter what I do, there's just no way to compete with a ghost.

No. That is not our story. I'll make him fall in love with me slowly, with guitar strums and soft kisses. I'll cook him dinner and make sure he goes to his AA meetings, and tell him how proud I am of him. I'll be the living force, the light, the salvation that fills up a house that was once a tomb.

I reach up to give him the lightest, gentlest kiss. "I don't think this is a good idea," I say.

My body is ablaze with protest, but I guide his hands away from my jeans and I sit up, forcing him to come up with me.

He stares straight ahead at the liquid gleaming in the bottles on the coffee table, and I think he might cry, but he only says, "What am I doing, Jade?"

I wrap my arm around his back, tuck my chin up on his shoulder. It's a sweet gesture. I'm patient. I care more about his cracked heart than my own needs. I am not a one-night stand. I am his one love, and we were brought together by fate. Call it God if you like.

He tilts his head against mine, and we sit like that for a long time, until the lust is gone and there's something new forming in its place. Right now, it's a fragile stem—our love—but soon it will be towering and great and impossible to escape.

8

AN OPPORTUNITY HAS BEEN GIFTED TO ME. I HELP EDISON down the hall and into bed. I won't get a good look at the bedroom tonight because I don't want to turn on the light and wake him. If he comes out of his drunken haze, he might regain enough sense to ask me to go home, and I'd lose this rare opportunity to be alone with unfettered access to his things.

He's pliable and trusting as I guide him onto the mattress and draw the comforter up to his shoulders. I position him on his side. I'll leave the door open just in case he calls out.

"Good night," I whisper, and lean in to kiss his forehead.

He grasps my wrist, and when I look at him, his eyes are open and they catch the scant light coming from down the hall. A tired smile spreads across his lips, and he's still smiling when his eyes close and his hand falls slack.

Affection blooms in my heart for him. My sweet broken thing.

It's a small house, but perfect for a young married couple. If there were ever any family photos on the wall, they're gone now. The hallway bears the generic scenic photography one would find in a waiting room. Landscapes, mountain ranges, cacti against the setting sun.

There's no rhyme or reason to any of it. Edison isn't a decorator. Rather, his passion is in the structure of the house itself. The living room is outfitted with antique wooden beams that surely aren't original to the house. The floors are aged hardwood, polished dark. The kitchen has brick walls, each one of them distressed and discolored. Edison rescued them from a demolished building. He picked them up one by one and decided they were beautiful.

But Sheila is still here too. She liked lace, it would seem. A lace-trimmed towel draped over the stove handle, and a lace-trimmed oven mitt—teal blue—shining out against the warm kitchen colors from where it hangs on a hook by the sink.

I pour out the bottles of Jack and I take them to the recycling bin in the garage. In the morning, he won't want to see them. They'll only embarrass him, and I can't have him associating any of those uncomfortable feelings with my presence. Instead, they'll be out of sight and out of mind until later in the week when he's taking the recycling to the curb. He'll see the bottles, empty and neatly placed, and think how sweet it was for me to clean them up and not say a word about it. I will be a tomb to his secrets, and I'll never judge him. I will be everything he was looking for that day he walked into the diner. The only one who could ever love him the way that he needs.

When Edison has been asleep for a while and I'm positive he won't wake up, I crouch by the bookshelf and peel one photo album away from the others. I'll put it back exactly where it was, between a serial romance novel and a hardcover photography book of scenic Japan.

All the photos are square-shaped, some of them heavily filtered, and I know these came from Sheila's Instagram because this is not how Edison sees the world. Looking around his house taught me that he sees things simply, as they are. He doesn't embellish, and he only lingers on details to enhance their natural shine, not filter them with too-bright colors.

I can't pull out my phone and search for Sheila's profile because I am always careful about my search history. But she was thoughtful enough to compile her life story for me, a gift to the next woman who will take care of the man she so loved.

I carefully turn the pages of their early life together. They were married on a beach on an overcast day, holding hands beneath a floral trellis while a minister fed them their vows. He wore dress shoes, and she was barefoot in a short white dress and a crown of flowers.

To my great relief, Sheila looks nothing like me. Taking the place of a dead spouse would be far more trouble than I'd hoped for, particularly if Edison had a type. Sheila is much shorter than him, whereas I come up past his shoulder. Her hair is pale blond and curly, and she has bright eyes that make her look just like a doll.

My own hair is dark and stubbornly wavy. My sisters and I maintain our identical appearance, and since this is my kill, I got to pick how we would look—right down to the nail polish we'd wear. When Moody gets her way, she always makes us dye it blond, or once, a pale blue that never fully set and stained our pillowcases for months.

Sheila was wrong for Edison. Too pristine, too virtuous. From her pictures alone I can tell what sort of person she was. She was sober for five years, and she judged him for it. When he told her that he was exhausted or that he was hurting, she didn't listen to him. She didn't tell him to put his feet up or hold him or bring him a mug of tea. She dragged him out for morning runs, and to pottery classes, and out to dinner with friends. Distraction is its own addiction, and that's what their love was.

When she died, suddenly he had no one to tell him what to do with his time between all those church visits, and now he's starting to break again. I've come just at the perfect time.

Once I replace the wedding album, I reach for a new one. The first several pages are travel photos. An airplane wing against the clouds. Two entwined hands with wedding rings on the armrest. Sheila gazing wistfully into the distance within a beam of window light. A blurry shot of Edison adjusting his cuff.

I look through all six of the albums, but I learn too much about Sheila and nothing about Edison. Sheila was all about appearances. She took only the pretty moments, and she and Edison existed in a vacuum. There are no shots of family or friends, not even at her wedding. There is one shot of her flower girl: a blond preteen with dark eyelashes staring down at a satin pillow with two rings on it.

After I've wiped my fingerprints and put the final album back in its place, I go back to exploring. Two bathrooms, one decorated to impress guests—black and gold cloth roses, a satin shower curtain—and one that looks more lived-in. I step into the latter and close the door, turning the knob to make as little noise as possible.

It's less impressive, with pale blue walls, no windows, and a glass shower door. This is the one Edison uses. I slide the glass door on its track, and when I step inside the stall, I can smell him. The faint damp of his last shower, an uncapped bottle of shampoo that fills the tiny space with a cologne scent.

This is where he's alone. Completely alone.

I feel dizzy with the love I have for him. Moody and Iris have never felt this, because if they understood this force pulsing though my arteries and veins, they wouldn't have told me to go find someone else. Yes, Edison is broken, but he was given to me. Someone carried him and nurtured him and birthed him out into this world for me to find.

From down the hallway I hear the creak of a door, then the shuffle of bare feet on the hardwood. I ease out of the shower. I flush the toilet and run the sink.

"Jade?" Edison's voice is soft. When I open the door, he stares back at me in a twilight, his face pale. "You're still here."

"Of course I am," I say. His expression is unreadable. I don't know how much of this he'll remember tomorrow, but in whatever memories he does have of me, I'll be speaking and touching him with great care. "I want to make sure you're all right."

He rushes past me to vomit in the toilet. I kneel beside him, rub his back. He murmurs something about not being able to drink like he used to. I don't say anything. I have plenty of experience taking care of someone in this state. Another sort of mess I've learned how to clean.

At thirteen, I exhausted Elaine's good graces and it was with great sorrow that she told me, "I just can't have you in this house anymore."

I became a ward of the state once again, but what should have been one of the worst days of my life was one of the best, because I was dumped into the same group home as Moody. We collapsed into each other's arms and we were inseparable for nearly a year, until she was shipped off to a home for troubled teens when she stabbed one of the boys with a ballpoint pen. Nobody bothered to ask her why she'd done it, what he'd tried—unsuccessfully—to do to her when he thought she was asleep.

For two years, I cycled through group homes and temporary placements. For a few months, at age fifteen, I was lucky enough to be within two miles of Iris, who never let me see where she was living but would meet me at my bedroom window every night. We would walk the same block over and over until the sun came up, just grateful for each other's company. No matter where I lived in those transitory years, I didn't bother to unpack. I barely spoke—there was no point. The revolving door of faces, some kind and others cruel, meant nothing to me.

I was returned to Elaine when I was sixteen. She ran into me by chance outside the grocery store where I had a summer job gathering carts and stocking shelves, and she asked me how I'd been. I looked like shit. My hair was stringy; I was the skinniest I'd ever been; there was a bruise on my arm the size of a baseball.

"Oh, honey," she'd said. She hugged me so gently, as though I might crumble and break. When she couldn't see my face, I closed my eyes and breathed in the familiar smell of her, like fresh-baked cinnamon bread and dish soap. Her guilt at giving me up had been plaguing her, even though I couldn't blame her for getting rid of me. But in the time since I'd been away, my elder foster brother, Colin, had become an alcoholic and graduated to cocaine. I liked him. He made me laugh, and he had a good heart even if he cursed like a trucker.

I'd always gotten along with him, and Elaine wanted to take me back on the condition that I'd keep an eye on him. Six months later, when he ODed in the bathtub, I'd be the one to find him, so I suppose her instincts were correct. Pulling him out of the water and doing what the 911 operator instructed me to do was a blur, but somehow he survived.

I was the only one Colin talked to most of the time, because I didn't yell at him to get help and I'd give him whatever money I had when he asked.

I nursed Colin through countless withdrawals, and I learned that the worst thing you can do is talk. All he ever wanted was a cold cloth for his face and to not be judged. "You're looking rough, kiddo," I used to tell him, and for some reason it always made him smile.

I don't talk about my time with Elaine, but especially not Colin. After all my sisters have done for me, it would kill them to know how much I love those outsiders. It would kill them to know that when Colin referred to me as his sister, I never corrected him. But even so, I carry everything I've learned from my time with them, and Edison's state right now is nothing I can't handle.

When Edison is done being sick, I wipe his face with a damp cloth and guide him back to bed. I turn for the door, but he grabs my wrist. His skin is clammy and hot. "Don't let me get behind the wheel," he slurs, barely conscious. "Don't let me go over there."

"Where?" I ask, gentle like the guardian angel he's imagining I am in this moment.

"I'll kill him," he whispers, his eyes dark and sad. "I'll do it."

My heart flutters desperately. He is giving me a secret he would never confess if he were in his right mind, and already I'm losing him to sleep. *Stay with me*, I want to beg him. *Tell me what's hurting you. Tell me what's in that head of yours.* But all I say is "Who?"

Edison doesn't answer me with words. A visceral hatred paints his face, and I have never seen anything so ugly and so beautiful. His sweetness and innocence are gone, revealing something I know as intimately as myself, because I have it too.

"Don't let me," he says. "Promise me."

I sweep my knuckles against his forehead. "I promise," I say. "I'm here. I've got you."

He's asleep as soon as the words are said, and I stand watching him in the shadows of his room for a long time. When I finally leave him, I curl up on the couch in the living room and I listen to the sound of him breathing.

I dream that I'm in his lungs. Endless blooms of red and black throbbing with the force of every breath.

It's the quiet that wakes me in the morning. No TV forever murmuring down in the living room, no throbbing music from the wall I share with Dara and Tim. Instead, there's the soft *whoosh* and then the trickle of coffee being poured out.

Edison emerges from the kitchen, his damp curls backlit by the morning sun. He's wearing a fitted gray shirt and black boxers, and he smells like coffee grounds and freshly showered skin.

"Hey," he says, and at his contrite expression I go soft. He is so beautiful. Shadows stretch across the lean muscles of his arms. Last night, I only got a taste of what it was like to be held by him, and already I'm aching for more. *In time*, I tell myself.

More intriguing than the physical are the words he muttered when I brought him back to bed. There's someone out there he wants to destroy. Left uninhibited, in a world without laws, he would. I could teach him how to get away with it. I could show him how to clean up and secure an alibi.

"Hey, yourself," I say, and as I smile back, I wonder if he has it in him. He doesn't even remember that he said it, I can tell. He's back to the guarded man he becomes when he emerges from his front door each morning. He doesn't trust me just yet.

"How do you like your coffee?"

"Black," I say, and I'm rewarded by a wink. He disappears into the kitchen and I hear him grabbing a second mug from the cabinet. I found the shelf where he keeps them last night, and he only has three: a his-and-hers set bearing the logo of a Las Vegas casino, and a blue Christmas mug with a snowman wearing a Santa hat.

He brings me the Santa hat mug, and I notice that he keeps the HIS mug cupped in his palm so that only the plain back of it is facing me.

"I'm sorry—" he says, at the same time that I ask him how he's feeling.

We both laugh. I don't even plan it. The breathy sound just comes out of me, because I'm so happy I could burst with it. Last night, I was strong. I did what was best for us both, and because I didn't give in and let him make a drunken mistake, he's glad to see me. He's brought me coffee and asked me how I take it.

He sits on the recliner adjacent to the couch, and he reaches over to tuck a piece of hair back behind my ear. My lips part. I want more of his touch. I want his hands grasping my hips again, his mouth on my neck. But I only smile and take a sip. The coffee is bitter and dark, and it's exactly what I need to keep my bearings.

"I'm sorry for whatever I said last night," Edison tells me. "Or—or did."

Now it's my turn to reach out. I put my hand over his on his thigh. His knuckles are calloused, and his hand so much larger than my own that I can barely wrap my fingers around it. His skin is bronzed from the hours he spends doing construction in the baking sun. Mine is shock pale by comparison because I slather myself in sunblock and spend so much of my life undercover. His hands have built and carried and created. Mine have dismembered and buried and destroyed. But I work in secret and every inch of me looks the part of the helpless girl I've been playing since I was a child.

This would make a lovely photo, I think. We don't need the wedding bands or the airplane armrest. We just fit as we are.

"You were a perfect gentleman," I assure him.

He stares down at our hands, and I wonder what he's thinking. His expression is soft, his lips slightly upturned.

"I have to get to a meeting," he says after a long silence. "I have the day off, but I don't blame you if you want to get home. After last night, I mean, but I'd like to see you—if—"

"Edison." At my interruption, he looks at me. I'm smiling. "Just ask me out."

He laughs into his coffee and then takes a long sip. After taking a moment to gather his thoughts, he says, much more smoothly, "There's a fair in town for the summer. I'd love to take you."

I drove past this on my way into town. A giant Ferris wheel and a roller coaster. Music, laughter. It's perfect, like a scene right out of a romantic movie. "Okay." At my nod, his eyes brighten. Yesterday, he was alone, mourning his love and drowning in alcohol. Today, there's sunlight and hope again.

I draw my hand back away from his. Let him feel my absence. Let him miss me a little bit.

He walks me to the door, and as I turn to leave, he captures my wrist, spinning me to face him. Softly, he lifts my chin with a finger. For a breath we stare at each other. He smells like the body wash in the shower, and coffee, and aftershave. His angled jaw is smooth now, and his eyes are bright with morning sun.

His hand grips my waist, and the way he squeezes me makes my knees go weak.

This time, when we kiss, he's with me. There are no ghosts. No alcohol. Nothing to regret.

"I'll see you later," he murmurs when I draw back. I reach up and sweep my fingers through his damp hair, and his hazy smile brightens. He waits for me to get in my car and back out into the street before he goes inside, turning once to watch me drive away.

When I turn at the stop sign, a girlish squeak comes out of me. I drive home in a manic excitement, licking my lips to catch the lingering flavor of his coffee.

I do a terrible thing on the drive home, and it's something I could never confess to my sisters. I dream of pinning Edison to the ground to kill him, and then, when his eyes are full of fear, I would laugh instead. Kiss him. Melt my muscles against his.

I dream of carrying his child inside me, and getting married in a venue with sweeping windows and a view of the Arizona mountains. Mornings lingering in bed. Vacations. Twining our fingers together over the Aleutians. Napping with my head on his chest on a warm beach as he twirls my hair around his fingers and breathes slow.

I dream of helping him to kill this mysterious figure who has wronged him. I would share Edison's hatred of whoever it is, and our love would only deepen to have such a secret. We'd never say a word about it. Only a loaded glance as we drove by the spot where we buried him, his fingers tightening gratefully in mine, so happy that he's found me.

By the time I pull into my parking space, I've spent a lifetime with him.

I look up at the stairs leading to my front door. No Dara out smoking on the balcony. The curtains are drawn. They're deep red, lined by a sheer white layer that makes her apartment always appear to be on fire.

Even though Dara isn't outside, I'm quiet when I ascend the stairs. She never misses a beat, and if she knows I've been out all night, she'll want details. After recording that "Stairway to Heaven" clip, she's invested.

I make it inside, and Moody is on me the second I've closed the door. "Where the hell have you been?" she demands through gritted teeth. She's still wearing the Rolling Stones T-shirt she had on last night when I left, and her hair is still in the same neat ponytail. She hasn't gone to bed.

The worry in her eyes nettles me, but I haven't forgotten that I'm still mad at my sisters, tired of being treated like a pet hamster they can keep in a tank. I square my shoulders. "I was with Edison."

Iris comes thundering down the stairs. She's brandishing her burner phone like an accusation. "You know how this is supposed to work," she hisses. Her voice is a rasp so that the neighbors won't hear. Ever aware of her surroundings, Iris is cool and collected even when her eyes are filled with rage. "You can't just disappear all night, Sissy. I was this close to going out and looking for you."

I stare at her. Cunning Iris, who always needs to be in control. She fought with all the violence in her body to keep us together when we were kids. The first time a social worker came to separate us, when we were five, Iris latched onto his back and bit his ear so hard that it bled. He screamed and tried to throw her, but she held on, and it took both of our foster parents and their teenage son to pry Iris away. She was spitting and writhing like a snake, her eyes black with rage.

After I arrived at my new foster placement, I didn't unpack for a month. I was so sure Iris would come scaling the trellis to whisk me away in the middle of the night. But she couldn't. The day we were separated, the three of us learned how big the world is. Filled with vast turns and chasms, caves and valleys. We could scream and scream, and the sounds would never find one another.

Now she stares at me in much the same way, because for just a few hours, I made her feel like that terrified little girl again. She didn't know if I was hurt, or dead, or had driven into a lake and couldn't shatter the windows of my car in time.

I don't tell her that I feel some satisfaction, mixed in with my shame. I'm twenty-five years old. I can disappear for a few hours if I want to, and I don't have to pick up the phone just because she wants to know where I am.

"I was with Edison," I tell her. Moody comes to stand behind Iris, and her own expression is more contemplative, one eyebrow furrowed, arms crossed and shoulders hunched. Moody shares in Iris's worry, but she doesn't judge me. She understands, in her inexplicable way, and watches me now with a hint of admiration. Always caught in the cleanup, I've never shown my own interest in killing, and she's proud of me. Respects what she sees. "And I have to go take a shower now. We've got a date later."

Moody frowns. "You didn't sleep with him already, Sissy."

"No." The accusation rattles me more than I was prepared for, and I clear my throat. "No. It was nothing like that. He needed someone to talk to."

It may not sound believable, but it doesn't matter because my sisters can see that I'm telling the truth. When Iris finally speaks, her voice is not exactly calmer, but tentative, like she's a buzzard circling carrion. "What's the date? Where are you going?"

"I can handle this, Iris." I square my shoulders, and immediately I feel foolish in my attempt to counter her ferocity. Behind her, Moody gives me a pitying expression, as though I need training wheels to pull this off. But I don't care. Edison is mine. Before we came here, all three of us agreed that it was my turn.

"I thought you would be happy," I say to Iris. "What was it you said to me the last time? That I was too soft?" She said those words exactly. I remember, because I was packing her lover's limbs and torso into trash bags and duct-taping them crossways like Christmas presents. I did everything for her but tie a bow. That lover was supposed to have been for me, but I didn't feel right about making him mine. I hated his aftershave when he sat down on the bus bench beside me, and I was so anxious that I spilled my coffee all over his shoes. "There you are!" Iris had called as she sprinted out to rescue me, and she introduced herself to the victim before apologizing for her clumsy sister.

He'd grinned in a way I suppose he thought was charming and said, "I must be seeing double."

But Edison isn't anything like him. He's different. This whole mission is different, and I'm in complete control.

Now Iris puts her hands on my shoulders. But there's no force to her grip. She's taking the killing-with-kindness approach. "I think Jade needs a twin," she says.

"No!" I hate that I sound like a petulant child. "I don't need you for this."

"You broke our cardinal rule," Moody says, being practical. "We always check in with each other. When we didn't hear from you last night, we didn't know what to think, Sissy. We were about five minutes away from going out to look for you. We would have been seen, and we would have had to abort everything and start over."

I think—impractically—of the man we buried up in the Arizona wilderness off that hiking trail. He's the only one in Rainwood to have seen two identical sisters, and he died for our secret.

"I'm sorry that I made you worry," I say, looking alternately at each of them so they'll see that I mean it. I don't add that I'm hurt they think so little of me. I may not have killed anyone yet, but a lifetime in the foster system taught me how to take care of myself. When he was deep into his addiction, I protected Colin from his own dealer. Foster Brother Dearest was built like a linebacker but he didn't have much grit, and he knew I carried a knife, so he asked me to come along. He was short on cash and his dealer thought he could have a few minutes with me instead. The dealer is lucky that his surgeon was able to reattach his finger.

I'm aware of how I look: tall, but petite. A rounded chin and big doe eyes. I know that I come across like easy prey. Even though we're all identical, I *look* like the baby of us three. Like I would trust a kindly trucker to give me a ride home, like I give everyone the benefit of the doubt, and I close my eyes at horror movies. But my sisters know me. We've all had to survive on our own, and we all made it this far intact.

In the interest of keeping the peace, I tell Iris and Moody exactly where I'll be and I promise to check in with them. Moody is quick to point out that they've always done as much for me. But I don't tell them about last night with Edison because some selfish, greedy little part of me wants to keep it all to myself. If they knew how gentle he was, and that his hands immediately stopped when he sensed my hesitation, they would understand just how safe I was in his house. The only predator in those four walls last night was me.

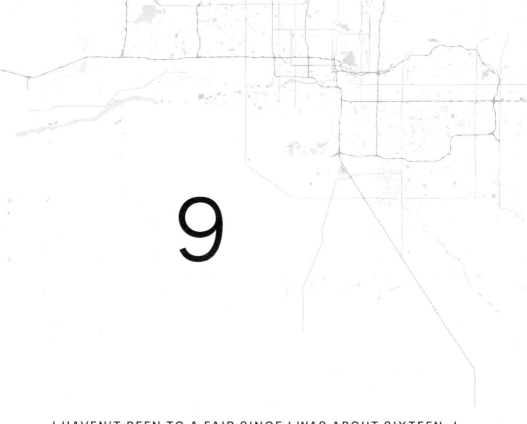

9

I HAVEN'T BEEN TO A FAIR SINCE I WAS ABOUT SIXTEEN. I
was with Moody. Just Moody and not Iris, who had been placed in a
group home fifty miles away. "I have something for us," Moody whispered when we met up by the fried-dough stand. She opened her
purse and showed me two small white tablets in a plastic ziplock bag.

"Baby aspirin?" I guessed, and she laughed and hugged me.

"X, you idiot," she said, and took my hands. "I wanted us to try it
together."

The pills, she later told me, were twenty dollars apiece, and she
wouldn't have had enough money to get one for Iris anyway. We made
a vow never to tell her about it, and nearly a decade later we still
haven't.

We rode the Ferris wheel, and we were at the top when it came to
a halt. Twilight was setting in, and the sky glowed an unearthly neon

pink. The lights were giggling and whispering far below our feet. Moody coiled her arms around mine, a warm body against the chilly September air. She had bleached all the color out of her hair, and the tips were still faintly pink with traces of blue. Kool-Aid.

A wave of incredible happiness overtook me while we were stuck there. We'd found each other. Soon enough we'd be torn away again, but for now we were sisters.

"I can read your thoughts," she whispered.

"What am I thinking?" I'd asked.

She nodded to the car ahead of us. A pair of teenage boys was hanging over the railing, trying to spit on the people below them. "That if they tried to hurt me, you'd kill them."

I couldn't remember what I'd been thinking, but I liked Moody's thought more than anything I could have come up with myself. In my delirium it seemed romantic, grasping their greasy over-gelled hair and cutting their throats with my knife because they'd hurt my sister. I didn't want anyone to touch Moody or Iris. I hated everyone who had torn us apart, every schoolyard bully who made fun of our clothes, our unwashed hair. Every timid social worker who didn't fight to keep us together.

The romance turned to anger, and the anger circled back around to the love I had for them. A love that strangled me and cut me deep.

"I would kill them," I agreed as we watched the boys laugh and nudge each other. Moody had a hunger in her eyes, and I felt it too. I squeezed myself closer to her, so close that it was like we were the same person with the same thoughts. "I'd kill anyone for you."

I LOVE THE DESERT—who knew? Rainwood is an ironic name, considering the air is impossibly dry, and seeing a tree is a rare event out here. Every city block is like a blank page made of sand and sky. Then the rides of the town fair emerge like simple ink lines against a blue canvas. If I'd grown up in the desert, I would have been an artist. A writer. With so much space around me, I'm constantly dreaming of all the ways I could fill it up.

Edison finds me after I've parked my car and made it to the entrance at the chain-link fence that borders the fair. When I'm close, he takes a step to bridge the space between us, and he reaches for my hands. "Hey."

His eyes have changed, and right away I know that I handled everything perfectly the night before. He was worried that he'd scared me away, or worse, that I would judge him, but I'm still here. He looks at me now in a way that he didn't before last night, and when he catches me searching his gaze, I kiss him. *We've found each other*, my kiss says. *It's all right now.*

I wait until we're through the gate before I ask, "How was your meeting?"

He smiles at his shoes, scratches at the back of his head. "Coffee and sob stories." He looks at me. "By which I mean I was the one sobbing." I laugh, and the gratifying expression he gives me is a gift. "Thank you," he says. "For this morning, and last night."

Don't let him wallow, I remind myself. There's a thin line before he starts to associate me with his cathartic confessions and sees me as a sister or a friend. But it's an act of great restraint for me not to ask him. *Tell me everything*, something within me is begging him. I want to see every sharp angle of his pain. The day he found out his wife was gone, and their dreams dead with her. Every woman from that church to come by with food and smiles and love. I want to climb inside his head and watch his memories playing out all around me. Hundreds of Edisons, all the different timbres of his voice.

"Are you close to your family?" I ask, because it's something I can learn about him instead. "Parents? Siblings?"

"No siblings," he says. "My mother died when I was young."

"I'm sorry," I say, and he shakes his head because he's heard this a million times.

"I don't remember her. I was a baby," he says. "And my father. He's . . . around. We don't really keep in touch."

He's alone, like I was whenever Moody and Iris had been torn from me. I want to tell him this. *I was left in a stroller at a rest stop, and whoever put me there never came back.*

My parents abandoned me, but I have my sisters. Moody and Iris are a religion, a sanctuary from the storm.

I weave my fingers between Edison's and draw him closer. All he had was a church and pictures of his dead wife, but now he has me. I'll be his faith, his sanctuary, the arteries that encase his lonely heart.

When we walk, he rests his hand on the small of my back. I think of the beauty in his eyes as sleep began to take him last night. That delicious, fearsome rage when he murmured about killing someone. *Who was it?* I look at him now, his face guarded, pleasant. *Who hurt you?*

I don't ask him. Not yet. I could fill this entire fair with all the things I wish to know about him.

We spend the afternoon burning in the Arizona sun, laughing, kissing in shy bursts as we wait in the line for the merry-go-round. He moves forward and surprises me with a kiss to my forehead. His lips linger and his arms cross around my back. I lean into him, inhaling the sunlight and heat in the soft cotton of his shirt.

In answer, I tuck my head in the slope of his neck and leave a trail of kisses there. The line has started to move, and we shuffle forward, still locked together. *I've found you. It's okay.* I kiss his flushed skin again, and electricity moves through me. I've never been held like this. Grabbed, yes. Groped in cars because I needed money or a ride. Kissed clumsily in empty hallways of my high school, and behind the restaurant where my boyfriend worked a few years ago, right before Iris made her first kill—her old guidance counselor turned secret lover because he was forty-something and married—and we had to skip town.

I was angry with Iris when she did it. I'd planned to give my boyfriend my virginity that weekend while his parents were away, but then I got the frantic phone call saying they needed my help. We left town just as soon as we'd cleaned up. That was the night that changed everything for all of us. The night we all forfeited any chance of having a normal relationship with a lover, and became murderers instead.

I'm grateful for Iris's poor timing now, grateful for the six years I've spent hopping from town to town, cleaning up my sisters' messes, because it led me here.

We spend our first day together, Edison and I, and we never run out of things to talk about. We're sitting on a picnic bench, eating ice-cream cones, when the sky turns gold and then deep gray with early evening. The air has cooled, but my skin is pink and hot from the afternoon in the sun.

I look at Edison, who is staring straight ahead at the Ferris wheel turning lazily against the horizon. He has the most beautiful throat. Despite the stubble at his chin, he keeps his neck entirely smooth. Muscles hint below the skin like ripples on a calm sea. His Adam's apple swims within him as he breathes.

When I kill him, it won't be like Iris, who leaves a sharp red line across her lovers' throats, their eyes red and bulging as they stare into the hereafter with tears on their cheeks. Or like Moody, who destroys them by tearing into their vital veins, making the cleanup a living hell.

Edison is too lovely for that. I'll kill him gently, kill him slow. I've thought of giving him something to take the edge off, but that isn't right. I want him fully with me when I do it. We'll be in bed, our bodies warm and spent, sweat at the line where our hair meets the backs of our necks. The air will smell like us, and we'll be drowning, delirious with love. When I climb on top of him, he'll reach for me, smiling lazily. What I'll know, and what he will soon learn, is that we've already been together for the last time.

"Jade?" Edison's voice brings me out of his bed and back to the fair. I slap at a mosquito that's sucking on my shoulder.

"Yeah?" I look at him, and I realize he must have been trying to get my attention for a while. *Stop daydreaming, Sissy. Pay attention.*

"I just asked if you've been to Arizona before."

I shake my head. "I've moved around a lot." I've been finding little ways to tell Edison the truth even as I lie to him. "California is where I was born, but I've never really felt at home there. I'm not sure how long I'll be here." I can't tell him outright that I'll be staying here for the next six months. For all the passion brewing between us, we haven't known each other a week, and I can't go scaring him off with talk of moving in and taking his dead wife's place. Not yet.

He's still looking at my face, a slight smile on his lips, a bit of strawberry ice cream in the crease. He's got a square jaw and a permanent five-o'clock shadow, but in glimpses like these I can see how he must have once looked as a little boy, inordinately vulnerable and sweet. His mother was gone and his father didn't love him enough, and there he was, looking for someone to come along and be his home.

I have a thought I shouldn't: Edison and me as children. I see him on the playground down the block from one of my first group homes. My sisters have just been taken away, and I can see that he's lonely too. Children don't say as much, but they can smell emotions like bloodhounds. They can see misery, see loss at such a level that it frightens the words right out of them. I see his gentle brown eyes and he sees the dried tears on my cheeks, and we know before we've even approached that we've just saved each other.

I could have loved that Edison forever. We could have spared each other a lifetime of searching. Rather than shyly getting to know each other through songs and drunken late-night confessions, we would be well past needing to say anything at all by now.

But I will never have a lifetime with Edison, and Edison will never have any kind of a lifetime at all. I reach out and touch the drop of strawberry ice cream with my thumb, capturing it and bringing it to my own mouth for a taste of him.

"Jade," he says, "I—"

"*There* you are," a voice calls through the waning crowd, and I go rigid. It's dark out now, the sun replaced by the neon floodlights set up around us. But when I turn my head, I recognize the figure sprinting toward us even though her face is in the shadows. Her long dark ponytail bounces from shoulder to shoulder, the exact same length as my own, which is wound into a loose bun.

Edison doesn't understand what's happening until Iris comes into the light, and he sees a face that's identical to my own.

"Hey," Iris says, out of breath from her jog. She's faking it. I've seen her run ten miles at a time on the treadmill while belting out the lyrics of whatever she's playing on her headphones. She wants to look vulnerable, endearing. She's wearing a baggy gray T-shirt. This is deliberate. She's letting me be the beautiful one, in my formfitting sundress—white with little strawberry buds.

Half a dozen people are killed by carnival rides every year. If I shove Iris at the Tilt-A-Whirl, maybe I'll get lucky and a stray foot will knock her head off.

"Sorry to interrupt." Iris flashes a brilliant smile and holds her hand out to Edison. He stands as he takes it, ever the gentleman. Rage burns in me as I watch her manicured little fingers coil around his broad palm. "I'm Jade's sister, but you probably guessed." She gives a flirtatious laugh. "I'm Lisa."

Lisa Canter. A name on one of the random unused IDs in our pile. Colin made them up for me the last time I saw him because he owed me more than one favor. Iris is wearing a plain wedding band. A nice touch to say she's off the market, and to make it easier for Edison to tell us apart. We learned little tricks like that when we needed to distinguish ourselves from one another—clip-on earrings, necklaces, rings—because even our foster parents couldn't tell us apart. Besides which, jewelry can be exchanged. I slip on that ring and just like that we'll have traded places.

Colin couldn't tell Moody from Iris, but he always knew me, because I'd spent so many years drifting in and out of his house. We were both the problem children in an otherwise perfect family. Joking together in the pews until Elaine hissed at us, which only made it that much harder not to laugh. And then later, scraping him up from the bathroom floor and dragging him to bed so he could come down. "Your sisters are psychopaths," he murmured in his delirium on one such night, shaking with withdrawal. This was years before we ever killed anyone, or did more than fantasize about it, but maybe he always saw something. I drew up my knees and told him I was a psychopath too. "Yeah, but I like you." He'd reached for my hand before he fell into an unreachable sleep.

Edison will come to know me. No one can love him like me, touch him like me.

"You said you had sisters, but you didn't tell me you were a twin," Edison says, looking at me. "I thought you said they were both older."

"Oh, I am older," Iris says. "By about a minute or two." She lets go of him, her eyes on me as she does it. There's not a drop of triumph in her gaze, but I know that's part of the act. We didn't talk about this. We didn't plan this. I am getting too defiant, she's telling me. Too unpredictable. "Jade, I came to get the car keys. I need to run to the store." The fucking store. "You don't mind riding the bike home, do you?"

There was a rusted ten-speed left behind by a previous tenant in the laundry room. I assume Iris cleared the cobwebs off the seat before parking herself atop it.

"Of course not," I say, all smiles. The Tilt-A-Whirl is only a few yards away.

"You're the sweetest," she tells me. Her eyes change when she looks at Edison, like she's appraising him. He isn't her type. She likes the gym rats, sexually charged and handsy. The ones who can wrap her waist in their hands and twirl her around. They're nothing like any of the men she used to date, and in stark contrast to the guidance counselor who was her first kill. She isn't attracted to them and she says the sex is terrible, but the behemoths are more of a challenge.

She stays only a minute longer, to tell Edison she's charmed to have met him and crack a joke about him not keeping me out too late. "Just text me if you're not going to be coming home," she says, and only I would recognize the edge in her tone.

I watch her walk away, swinging her hips in a faded pair of black leggings, and all I can think is that she touched him. She touched my Edison with the same hand she used to make her last kill. She wounded herself on the garrote and I made her let me treat it, because if it got infected, we couldn't very well go to a doctor after a man she was associated with had just been murdered. She sat on the toilet lid while I hunched over the sink, flushing it with antibacterial soap, patting it dry, and then plastering a clear bandage over it. Both of us entirely trusting, knowing we had it in us to kill a man twice our size, but that we'd sooner die than let any harm come to each other.

The betrayal cuts deeper than any salve could heal.

Edison is careful about how he lays the bike in his trunk, even though the bike is fit for a scrapyard. He wants to take me somewhere for dinner, but I tell him I'm getting a migraine so that he'll take me home and won't try to follow me inside.

My anger is a poison that muffles the world. I barely hear what Edison is saying as he drives, barely hear myself giving him the directions. It's a bit early to be telling him where I live—he might show up unexpectedly—but it would be more suspicious if I refused when he insisted on giving me a ride. He doesn't want me to take my bike five miles in the dark. It's a crazy world and you never know what's out there at night, he tells me. Last week a man went missing when his truck was found abandoned on the side of the road.

10

IT TAKES A WEEK FOR ME TO FORGIVE IRIS, AND EVEN then, it's only in the interest of keeping things uncomplicated. Moody is ever the peacemaker, and she points out that Lisa can be a helpful addition to my mission if I allow it. I know that I'm being selfish. I don't want to share Edison at all, but I can't come out and say as much, emotional thing that I am. If my sisters knew I was dreaming up little fantasies of a future with Edison, they would stop everything right now. End our lease, pack up the car, drag me someplace far from here, like Minnesota. Or Dubai.

I can't have that. *Focus on the positives, Sissy.* I brush my teeth in the morning and regard my rumpled reflection. I have six months with Edison. Six delicious, glorious months, and the best is yet to come. At the end of our first month together, he'll realize he loves me. He'll tell me, but I won't return his feelings. I'll make him wait. I'll come to his house in the middle of the night—maybe I'll be crying, or my car will have broken down and my phone will be dead. Vulnerable, helpless, I'll rush to him and he'll save me, and that's when I'll confess that I love him too. We'll tumble into bed and it will be everything I've waited my whole life for.

I haven't seen him since that evening at the fair, and sometimes I don't reply to his texts just to see how long it will take him to send another.

Last night, I called him when I knew he'd already be in bed. He was dozing, and his voice was warm like a mug of tea and honey. I asked him when his next meeting was. I told him I was proud of him for being strong. He laughed, a slow humming sound. "Where did you come from?" he asked, his voice starting to fade. I knew he'd fallen asleep by the way he breathed, and I lay in bed listening to him for a long while, until I heard one of my sisters coming up the stairs.

This morning, I'm choosing to be happy. Edison texted me good morning, there's a church cookout on the Fourth of July and would I like to go? Of course. Three smiley emojis. I'm jubilant. Sick with anticipation because Thursday is four days away and I'll get to kiss him again, get to feel him slipping his hands under my shirt the way he does when he holds me for long seconds.

Moody and Iris are at the kitchen counter sharing a bowl of cereal. I grab a granola bar from the cabinet and a bottle of water from the fridge. "I'm going out," I say. "I'll take the bike." I need the exercise. I need to do something with my energy. I can only spend so much time in this condo with my heart and my mind fit to burst with the excitement of what's to come. Not like Moody, who could go months without saying a word if it weren't for us. She relives her kills, smiling to herself, twirling her hair and staring off.

And Iris, who turns oddly solemn after a kill. In the months leading up to it, she's all eagerness, tapping her feet when she sits, knitting to keep her hands busy, snapping at us for the smallest offenses. Once it's done, she turns quiet. She sleeps for days at a time, emerging only to use the bathroom and force something down so she doesn't starve. It's a full-soul purge, she says.

"Got a date?" Iris asks.

"I'm giving him time to miss me," I say. "Just getting some exercise."

Moody tosses me a retractable box cutter and I catch it with one hand. "Lots of sickos out there," she says. "Did you hear about that man who went missing by the ten-mile marker?"

I stuff the blade in the pocket of my pink leggings. "Nope."

It's hot outside. The kind of searing sunlight that makes me grateful Arizona isn't known for its humidity. But once I'm pedaling, I'm cooled by the breeze of my own motion. Rainwood is a small town with long stretches of barren road that's perfect for solitude. Just the cacti, brush, dirt, and me. My true church.

Thoughts of Edison come to me here in all this brilliant open space. I don't know yet how Edison's murder will affect me. I've given great thought to how it will affect sweet, compassionate Jade. Walking up the church steps, organizing search parties, begging the police to take it seriously, falling into Jeannie's arms as she pets my hair and shushes me, a daughter to her.

I ride for a long time and don't see so much as a car passing by, so when I notice the figure in the distance, it's an immediate intrusion. Edison floats away from me like vapors on the air.

The figure is tall, holding a bag that dangles limply from one hand, and walking back from the gas station a quarter mile away.

When I get closer, I see the short dark hair, the effortless curves and confident stride. "Dara," I call out, and she turns her head. She stops walking when she sees me and watches as I skid to a stop in the dirt beside her.

Something is wrong. Her eyes are bleary, and her smile doesn't rise up all the way. Normally she has a magnanimous smile, shining with confidence, illuminating her eyes. She throws herself at the world like a dare. But today she's subdued, and she is too exhausted to feign otherwise.

"I saw your sister yesterday," Dara says by way of greeting. "Lisa. She seems nice. Had no idea she was staying with you."

Yesterday, Moody donned Lisa's persona and went out to water the potted plants we bought as an excuse to be outside, should we ever need to eavesdrop. She introduced herself to Dara and said she'll be visiting for a few weeks to help Jade with their dear aunt's affairs. We can smell Dara's cigarettes from the living room, and Moody was curious about her. Moody's prognosis: Something is off about her. She's always home and she knows everyone's business. She is far too young and pretty for this.

I didn't tell my sisters about the money Dara withdrew from the ATM at Safeway. They would have wanted to take it after Edison's murder. We never take anything from our victims—no trophies. My own rule. That's a sure way to get caught. We come into town, kill our victim, dispose of him, and speed off with only the memory to keep us satisfied.

After we were found abandoned in our stroller, donations poured in. It was a solid year before interest waned, and then again when we were five, we were the subject of a "Where Are They Now?" episode of a daytime talk show. I barely remember being paraded with my sisters on the stage and being gifted a new tricycle—an offering for our exploitation.

The donations were put into a trust for when we turned eighteen.

A cool three million dollars, which we only touch every other year or so when we return to Fresno to visit the bank in person. We take enough cash to get us through the year, but if a crime of opportunity arises, we steal cash elsewhere to make our funds last. Tips from restaurant tables, off the dressers of people we befriend, things like that.

But Dara—she needs that money. I can't figure out what for just yet, but I know she doesn't do anything without a reason. If it went missing, she would know immediately. She would figure out who had access to it, and how they knew she'd even withdrawn it from the ATM. I'm positive even her husband doesn't know.

"A bit hot to be walking, isn't it?" I say. "I would have given you a ride if you needed."

It's 105 degrees, and we're both glistening, but she hardly seems to notice. "That's okay." She raises the bag like it's an explanation. Through the thin plastic I see a carton of menthols, an extra-large energy drink, and a bag of Combos. "I needed snacks."

Nobody walks four miles round trip in this weather for junk food. The gas station, I recall, also has an ATM by the door. Dara isn't carrying a purse, but I glance at the pockets of her denim shorts and think I see the square outline of folded cash. I move my eyes back up to her face before she notices. If I ask her about the money, she'll never tell me. But if you want someone to confess, the best way to do it is to start talking about yourself. Get their guard down, make them see you as the vulnerable one.

"That video you recorded for Edison worked," I say. I smile conspiratorially, pretending not to see how puffy and pink her eyes are. "You're right. That song is magic."

She pokes me in the shoulder, and the force sends me back a step, my hips still straddling the bike. "I told you! What did he say?"

We start walking, me wheeling the bike between us. The small barrier it provides will make her feel safe.

Dara *is* safe with me. I have no reason to hurt her. I like her, and she helped me break the ice with Edison. She's the eyes and ears of our little subdivision, and she knows everyone's comings and goings. Doubtless she saw Edison drop me off last week after the fair. Edison parked under the only working streetlamp, and if Dara was looking through her blinds as she often does when she hears an engine, she'd have seen me lean over, take his face in my hands, and kiss him. A chaste kiss with our tongues kept in our own mouths. The kiss of a new, blossoming love.

I tell her about Edison's recovery, and she frowns sympathetically. "Good for him," she says, not a hint of judgment.

"My mother wouldn't like him," I say, because I want to build a bridge so Dara will tell me about her family. She's in a passionate marriage and living next door to me in that dump. If anyone out there loves her, they have feelings about that. Her parents hate Tim because he's always dressed in expensive suits to go to a job that doesn't afford their precious daughter the life she deserves. She's wasting her youth, her brain. Or Dara is their golden child who could do no wrong, and they want her to be happy. Her parents call her every weekend and pester her for a grandchild. They think she quit smoking last year.

I can't read Dara. She may be a hundred different things. A thousand. She's intriguing like the music that thunders into my apartment through the wall, a melody I've heard before but can't quite catch.

"Are you close to your parents?" Dara asks.

"No," I say. A small bit of the truth before I go for the lie. "They judge everything I do."

Maybe this isn't entirely untrue. If my parents are alive out there, they wouldn't approve of the way Moody, Iris, and I live our lives. But then again, they abandoned us without so much as a note to tell whoever found us what our names were supposed to be.

"We moved here for Tim's family." She sighs, and I can hear that she's aggrieved. Dara isn't the sort to get mad or to push back. I can tell that much already. But she makes her displeasure known, even if there's no one around to acknowledge it. She's chatty with the neighbors, but she doesn't seem to have any true friends. I've overheard her phone calls as she sits on the balcony outside her unit. She only ever calls her parents.

Tim has trapped her here. His beautiful wife all alone in the desert, where she's his and his alone.

Dara stares out at the desert for a long while, and when she suddenly spins to face me, my heart leaps anxiously. "Can I ask you for a favor?"

"Of course." My heart thuds. She's going to tell me something, gift me some piece of what's happening in that head of hers. We stop walking, and she digs into her pocket and extracts the wad of bills I'd already suspected was in there.

I pretend I'm not astonished by the sight of it. Not because it's easily five hundred dollars—the maximum withdrawal that particular ATM allows—but because she trusts me enough to let me see.

"Can I hide this at your place?" she asks. We've stopped walking, and the sun is beating down on my shoulders, my neck. Even with sunblock, I'm always sunburned in this place.

I don't answer Dara's question right away. Uneasy at my silence, she charges on. "It's not for anything sketchy. It's just, I've been sending money to my parents at the end of every month. Tim hates it. We had a big argument last week when he found the money in an envelope, and he made me put it all back into our savings."

Her parents. So, she's the dutiful child, then, trapped between her devotion to them and her loyalty to an exasperated spouse. *What else is eating at you?* I want to ask her. A fight about money shouldn't be enough to make her this upset. But she's said all she's going to, and for now, it's enough. The rest will come later. Like Edison, Dara is a long-term project. I need her to trust me; I need to be the shoulder she can lean on, the one who doesn't take too much or give too little. That way, when Edison is gone, she'll be my primary character witness. *Jade loved him; Jade is a caring person who couldn't hurt a soul; with Jade, you always know where you stand; she couldn't lie to save her life.*

If Tim doesn't support her, I will. I'll be the friend she can turn to when he's being unreasonable, when she's down to her last cigarette and she has no one else.

For a long moment we stand there, the only beings in this burning wasteland, the green bills pinioned between us. Dara is giving me something much more precious than money. She's giving me her friendship. On the other side of her unit, a woman named Mrs. Keltch has lived there for more than a decade. She comes out sometimes and makes a fuss about how bad those cigarettes are for Dara's skin, and occasionally to pour us a glass of boxed wine. Mrs. Keltch doesn't know about the money Dara is hiding from Tim. No one in the world knows but me.

Finally, I take the money and I tuck it into my own pocket beside the box cutter and my keys. I pretend that something ceremonial didn't just happen. "Sure," I say. "No problem." A pause. "Hey, I don't know if church is your thing, but there's a Fourth of July cookout on Thursday." I am giving Dara something equally precious: an opportunity to meet my Edison.

"Don't worry," I say. "I'm not going to try to recruit you or anything."

She laughs, and it's the lightest her voice has sounded all day. "Oh, honey, believe me, I'm not worried about being recruited."

"Is that a yes?"

She throws her arms up. "Why not?" she says. "Can I bring Tim? He works so much—he really needs a social life, even if it is a G-rated soiree."

"Of course. Tell him it will be PG-13," I say. "You might hear an errant *holy shit* or two."

"Just so long as it's holy," she says.

We're laughing and the air is lighter when we start walking again. I know that something powerful has just happened between us. We've just given each other a tiny piece of our trust.

I have decided I want Dara to know him. When Edison is dead and gone, and I'm lost in my grief, Dara will comfort me. She'll come into the apartment and sit on the edge of the couch where I'm curled up. She'll bring in the smell of her sangria hair conditioner and menthols, and she'll put a hand on my shoulder. She'll remind me that I have to eat, that life still goes on. She'll open the curtains and fill the room with sun. When I'm strong enough to speak, we'll share memories of him. In my darkest hour, I'll have a friend.

11

I DON'T LIKE TIM.

He's a calm, quiet, stoic thing beside his wife's effervescence. His eyes are pale blue, but they're dark in a way that doesn't have a logical explanation. It's as though the light never fully touches him. He doesn't talk much.

Still, I pretend to think he's delightful. I introduce Dara and Tim to Edison at the picnic as "the world's best neighbors."

"Hardly," Dara says, shaking his hand. "We're really loud. Jade is just being sweet." There's a gleam in Edison's eye when he looks at me over the top of Dara's head. He thinks I'm sweet too.

I was worried about abandoning Dara at this party to steal off with Edison, but she's at home in crowds. I hear someone laugh at a joke she's told by the bowl of sherbet punch. Tim stands beside her like a shadow, looking uncomfortable in his ironed blue T-shirt and khakis. Someday, I would like to know their story. Dara doesn't make a move that he isn't watching, and I think it's because he knows how mismatched their love is.

When I look to Edison, he's watching them too. "They seem nice," he says. He hands me a bottle of water that's ice-cold and drenched from being in the cooler. I press it to the back of my neck gratefully before I take a sip.

"Did you bring your guitar?" he asks. "Maybe you could sing something."

"I don't want to sing in front of all these people," I say.

"Sing something for me, then." He tucks a stray lock of hair out of my eyes. "I love your voice."

I smile. Warmth spreads across my face. "Later," I say.

All day, I play a tug-of-war with Edison's attention. He kisses me, and then I leave him to check on Dara, or to talk to Jeannie, or to take water to the boys in the high school band playing up on the stage. I catch Edison's gaze from across the sea of faces and he looks up immediately, sensing it every time. We're connected, he and I. He knows that something pulls us together—even if he doesn't know what it is.

The church combines its party with the community center, and while the church doesn't bring alcohol, the community center comes supplied with their own coolers. People are milling about all around him, holding sweating bottles of beer, plastic cups of wine and drinks with crescent ice cubes. I stand on tiptoe behind him and softly ask, "Are you doing okay?" He knows what I mean.

He takes my hand and kisses it. "Yes."

"I'm proud of you," I say. "I really am."

He turns to face me. His finger coils around a lock of my long dark hair just as Jeannie calls out, "Jade!" and starts waving me over. "Do you have a spare guitar pick in your car by any chance, honey?"

I run off to help her, leaving Edison with empty hands and a loaded grin. He loves Jeannie—she dotes on him like a mother. But still, I wonder if he would fantasize about killing her for interrupting our little kiss. I'm still carrying his secret, those drunken words he murmured that night. Someone out there has provoked his wrath. Awoken that darkness inside him that none of the fine, upstanding citizens of this cozy desert town would suspect.

When the sun begins to set, I stop depriving myself and go to him. He brought a beach towel for us to sit on for the fireworks show. It's an orange-and-white Hawaiian floral print, faded and frayed from years of machine washings. Sheila sat with him on this towel. He kissed her here, and held her under dozens of burning rainbow lights.

That he would share something so meaningful and intimate is not lost on me. When he wraps an arm around me, I snuggle myself close. Fuck, he smells so good. Not a drop of cologne. Laundry detergent and summer heat are caught in the fibers of his shirt. He rests his chin on top of my head, making me feel small and protected.

Darkness falls fast. Things chirp distantly in the brush, and from here I can see the mountain where my sisters and I buried the trucker. It stands just a bit taller than the surrounding ones, sharp and jagged and black against the emerging stars.

It's been about two weeks. The trucker is unrecognizable now; even if a search party thought to unearth him from the hiking trail, they would need dental records to find him, and his teeth are long gone. He's in active decay, with his organs leaking out through his orifices and his skin shriveling up.

If you can hide a body for a week and a half, and if you carve out any identifying details like teeth or tattoos, it becomes mostly unrecognizable. The organs decompose and the skin discolors. Give it a month or two in this heat and you're looking for a skeleton. I haven't followed the man's story on the news. They say his name and they show his picture, but he isn't that thing anymore.

From her spot several rows ahead, Dara turns her head to look for me. Tim's got an arm around her. He says something to her, but she isn't paying attention. At last she finds me and flashes me a wicked grin, waggling her eyebrows at Edison. My ears turn hot.

The sky lights up with an explosion of color and sound, and it takes my breath away. I'm not expecting it when Edison grabs my chin and turns my head to face him. He kisses me hungrily, greedily, counter to the way I've teased him by keeping myself away all afternoon. My stomach flutters and flips. Tonight is the night. I wanted to wait a bit longer, but my man is all surprises. Fits and bursts of this strange passion are alive between us. We want each other so badly it's like a rage brewing—an undercurrent—and if I don't give in, if I let tonight end abruptly, I will never again get such a chance.

The fireworks are still thundering like ethereal drums when Edison pulls us to our feet. We take three steps before I stoop to grab the towel in my fist. It trails in the desert dirt as we sprint to Edison's car.

He speeds through empty roads and I roll down my window to let the cool night air flood me. My skin swells with goose bumps, one hand raking through the air and the other holding his warm calloused hand. We don't talk. We don't have to.

The last time I was in his house, he was broken. He wanted me, but he wasn't ready yet. This time, when we giggle and scurry up the steps, he is open. His heart laid bare. "Jade," he growls, and the door slams shut behind us.

His dead wife sleeps forever in the albums in the fireplace. A clock ticks in the kitchen, shaped like a teacup and in need of a dusting. It's just us, alone in this island that has materialized so quickly around us. We're kissing as we move down the hallway, frenzied, dizzy, and then suddenly we're standing on the threshold of his bedroom and he draws back. Moonlight comes in through the window, painting him silver.

He's all softness now. He brushes his knuckles against my cheek, and his eyes are full as he watches me. "Hey."

I tilt my face into his waiting palm. "Hey."

Edison has been with other women—Sheila at the very least. He hasn't asked about me, but he must assume Jade has done this before. A free-spirited singer who adapts easily wherever she may roam. I'm not going to tell him that he's my first. I may be more emotional than my sisters, but I'm less likely to act on those emotions. I've saved myself for the right kill. Saved myself for him.

He lets out a nervous breath of a laugh, and it only makes me want him more. I rake my fingers between his and he pins me to the doorframe for another kiss.

He lifts me up, and I let out a startled shriek as he spins me around and drops me on the bed. I'm laughing and he's laughing when he crawls over me, our loud breathing silenced when we kiss. Buttons, zippers, collars being pulled over our heads. His stomach is warm and rock solid against mine.

His tongue grazes my earlobe and I shudder. "Jade?"

I look at his eyes, dark and heavy in the moonlight. He understands even in his fevered desire that he still is getting to know me, that I have my own cues, my own wants. I am not the other girls who have been in this bed. He seeks my eyes and I realize he's asking my permission. In answer, I take his face in my hands. "Yes," I rasp, a plea.

It hurts, having him inside me, but I hardly notice. His hand is on the side of my throat, thumb tracing my jaw and then my lower lip. My eyes flutter and I lose myself for a moment, drown in my happiness that he's with me and that he's mine. He was surrounded by alcohol and temptation all day, but he didn't have one blessed drop, because he wanted to be here with me. Ready, unlike the last time.

To everything I've ever wanted, every night I've spent lost, every moment of my life that I've been in mourning, or frightened, humiliated, desperate, he is the answer. He is the thing I never had the words for. And now his presence fills an emptiness so deep within me I could never bring myself to face it before. I'm not supposed to fall in love with him, and I haven't. *Love* is not the word for this. Love is a blur, a smear of color in the distance, so far behind me now.

He calls for Jade and I pretend he's calling my name in his rising crescendo. His prayer.

Sissy, I think. *That's my name. Call me that.*

Jade had lovers. Jade had boyfriends. Experiences. But I've only ever had this, and one moment with Edison is more than a lifetime of Jade's hollow lovers could give me.

He slides one hand down the length of me until he's brought it between us. His calloused fingers touch a part of me that makes my skin go hot. My eyes flutter. My head lists. He grips the side of my throat, his thumb digging into my pulse. "Look at me," he murmurs. The vulnerable plea in his voice undoes me. "Look at me, Jade."

"That's not—"

His touch turns rapid and my body arches in anticipation, a terrible ecstasy that makes me abandon logic. *You'll have to kill him*, I think furiously. I grasp his forearms so tightly his skin reddens around my fingertips; his pupils expand when I call his name. These are sensory reactions because he's alive and I'm alive. All his veins and arteries are flowing with his beautiful life-bringing blood.

He'll die. You'll bury him.

But this moment is here, and it's ours, and nothing has ever felt like this. When he cries out, I cover his mouth with my hand, not to stifle his sounds but to catch them, so that I might carry them inside me and keep them when he's gone.

MORNING LIGHT FILLS THE room, but I don't stir. I don't lift my head from where it rests above Edison's beating heart. My hair is coiled around his fingers, and he holds me with an arm around my waist.

There's a soft buzz from my jeans pocket, wadded at the foot of the bed. I extend my arm to reach for it carefully. Edison tightens his grip on me and sighs. I go still. When he doesn't wake, I grab my burner phone from my pocket.

There's a text from Moody. I didn't add anyone to my contacts, but I memorized the last four digits of my sisters' respective numbers.

> Up all night singing psalms with the
> church boy, Sis?

> Fuck off.

There, now she knows I'm still alive. I delete the messages and power the phone off before I put it back. The clock on Edison's bedside table reads six forty-five. In fifteen minutes, his alarm will sound and he'll have to get ready for work. The world doesn't stop even when wonderful things happen.

I force myself to get out of bed. I make my way to the kitchen and pour water into the Keurig. When he wakes up, I want him to realize the bed is empty. He'll panic, think I've left him. He'll realize how much he needs me and worry that he's lost me, that last night was too much. And then he'll smell the coffee and hear me moving around in the kitchen, wearing his T-shirt that comes halfway down my thighs, my collarbone exposed. He'll want me all over again, but there won't be time, and I'll live inside his thoughts all day.

While I wait for the coffee, I browse the fridge. Edison is the quintessential bachelor. A take-out carton of fried rice, an open box of baking soda, a splash of milk left in the carton, and some eggs. I can work with this. I find a potato next to a brown banana on a cutting board by the sink, and some olive oil by the stove. The bottle is covered in dust, and I run it under the faucet, exposing the date stamped on the bottom. Only a month past its expiration.

By the time I hear Edison's alarm go off, the diced potatoes are browning on the skillet and the eggs and milk are scrambled in a bowl, waiting to be cooked. I grab the snowman mug and press the button on the Keurig.

I'm singing when he finally makes his way into the kitchen. I don't turn to greet him, and I wait, my nerves standing on edge, as he coils his arms around me and kisses the side of my neck. "Morning." His voice is gruff. His fingers tighten against my hip.

"Hi." The world is spinning only for us. "I made you coffee."

"Coffee and breakfast," he says, and my body feels cold when he moves away.

"Oh, did you want some? I was making this for me."

He laughs, kisses the back of my head as I pour the eggs onto the skillet. He hasn't told me that he loves me. It's too soon; he doesn't even realize yet that he does. We're in the early stages, filled with comfortable silence and devious kisses. He'll think about me all day at work. The shape of my mouth, the rasp in my voice when I cried his name. All of me laid out before him for the taking. He'll think of the ways he's touched me, and the unexplored ways he still wants to.

I have to let him want me. Don't text first, not even to ask how his day is going. Be aloof, but not cold. Mysterious but intrigued.

I don't make myself a cup of coffee because the only two mugs left in the cabinet say HIS and HERS on them, and I don't want to remind Edison that he's a widower. I pour a glass of water from the tap instead, and I bring the plates to the table.

"Looks amazing," Edison says, inhaling deep. "I don't know how you managed to whip this up. I didn't think I had any food in the house."

Morning light fills his messy hair, and it takes all my willpower not to stare at him.

"I have a meeting before work," he says.

I reach across the table and put my hand on his. My thumb traces little circles in the space between his thumb and forefinger. *Good,* my touch says. *Stay strong for me. Come home to me.*

He meets my gaze, all warmth and a mischievous smile. "Last night was— I'm still breathless."

A warm feeling fills my chest, and I look down at our joined hands and then at him. It's too soon to use a word like *love,* but we're shrouded in a beam of morning sun, and it's the perfect time to ask him the question that's been tormenting me. "Edison," I say. "That first night I came over, you said something about—"

A sound in the living room captures both of our attention. Keys jingling and then the front door swinging open.

I give Edison a confused look and he stands, his arm outstretched to keep me behind him. I don't have my box cutter. *Sloppy.* It's in my jeans pocket on the bed.

"Eddie?" At the voice, Edison relaxes and lets out a relieved laugh. His arm drops back to his side. I follow him to the threshold, and from here I can see right through the living room to the figure standing at the front door.

"Sades? What are you doing here?"

Immediately, I recognize her as the flower girl from the wedding album. She's older now than she was in the pictures—at least thirteen. What the fuck is she doing here? Wearing a blue tank dress, her blond hair piled into a messy bun. She drops the bright purple backpack from her shoulder and launches herself at him, erupting with a sob.

"Hey, hey, it's all right," Edison whispers to her. "It's all right."

She's small in his arms. A little damsel in distress wearing neon pink Converse sneakers. A knife tearing through the fabric of our perfect morning. She's left the door open, heat and sunlight and insect buzzing filling up the house. Her presence invades every corner of the tidy home, and a tornado may as well have wrested its way inside.

At last, Edison draws back. He wipes at her tears with his thumb, and for the first time, I see the girl's impossibly blue eyes. So starry and piercing they're like a scream. They were downcast in the only photo I saw of her, hidden by her burden of blond lashes. But I see the resemblance now. It's as though Sheila herself has just walked through the door.

I don't move, and it's a good thing Edison's back is to me, because it takes a moment for me to wipe the stunned look off my face. The little interloper sees it, though, and her expression goes slack when she notices me standing in the doorway in Edison's shirt.

Edison sees the girl's confusion and remembers that I'm still here. By the time he's turned to face me, I'm wearing a pleasant smile.

I already know what he's going to say.

"Jade, this is Sadie. My stepdaughter."

12

THEY HAVE NICKNAMES FOR EACH OTHER: EDDIE AND Sades.

Sadie stopped crying when she realized she had an unwanted audience in me. I went into the bedroom to give them some time alone, but I left the door open and listened to every word they said. The acoustics in Edison's open-concept house made this an easy task. This month is the anniversary of her dear mother's death and she can't take it at her father's house. He's too overbearing, positively obsessed with what she's doing and whom she's talking to. He won't stop harping on her about taking summer classes to keep her grades up, and she had to be with family. Someone who understood. Edison. Her mother's one true love.

Edison didn't tell her he had to go to an AA meeting, I noticed. He only said he had to be at work early today—a contract installing a hot tub at a new development in town. And then he came to the bedroom to whisper an apology to me and say that he'd drive me back to my car and that he'd call me on his lunch break.

Sadie was on the couch with her iPad when I left. She was eating the scrambled eggs and potatoes I made, and drinking tap water out of her mother's HERS mug. She didn't look up when I made for the door, pretending to be too engrossed in the streaming show she was watching to notice me, but, oh, she knew I was there.

If the holy glowing ghost of Edison's wife herself had burst through that door, it couldn't have been worse than this. Sadie may not be a woman just yet, but she's old enough to be smart. If Edison had a dim-witted stepson or a neighbor with a crush, I would know what to do. But a doting stepdaughter will see through the veils. She'll want to protect him.

IRIS ISN'T HOME WHEN I return to the condo, but Moody is on our shared laptop watching a cooking show and eating chocolate chip cookies right out of the bag. She senses my anxiety even before I've said anything and closes the laptop with a soft slam. "What happened? You slept with him?"

I hesitate, wishing Iris were here. I swear she invented Jade's twin, Lisa, just to get out of the house. It's been months since her last kill and she's past the mopey phase and onto the energetic second wind she gets when it's no longer her turn. Like she's a kid out of school for the summer, gifted with more time than she knows what to do with.

But she's also whom I'd rather talk to about this. Iris is uncomplicated about murder. She sees it practically and responsibly, the same way that I see the cleanup. There's a right way and a wrong way to do it. Clean mark, clean kill, clean disposal.

Moody is messy and impulsive. If she thought we could get away with it, she'd drown every neighbor who lets his dog shit on our grass, follow home every soccer mom who cuts her off in traffic and hang her by the emergency release cord in the garage. Her violent mood swings are why Iris and I gifted her with her name. Long before our talk of murder, when we were only children, one never knew what to expect of her. She's sloppy because she knows that I'm here to fix it. She's hardly the one to turn to for advice about keeping things simple.

"Sis?"

"It's nothing," I say.

"Bullshit, it's nothing. Sit down." She throws the bag of cookies at me, and I just barely catch it. "Have a snack. Tell me what's up."

"Promise not to get dictatorial," I say. She only smirks at me. I slump into the ratty armchair. "Edison may not be as alone as I thought."

"Ex-girlfriend?" Moody guesses. "Cunty sister?" At my grim expression, she begins to look concerned.

"Stepdaughter," I say.

"Oh. Fuck. How old?"

"Thirteen."

"I thought his wife was dead. Why is her kid still coming around?"

"I didn't even know she had a kid," I say. "The narcissist didn't have any pics of her own daughter in most of the photo albums. It was all beach shots and sunsets."

Moody considers. She raises the volume on the TV to conceal our voices. "Can you get rid of her?"

"I'm not going to kill her, Moods."

"I didn't mean like that, you idiot," she says. "Make her go back to her family."

Back to her family, or over the edge of a cliff. The way the girl breezed right into Edison's house like she owned the place and ate the breakfast I made him. Knew where he kept the mugs and what the Wi-Fi password was. Looked at me like I came bearing a plague. *That's right*, I'd thought, willing her to read my mind as we stared each other down. *I'm here now, and there's no room for you.*

Moody sees my expression and says, "Calm down, Sissy. Iris will be back soon. Then you and I will go see what we're dealing with."

"She's in summer school," I say. "I drove by the junior high on the way home. Classes start at ten. It's walking distance from Edison's place."

It took all my restraint not to check Facebook for the girl's profile, but I can't have her in my search history. Nothing will happen to her. But you never know when leaving a trail will come back to haunt you, and the less in your search history, the better.

By the time Iris returns home, two hours later and bearing a fresh loaf of bread from the patisserie, my shock has worn off. I'm ready to be rational.

Moody puts on the wedding band and becomes Lisa. She wears her oversize sunglasses and forces me to take a shower before we go out. Says it will help me compose myself, and she's right—it does.

"Montana had a meddlesome ex," Moody says as she drives us toward the junior high. She's talking about her first kill. His real name is already lost to her, or maybe she just doesn't want to say it. "I thought she'd ruin everything. Kept writing him these weepy drunk texts at four in the morning. You know, one time that asshole grabbed his phone and texted her back while I was on top of him."

Her rage flares, but then she smiles at the memory. The kill in Montana was her perfect match. Irrational, emotional, addictive. They were all over each other—he pawed at her in the restaurant right in front of me, shoved his hand up her dress and his tongue in her mouth. And then the next minute, some small offense—he looked at the waitress a beat too long, or she flirted with a man at a red light—and the gloves came off.

Moody slams her palm against the steering wheel, two fingers raised as though she's holding a phantom cigarette. "That fucker cheated on me with her. He denied it right to the very end. Even when he was bleeding out. He slapped me in the face with the last of his strength and told me I was crazy. He thinks that's why I killed him—jealousy." She laughs angrily.

I don't tell Moody that I remember all this and there's no need for her to tell me. Instead, I watch her with fascination as she relives it. She's no longer talking to me, and she's no longer in this car. She's back in that maelstrom of a relationship, kissing him, cutting him open, wrestling his bloody form around the tiny bathroom like dancers in the final act of a gruesome play.

If Montana were still alive, he would have broken her heart eventually. He would have left her, or she would have given up on him. But in death he hasn't left her at all. He'll be the hot flush in her cheeks, the faraway stare in her eyes, for as long as she lives with the memory. It's better this way.

Edison will be my Arizona. I won't speak his name once he's gone, but I'll carry it. I'll smile and think about his touch, and no one will know my secret. I'll go back to him over and over in my head. Last night will be the first loud chord in our desperate song, all muscle and sweat and that helpless gasp he gave me as he fell, and fell.

"Did you want to kill Montana's ex?" I say.

"Of course," Moody says, coming back down to earth again. "But she wasn't the one. We only do one at a time; otherwise that's how mistakes happen."

More than one is too messy, but also, it ruins the intimacy. Makes it less special, like having two birthday parties on the same day.

"Do you want to kill that little girl?" Moody's voice is breezy. She's telling me that she wouldn't judge me if I said yes. No one in this world knows me like Moody, not even Iris. After that day we daydreamed about murdering those boys on the Ferris wheel, we wrote stories about all the vicious things we could do. Some of them we wanted, and others were just fun to pretend. We swapped notebooks and wrote on top of each other's sentences between the lines, our words kindling on a fire that had always been burning inside us. Moody is my best friend, my mirror soul. She loves me more than Montana and I love her more than Edison. Love her like breathing.

"No," I answer. Edison loves his stepdaughter, and this makes her a rival. It makes me angry. Sadie is a lightning bolt shot across my clear blue sky. She is the rumble of a coming storm that will flood my carefully laid plans. But the thought of harm coming to her upsets me in a way that I don't have words for. It's not logical. I should have daydreams of backing over her with my car as she sunbathes in the driveway, or taking her to the public pool and drowning her so that Edison will find her floating—a punishment, a sacrament. *Love me. Love only me.*

These thoughts damage me in some inexplicable way because she is a piece of Edison's heart and that makes her precious. Even if I wish she weren't.

I tell Moody something that will be easier to explain. "I don't want to spend my limited time with Edison consoling him because something happened to her."

"That's smart," she says, and pulls the car over. "Nobody wants a buzzkill." We blend in with all the others parked here. The junior high is on a city grid across the street from several little shops.

The little lightning bolt is standing on the sidewalk. I recognize her purple backpack and her neon pink shoes. She's talking to a wiry boy whose braces I can see from here. They stand close, and he brushes his hand down the side of her arm and nods soberly at whatever she is saying. He's comforting her. She is a tiny queen in perpetual dismay. Already she has learned the power she has over males, because she is beautiful and she knows how to be vulnerable.

A small group of kids assembles and they make their way inside. But even then, she stands out. Her long light ponytail is flickering behind her.

Moody has said nothing this whole time, but she doubtless knew which girl was Sadie by the way I was staring at her. "Come on," she says now, putting the car in gear. "We've got a couple of hours before she gets out. We'll get lunch."

We find a food cart two blocks away in the parking lot with the Safeway. Kebabs, sodas, and bags of chips. Comfort food. Thinking food. Nearly all our problems have been solved over takeout. Moody treats us both, and for the first time since coming here, I'm glad my sisters created Lisa without consulting me. I'm grateful that I have someone to confide in while we're out in the daylight, even if she can't give me any advice.

It's too hot to eat outside, so we climb back into the car and crank the AC. When my phone begins rattling in the cup holder, Edison's name appears on the screen. Moody mouths the word *speaker* to me.

I set the phone on the armrest between us and answer the call. "Hey!"

"Hey, you." Edison's voice is swooning and soft, and it sends a flutter between my legs. Last night changed something between us. We know each other in a new way. I hope it will be like this right up until the end—meaningful glances across a crowded room, a particular thrum in his voice when he's thinking of how I felt in his arms.

Moody lowers her eyebrows and looks at me with a mouth full of sour-cream-and-onion chips.

"How's work?" I ask him. My tone is light, upbeat. I'm happy to hear from him. I want the mundane details. "Did you make your meeting in time?"

"The meeting was . . . great." He packs so much relief into that word. *Great.* He's back on the wagon, on the mend, falling in love with me. "And listen, I'm sorry about Sadie showing up like that. It must have been a shock."

Sadie. The name freezes me, fills me with overwhelming sadness, because there is no way to undo her. Even if she returns to her father and stops coming around. Even if I bury her beside the ill-fated trucker, she would be present. Edison will love her. Miss her. Worry for her if she disappears. She is worse than a dead wife or an ex-lover or a best friend. She radiates purity and innocence and no matter what I may do, I will never be the only love in Edison's heart.

Moody sees my expression and rushes in to save me. She grabs my phone, holding it closer to her face. "Not at all," she says, mimicking my inflections perfectly. Unconsciously she begins to twirl her pony-tail the way that I often do. "This month makes a year, and she's so young. Poor kid."

I can hear Edison's smile when he says, "Thank you." And then, "I haven't been able to think straight all day, I'm so worried about her. She should be spending time with her dad. He and I had a long talk after Sheila's . . . passing." The hesitation in his voice tears open my jealousy anew. "He thinks it's for the best that she stops coming around as much now."

Good. Do that. Tell her to go home. She's not your daughter. Let her family handle it. I start to speak, but my sister reaches out and clamps her hand over my mouth.

"Oh God, Edison. How do you feel about that?" says Moody. Brilliant, amazing, wonderful Moody, who is rescuing me from my own bitter emotions.

There's a pause. A sharp breath. Edison's voice comes with great strain, and I realize that he's holding back tears. "I don't want her to think I abandoned her," he says. "She just wants to feel close to her mom."

Edison. I want to go to him. I want to speed out of this parking lot to the construction site and find him where he's huddled in the shadow of the new development, cradling his phone. Take his face in my hands, kiss him, draw his head to my chest, and let him cry. Tell him to let all of it out, to hold on to me, I'll fix this, I'll make it better.

"I was thinking about leaving work early to pick her up," Edison goes on. He's pulled it together again. "I don't want her walking home in this heat. It's supposed to get well into the hundreds."

I pry Moody's hand away from my mouth and say, "I'll get her if you want."

"Really?"

"Yeah." All my effort to sound like I haven't given Sadie any thought at all, that I haven't been stalking her all morning while thoughts of her demise filled my head. "I was just dealing with the attorney for my aunt's estate. I'm free the rest of the day."

"That's—that would be great, Jade. Thank you."

I've made him happy and my heart sings. I see what his little love means to him and I will treat her with care, like the valuable thing she is.

"Maybe we should have her over for dinner tonight, if her dad is fine with it," I say. "One little meal couldn't hurt, right? We can take out some photos if you have any. Maybe watch a movie."

"Wow," Edison says. There's a long silence. Moody glowers at me.

Too much, Sissy. But I know what I'm doing. I am the best liar of us three, and there's no great secret to it. If you want to be convincing, say the exact opposite of what you believe, and say it emphatically. It will sound like the truth.

"That would be—wow—yes," Edison says, and I square my shoulders and give Moody a triumphant smile.

"Where's Sadie's school?" I ask him. Her name is sandpaper in my throat. My own body seems to know I shouldn't be saying it.

Edison gives me the directions and I pretend I'm writing them down. After we hang up, I shove Moody out from behind the wheel.

"Don't speed," she warns as I make our way back to the condo. "We can't afford to get pulled over."

We have the world's cleanest records, we three. Not so much as a parking ticket. In our group homes, while the other children got into fights that tumbled from bedroom to hallway and down the stairs, we bided our time. If someone wronged us, we waited. We got them when they were alone and put the fear of God into them so they would never tell a soul. Once you know how to play by the rules, you can get away with anything.

I'm at the junior high ten minutes early. I can't risk the little lightning bolt already being on her way home. It's a small square building. White with small windows, all of them open, with box fans spinning furiously. An unremarkable place in an unremarkable town where nothing ever happens.

When Edison is dead, it's my every intention for nobody to find him. It isn't that I'm worried his body will bear some clues and I'll get caught. It's because I want him to be left to rest, to hear the happy lives thrumming above him. He'll be forever interred beneath the pavement of a cozy new subdivision where children will chase one another, shrieking giggles, and young loves will excitedly take the keys from their real estate agent. He'll be near neatly culled gardens, window boxes, the gentle murmurs of music wafting from backyard parties on clear summer nights. He'll be at peace.

If Sadie is good, I'll take her there. I won't tell her what for. I'll pretend to get lost on the way to a restaurant and pull in to turn the car around at the cul-de-sac. I'll stop for a minute, roll down the windows, and close my eyes like I'm smelling the breeze. She'll ask me what I'm doing, and I'll say that it's nothing.

The double doors open and the small crowd of children files out. Awkward, lanky, pimply, rotund. There is only one boy here with beauty and Sadie has found him. They emerge last, smiling and talking without looking at each other, his braces glinting. She has him wrapped around her finger. She'll break his heart, though, because young love never lasts. Love—especially the adolescent kind—is a form of murder. It lures, it promises, and then it destroys.

"Sadie!"

Her head whips in my direction, and her eyes are two sharp blue stones. She turns wary, and the boy at her side says something to her. She shakes her head.

I wave, flashing a bright smile. She approaches me like a death row inmate on her last walk. Arms at her sides, fists balled, shoulders stiff.

"Hi," I say. "Remember me from this morning? Jade."

"What are you doing here?" She has a soft voice. She's cautious, which is how I know she's a smart one.

"Edison was worried about you," I say, offering his name up to put her at ease. "He didn't want you walking home in this heat."

She grips the strap of her backpack, hefting its weight against her back. The boy stands at a wary distance, a guardian angel watching over her. *She will break you, you poor, dumb thing.*

"I'm all right," she says. "It's only a few blocks."

My smile turns soft, not quite pleading. "You'd really be doing me a favor if you let me take you," I say. "Edison is all in knots about that man who went missing. He just wants you to be safe."

Sadie shrugs out of her backpack and retrieves her phone from a side pocket. She turns away from me, tapping a message. It sends with a *whoosh*. A few seconds later, I hear the chime of the reply come in.

Clever girl. She texted Edison to make sure my story checked out. Later tonight, when Edison leaves his phone unattended, I'll scroll through his messages and find out exactly what she said to him. He doesn't keep a passcode on his phone because he is trusting. Muscular, tall, confident, male. The world hasn't treated him the way it has treated even the youngest of girls, and so he never learned caution.

I wait patiently as Sadie says goodbye to the boy. She waves to the others who are clustered on the sidewalk, and then she tosses her backpack on the floor at her feet when she climbs in. The air conditioner blows the fine tendrils of hair around her face. She's all sunlight colors, and she resembles her mother, but at the same time she's a different energy. Sheila was gregarious and flashy with manicured nails and makeup, but Sadie is elusive and reserved in that way that will make men want her for all her life.

"Thanks for the ride," she says.

"Tell me where to turn," I say. "Not used to this area."

We ride in silence. I don't even turn on the radio; I'm waiting to see if she'll help herself to the dial, but she doesn't. She only sits hunched and staring straight ahead. "Take a left here," she says, so softly I almost can't hear her over the whirring of the AC.

She wants to look at me, but she doesn't. She's filled with questions, the least of which are not who I am and where the hell I've come from. Edison hasn't mentioned me. I'm not on social media. Three weeks ago, I didn't exist.

I don't make small talk. I don't care what grade she's in, or the name of that boy, or what she likes to do for fun. Watching her interact with her peers has already told me what I needed to know about her anyway.

"How did you meet my stepdad?" she asks. She glances at me for a second, but I keep my eyes on the road.

"We go to the same church," I say.

"Oh." She flattens the hem of her dress. "Do you like him?"

I've already answered one question, and that was to establish some trust. Answering another would give her too much control.

"Do you like stir-fry?" I ask her, putting on my friendliest tone. "Because I'm a great cook"—she already knows this; she scarfed down the breakfast I made—"and I was thinking it would be fun if you had dinner with Edison and me tonight."

She looks at me again, and this time I see her eyes narrow, her mouth pucker in thought. She'll come, I already know, because she loves Edison. She feels how magnetic he is, the father she wishes she had instead of the overbearing one she's got. She'll come because she hates the thought of a woman who is not her dear mother stealing kisses as she stirs the eggs at the kitchen stove, making him laugh, squeezing his hand on the armrest in the car as he drives her home.

Sadie is young. Still innocent. She could never guess at how different Edison's loneliness and longing are from her own. Last night, the way he reached for me, the things he murmured in my ear, the unspoken promise I gave him that he doesn't have to be alone. I'm here now. I'm filling in all the spaces in his heart and in his bed.

She is hoping that I'll go away, and this already gives me the advantage, because I know that she's just as permanent a fixture in his life as I am now. *We all have a role to play, little lightning bolt.* Rather than push her away, I'll find a use for her.

13

WITH THREE HOURS TO SPARE UNTIL EDISON GETS OUT OF
work, I find myself wanting to talk to my only friend here. Dara has
become a constant in the weeks since I've come to Rainwood, always
manifesting in places—on the side of the road with a grocery bag, or
out on the porch tapping away on her phone, overhearing everything.
She's wise for her twenty-six years—like me, she understands that
there are some questions best not asked. Although she never misses a
beat, she doesn't pry about where I'm from or what I'm doing here,
and I don't ask her about her parents down in Florida or why she's
sending them so much money. I just hide the cash she hands me under
the upholstery in the trunk of the car. The less we say, the more we
come to understand each other.

But now that Sadie has entered the fray, I have something to talk
to my neighbor about. A genuine Jade problem. How to contend with
the child of your new love's dead wife. She isn't outside when I come

home, but I can hear the soft murmur of a TV when I approach her door and knock.

It takes a full minute for her to come to the door, looking so bleary and rumpled that I wonder if I've woken her up, even though it's well past two p.m.

"Oh, hey," she says, smiling but not opening the door all the way. I can just make out the living room behind her. It's identical to my own, but with red suede couches to match the curtains, and the television is placed on the other side of the room. A three-wick candle burns on the coffee table beside a little orange pill bottle. Cinnamon spice. A dying trail of smoke wafts from an ashtray in a straight line. "Sorry. I just took a painkiller, so I'm fuzzy. I was about to take a nap."

Her voice is heavy, her eyes filled with their usual warmth, but glazed over.

Something isn't right. A nettling churn in my stomach warns me. Dara does not nap in the afternoons, does not take pills that make her hazy. She's not an addict, and she's in control of her shit. I've seen her nearly every day, and I know what to look for.

She picks up on my suspicion and brings her left arm out of its hiding place behind the door. Her wrist is in a splint, her index and middle fingers taped together inside a metal brace. Deep bruises darken the swollen skin around them.

"Brittle bone disease," she says. "I'm lucky it's as mild as it is. Lots of people die. I just break bones like little twigs if I'm not careful."

For a pivotal moment, we stare at each other. Two liars in a world of fools. And I could almost believe she knows what I am. She's challenging me, daring me to call her on her bullshit so that she can call me on mine. A game of *I won't tell if you won't.*

But then she shifts her weight and I see how vulnerable and uneasy she is.

"Can I come in?" I ask.

"Now's really not—"

"Dara." My tone is soft, but it cuts through her. To her credit, she holds our stare. Chin jutted, eyes defiant. I put my hand on the door. She'll have to crush my fingers if she wants to close it, because they're not moving.

She peers out, looking in both directions to see if any neighbors are watching us. They aren't. The parking lot is mostly empty, everyone at work. She purses her lips and gives me the barest nod, then moves out of my way.

I close the door behind us once I'm inside. Dara returns to her blanket on the couch and wraps herself up. The window unit AC roars by the kitchen nook. Apart from the little nest Dara has made for herself in the living room, the unit is immaculate. The kitchen is even cleaner than ours, which is impressive, given that my sisters and I are used to leaving as little trace of life as possible.

Rather than the dingy shag carpet in my unit, Dara's living room has beige linoleum meant to look like marble tile. There's a jar candle and a wooden bowl of apples on the counter, the only sign that anyone uses the kitchen at all. On the walls are framed montages of Dara and Tim. Some in black and white, most in color, all of them taken in isolation as though they've spent their marriage stranded on a deserted island. They look happy, in love, smiling as they kiss.

I sit on a leather recliner in the same spot as the ratty hideous one in my own unit. Across from me, Dara crosses her long legs and reaches for a cigarette. She flicks the lighter, coaxing out the flame. With nowhere for the smoke to go, it's overwhelming and my eyes water.

"I know what you're thinking," she says, her voice muffled. "Everyone thinks that. But Tim wouldn't hurt me. I can't even go to the doctor when I sprain something because that's the first thing they think."

"Okay," I say. *You liar, Dara. You fucking liar.*

Moody's words come back to me now, a meditation in the frenzy that's forming in my head. *There can only be one.* I could kill Tim easily. He's taller than me, but he isn't very solid. His muscles are far leaner than Edison's. Dara could knock him out herself if she really wanted to, but he knows that her love for him makes her foolish and she won't fight back. He's captured her here, away from her family, with no car, nothing to do all day but walk in the boiling heat to buy gummy bears and Red Bull.

There's seven hundred dollars cash hidden in the trunk of my car right now. I counted it.

That money isn't for her parents; it's in case she works up the nerve to leave him. It isn't enough. It won't even get her out of town.

Iris and Moody would say it isn't my business. Dara is hardly the first neighbor who's had a problem that could have been solved with a dead spouse.

Dara is smart. I'll have to give her situation a lot of careful consideration. She'll never let me help her, but there are ways I can make her help herself. I just need time to think.

"So," she says. "What's up? To what do I owe the pleasure of your visit?"

There's no sarcasm to her words. She gives me a sweet smile, and I wonder if she knows how powerful she is. How much she could do in this world if she got out. She could model. Put dying hospice patients at ease. With her body I bet she could dance. Serve fast food to grumpy patrons—fucking anything. Something. But she has to get out of this shitty complex once in a while first.

I don't say any of this. Dara must trust me, and she won't do that if I push her now. So I say, "Edison has a stepdaughter. She's in junior high."

She sucks a long drag of her cigarette. "He's married?" No judgment or incredulity.

"Widowed," I tell her. "But it's only been a year, and I guess he's pretty close to her kid."

"That's not so bad," she says. "He's good with kids. You want that."

The little orange bottle of fentanyl on the coffee table is in Tim's name, not hers. Timothy Sutton. What does he tell the doctors to get it? An old sports injury? Headaches? He hurts his wife and then he brings her splints and bandages and pain pills as penance. Pours her tea, says he's sorry, fixes her up so that she forgets who broke her in the first place.

"I'm trying to get along with her, but I know she hates me," I say.

"You're not trying to impress her," Dara says simply. "You don't have to. She's not his kid. She'll go away eventually." She points her cigarette at me and then taps the ashes into the tray. "You're trying to impress *him* by getting in her good graces. Admit it."

I shrug. "Is it that obvious?"

"You really like this guy, don't you?" she says.

"It's early," I admit, "but he's the one."

I wanted to ask Dara how she knew Tim was the one. That was part of why I came over here. What did she see in that scrawny blond boy that ignited so much passion in her? I've seen the way they kiss. At the church picnic, during the fireworks, she grabbed at him like he was a life raft in a violent storm.

But now I realize that he lured her in slowly. He plied her with promises and nice words. He got her far away from her family. He puts on a suit and tie and tells her that one day he'll buy her the house she's dreamed of. She has given him all the love she should be dispersing to the others in her life, because he's taken the others away.

"My advice, you're on the right track," Dara says. "His step-kid will come around for a while because he makes her feel close to her mom. But she'll move on. Find some friends in high school and realize it's fucking weird to keep hanging around her ex-stepdad. All you have to do is show Edison you're okay with it."

It usually sets me on edge when other women say his name, but not Dara. She handles it with all the care it deserves. She knows what he means to me.

She's down to the end of her cigarette, and when she sets it in the ashtray, her eyelids are drooping. She coils the blanket around herself and leans back against the cushion. "I only took half a pill, but these things make me so damn tired." She yawns.

I watch her fall asleep. Her arm goes slack, wounded wrist splayed out beside her on the couch. Awake and active, she's a force. Lovely and bubbly with a mouth like a trucker. But here and now she's small. Like a lost kitten. Or a baby left abandoned in a stroller at a rest stop.

I take the ashtray and scrape the contents out in the trash, refill the empty glass on the end table and leave it beside her. Then I sit on the arm of the couch and rake my fingers through her soft black hair. She's a rare mind, a loyal soul, a precious thing. But I can't ride in on a white horse and save her. She would never let me and never forgive me for trying. Tearing him forcefully out of her life wouldn't give her freedom—only leave her with a gaping, bleeding wound and about a thousand awful things to fill it with.

But still, I imagine how easy it would be to end him. Quiet and quick. With a shoelace or a razor, his blood ribboning into warm bath-water. I could strangle him with the strap of the designer handbags he buys her in penance.

"Oh, Dara," I whisper. She doesn't hear me, lost in a deathlike sleep. "Say the word and I'll do it."

14

I PULL INTO EDISON'S DRIVEWAY A HALF HOUR AFTER HE'S home from work. My car blocks him in so that he won't be able to leave to pick up Sadie from her dad's. We'll have to go together in my car. The five-minute commute will give us a chance to talk. I'll put my hand on his arm and tell him that we need to honor her father's wishes. It isn't healthy for her to come here every time she's sad.

Edison already knows this. There's a spare room in his house, and it belonged to Sadie once, but not anymore. There's a twin bed with a neutral gray bedspread, thumbtack holes on the walls where posters used to be, a wooden dresser with the remnants of band stickers that have been scraped off. I'd seen the room that first night, as Edison slept off the Jack Daniel's, and I'd assumed the furniture was second-hand and the holes were from a previous owner, but to know that Edison has purged the room of Sadie's presence is better. She may always have a place in his heart, but not under his roof; he wants her to move on.

I won't try to get rid of her. She'll keep coming back around for the rest of Edison's short life, but she'll mark the past while I become his future. She'll move farther and farther away until she's little more than a gleam in his eye.

Once he's dead, I'll reel her back to me. Console her and make sure she's eating okay. I'll tell her I'm sorry that we've never really gotten along, she and I, but that I'm here for her if she'll be here for me. I'll need her trust when the cops come sniffing around.

I make my way up to the door, unsure whether to knock or try opening the door and letting myself in. I decide to knock; I'm a gentle force creeping up on him slow. Not too much all at once.

Voices murmur inside. Footsteps approach. The door swings open, and instead of Edison—sweaty from work, dirt smudged all over his fitted T-shirt, his arms open to embrace me—the little lightning bolt is the one standing before me.

The persistent thing. Walked all the way back here after I dropped her off at her dad's and specifically told her that dinner would be at seven thirty. It's six fifteen.

Sadie doesn't smile at me. She shrugs by way of greeting and wanders back into the bright depths of the living room, grazing on the bruised banana from the kitchen. Edison emerges from the hallway, tugging a clean shirt over his head. He only likes to shower in the mornings. At night, he smells of the day's sunlight and sweat, a rugged must that mixes with his faint cologne. The bedsheets smell of him.

He pulls me into his arms, and I forget about my irritation that the little lightning bolt was a step ahead of me this time. I'm carrying a grocery bag in one hand. Fresh broccoli, a can of baby corn, organic steroid-free chicken breast, no additives, no fillers. I'd hoped to bring

Dara to the store with me so we'd have more time to talk about this Sadie situation, but I knew that was out the moment she opened the door.

She was still sleeping when I left her. I checked the bottle, and she had told me the truth: she had only taken half a fentanyl. There was one pill split clean in half among the others. She tries so hard to be careful, not to protect herself but to protect him. As I browsed the fresh carrots in the produce section, I imagined how gratifying it would be to wait for him behind the door, fire extinguisher in hand, and to bash in his skull with it. Drag him inside, check if he still had a pulse, and then wait for him to wake up. As he lay at my feet, weak, bruised, groaning in pain, I'd give him a list of all his sins and why they meant I was going to dismember him.

But instead, he will come home to a beautiful wife dozing on the couch. He'll bring her flowers, chocolates, tell her he spent the day positively wracked with guilt. She'll forgive him, kiss him.

I want him to die.

But this is exactly the sort of thing Moody and Iris worry about when it comes to me. There's no shortage of people who deserve to die, and if I tried to kill them all, I'd be caught in a heartbeat; we'd all go down together if one of us did. For murder to be committed well, it must first be an act of love. And so many vile people in this world are not worth loving. The key is to find someone who is, and to give that person all your heart. Kill them with passion, bury them with love, obsess over every detail the way that only a lover could, and you won't make a careless mistake.

Tim belongs to Dara the way that Edison belongs to me. His fate is in her hands. She is choosing to squander her strength and love him instead, and I can't control that. I can't make her see what it's doing to her.

Edison kisses me. "Sadie's going to pick out a movie for us."

I smile at him. "Great. Perfect."

I get to work in the kitchen. Edison orbits in and out, pouring me ice water in a long-stemmed wineglass and telling me how great what I'm cooking smells. He sits on the couch beside Sadie, and she plucks one of her earbuds out to talk to him.

This is what it would be like to have a family with him. Worried about how well I'm seasoning the chicken, the smell of his cologne in the fabric of my shirt, a child's voice giggling with him in the next room. They would have been beautiful, a boy and a girl, one with brown eyes and one with green, both of them tall and broad like us.

"What are you smiling about?" Edison raps his knuckle gently on my cheek.

"Just you."

When dinner is ready, I serve it up on the large white plates I find in the cabinet. We eat on the couch because Sadie wants to watch a movie and Edison wants to make Sadie happy. The little lightning bolt sits squarely between us, leaving half a cushion's distance between herself and me. She doesn't realize that her test will only work out in my favor. After we take her home, Edison will thank me for being so patient with her, for being sweet. We'll topple into bed and I'll show him how perfect we are for each other.

Sadie picks *Snow White* for us to watch. It's digitally restored, and the fair princess is all soft lines and gentle ballads. The evil step-mother glowers down from her throne, doomed to fail.

The message is a little on the nose, but she's a smart girl. I'll have to be extra cautious around her. She doesn't afford me much chance to do this. She barely looks at me all evening. She huddles close to Edison, determined to prove that he belonged to her first.

"Thanks for dinner," she says, when the credits are rolling and I stand to collect the plates.

"It was great, Jade," Edison says, slapping his hand to his taut stomach. "It's been a long time since I've had a home-cooked meal."

"I know," I tease him. "I've seen your fridge." I wish he would call me by a nickname—anything but Jade. But Edison sees something valuable in my nom de plume because he associates it with me. It's beautiful to him, and it sparks a recognition like the first chords of a favorite song.

It hurts in some inexplicable way that I can't tell him I'm Sissy. That isn't my legal name, the one that the state gave me when I was found abandoned. It isn't the name I wrote on my tests at school, or when I was applying for jobs at sixteen. It isn't even what my foster families called me. But it's the most important name I carry. My sisters gifted it to me because I was the baby, the littlest sister, and it stuck. Moody got her nickname shortly after. And Iris picked her nickname for herself.

When we were ten, Iris was placed with an elderly foster mother, and it was the only placement she liked because there were no other children and the woman had no spouse. Most of Iris's placements were a mystery to Moody and me, but I saw the change in her each time we were reunited for visits. I saw her anger building, her childhood powerlessness slowly morphing into something sharp. But in this place, where she spent nine tranquil months, she was as close as she'd ever be to a typical, happy child. The woman lived behind her flower shop and she taught Iris all about botany. The irises she sold were a deep indigo, bold and stark. There were more than two hundred species of them, the old woman told her. They were a favorite in gardens, and soft to touch, but all of them are deadly.

"Did you do your homework?" Edison asks.

"Yes," Sadie tells him. Her voice is bright and sweet when she talks to him. Familiar. Nothing at all like the shy mumbles she's given me thus far.

I bring the plates to the sink, and as soon as I run the water, Edison calls out, "Jade, don't wash the dishes. You've done too much already."

"I don't mind," I say. I work a smudge off his plate with my thumb. I want to cook for him, bring him a cold glass of soda as he puts his feet up on the couch. I want to take his clothes out of the dryer—his work shirts, his church clothes, all the little traces of his presence, and press them to myself as I fold them up and arrange them in neat rows.

When his body is lying lifeless before me, I'll take care of him in much the same way. I'll trim my DNA off his fingernails and I'll tell him that I forgive him for scratching and fighting me. I know it isn't his fault. I know it's just the stubborn instinct to survive. I'll remove his clothes and launder them. I'll wipe away the waste that he expels. I'll pull his teeth with the pliers from his toolbox in the garage.

I would like to keep him whole and bury him in one piece. I'll have to fold him, knees to chest, so that he's as small as possible when rigor mortis sets in. He'll be easier to transport that way. He'll fit neatly in the fifty-gallon trash bags he keeps in the garage for his construction waste.

Sadie is so quiet that I don't hear her approaching until she's standing beside me. "I can do the dishes," she says, and I know that Edison told her to come in here and help me.

"Thanks, honey," I say, although every inch of her is an intrusion. "You wash and I'll dry. How's that?"

She nods, staring down at the drain.

"Eddie said you like to sing." It surprises me when Sadie opens her mouth; she's been so quiet all night.

"Just a little here and there," I say.

She nods. "That's cool."

I study her. Graceful swan neck, hair in every shade of yellow and white and gold. Pert nose. All shyness. The kind of child who will impress mothers when their sons bring her home after school. *Can I help you clean up, Mrs. so-and-so? We're just doing our homework. Oh yes, I'd love to stay for dinner.*

"Do you like music?" I ask, because this is a chance for us to connect and for me to score a point with Edison. Of course she likes music. Everyone on the planet does.

"I play violin at school." Was that—is that a smile on her face? It's gone already. "I'm not very good."

"I have a guitar," I tell her, and it is a victory when she looks at me with light in her eyes. Music, she is drawn to. I will have to test this. When her favorite songs are playing on the radio, does she let herself go and sing more than she speaks?

"Hey, Sades, it's getting late, kiddo." Edison is in the doorway. "I told your dad I'd have you back by ten."

It's nine forty-five. "Oh," I say, wincing apologetically. "Edison, I think my car is blocking you in. Do you want me to take her?"

Edison looks at Sadie, who shrugs. She's retreated back into herself. She doesn't want to commit to an answer, doesn't want to be the reason that anything does or does not happen.

Sadie hands me the last dish, and I nudge her with my elbow conspiratorially. We're going to be friends, I've decided. I'm going to learn about the violin and the music she likes, and I'm going to make her trust me. "Go get your shoes and meet me in the car."

Once Sadie has gone outside, Edison grasps my wrist and reels me to him. "Thank you for being so patient with her," he says. He nudges my forehead with his, and my arms go up around his shoulders, our bodies swaying in our own little dance.

"She's a good kid," I say.

"Disney movies were a special thing she had with her mom," he tells me. "I know cartoons weren't what you had in mind, so thank you."

There are hundreds of Disney movies in this world, and Sadie chose the one with the noteworthy evil stepmother, but I don't say that. Edison didn't care, and all that matters is what he thinks. Doting, pure, trusting Edison. I kiss him and he growls, a sound that fills me up. His fingers dig into my hips and he hoists me onto the counter, kisses me deep.

My breathing is ragged. My hand scrapes the stubble on his jaw. Our eyes meet, full and wanting, squeezing every drop out of the first moment we've had alone together since last night. All day I've wanted him, and yet I've barely had any time to think of him with all I've had to deal with between Dara and the situation with the little lightning bolt. *Not to worry, love,* I promise him, my lips around his earlobe, my tongue awakening goose bumps on his neck. *We're only getting started. There is so much more I can do for you.*

"She'll wonder where I am," I say. "I should go." I tear myself away and leave him wanting. I look over my shoulder and see the astonished, delirious happiness on his face.

He'll wait for me. He'll be right here where I want him.

In the car, I turn on the radio. I have five minutes to learn something new about Sadie. So far, I know that she doesn't interject and so it's hard to know what she's thinking. I scroll through a rock station, a catchy pop song that's been playing on every store radio for weeks, and find Sarah McLachlan on a static-filled AM station. "Possession," a rare treat, and one of deep kismet. Like "Stairway to Heaven," it's magic.

Midway through the second chorus, Sadie gifts me with her thoughts. "This is pretty."

The song is older than both of us, long before her 1997 hit "Angel" would become the official anthem of sad ASPCA commercials.

Sadie is humming, having already picked up the melody. A high soprano I would have pegged her for.

A lot of people think "Possession" is a love song, but it's based on the myriad of love letters from an obsessed fan. He sued her, but then offed himself before anything could come of it. It was a deluded love. He let it overwhelm him because he could only see her from afar—a little songbird he would never cage. The lawsuit was a last desperate grasp at having her near him.

Celebrities are a terrible target. They'll never love you. But there were so many beautiful women he could have found down here on earth, out of the stage lights. Rather than thousands of letters, he should have waited. He should have let that lust, that agony, that love, collect within him until he thought the weight of it would crush him. He should have channeled it into a single kiss beneath an umbrella on a rainy afternoon, a squeeze of his lover's hand. He might have survived then.

I think Sadie can hear how sad this song is. She has big eyes like a Precious Moments figurine, and they're thoughtful now. She doesn't share whatever she's thinking, because she's a careful one. Bonding with her will be a slow project, ultimately rewarding. When Edison goes missing, she'll come to me with tears in her eyes. She won't fling herself into my arms the way she did for Edison, but rather she'll show her grief to me with the steady understanding that we must address our sadness if we're going to be strong enough to go out there and look for him.

I pull into the driveway just as the music trails off and gives way to a commercial for a used-car dealership. She thanks me for the ride. The front door opens before she's even halfway up the walk. Her father, sharply dressed, stands in the rectangle of light. The humorless expression on his face tells me everything I need to know about why Sadie can't stand being home. *Fun time is over now. You have exams coming up.*

This time, when I return to Edison, I don't knock. He's in his favorite recliner, soda can in hand, and he looks up when I let myself in. "You really should lock your door, you know," I say.

In answer, he holds out his arms to me. I sink into his lap, and my head fits perfectly in the space between his chest and his chin. "Don't worry," he says. "I'll protect you if anyone breaks in." He chuckles at his own joke, a rumbling vibrato in his chest, but he falls silent when he sees the look in my eyes.

I kiss him the way that we did in the kitchen, and the air changes around us. He raises the remote and shuts off the television.

"You're not like them," I say against his mouth. "From church."

He reaches behind my head and slides the elastic from my ponytail so gently I barely feel it; my hair falls around my shoulders, and he holds it between his fingers.

"Neither are you," he says.

I want to tell Edison the truth, which is that I loved him the moment he came into that diner. Alone, searching for something. Searching for me. I've been all across the West Coast with my sisters, and I traveled a thousand miles just to find him.

That he's here, solid, in my arms, astounds me.

He nudges my chin with his knuckle, tracing his thumb across my lower lip. "What are you thinking?"

How beautiful the need in your eyes would be if I wrapped my hands around your throat. The silent, desperate begging. I'd let go just before I nearly lost him, hold him as he gasped air back into his lungs. Tell him he's mine, wrap my legs around him. Make him see how much he needs me.

My mouth closes around his thumb, my tongue stealing a taste of the salt of his skin. "I'll never tell," I say.

"What is it?" His voice is low and heavy with need. He wants all of Jade—every inch of her body, every thought in her head, every word that she forgets to say out loud. He keeps them like bits of sea glass so that he might hold them and think of Jade when she's not near. But how I want him to know me. The first love of my life, and, I deeply suspect, the only.

I hold his face in my hands, the stubble of his cheeks biting into my skin. He is softness with secret edges, little bits of pain I unwrap like gifts. As I draw nearer, he closes his eyes, expecting a kiss. But I stop when our mouths are just a hairsbreadth apart. "I want you to tell me who hurt you," I whisper.

"What?" His eyes open, still dark with longing.

"That night you were drunk, I put you to bed, and you said, 'Don't let me go over there. I'll kill him.'" I stroke the tender skin under his eye with my thumb. "You were so sad."

He studies me, his gaze moving from my eyes to my mouth. When he tries to stand, I tighten my thighs around his hips, rooting him to the chair. I'm careful not to use too much strength, not enough to frighten him, but enough to show him that he can't escape me.

Tell me. Tell me what he did so I can hate him too.

He lets out a long, deep breath. The look in his eyes says that he's relenting, and I can see that he's gifting me with something important. Something he would never share with those beautiful women from church, or Sadie, or even Jeannie, who has a motherly way of putting him at ease. Something that has lived alone in his head like a caged monster. "I'd have to show you."

Moments later, we're riding in silence in Edison's green Buick. It smells like him, like sun-warmed skin and that musty sweet cologne that drives me wild.

He holds the wheel in one hand, his grip relaxed. His eyes are fixed, though, and his jaw is tight. I reach over and weave my fingers through his. Whatever it is, he won't scare me away. I'm here. I'm with him.

Edison uses the turn signal dutifully, even though the roads are empty. We veer onto a suburban grid with manicured lawns amid the desert landscape. He pulls onto the shoulder and shuts the engine.

"You see that house?" He nods to a one-story mid-century modern across the street. It has a slanted roof, and its left side is comprised entirely of windows. Plain white curtains are drawn, but I can see a silhouette moving back and forth, stopping to clean up, perhaps after a party. Edison doesn't wait for me to answer, and I suspect he wouldn't hear me even if he did. He is lost in whatever storm brews inside him. "He killed my wife."

I look at him. He's hidden his sadness, replacing it instead with the hard set of a clenched jaw. But I feel his pain anyway. It ripples through me, a cold breeze, making me want to hold him.

"Just turned twenty this year. He comes from money. His parents pay the rent on this place for him."

I'm impressed with the amount of research he's done, and I want to ask him if he used his own computer for this, but I don't speak. I barely breathe. Usually, Edison is guarded. Like me, he presents a cultivated side of himself to the world. But in this moment, he can't restrain whatever mystery he keeps shrouded in the daylight. His fist tightens under my fingers.

"I come here," he says. "I park right here and I watch him sometimes. I think about all the ways I could kill him." He's living one such fantasy right now. I see the shift in him. The focus. The cool, steady anger that he channels. Like Iris tightening the garrote. Like me dismembering the limbs and scrubbing the blood from the grout.

When he finally looks at me, my blood runs hot with desire. With desperation. "I would never do it," he says. "I just like knowing that I could."

The moment passes, and vulnerability takes the place of his confession. He realizes how this looks—alone in his car on a dark street, with me, a woman he's only just met, entirely at his mercy. I must be frightened of him now, he's thinking. He must have ruined everything.

His fist loosens under my grasp and he tries to pull away so that he can put the car back in drive and take me home. I tighten my hold on him and feel gratification at the surprise on his face when he realizes I'm the one who won't let him go.

Softly, I ask, "What would you do to him?"

I don't let him see my own darkness. I don't smile, even though I want to. This moment is about him. He lives such a quiet life—work, church, AA meetings. He lives in a house filled with picture albums that gather dust, and sharp reminders of a woman he loved and a life he lost. He carries this hatred all alone.

But I'm here now. "Tell me, Edison."

He looks away from me, to a streetlamp that flickers in the distance, swarming with moths. Foolish, emotional Sissy. I've gone too far again. If my sisters were here, they'd warn that my helpless romance was going to be the doom of us all, that I'm laying it on too thick, that no man will ever love me if I throw myself at him.

He turns my palm in both his hands, and he traces his fingertip down the line that leads to my wrist. There, he presses down to feel my pulse. Alive. I'm alive. Like him. Hours ago, I was in his bed and he was making me come, and now I'm opening myself to hear his ugliest secrets. Practically begging him to tell me.

"You must think I'm fucked up," he says.

I unbuckle my seat belt and lean over the console to take his face in my hands. "Hey," I say. "That man in there destroyed your life. He doesn't even have to answer for it. Gets to carry on, probably have his own family someday. You have a right to be angry."

God, the way he looks at me. That helpless pleading, that mix of confusion and desire. *Who are you?* his eyes say. *Who sent you to me?*

His hand goes to my waist, fingers kneading softly into my skin. Exploring me, feeling the bones buried within me.

I remind myself of the burial site I've lovingly planned out for him, but suddenly it doesn't seem like enough. When he's near me like this, with his fingers teasing the inside of my thigh, a dangerous thing starts to happen to me. Love is necessary and lust is the ultimate test. *Stay strong, Sissy. Follow through and he'll be yours forever. He'll never leave you. It has to be this way.*

"My God," he says, breathless. "What are you doing to me?"

I look at his eyes, and for one maddened, helpless moment I think he can see what I'm really thinking. That violent edge I want to test.

I lean over the console. He rakes his hands through my hair, watching heavy-lidded as I unzip his jeans. He wore them to work, new smudges of desert dust in the stitching. He wore them all day while he was thinking of me.

"Jade—"

"Shh." His jeans are bunched below his knees. His skin is hot. He shudders when I brush my fingertips across him lightly. He holds my hair like it's the only thing keeping him from falling. When he gives it a tug, it ignites me. *Pull harder,* I think. *Fight me.* But he doesn't, because I'm not the object of his rage. I'm not the one who killed his wife. I am Jade, and he wants to protect me. Sweet, dulcet Jade, who just may be full of surprises yet. His eyes are on my tongue as it moves slowly across my lips. "Let me show you," I say. "Let me show you what I can do to you."

HOURS LATER, I DON'T sleep as Edison dozes with his arms around me. He drove us back to his house, and I'd let out a shriek as he hoisted me into his arms and spirited me to his bed. We didn't say a word to each other this time. We'd only stared into each other as we moved, frantic for each other, gasping.

He was so vulnerable, even with his arms so taut with muscle. He's got the physique to kill a man if only he indulged that side of himself. He could kick open the door, storm that man's living room, and be done with it in seconds. A hurricane of fists and blood and raw hatred.

But instead, he turned that energy toward me, cradling the top of my head in his palm and handling me like something precious. The strong angles in his face clenched, but his eyes gentled as he focused on my face. I could almost believe he felt the real me when he let out that guttural cry. For one moment we were the same. Broken and hideously strong, all darkness inside.

After, he'd collapsed beside me, pelting my throat and my collarbone with kisses while I held him. *It's okay,* I was telling him with my embrace. *I'll keep you safe. I'll protect you from yourself.*

Nervous energy buzzes through my blood even now, and I can't believe that it's finally happening. It's as though we've willed each other into existence. To think that every lonely hour of my life, he was here and it was just a matter of finding him.

His mouth is parted, his body prone and trusting beneath me.

Slowly, I stretch my arm out, my fingers grasping at his phone on the bedside table. The brightness of the screen makes me wince. His wallpaper is a photo of the mountains beyond a barren desert, and I think that I'll suggest a hike sometime.

He doesn't so much as stir beneath me, and I scroll through his messages. There isn't much. Alerts about login attempts on his iPad from back in February, arrangements to meet his father for dinner on Christmas Eve, messages of support from friends he's made at AA, me asking him if he likes water chestnuts for tonight's stir-fry. And a text from Sadie.

At 12:02 p.m.: Did you send your girlfriend?

His immediate reply: Yes—just want you to be safe.

15

BY MID-AUGUST, THE HEAT IS SWELTERING. MOODY IS slumped on a barstool that she's dragged over to the air conditioner, groaning. "When it's my turn again," she says, "we're going back up north. I've always wanted to kill someone in the snow."

The image is romantic. Blood splayed out upon an untouched field of pure white. Doing it at night would be best, I think. Somewhere under a cloudless sky so that the stars make it bright enough to see. A clean swipe of a serrated blade on a carotid artery.

"The cleanup would be a nightmare," I say, pouring ice cubes into my glass. Snow has a way of burying things, but when it melts, it leaves them all exposed. The blood won't wash away—not entirely— and it will be too hard to see what may have been dropped or left behind.

"I want one of those—what are they?—MMA fighters next time,"

Moody says. "Mixed martial arts. Really aggressive. Raging mommy issues."

Moody has three kills under her belt now. Each time, Moody has a vision for the lover she'll find, and then he manifests as though from a catalog.

"We'll dye our hair too," she says. "I miss being blond."

I feel a twinge in my chest. I'm two months into my time with Edison. More than a third of our time together has passed. I don't ask my sisters if this grief is normal, if they've felt it too. There can be no quantifier. They suspect that I'm hoarding too much of Edison to myself, and so I look for details I can give them, like the hikes we've started taking in the mountains. I freeze water bottles for us the night before and wrap them in foil so they'll stay cold. And I tell them that his stepdaughter has stopped coming around as much, but when she appears, she brings her violin and I follow along on my guitar.

I don't tell them about the way the sex with him makes me feel, how I can never sleep afterward and how I lie in the darkness studying every inch of him. His thick brows, the curl that falls across his forehead when he sleeps, the way my cheek fits into the slope of his biceps. I don't tell them that I can't imagine how the world will make sense without him.

Dread in my stomach when Iris comes downstairs, hair drenched from her shower. She can always sense when I've been thinking too much. She reads it on my face like pages from a romance novel.

She sits beside me on the couch, so close her damp arm presses into mine. Fragrant soap, red skin from the scalding water. Unlike Moody, she loves the heat, and she's radiant, her pink cheeks glowing.

"What's up, Sis? You feeling all right?" She presses the back of her palm to my forehead, the side of my face. "You're looking a little glassy."

"She's in love," Moody says, not turning away from the AC as it blows on her face.

I am in love, it's true. I think of Edison and my knees shake, my chest hurts, my eyes water. It's like having the flu and winning the lottery every day of my life. I mourn him even though he's still alive; if I call him right now while he's at work, he'll answer on the second ring and I'll hear the smile in his voice.

Edison is alive. I savor the thought and how it feels for this to be true. We'll have Christmas together and then I'll kill him on New Year's Eve. An hour before midnight, I'll lead him to bed. I'll make the most of our last time together. And then I'll do it. I'm not entirely sure how I'll make him stop breathing. If I strangle him, he'll fight me, but I'll have the advantage because I'll be sitting on his chest. If I cut his throat, he'll stare up at me in stunned silence, his mouth puckering and gaping like a fish out of water.

Iris is watching me. She frowns and hands me the glass of ice water I've brought to the coffee table. It's an unspoken offering, her way of trying to console me.

It frightens me the way that Iris can see right through me. She gets up, opens a drawer in the kitchen, and returns wearing Lisa's wedding band. "Do you want to get ice cream?" she asks me, quietly so that Moody won't hear over the whirring of the AC.

She's in rare form today, a doting older sister trying to comfort me rather than lecture me. She's worried that I'll end up like her once Edison is dead, hiding under my blanket like it's a burial shroud and not emerging for weeks and weeks. But it's different. It's something that I don't have words for. I'm already in mourning for Edison and the life we'll never lead, the conversations we'll never have.

It will go away, I tell myself. He'll always be the most special because he's my first, but he's only human. Bones and skin.

"Sure," I say, even though I don't want ice cream and even though I don't want to leave this room. It's because I don't want to get up that I have to.

I follow Iris outside and I lock the door to make it look like nobody will be home with Jade and Lisa gone.

Dara is lounging on her favorite plastic chair, facing the balcony where she can see everything. She's playing some game on her phone, but she raises a hand when I wave at her.

I like to think we've gotten closer since I learned about Tim. She still won't admit to the monster she married, but I keep an eye on her for bruises, for any slight change in her posture. There's been nothing. I haven't asked, because she's onto me, both of us trapped in this silent game of her own design. The closer I look, the better she'll hide it.

Dara must think I'm trying aggressively to save her soul, because I've been taking her to every church function that I can. Picnics, baptisms because I'm in the choir and I say I want her in the audience to alleviate my stage jitters, Saturday fellowship drive-in-movie night. The latter is a particular testament to our friendship, because I let Edison take Sadie in his own car while Dara and I stuff our faces with candy and talk through the entire thing. I am giving her precious hours I could be spending with my man while our time together is ticking, because I want her to be okay when I leave this place.

There's a man at the church who flirts with her. Liam. He's twenty-four, in medical school. He wants to be a neurologist. He's about twice Tim's size, but gentle as a lamb, with a soft voice. When Dara talks, he shuts his mouth and listens to her, rapt. Dara pretends there's nothing there, but I've seen the way she smiles and lowers her eyes when the two of them congregate beside the coffee urns.

It's that easy, I want to tell her. *There are so many out there who would grab the world in a fist and give it to you.*

"Still trying to make a Christian out of the nonbelieving neighbor?" Iris asks, climbing into the driver's seat.

"I am just being thorough," I say, and slam my passenger-side door. "I'll need friends after it's done."

"Uh-huh." She leans forward to have a better view of Dara, high up on her balcony. "And this has nothing to do with the fact that Mr. Wonderful beats the shit out of her, right?"

One night while I was away sleeping at Edison's, Moody and Iris told me that the power went out. As soon as the music stopped blasting from Tim and Dara's apartment, they heard Tim shouting. The sound of something shattering against the wall. It was so brutal that my sisters pressed their ears to the wall because they thought he might kill her. "To her credit, she didn't cry," Moody had told me; after her own nightmarish experiences in group homes, she has a lot of respect for anyone who can go through hell without breaking down.

I'm relieved that I didn't have to be the one to tell them about Tim. I'm already burdened enough hiding all three thousand dollars of Dara's cash under the upholstery of the trunk. It's the one place my sisters will never think to look.

I don't answer Iris's question; she puts the car in gear and we ride in silence. I've never seen as many food trucks as I have in Rainwood. There's an ice-cream truck that's taken up permanent residence outside a thrift store on the main thoroughfare. I've only been there once, but they pile an unholy amount of sprinkles on their cones.

Not wanting to make a mess in the car, Iris and I sit on a bench in the shade of the thrift shop, ice cream dripping onto the napkins wadded in our hands.

I wish Iris would come out with whatever it is she wants to say. She handles me like I'm made of glass sometimes, especially after I screwed it up with the man who should have been my first kill. "I couldn't do it," I'd told her that night as we conspired in our apartment. "He was all wrong. It wasn't me. It was him."

Now Iris takes a gentler approach. "Has he told you he loves you yet?" she asks me. "You haven't said."

"No," I say, doing my best not to be terse with her.

"Really? After two months?" She licks the chocolate ice cream around the rim of the cone and then bites mercilessly into the scoop. I watch goose bumps rise on her arms from the shock of the cold. "That's a little slow. How's the sex?"

I've labored not to make a big deal of Edison being my first. Years ago, long before we ever thought we'd kill a soul, I saw what boys did to my sisters. Made them irrational, jealous, sad. When I got my driver's license at seventeen, Moody made me follow her boyfriend around Fresno for a week straight because she was positive he was cheating on her. Damn near impossible to be inconspicuous when you're following a man in a part of town with about three other people in it.

And when Iris killed her ex–guidance counselor, I realized it was so much easier to come in and clean the blood from the walls than to mend my sister's broken heart afterward. It was the only messy kill Iris ever made, enraged by her love for him, her hatred that he wouldn't leave his wife and children to give her all the things he promised. After him, Iris became so much smarter about her marks. She chose men who adored her but meant nothing to her, so that she could handle their demises with intelligence and grace.

"He's just being careful," I say. "He still misses his wife."

Edison's sensitivity has been useful to me. He believed Sheila was his soul mate, and he blames himself for not protecting her. If he'd been there to put the spare tire on her car, she wouldn't have been hiking that stretch of highway and she'd still be alive. But she's gone, and in her place is me. He is so careful when he kisses me, drawing back to seek my eyes for permission, watching my face to be sure that I'm with him. In his bed, he pushes his palm to my chest to feel my heart. He makes me his queen. He falls asleep holding me.

Even though I could kill any intruder who broke into his house in the middle of the night to overpower us, I let him shield me. I turn into something delicate and sweet. I sleep wrapped in the steel of his arms and make myself small.

I drink it like rain. I've never been anyone's precious thing.

Iris takes my hand. She weaves her fingers between mine. "Sissy, everything I've done has been to protect you. Both of you."

I stare down at our hands. Identical pink nail polish. She held my hand just like this when we were five and the social worker was prying her away. We were so small then. I screamed her name—the legal name she no longer uses—over and over. She was the one with the ferocity. The one who bit and scratched and screamed until she got her way. She was my hero, but now I can look back and see that she was as powerless as me.

"When he's gone, you have to talk to me," she says. "Don't get lost in your head."

I nod, but her gaze is relentless, and I'm forced to look into her green eyes.

"Don't screw this up for yourself by loving him the wrong way," she says. "You don't have a lifetime to let him sort his shit out. You need to go to him and make him say it."

"I have four months, Iris," I say, bristling.

"Yes, and they'll speed by." She squeezes my hand. I watch as a drop of chocolate ice cream falls to the bench between us. "Get everything that you can out of this, Sis. If there's anything you want to say, anything you want *him* to say, any fucking position you want to try in bed—do it. Do everything. That's the only way to get out of this without being haunted by regret."

Everything. So small a word for what I want with Edison. Still, I know that Iris is only trying to guide me. I want a full love with Edison. Eager kisses, grasping at each other in desperation. I want him to gasp for me, cry for me, murmur for me as he falls asleep.

Edison and I will never have two beautiful little children who look like us. There's a finite number of hikes and movies and lazy mornings lingering in bed. When he's gone, I can't have him back. I can only have the memories we've created, playing over on a flickering film reel in my mind.

How do I want him to tell me he loves me? I already know the answer to that. I want him to need me so much that it terrifies him. The way that it already terrifies me.

16

LOVE, I'M LEARNING, IS NOT A SUDDEN REVELATION. I love Edison, but I look back and can't be certain when it started. I love him when he sleeps with a hand on my hip, and when I hear the text chime on my phone and I know it's him. I love him when he's near me, but especially when I don't know where he is or what he's thinking.

The air-conditioning in the church is on full blast, but Pastor McDaniel looks especially wilted today at the pulpit. The sermon is about putting value on worldly things. Build your castle on a rock, he says. On salvation. The grandest palace built on dunes of sand will wash away.

Edison reaches over and puts a hand on my knee. We arrived late and slipped into a pew in the last row. We're beyond the range of the AC and I fan myself with a pamphlet with all the upcoming get-togethers through the rest of the year. A youth Bible campout with outdoor movies next week. A devotional family-style dinner in September. Christmas pageants all through December.

We'll skip the New Year's Eve service. That will be our last night together and I want us to be alone.

Edison's hand slides up my thigh, one finger moving under the hem of my blue dress. Tiny white ships ripple in the fabric at the movement.

I look at him. His eyes are straight ahead, and he cants his head thoughtfully, as though considering the sermon.

His hand moves, even as the rest of him is still. He's in his white dress shirt, the buttons gleaming and pristine. His hair is combed neatly, and that one rebellious curl has escaped again. The one that hints at something wild lurking within.

Curiosity turns to desire as I watch him, and I know that he feels my eyes. There's just the faintest hint of a wicked smile on his lips. I can see his teeth. To everyone else, we're just another couple sitting alone in the back row, where the AC doesn't cool us. I don't move. Don't make a sound as his hand moves up and up.

Heat rushes to my face when he touches me. One finger slips inside me and then another. I grasp the edge of the pew. The sermon drones on, the dull beat of some distant song as the world spins on.

Edison betrays nothing, mischievous thing that he is. When I grab the fabric of his dress pants, his smile twitches and that's all he gives me.

My back arches. I hold my breath because I'm sure that if I let it out, I'll scream. He's managed to surprise me. He's decided that he can't resist me. That he wants to see what I'll do, just how far he can take me. I live in his head—not Jade, but me. The real me. He sees somewhere in my words and in my face that I'm more than this sweet church girl who sings "Ave Maria" and strums her guitar.

How much does he see? When did I let it slip?

I shudder, claw at his wrist with both hands. I go to pieces, flushed and spent all without making a sound. He draws his hand away, leaving me to melt.

McDaniel asks us to stand and turn to page forty-five in our book of psalms. There's an electric energy here and he feels God in this room today and he wants us all to sing.

My legs are rubbery, and Edison grabs my arm and hauls me to my feet, breathing out a laugh at the way I stumble and fall against him. His. I'm his, and he knows it.

He lets out a little cough and brings his fist to his mouth. His tongue moves across his fingertips, tasting me.

I hold the hymnal between us and we both sing, and he knows that he's won. He knows how much I want to grab him and take him out of here, the things I'll do to him later when we're alone. But all I can do now is stand in this overheated church, reeling, wanting, stunned by how much I love him. He scares the living hell out of me.

THE LAUNDRY ROOM IS the closest thing to a basement you can find out here in the desert. It's where every past tenant has apparently stored their useless crap. But growing up with nothing, my sisters and I have learned to be alchemists of broken things. With an old dust-coated phone book from 2007, Moody was able to prop up the archaic dryer so that it runs without rattling across the cement floor. Iris worked the rust out of the silver bicycle with baking soda and lemon juice, and now it gleams like new.

Here I stand now, staring at a small piece of plywood and a discolored cardboard box of nails. They caught my attention a while ago, while I was sitting on the washing machine, waiting for my clothes to be ready for the dryer. It's time to put them to use. Edison would use something like this to lay the foundation for a porch, or a new hardwood floor. I have something else in mind.

It isn't Iris who pushed me into coaxing a confession of love out of Edison. Rather, it's the thought that time is slipping by. Outside, the sun is going down, and the brush along the desert plain is on fire with pink and gold. The mood-ring sky is pale blue until the clean line where it becomes suddenly dark, deep and deadly like the Mariana Trench on a satellite picture.

If I want to love Edison, I must do it—as all other things regarding him—ruthlessly. I kneel on the concrete and set the board before me. When I grab the hammer from where it's been abandoned against the wall, it's heavy with grit, the grime coming off on my palm. I hammer four nails into the board. Rusted, bent, long as a human finger. When I'm through, I put everything back where I found it, taking only the board with me.

I feel the first drop of rain as I'm laying the board in the trunk. It lands on my nose and rolls down my cheek before it's gone. I hold my palm up, astonished that the weather would turn at such a perfect and romantic time. When I pull out of the parking lot, it's started to pour.

I drive too fast. I know that. But I've yet to see a single state trooper out on this stretch of road. Rainwood itself is asleep most days, a town in which nothing ever happens. That is, except for the man who went missing back in June. Edison didn't know him, never heard the name. But still, he's been in knots about it. I've tried to tell him that it probably isn't what he's thinking. The man just wanted to escape his debts, or get away from his wife. He's probably at a casino in Vegas right now living the high life with a beautiful woman on each arm.

I couldn't have imagined I'd find a man as sensitive as Edison. He worries about Sadie walking home and me driving at night. I text him when I get where I'm going and I promise him we'll be okay, and he eases in my arms and gives me that smile that warms the darkness in me.

I roll to a stop at the ten-mile marker. I put the car in park. There's no one here but me, especially now that it's after dark and everyone is home from work. No Good Samaritans will come and ask me if I need some help. A jump, a spare, a tow.

I get the board out of the trunk, pushing away the hair fallen into my face by the rain. I lay it in the street a few yards ahead of my car, jagged nails sticking up, and then I get back behind the wheel.

"Ave Maria" is playing on my phone, plugged into the car so that it throbs through the speakers. I start to sing quietly along. My sisters being torn from me. The sadness in Elaine's eyes when she tried so hard to love me but I refused to let her be my mother, refused to be what she needed when there was no way to fill the void in my own life left by Moody and Iris. The stories I wrote in my journal—my secret journal, the one I never showed my sisters—about a mother who could sing like me, a father who hoisted me up on his shoulders and loved me. All the moments I hurt, or wished for something that would never come. "Ave Maria" makes these things flow through me like nothing else, and I need to be crying when he comes to me.

But the tears don't appear until I let myself look at the construction site. There are more trucks parked in the dirt now, and houses have started being built. Wooden skeletons waiting for walls and warmth and life. Edison will be buried somewhere along that dusty trail of tire treads. I'll lay him down gently. I'll kiss him goodbye and cover him with dirt.

"Our time will come to an end." I make myself say it as the song loops back around for a second time. My cheeks are wet and I draw a shuddering breath. I sob and cup my hand over my mouth, startled by the ugliness of the sound. My voice cracks when I whisper the words again. "Our time will come to an end."

I throw the car in reverse, speeding fifty yards back. Stop. Put it in drive. The average car can go zero to sixty in five seconds, and that's more than enough. My vision is blurry and wet, and the starlight drips down all around me with the rain. I take a deep breath and slam on the gas. I feel the tire blow out when it hits the board. The car spins and I clutch at the wheel. *Go slack*, I remind myself. Limp bodies incur the least damage in accidents. That's why drunks walk away from their own accidents unscathed while everyone else ends up injured or dead. But it's over in the time it takes me to think the words.

I scream. Something slams into me and I'm blinded by the brightness of it. White and red. Rain pounding angrily on the metal roof.

The airbag. I make myself think the word. *Focus*, but I can't. Tears all over my face. I touch my forehead and my palm comes away slick with deep, dark blood.

My hands are shaking so furiously that it takes too long for me to dig into my jeans for my phone. Before I left, I put it in my pocket, not my purse, because I knew that I might lose my purse in the impact. I have no idea if this is true because I can't make myself see anything but what's immediately in front of me. Numbness creeps at the edges of my mind. "Ave Maria" has stopped playing, and I realize that I turned the car off, or it shut itself off. I don't know.

I call Edison. He will pick up by the second ring the way he always does. He'll come and save me and I'll tell him I love him, and he'll say he loves me too. He has to. I am delivering myself right into his arms so that he can rescue me.

"Hey, you," he says, and at the sound of his voice I start to cry again. He's in his house with the light from his window glowing out onto the barren lawn. He's waiting for the pizza to be delivered because I'm supposed to be coming over to watch the first season of a new show that's got great reviews.

I try to say his name, but only a squeak comes out.

"Jade?" There was television noise in the background, but it's gone now. He's standing up, holding the phone closer to his face. "What's wrong?"

"Edison," I choke out. "There was an accident."

"Where are you?" His voice is something I don't recognize. Because I love him, I am giving him a gift: the chance to save me the way that he couldn't save his wife.

When I tell Edison I'm at the ten-mile marker, I don't realize how far I've spun out. I stumble out of the car and into the rain, and I can barely see the construction site from here. One lone crane reaches victorious toward the waxing moon. I collapse to my knees on the pavement. My vision roils, and I double over and vomit. I didn't know that it would be like this, with so much blood, my mind so hazy.

"Jade!" When I look up, I see him. A silhouette cutting through the rain, backlit by his high beams. I try to crawl away from my vomit. I don't want him to see it, but my limbs have gone rubbery and all I can do is moan.

His hands are under my arms. "What are you doing out on the road?" he's asking me. "Why did you get out of the car?"

In my delirium I tell him the truth: "I was waiting for you."

"Jade." He lifts me into his arms. He peels the hair from my face. "I've got you. I'm right here, Jade." In this moment, that's my name. That's who I am, because he's willed me into being. I'm in this place for him. Only him.

175

He wraps me in the blanket that he keeps in his trunk. It's a soft fleece, bright red, nothing like the shade of the blood I'm getting all over it.

"It's going to be okay," he tells me, buckling me into the passenger seat. "I'm taking you to the hospital."

"No," I groan. It wasn't supposed to be this ugly. There wasn't supposed to be any blood. I was only supposed to blow out the tire and tell him I'd sprained my wrist. He would lift me by the hips and sit me up on the bathroom counter and patch me up with the brace he keeps for his construction injuries, and fuss over me, and bring me to bed and make love to me. And then, thankful I'm safe, he's supposed to tell me that he loves me, that he doesn't know what he would have done if anything had happened to me.

I don't realize my eyes are closed until I feel him grab my chin, pulling me back to consciousness, back to him. He's got that look about him. I saw it the night we drove to stake out his wife's killer. Only, with me, he doesn't seek to destroy. A weary smile rises on my lips.

"Don't you dare close your eyes on me," he demands. His voice is so strong that even if I were to die right here, his ferocity would be enough to bring me back. "You're going to stay awake and I'm going to do the rest." He grabs my shoulders, digging into my skin. "You aren't going to leave me. Do you understand?"

I reach up and put my hand over his. "Yes," I manage. I wouldn't close my eyes again for the world; I'm too afraid that he isn't real and that this beautiful bright desert town is all a dream.

He gets behind the wheel and I watch him. His jaw is tight. The construction site is behind him, encased by the window like a picture in a frame.

"Edison."

He fumbles through the folds of the blanket and grabs my hand. He drives like hell, the engine of his ancient car straining noisily as we speed through the empty roads. He goes through stop signs, disregards the lights. I know, from being a passenger in Moody's car when we were in high school, that we must be doing at least a hundred.

"It's just two more miles," he tells me. He's laser focused. Like my sisters going for a kill. Like me dismembering the pieces and scouring for evidence. He clenches my hand, and the pain of his crushing embrace only heightens my desire for him. I can feel the rawness of his fear. If the doctors couldn't save me, he'd park outside their houses, watch them move inside as he schemed. How would he kill them? Something efficient, I think, but violent. And as he straddled them in the debris of a frenzied struggle, he would demand to know why they couldn't keep me alive. He couldn't lose me, too. He never even got the chance to tell me he loved me, and it was all their fault, and he had to do it. For me.

He parks right in front of the emergency room in the loading zone. He's going to get towed if he doesn't move, but he doesn't care. The car is still running when he comes around to the passenger side and lifts me, a cocoon in his red blanket. My forehead rests against his throat and I feel his heart beating wild.

I wince when the fluorescent lights inside the building meet my eyes. Everything is moving too fast, and then slow. The place is empty because this is the middle of nowhere. Someone brings a wheelchair and Edison sets me down. He jogs to keep up with the nurse who's wheeling me down a hallway, telling her about the accident, how damaged the car was, how bad it seemed. I slammed into the mile marker sign and bent the post. Things I never bothered to look over my shoulder and check for myself because I was too busy looking to the horizon and waiting for him to come to me.

"There was something in the road," he says. "There's construction nearby."

The nurse tells him to go back to the waiting area, that she'll come out soon. But he doesn't go. Once I'm in my room, I see him pacing on the other side of the window.

I should be telling him I love him. We should be in his bed by now. That's what I'm thinking when a nurse comes and puts an arm around his back and leads him away.

"Can you climb up onto the bed?" my nurse asks me. But I wobble so much that she holds me by the shoulders and tells me, never mind; we can do this part right where I am. She just needs to take a little blood and then someone will come and take me for my X-ray.

She draws a full vial, dabs at my forehead with gauze and peroxide, and gives me a smile.

All I can think is that my sisters are going to be so angry about what I've done to the car. We pay cash for everything, and the damage will be at least three months of rent, and what was I thinking? Couldn't I have just crashed the damn bike into a ditch instead? Or discussed this little plan with them first at least?

And that's saying nothing about the medical bills, which will also have to be paid in cash because Jade Johnson doesn't have insurance and we don't want them running our fake license.

This will all be worth it, I tell myself. The way Edison looked over his shoulder at me as the nurse forced him down the hall. The way he held me and carried me through the rain. He loves me. If he didn't know it before, he knows it now. When we get out of here, he'll take me back to his bed. He'll prop pillows behind my head and watch over me as I sleep, fretting, thinking how broken he would be without me. In the morning, I'll open my eyes and there he'll be beside me. I'll tell him that I'm sorry for scaring him and promise not to do it again. And somewhere in the brilliant sunlight that can only come after such a stormy night, we'll confess our love.

It seems an hour passes before a different nurse comes into my room. "All right, then," she says, staring at the chart propped against her forearm. "How far along are you?"

I don't understand the question. The nurse looks up, and when she sees the bewildered look on my face, she softens. "Your baby, honey," she says. "How long have you been pregnant?"

17

IT'S ONE O'CLOCK IN THE MORNING WHEN WE'RE FINALLY out of the emergency room. Edison arranged for the car to be towed to the mechanic. They'll get us a quote for the repairs in the morning, he tells me when I ask him. And then he kisses my forehead, beside the browning gauze, and says it's not important. He'll take care of it. He'll take care of everything. But I beg him to bring me to the mechanic so that we can find my purse. I can't have them running my license and realizing it's a fake, but I tell Edison I'll need my keys.

The building is closed, but there's my Honda with its mangled hood resting in a row of other damaged cars. Edison finds my purse in the back seat. My phone is ringing when he brings it to me. I hear the musical chime, muffled by all my things, the tube of matcha ChapStick, my wallet with my fake ID, and a travel pack of tampons because I was expecting my period sometime this week.

I'm too numb to wonder who could be calling me so late. My sisters would never use this number, besides which, they expect me to be spending the night with Edison and won't be concerned that I haven't been in touch. The little details that usually bring me comfort are evading me right now. The ringing stops. The door opens and Edison sits behind the wheel.

He doesn't know that his baby is inside me. He'll never know. That detail floats away with all the rest—the car crash, the ache in my head, my wild love for him. All of it is a blur.

"Are you sure I can't take you back to my place?" Edison cups my cheek. When I left my apartment this evening, sleeping beside him was everything I wanted. But now the thought of being near him frightens me. *We could run away.* I open my mouth and those words are on the edge of my tongue. I know how to make us disappear. We could go someplace we've never been and rent a house with window boxes and an ornate door knocker. He could rest his head on my stomach and feel the movement inside.

Stop dreaming, you idiot. In my mind, the baby falls out from between my legs, slimy and screaming, and I don't know what to do with it. I'm afraid, even in my own imagination, to pick it up, to clear away the blood and see if its face looks anything like mine, to know if I'm capable of loving it.

"Jade?" There's a worry line on Edison's forehead that I've never seen before.

"I want to sleep in my own bed," I say, and it pains me to tell him such a lie. But I can't be emotional right now. This is too important, and I need time to think.

As Edison drives back to my apartment, I watch his face in the flicker of the passing streetlamps. He looks about ten years older than he did yesterday. His eyes are bleary, his fingers clutching the wheel. But his grip softens when I reach out and put my hand over his.

"I'm sorry I scared you," I say.

"Jade, I—" His voice chokes off. He gives himself a few seconds. "This could have been so much worse, and I couldn't take it if—"

He can't finish, too afraid that saying it out loud will manifest it.

This moment will live inside of me forever. Those beautiful words will warm me for the rest of my life.

"All I could think about was you," I tell him in a soft voice. "When the car stopped spinning and I realized I was alone out there, I knew that I just had to call you and you'd come."

He brings my hand to his lips and kisses my palm, hard. This was his greatest fear. He imagines it every time I leave him, and only breathes a sigh of relief once I text him that I've gotten home safely.

"I love you so much, Jade," he says, too caught up in the moment to maintain his defenses. If he caught me by surprise in that church, I've repaid him here. We are full of surprises, my love and I.

This can't last forever, Sissy, I have to remind myself. We are lucky to have found each other. We'll burn for a short while, but the fire is hot and bright and wild. It's a short love, but a rare love. Once in a lifetime.

"Really?" My heart fills up with more heat and light than the sun.

He nods, brings his hand back to the steering wheel with my fingers still in his. "Yeah." His voice is tight. "I love everything about you. I love the way you grab the headboard with both hands when I go down on you, and the taste of coffee in your mouth when you kiss me in the morning. I love your fucking smile. It drives me wild, Jade. That day in the church, you smiled while you sang to me and it set me on fire."

He knew. He knew that I'd come for him. We were always on this course and we'd waited all our lives to finally crash like two asteroids in an empty galaxy.

183

I don't say anything for a long time, and he glances at me. When he sees the tired smile on my face, relief floods through his features. No, his confession hasn't scared me away.

"I love you too," I say.

The rain drums all around us, composing a song.

Now that the adrenaline has died down, my muscles have started to ache. My neck hurts, and my head is starting to throb. But I will relive this night a thousand times after Edison is gone. I'll remember how beautiful he was, how gentle his calloused hands, the protective watchfulness of his eyes. I'll remember his child curled up inside me.

"There can never be another you," I tell him. He smiles, taking this as a sweet declaration made in my delirious state. But the words are the truth, and I needed to say them.

By the time Edison pulls into my parking space, I can barely keep my eyes open. He sweeps me into his arms and carries me up the stairs, using the blanket to protect me from the rain. He sets me down only once I've fished the keys out of my purse, but I stop him with a hand to his chest when he tries to follow me inside.

"Lisa is sleeping," I say. "I don't want to wake her up."

"You need someone to look after you," he says. "Your head—"

"The nurses said nothing was broken," I remind him. "I just need to take a couple of aspirin and get some sleep." I kiss him before he can argue. "Good night."

The ghost of my original plan is still in play. No, we won't sleep beside each other, but he'll spend the night thinking of me, loving me.

I'll go to him just as soon as I figure this out. I'll have my sisters to contend with first, and then the car, and the matter of paying for all of it.

And then the other thing. The one I can't put words to just yet. There's a blurred image of a baby's face that won't come into focus in my mind, and I try to push it away but something else within me clings to it.

Once Edison has left, I move through the house silently. My sisters will be fast asleep by now, and if they knew I let Edison come all the way up to the front door, they'd be furious. *What if we were down here, Sissy? What if he saw us?*

My phone starts ringing again, and this time I fumble for it immediately and put it on mute so that the noise won't wake my sisters.

Twenty-seven missed calls, all of them from Dara.

A new terror takes hold of me, and I drop my purse on the couch and I go to her. *He's done it*, I'm thinking as I take the three strides to her front door. He's finally hurt her so badly that she wants to run away. She has no one else to call. Her parents are in Florida, and her little brother is in Dubai for a year as a college exchange student. She would never confide in the nosy biddies in our complex, or the judgmental lady across the parking lot who keeps telling her that her music is too loud. Although it may come to her great detriment, all she has is me.

I knock quietly. Two brief raps with the knuckle of my index finger. There's the glow of a light through the curtains, which are too thick for me to make out any silhouettes inside.

The door opens an inch, and Dara peers out at me. There's blood smeared all over her face and her left eye is swollen, bruised deep purple against her skin.

"What did he do to you?" I growl.

Tears all over her cheeks. "Jade?" she whispers, her voice broken. "I—I need your help."

"Let me in," I say, but when I try to open the door, she holds it in place with her foot.

"I'm in trouble," she says. "I—"

I know she wants me to see whatever's happened in that apartment. She didn't call me nearly thirty times just to show me the outside of her front door. I've never seen her like this, shaking and small, and I force myself to tamp down my rage so that I can reason with her. "Dara, whatever it is, I can help you. But you have to let me."

"No." Fresh tears well up in her eyes. "No, no, no." She sobs, and I suspect those words aren't meant for me. When she wipes her hands across her face, I take the opportunity to push the door open. This time, she doesn't stop me. She tumbles out of the way, her back pressed against the wall.

The coffee table is upended, candle wax caked in splatters on the linoleum. The television is broken, spider cracks on the screen. Dara's yellow flip-flop is wedged between the couch cushions, and I can see that she must have been running from him, crawling over the couch to put a barrier between herself and his monstrous wrath.

I close the door and lock it. She is cradling her left wrist, which is swollen like her eye. "Dara." I stand in front of her and brush my thumb across her cracked, bleeding lip. "Where is he?"

Her eyes give her away. She looks over my shoulder to the kitchenette. There's a bare leg sticking out from around the island with the bar counter. Pale and thin and unmoving.

I walk slowly, Dara whimpering in agony behind me. When I step into the kitchen I see what she's crying about. Tim is slumped against the cabinet below the kitchen sink, trembling, blood pooled around the hilt of the steak knife wedged into his chest.

He looks at me with bloodshot eyes, blood dribbling down from the side of his mouth.

"Help," he whispers, sound barely leaving his lips. "Help me."

Dara is chewing on her knuckle, pacing. She grasps her hair in her fist and then flails, as though the violence of this night is a cobweb she can shake herself free of.

"I didn't want to," she says. "I swear I didn't want to."

"Yes, you did," I say. Nobody stabs someone in the chest unless they mean it. "If you lie to yourself, this will be a lot harder than it needs to be."

She presses her palms to her eyes. "God."

"Hey." My voice is gentle, the way I would speak to my child if I could ever hold it in my arms. I take her elbows with careful hands, but she still flinches. She looks at me. "You have a choice to make."

Even in her grief, Dara is too strong to succumb to hysteria. She's in her right mind. He's come for her a hundred times before, and she's subsisted on the promises and apology gifts. He buys her designer purses and shows her real estate listings for homes they'll be able to afford one day. But somewhere in there, he started to push her too far. She started to think about where the weapons were, how she would do it if she really had to.

Tim might be a goner no matter what. The blood in his mouth means that he's bleeding internally, and if he could have been saved, it would have been sometime in the last hour while Dara was calling me instead. But if Dara regrets this later, and she didn't try, I know that it will only haunt her. She'll make a saint of him and forget what he did to make her stab him. "We can call an ambulance and tell the police it was self-defense," I say. "They'll take photos of you. They'll see what he did to you and we'll get you a good lawyer. You might go away. It might be really, really bad. But maybe the hospital can save him if we act now."

She takes a shuddering breath and looks at him.

"Or we can make all of this go away, you and me together," I tell her. "But it has to be your decision. Do you understand?"

"I want to call the ambulance," she whispers.

"You're sure?"

She nods, swallows hard. I grab her phone from where it's sitting on the counter smeared with blood. I place it in her trembling hands. "Say it just happened," I instruct her. "Act like you called them right away."

She unlocks her phone, and Tim gurgles and spits. After hanging on for nearly an hour, he's finally starting to lose consciousness. "Move—" he rasps. "Move faster, you fucking—psycho."

Dara studies him anew, this man she vowed to honor and love. This man who puts on a suit and tie in the morning and kisses her at the door. This man who breaks her over and over, until she can't believe there's anyone out there who would love her like she deserves.

She locks her phone and sets it back on the counter.

18

IT TAKES THIRTY MORE MINUTES FOR TIM TO DIE. BY THE
time his chest stops heaving, Dara is completely drained. Her skin is
ashen and her leg is shaking, knee bobbing furiously up and down.

I sit on the adjacent barstool facing her, and I wait for her to
understand that Tim isn't going to draw another breath. The realiza-
tion comes when she squeezes her eyes shut and bows her head.

"What the fuck?" she whispers.

I don't tell her what I'm thinking, which is that she made the right
choice. When she answered that door, coated in blood, my heart
about stopped. I don't tell her that I've never had a friend who could
scare me like this except for Colin, who flatlined once between rehab
stints. I don't tell her that she couldn't have done a more beautiful
thing to free herself if I'd given her written instructions.

"What the fuck," she says again. "I just killed my husband—I—"

"Dara." At the firmness of my voice, she snaps out of it and looks at me. Her brow furrows; she's just noticing my own bruises and the bandage on my forehead. Now that the adrenaline has worn down and the world hasn't ended, little details are starting to make sense to her again. "Take your clothes off and leave them on the kitchen floor. Then get in the shower and scrub every last inch. Don't touch the railing or the doorknobs. Don't even get a towel until you've cleaned off all the blood."

If my instructions are strange to her, she doesn't let on. "What's going to happen to him?"

"I'll take care of him," I say. For the first time, skepticism mars her features. And then incredulity that I can be so calm.

But she does as I say. I look away as she slides out of the pink tank top and shorts she was wearing—pajamas she had put on expecting to go to sleep before Tim balled his fists for the last time. She leaves them in a pile on the floor. We wear almost the same size and her clothes can pass easily for mine. I'll wash the blood out with dish soap first. Then I'll clean them with my own laundry. I'll fold them and put them in a trash bag with some other clothes and dump them in a donation bin. They'll be on their way overseas just as soon as the next pickup arrives.

Water runs through the pipes as Dara showers upstairs. A wave of dizziness and fatigue overtakes me when I kneel beside the ill-fated Tim. The dull ache in my head has become a persistent throb. My muscles are begging for rest. But I must move quickly. Rigor mortis can begin as soon as an hour after death, and once his body goes stiff, it will become a lot harder to manipulate.

Dara and Tim order weekly meal kits that are left in a temperature-controlled box by their door. Filet mignon, seared ahi tuna, braised organic vegetables. And because they're such avid chefs, they have a full supply of cutlery, including a hefty butcher knife stuck to a magnetic strip above the stove. I'm grateful Dara didn't use this one to kill him. It would have done the job, but it also would have left a considerable mess. As it is, she stabbed him once and it's a clean wound. Right through the chest with a serrated knife from the block. I'm amazed that he lasted as long as he did.

Her bloody handprints are all over his bare chest. She knelt down to help him, cupped his cheek. She had tried to stop the bleeding, and she'd gripped the hilt of the knife with her bloody fingers, but then thought better of pulling it out.

Dara. She's strong. She'll survive this. But the shock will wear off in the coming days and I'll have to keep her close to make sure she doesn't have a crisis of conscience and go to the police. I'm not dismembering her piece-of-shit husband only for her to throw her life away in a federal prison.

As I get to work, I make a mental checklist of instructions for her: Call your parents just to ask how they're doing. Email your brother like normal. Don't touch your bank accounts. Don't report him missing. Don't impersonate him by using his phone or checking his email. Don't go out on the balcony until that black eye and split lip are healed, and if anyone asks where you've been, say you've had a stomach flu. Tim isn't dead. Tim just left, and you're sure he'll be back.

I take off all my clothes, fold them neatly on the couch in the living room where there's no blood, and get to work.

When dismembering a body, a common mistake is to hack away at it in haste and hope for the best. Bones will fracture this way, but without a saw they won't sever in the way you need them to. It's much cleaner to feel for the joints and hack away at the cartilage. A few sharp, swift swings of the butcher knife and I've detached his arms at the shoulder.

If I had more time, I'd hang him over the counter with his head toward the floor, slit him from ear to ear, and let the blood drain into a basin. The human body can hold approximately one and a half gallons of blood—10 percent of his body weight—and getting rid of it makes dismemberment a hell of a lot easier. But without the heart to pump the blood to the wound, it would trickle out slowly, and we don't have the hours to squander.

I move quickly. It's arduous work. We're moving against the morning, and there won't be time to clean thoroughly before disposing of him. I'll clean the visible blood with dish soap and hot water, get all the detached pieces wrapped securely in bags, and come back to clean the cabinets and floor properly once Tim is laid to rest. Most domestic murders are committed in the kitchen or the bedroom, and if Tim's family reports him missing, the police will be here with luminol and cadaver dogs before the ink can dry on the warrant.

Dara takes a long shower. The water must be ice-cold by now, but I don't go to check on her. She needs to work through the shock of what she's done, make her peace with it, and then compose herself, because I'll need her help getting rid of him.

Torso, head, arms, shins, thighs. Everything is laid out and wrapped by the time the shower stops running. I glance at the clock above the stove. Nearly four o'clock.

I stand to wash the blood from my arms, and dizziness pounds at the inside of my skull. Before I realize what's coming, bile burns at my throat and I vomit into the sink. The tang of blood has never smelled so strong. My muscles have never ached like this. Sweat drips from my face in heavy drops. *Pull it together, Sissy.*

Plans and logic come to comfort me as they always do. Get back to work. Stay organized. I put my clothes back on.

Dara comes downstairs just as I've rinsed the last of the vomit down the drain, using the hose attachment to direct the last of it. She heard me, and sympathy joins the blend of traumatized emotions on her face. This concussion and my unexpected condition have afforded me an advantage—Dara mistakes my illness for revulsion at what she's done and what I've been made to clean up.

She stands at the edge of the kitchenette as though the floor beyond the threshold might burn her, and she stares at the grim packages wrapped in solid black garbage bags on her floor.

"What do I do now?" Her voice is hoarse. She's pulled her wet hair back into twin French braids that stop at the nape of her neck, out of her face, ready to get to work. There's sadness in her dark eyes, but a renewed sense of calm as well.

I hope she realizes how practical she is—how mighty. I wonder how many times she's thought about this night, wondering if it would ever come, laying out the details in her head. Terrified as she was when she called me, she didn't panic. She didn't call the police or tear out the knife and stab him over and over. She did only as much as it would take to kill him, and then she waited for me.

"Do you have a box?" I say. "A really big one."

We load Tim's body into two fifty-gallon storage bins that Dara was using to store spare blankets in the hall closet. We haul him down the steps to the laundry room in two shifts, and then into the back seat of her car. The car that I've never seen her drive because Tim always takes it to work.

I tell Dara to wait in the passenger seat while I go inside to clean up the blood. She wants to come and help me, but I'm not convinced she's aware of what she's volunteering for. It was gruesome enough for her to carry the weight of him in those storage bins. If she has to look at his blood again, really look at the colors that were once inside him, she might break down again, and I need her to stay strong for what will come next.

The clock on the stove reads five o'clock. Sunrise is in one hour, and before that, the sky will start to lighten.

I'm ashamed of the rushed job I do cleaning up. I use the white kitchen towels to clean most of it. What a gift that they're white, because I'm able to pour bleach into the washing machine. Bleach isn't my favorite. It's conspicuous, but it's already here, which will work in Dara's favor, since it wasn't a recent purchase and it's formulated for laundry.

When we return, I'll launder them again with regular detergent, toss in some of Dara and Tim's other laundry for good measure, and instruct her to put the clothes away. Then I'll wash her pajamas. It will be okay. Time is wearing thin, but there's enough of it.

My vision roils with dark spots, and I clutch the edge of the washer as it rattles and whirs. *It's almost over and then you can sleep*, I tell myself. I've already done the hard part.

I think of Edison for the first time in hours. He won't call me because he thinks I'm resting. And—oh, how I wish I were. My entire body is starting to remember that it was in a car accident, and new pain flares every time I move.

When I climb into the driver's seat, Dara is shivering, hugging her arms tightly to her chest and soaked through with rain. Without saying anything, she hands me the keys, and we drive off. I don't turn on the headlights until we're well out of the parking lot.

"You look awful," she finally says, when we're a mile out.

"Ran my car into a ditch," I say. "It's nothing."

She nods. Shock is shifting, taking new shapes and colors within her. "Where are we going?" Her voice is hollow.

Edison and I have hiked all the mountain trails within a ten-mile radius. But they're lush with rivers and breathtaking views. Even the most barren parts of them run the risk of someone spotting a body.

All the worthwhile hiding spots are higher up, more treacherous to reach, and I'm operating at half capacity. He's going to be found if I leave any piece of him in the more accessible wilderness. I know that. The plastic bags in this desert heat will create a greenhouse effect that accelerates decomposition, but it only takes a hair of DNA from a willing family member to compare against the remains. And while I'll be long gone by the time his corpse may be found in the brush, Dara will forever be linked to him. She has the most to lose, and I'm doing this for her.

Dara is starting to panic. She's breathing faster, clutching the hem of her shorts in her fist, and we only have about thirty minutes before people start waking up for their morning commutes.

Think, Sissy.

"I know a place," I say.

The head will be the most important identifier. Although I've removed his teeth, a sketch artist will be able to draw a facial composite from his bone structure long after decomposition sets in. If I can make sure his head is never found, the other pieces won't be as damning.

I pull up to the playground behind the elementary school that's attached to Sadie's junior high. I already know there are no cameras here; I checked the day I picked her up. Tim's head goes into the trash barrel that's painted with a landscape and stick-figure children holding hands below a sunny sky. I paw through the existing trash and bury him under juice boxes, candy wrappers, wadded paper, and various other types of pedestrian trash. The barrel is almost full, which means the janitor will tie it off and carry it away first thing when the building opens. It will be on its way to the landfill by noon.

I consider the dumpsters downtown, behind the restaurants and apartments. The trash collection for our apartment complex is on

Mondays and Thursdays, and the town pickup goes by district, which means the city block with the Safeway is due for collection this afternoon.

I park behind the grocery store, and at my urgency, Dara snaps out of her trance and helps me to carry the severed pieces of her husband into the dumpster. We bury him amid coffee grounds, expired cans, runny produce, and rat droppings. This has to work, I tell myself. A dumpster burial has never been my modus operandi; there's the risk of being seen, or of the bags rolling out of the truck, but it's also the only way to ensure the body will be gone forever. Greater benefit but a stupid risk to take unless you have to.

If this were one of my or my sister's kills, it wouldn't matter that the body may be found in the wilderness or floating up from a lake after the marine wildlife has eaten away at the plastic. We'd be long gone by then, leaving behind only a fake identity. Besides which, to cement our alibi, one of us is always on a security camera at the time the murder is being committed.

Dara retches and then stands with her face canted to the falling rain.

"It's done," I tell her, my breathing ragged. I touch her arm. "Come on. Let's go back."

She starts crying again in the car, and I let her. The empty storage bins—stacked one inside the other—slide across the back seat.

I don't speak until the turn for our apartment complex comes up. "Bring the bins into the bathtub and wash them with one cup of bleach and hot water." The recommended amount for cleaning, not enough to leave a suspicious chemical stench. "Rinse them thoroughly with hot water. Then let them soak with a half-bottle of dish soap in each one. Dry them with paper towels. Put everything back."

I know it's not an ideal time to be giving her instructions, but it's important.

"Jade?" It's the first word she's spoken since before Tim's unceremonious but arduous burial. She looks at me as I pull into her parking space.

I turn off the ignition and turn to face her. Her eyes are moving up and down the length of me, her split lip quivering. I know what she wants to ask me, even though Dara herself doesn't seem to know how to ask it. She wants to know how a churchgoing musician from California can tie her hair back in a bun and set about such a grim task so calmly, how I didn't retch at the tang of blood as I arranged the pieces. Like I've done this before.

When she doesn't speak, I reach out and cup her cheek. She flinches at first, but then purses her mouth thoughtfully. This is it, all the comfort I can offer her, and she understands just how much she needs the reassurance.

I instruct her to put the towels in the dryer, and then wash them again with some other dirty laundry. Repeat three times. Don't forget about the storage bins. Don't panic and overbleach them, because the smell and the stains will be suspicious to police. You may not think forensic investigators will look through your closets, but they will. They'll think of everything, and two bins large enough to fit a human body leave no room for mistakes.

She takes the bins and enters her condo though the laundry room entrance, while I take the stairs to my front door. Twelve steps, but it feels like Mount Everest, I'm so exhausted.

The door swings open before I can reach for the knob. Moody must have been watching for me. Distantly, I remember that I left my purse and Edison's blanket on the couch.

I've never seen my sister look so frantic. "Sissy, what the hell happened to you?" she says, ushering me inside. The door closes behind me with a slam that rattles my brain inside my skull.

Everything hurts. I taste blood on my lips, and for a second I think it belongs to Tim, I missed a detail, I forgot something. But then Moody reaches forward and touches the bandage on my forehead, and I realize it's soaked through and dripping down my face.

"Where have you been?" she's asking me.

Moody's image triples. Two ghostly, translucent sisters with big horrified eyes standing behind her. I want to tell her everything, my dearest sister, my best friend in this world. I want to tell her that I've made so many horrible mistakes, that I won't know how to stop loving Edison when this is through and that we've created something I know I can't keep. That I've fallen in love with the desert and with the way the rain here smells like cheap perfume and the sky is always buzzing. That I wish I could keep all of it.

But I know that I can't.

The world turns blurry and spins, and I feel her small but steady hands catching me right as I collapse.

19

I DREAM THAT IT CRUMBLES INTO DUST AND DISSOLVES inside my womb.

This is the image that wakes me, an empty feeling replaced by one of turmoil as I regain consciousness. The thing inside me is still alive, and it frightens me that I feel relieved. I should be angry with it for intruding on my plans and for making me so weak.

"Get her some water," Moody is saying. "Bring the fan closer." She's kneeling beside me when I open my eyes, dabbing at my face with a cold wet cloth. "Sis?"

My feet are propped up on a pile of the ugly green throw pillows that came with the couches, and the oscillating fan from the bedroom is blowing a steady stream of cool air onto my face.

"Hey," Iris says, emerging from the kitchenette. She hands me a bottle of water, but I shake my head.

"What happened?" Moody is fussing over me with the damp cloth.

There's a bottle of peroxide and a newly opened package of bandages on the coffee table, and I realize she's changed my soaked hospital gauze.

"I crashed the car," I say, feeling guilty about my half-truth.

My head throbs and my muscles are taut with pain when I sit up. I tell my sisters about my proclamation of love with Edison, how my plan did not play out as expected but still left him melting in my palm. It was better than I could have hoped for, even, except for the expensive damage I'd just inflicted on our only vehicle.

Iris and Moody don't care about the car. Whatever it costs, we'll sort it out. The emergency room bills too. They only care about getting me well again. When one of us is broken, we all are.

Moody helps me into the shower and stands there—her clothes drenched—holding me up as I scrub the sweat from myself. She steadies me when I sway, and she works the shampoo through my hair. Iris took my clothes and I asked her to put them in the wash. I didn't get any of Tim's blood on them, but you can never be too careful.

I'm feeling better by the time the hot water runs cold. I wrap myself in a towel and sit on the toilet lid while Moody brushes my wet hair. She's being so sweet with me, like I'm a doll that turned up again after she thought she'd lost it for good.

My eyes close. I'm safe, the way I felt in the rare times my sisters were able to visit me at Elaine's, or we were placed in the same group home.

"What were you and the neighbor doing out last night?" she asks me, her voice gentle.

Dara. I knew I would have to share her secret with Moody and Iris—it's for her own protection that they know, so that we can help her if the police come around. There are still details to be sorted. I'll have to go back and work the kitchen over with something to oxidize the blood so it won't show up under the luminol spray. Peroxide is a favorite, but it will have to depend on what's already in her bathroom cabinet, because now is not the time for suspicious purchases, and one bottle won't do the job.

"Tim is dead," I say.

The brush stills in my hair. Moody takes a step back and looks at me. "Sissy," she rasps. "You didn't."

"Dara," I say.

Moody searches my eyes, and then something like a smile starts to form. "No," she says. "Really?"

"With a steak knife."

Moody lets out a long, low whistle as she resumes brushing my hair. "What'd you do with him?"

"All seven pieces of him are off to their final resting place at the city dump," I say. "Before you get mad, I know we said no dumpsters, but there wasn't time—"

"Hey. Sis." Moody kneels before me. Only when she takes my hands do I realize that I'm trembling. A wave of nausea pulses through me, but I force it down. "You know what you're doing," she says. "You did what was best. I trust you." She's giving me her rare gentle sweetness, which I haven't seen in months. When Iris fell into her typical depression after her last kill, we climbed onto the bed beside her and Moody doted on her like a mother hen.

I clean the blood and keep us safe, but Moody holds the three of us together. She's the foundation beam in our little family. Throughout my long and lonely childhood, all I ever wanted was for someone to love me and worry about me, but now, seeing the look on Moody's face, all I feel is guilt that I've scared her so.

I'm pregnant, Moods. I fucked up. I need you to help me fix it, because I don't think I'm strong enough to do it.

But the words don't come. Only an infuriating well of tears. Moody doesn't ask what's gotten into me, why I'm being so weak. She sits beside me, both of us crammed on the small oval lid, and she rocks and shushes me like I'm a child. We're nine years old again, huddled under the blanket of the bunk bed in our group home. I was so relieved when she arrived with her suitcase in that sea of cold, unfriendly faces that I sobbed myself to sleep while she whispered, "I'm here, I'm here," over and over like the chorus of a song.

"I love you," I tell her now. I need to say those words to someone who can feel them the way that I do. I need to say them to someone who will always stay.

IRIS IS NOT HAPPY when I tell her about Tim. She says she knew Dara would make trouble for us. But Iris, ever practical and collected, spends the morning dutifully prescribing me spoonfuls of peanut butter for the protein, a multivitamin, and an endless river of tea. "Maintaining her trust is even more important," she says, tucking the blanket around me on the couch. "Rest up and then go check on her. Make sure that girl doesn't crack."

Tim's not our kill, but if Dara has a crisis of conscience, he may as well be. We'll all go down for this. Fleeing would be easy enough. We never unpack our suitcases. Nothing in any of these cabinets belongs to us apart from the food. Our IDs are fake; we pay rent by stuffing cash into an envelope and dropping it in the deposit box by the mailroom. But the thought of leaving Dara to fend for herself gives me an uneasy feeling.

She's not your friend—she's Jade's, I remind myself.

I'm heartened by how calmly my sisters are taking the wrecked car and the new complication with Dara. But I still haven't told them the worst of it. I already know what they'll say.

Sis, sweetheart, you can't keep it.

We wouldn't be able to bring a baby with us.

It's not mine. I make myself think the words. I will say them over and over until I understand. It's a piece of Jade, and once we leave Arizona, Jade—and her lover, and her dreams, and all her pretty thoughts of love—must die.

It's not mine.

"Take a nap," Moody says. "You look like shit." She takes my phone as she heads for the stairs. "When your boyfriend calls to check on you, I'll handle it."

I push down the anxiety I feel at Moody taking even this small bit of control. *Don't be a child,* I tell myself. *Let her help you.* Moody knows that I'm exhausted and that I'm likely to make a mistake right now. We can't afford to be vulnerable with anyone but one another, the three of us.

My sisters love me in a way that no romantic partner ever could. They have seen me ugly, naked, covered in blood. They've read my journals, heard my loud and hideous laugh—the real laugh I give only when I'm not playing a role. And when the time comes, they'll see me in the depths of grief. Only once Edison's gone will I confess my great sin of wanting to keep him, of trying to dream up any possible way. They'll forgive me. They'll understand, tell me there's a lover or two they fantasized about running away with. It's just how it goes. It's these sacrifices that prove, over and again, our loyalty. Our trust.

If someone in this world had wanted us, our lives might have been different. But we learned the truth at the very beginning, which is that there are three of us—only three—and there will never be room for more.

I SPEND THE EARLY afternoon in and out of sleep, wrapped in a blanket and staring at the television. Every so often I hear the creak of their weight on the stairs as my sisters peek in on me. To check if I'm still breathing, I suppose. Disposing of a body is nothing I can't handle, but I've never had to do it when I was losing blood and half concussed. I hate how hollow and exhausted I feel, but it's a relief to take a break from Jade. To lie limp on the sofa and not think about how I'll murder Edison, or what aspects of our sex life I share with Moody and Iris when they ask.

I don't know how long I sleep, but when my eyes open, the sun is starting to set, a vivacious orange light streaming in through the closed blinds.

The TV is still on, the evening news crews gearing up to tell us of the day's tragedies. The anchor paces through a live feed of the desert wilderness. Police tape. Flashing lights. An ambulance idling on the shoulder, and a gurney carrying a body under a sheet.

My heart is thudding in my ears. I know that particular stretch of nothingness. I recognize the start of the hiking trail.

"Moody!" My voice is hysterical, and I command myself to remain steady. "Iris!"

My sisters thunder down the stairs, Moody clutching the tire iron we keep by the bed, Iris ready for a brawl with nothing but her bare fists. From the pitch of my cry, they were sure that we were in danger.

"Sissy?" Iris rasps.

Then they see the TV, and they understand. The headline at the bottom of the screen reads:

BODY FOUND ON HIKING TRAIL SET TO REOPEN THIS FALL

"Oh," Iris says, flopping onto the couch beside me. "Oh shit."

Bodies are always found. I knew this even as I labored to destroy the evidence and leave him somewhere that would buy us enough time. Of the six prior kills my sisters share between them, three have emerged, two of which have been identified. None of which have been linked to us. But we were long since out of town before they were uncovered.

"How bad is this, really?" Moody's voice betrays nothing, but I can feel the nervous energy within her. She paces, chewing on her lip. Sourly, I hope she feels a healthy dose of regret, because her impulsiveness is what got us into this mess. "Sissy makes sure we never leave any DNA. There's nothing linking him to us."

"Nobody saw you talking to him when he pulled over to help?" Iris asks. "Not a single car passed by?"

"No," Moody says.

"Think, Moods. Are you sure—"

"I told you!" Moody hisses. "I'm not fucking stupid. Nobody saw us."

"Well, if you're so smart, why did you make us kill him at all?" Iris fires back. "You knew we'd still be living here when he was found." Even if I hadn't set my sights on Edison before we killed the trucker, we wouldn't have been able to abandon the mission so early. Jade Johnson had only just put down a deposit for this rental, and if she had skipped town without spending a day in it, that would have raised more suspicions in a town as small as this. The landlord would have made a note that it was strange.

I hold up a hand and shush them. They stop bickering and look at me like I'm the only salvation in this world, and for them I may as well be.

The news has already transitioned to another topic. They won't have more to say about the missing man until he's been properly identified and the family has been notified. After several weeks in monsoon season, the discovery won't be pretty. Animals will have picked away most of the flesh. His teeth are long gone. After I removed them, I put them in a plastic bag and smashed them to bits with a hammer, flushed the dust down the toilet. Burned the plastic with a lighter and threw the husk of it away weeks and weeks ago.

"They'll identify him soon enough, if they haven't already," I say. "Nobody else has gone missing and not been accounted for." His photo will be on the news. His name will be released. His spouse, his kids, everyone who's ever bummed a cigarette off him, will have something to say for the cameras. "But there's nothing to tie him to us. We were on a stretch of road with no cameras. We didn't touch his truck. I'm positive we didn't leave any DNA on his body, but even if we did, our hair and fingerprints aren't in any police database. Nobody would be able to match it to us."

"So, we're okay," Moody exhales. "Good."

Iris shakes her head. "I don't trust it," she says. "We should get out of here. Abandon the plan and find you someone new."

Leave Edison. Leave the desert. I steel myself against the weight of it. "Leaving would be more suspicious than carrying on as normal," I tell her. "Jade has a life here. She has friends at church. Edison will try to find me."

"He'll try to find Jade," Iris corrects. "And he won't, because Jade isn't real."

The words sting. I know that Jade can't come with me when we leave this town, but the reminder that she'll blow away like dust breaks something inside of me.

Iris grips my wrist. When I look at her, there's determination in her eyes. This never amounts to anything good. Once Iris has made up her mind about something, it's easier to grind blood from stone than make her see things differently.

"You could kill Edison now," Moody tries to compromise. "We can make it look like a serial killer."

"What?" I squeak. I have to work to compose myself, but if Moody catches my slip, she doesn't comment.

"Dump him on another hiking trail," she says. "We'll do the same thing—hack out his teeth and roll him into the brush. But someplace more obvious where he gets found."

Her use of the word *we* when talking about Edison angers me more than anything else she's just said. She forces me to picture it: killing Edison—*my* Edison—in haste so that my sisters can help me haul him up some nondescript mountain. Chiseling his teeth and leaving him for the coyotes.

No lingering kiss before I take his breath away. No peaceful burial before they pour the asphalt in the new subdivision. No coming back to visit him when the homes are built and children are playing over his grave.

"No," I tell her. "That isn't the plan."

Iris gestures to the TV. "The plan's ruined, Sis. You need to take care of this, or we need to go."

I don't like this. "That trucker threw us off," I say. "This is the first time we broke our rules about who to kill, and look what it's done. Breaking another rule by leaving early will only get us caught. It's sloppy."

"It wouldn't be the first time we've had to abandon a kill," Moody says. "I had to give one up in Iowa because it turned out his brother was in law enforcement, remember? We all have to make sacrifices." I glare at her, and she frowns sympathetically at me. I don't buy her feigned penitence in the face of what she's cost me. She'd be all too happy for me to murder Edison in haste and lose my final months with him, just like she was happy when my preteen antics got me kicked out of Elaine's house and we were reunited in a group home. Moody loves me too much. She hates sharing me. There is no room for me to have any shred of happiness for myself.

"We don't do anything for now." I extend both arms to take my sister's hands. "The best thing is to stick to the plan. It's never failed us before." My eyes linger on Moody. "We don't act without planning, and only if we all agree. Same as before."

I hope they can't hear my wild heartbeat in the silence that follows my words. If they understood how deeply I cared about making things perfect with Edison, they would kill him themselves just to teach me a lesson about getting too attached.

"We work together," Moody says, and I catch the taunt in her voice. Her eyes stare into mine, and even though we're identical, I can see something distinctly Moody about that look she gives me. *Together* is the word she used. She knows there are things I haven't told her. She knows I'm hiding something.

After a moment, Iris shakes her head. "I don't have a good feeling about this," she says. "I think we should go."

I'm on borrowed time. My sisters want me to kill Edison or abandon him. To forfeit my last precious months with him. I'm walking the precarious tightrope of their patience, and I know that everything I do from here forward will have to be more transparent.

For the rest of the afternoon, we talk strategy. We corroborate our stories if anyone asks Jade or Lisa what they think of the man on the hiking trail. I'll attend the inevitable church prayer vigil with Edison to get a climate check. We will avoid the crime scene, avoid police at all costs, and we won't panic.

There's comfort in the planning, and I try to draw strength from that, rather than letting myself think of what will happen if I fail.

20

EARLY THE NEXT MORNING, I KNOCK ON DARA'S DOOR. It's been eerily quiet without her music thundering through the wall. I understand now that she used it to cover up so much of what was happening over there. I never heard her and Tim shouting. I never heard furniture being knocked over or punches being thrown. Only some dance melody I couldn't quite identify.

"Dara?" I call in a soft voice. "It's me."

There's no response, and the persistent, nettling worry I've had since I left her reaches a fever pitch. The car is still in its space, so she hasn't gone anywhere. But she could have hurt herself.

I knock again. I'll give her five seconds, and if she doesn't answer, I'll break in. "Dara—"

The door opens just a crack. She looks terrible, but not quite so bad as when I left her. Dark circles from a sleepless night join the bruises on her face, which have shifted and adopted new hues of yellow, purple, and gray. "Hi," I say, with the tone one might use with a baby bird that has fallen from its nest. "Can I come in?"

Wordlessly, she moves aside, and I'm able to nudge the door open. Her wrist is in the same brace I saw her wearing a few weeks back, though the swelling looks less angry.

There's a peppermint candle burning on the kitchen island. The place looks tidy again, her yellow sandals resting on the mud mat by the door. There's no stench of bleach. She didn't panic. Good girl.

"I'm making coffee," she says, her back already to me as she heads into the kitchenette. She stands over the spot where Tim's body was slumped only hours before and slides a mug under the spout of the Keurig. "How do you take it?" Her voice is flat, and it's as though she were sleepwalking.

Before I catch myself, I wonder if caffeine is bad for an unborn baby. If one sip is enough to kill it, or damage its heart.

It doesn't matter.

"Black," I say, even though I'm not sure I'll take a sip. I don't want to interrupt this fragile dance Dara is performing. I don't want to upset her when I don't know what might make her fall apart, if she will at all.

We sit on the barstools, and I watch Dara pour creamer into her mug.

"I cleaned the bins," she says after a long silence. "The way that you said. But after that, I didn't know what to do."

"We have to use cleaning chemicals that oxidize the bloodstains," I say. "It's the blood's response to oxygen that makes it show up on the chemicals forensics teams use."

Dara isn't looking at me. "Were you really into science in high school or something?"

"I've always liked watching true crime," I say. A partial truth.

There's a lot to be learned from forensics documentaries, and it's a hell of a lot less conspicuous than running a computer search. Hey, Siri, how do I get rid of a body? What's the best way to dismember a corpse? If the police confiscated my phone right now, they'd find searches for random celebrities, puzzle games, and bookmarked pages about the best restaurants to try in Scottsdale. I haven't shut it for a suspicious amount of time or disabled the Wi-Fi in the middle of the night. Nothing out of the ordinary.

"You must love what I did, then," Dara says. She laughs and then clasps both hands over her mouth. Her eyes go wide with terror. "Oh God," she says. "That was so horrible. I don't know what made me say that."

I glance at the clock over the stove. Just after one o'clock. In less than two hours, Edison will be on his way to take Jade and Lisa to the mechanic, and I want to make sure I'm ready. I don't want Moody to be alone with him. It isn't that I don't trust her, but that I selfishly want to scrape up every memory of Edison for myself. Later, when he's gone and we're looking back on this time, I won't be able to bear the thought of Moody or Iris having a single memory of my man that I wasn't present for. I want to relive every detail.

Which means I don't have much time. "Bring me every cleaner you have in the house," I say. "You're not going to buy anything new. Not even Windex. All of your purchases have to stay consistent. But we can make do."

While Dara is busying herself with the task at hand, I dump my untouched coffee down the sink. I crawl across the floor, checking under the cabinets and then inside them. I did a good job even in my addled state last night, because all the visible blood is gone. I work at fresh corpses the way that some work at needlepoint or knitting. It's taken years of practice, but I've learned where all the seams in the human body are—the vulnerable joints that come undone when you hack at them with enough force.

"If you have mouthwash or peroxide, bring that too," I call up the stairs.

The first time I did this, Iris left me with a startling mess. Her lover expelled what seemed like a gallon of waste. That, combined with the blood, left me feeling nauseous and light-headed. But Moody was busy taking care of Iris, who was reeling from the shock and still spattered with blood. The two of them went into the bathroom to clean up while I contended with the living room.

Peroxide-based mouthwash is what I ended up using for all the angel figurines. Combining it with some dish soap got the stains right out of the throw rug, before the washing machine did the rest of it. Even once the blood was gone, I went over everything thrice. I developed a method: Listerine, dish soap, peroxide. As the smell diminished with every round, it got much easier.

Once the body was gone, I went back to the apartment, feeling pleased with myself that I had aided my sister in erasing all signs of her tragic love life. But the worst was yet to come. After we dumped his body, she didn't speak for days, barely looked at us.

After a week of the silent treatment, I crawled into the bed beside her one morning, snuggled up against her back, and put my arms around her. She tensed but didn't push me away. "What can I do for you?" I asked. Moody was a shadow in the doorway, her arms folded where she stood in the predawn dim.

Iris was silent for a long time, and then she whispered, "I loved him, and you can't possibly know how this feels."

But I wanted to know. I wanted to climb inside her brain and sit beside her, because I loved her and I didn't want her to be trapped in that dark place by herself.

"Tell me," I whispered.

"I can't." Her voice was cracked. "He's gone and I'll never get him back."

"Fuck him, Iris. He broke your heart," Moody said, getting impatient. "If it'll make you feel better, I'll kill the first man I fall in love with too."

All these years later, I'm still not sure if Moody meant it, or if she ever relives that moment and wishes she had said something else. But it happened the way that it did, and very slowly, the promise took root.

Dara brings me a bottle of OxiClean, two full, unopened bottles of peroxide, and a mostly empty bottle of bathroom cleaner that smells far too abrasive and is useless to me because the strong smell of it will linger and there's nothing in it to treat blood. Dara leans against the refrigerator, arms folded, watching me.

"See what I'm doing?" I tell her, not looking up as I scour the baseboard under the cabinets with a damp rag. "Clean like this every day for a week. Just to make sure."

After a beat, Dara slumps to the floor and folds her legs. "I really loved him, you know," she says. "I thought I could go back to Florida for a few weeks. Spend some time with my parents and keep my phone off, so he'd worry about me. I wanted him to think—think that I'd left him for good, or maybe even that something had happened to me, like that man on the news who disappeared. If I really scared him, he would appreciate me when I came back. It would be like it was before things got so ugly." She whispers that last word, like she realizes it wouldn't be possible as she says it. If she left and came back a thousand more times, it would always turn ugly.

"You did the right thing," I tell her, and toss the rag into the sink.

She looks at me. "How can you say that?"

"There's someone out there who's desperate to love you," I say. "Someone who will make you so happy, you won't be hoarding your money and dreaming of running away. Someone who makes you want to stay all the time."

I give her these words because I know that Dara isn't like me. She doesn't have sisters who will give her the strange, unconditional love that comes from growing up the way Moody, Iris, and I did. But she's got something perhaps more powerful, which is the bravery to stay in one place. To build a life with someone and really give the long haul a shot.

I can see her with someone—maybe the man at the church who's been flirting with her, or some other tall, strong creature with kind eyes. I can see her conceiving a baby and being able to keep it, to hold it when it comes out and see if it has her long fingers and her dark eyes.

Dara will have a lifetime filled with chances at happiness. She'll live with the mystery of what each moment might bring her, and she'll grow from all of them. I want this for her. These things I can't have, because all my outcomes have already been determined.

"You aren't freaked out," Dara says. It's not a question.

I stop hunching over the newly scoured tiles and sit up to face her. Whenever I can, I give Dara the truth, much as I try to do with Edison. Deep in the make-believe existence of Jade Johnson, there is just the tiniest, thinnest thread that connects Dara and Edison to the real me—even if they can't know as much. So when I speak, I tell her the truth.

"If I had to come in here last night and find a dead body on the floor, I'm just thankful it wasn't yours."

Dara stares at me for a few seconds, and then tears fill her eyes and her entire face scrunches into a grimace. I advance on her cautiously, not quite touching her.

I want to tell her that she's going to be so much stronger for this. One day she'll look back and see that this was the only way. When she's in the arms of someone who sees her for all she's worth, and when she's living in a new place that smells like all her scented candles, where she doesn't have to blast music or keep the curtains drawn to hide the ugly bits. When her life is so full of beauty that she won't have to live on promises and platitudes. But I know that Dara is not like me, and that these words won't comfort her now. She has to slog through this despair, this guilt. She has to make a saint of the monster whose blood I spent last night scraping from the grout. Only in this way will she emerge.

I inch closer, and when I put an arm around her, she sinks into me. The way that a sister would, full of trust, her guard stripped away. Terrible wailing comes out of her, and I hold her head against my shoulder.

"You'll be okay," I tell her. "Dara, you'll be okay."

She shakes her head furiously. "No," she whispers. "I could have saved him."

"And then what?" I ask. "Let the doctors restore him to full strength so he can repay you?" I pull her away from me so that I can look into her eyes. "He was going to kill you."

"I was—going to—leave him." The words come out as hiccups. "That's what all the money was for."

"You would have gone back to him, or he would have followed you," I say. Maybe this isn't true. I don't know. But it's done now. Tim is dead, and if Dara can't make peace with what she's done, then it won't matter that he's in several pieces scattered throughout the state; she'll never truly escape him.

"I should go to the police," she says. "I—what I did—"

I say nothing, waiting for her to complete the sentence. I can't do it for her. Her face changes as she works it out, as she imagines herself marching into the police station and telling them that she's killed her husband. They'll ask if there was any record of abuse, and she'll have to tell them no, that she's never filed a report or pressed any charges. Yes, she has bruises, but those could be from anything. His family will want her to fry for what she's done. She'll spend the rest of her life behind bars.

She stares at me, and it breaks my heart that she's in so much pain. I sweep the hair out of her face, very gently. I want her to have a long life of soft touches and sweet words. I want her to know kindness and strength. I want her to have all the things that my sisters and I will never have. *Be strong.* I will the words into her. *Take this gift you've given to yourself.*

When her sobs have finally begun to quiet, I whisper, "Never forget the strength it took to do this."

21

MOODY AND I ARE SITTING ON THE BALCONY, WAITING for Edison to show up to take us to the mechanic. The day is overcast, still grumbling from last night's rain. The balconies on these condos are small, but even so, Moody scoots her chair closer to mine than she has to. Strands of her long brown hair brush against my arm. "How are things with the little one?" she asks, her voice so quiet that I can barely hear her. "You never gave me much of an update."

My entire body goes cold. I feel the color drain from my face, because for one horrible second I think she knows about the pregnancy. But then I realize she means Sadie and I recover, too late. Moody is looking at me with a furrow in her brow. "Sis?"

"Sorry." I rub at my temples. "My head is still aching from the crash. What were you saying?"

She searches my eyes, her own going dark. "The step-kid."

"Oh," I say. "Her. Okay, I think."

"So, she likes you," Moody says. "That's good."

"I suppose." My indifferent tone is one I've honed for years. When my sisters asked me about Colin or Elaine, and I knew it would break their hearts if I told them the truth. I still call Colin sometimes when I have a moment to myself, which happens about once every few months. I tell him I'm out seeing the country, visiting famous monuments and national parks. Other times, when I don't trust myself, I say nothing at all; I just call to make sure that he's still alive. I'll hold my breath and listen to him saying "Hello?" over and over, and I'll hang up when he says my name. In this age when nobody answers a phone call from an unknown number, he always picks up. He's always wondering where I am and if I'm okay.

Sadie is different, I tell myself. I don't care about Sadie. I can't. When we sit on the floor in the living room and I teach her how to strum the guitar, and she shows me how to rosin the bow of her violin, she is nothing more than a prop. Something I'll need to vouch for my character when Edison goes missing.

Moody is looking at me, and I pretend not to notice, acting like I'm in too much pain to concentrate on our conversation so that she'll let it go. But Moody isn't exactly known for letting things go. "Maybe you can use music to bond with her," she says. "Teach her how to carry a tune."

"I'm teaching her to play guitar," I say, because if I don't give Moody this much, she'll know I'm holding back. "I'm not here for Sadie," I add. "I wish she'd stop coming around and getting in the way so much." *Believe me*, I'm pleading with her. *Just this once, don't see right through me.*

Edison's car turns into the parking lot, and I stand up, relieved at the diversion.

I imagine that someone else took that missing trucker. Some burly, monstrous figure dragged him up that hiking trail and murdered him. I imagine that this sinister figure takes Edison too.

I would find Edison. I would go to him, loose the ropes that bind him, stop his bleeding with my bare hands, and say, *Who did this to you? Who did this? I'll kill him.* I would save him the way he saved me last night.

But there is no dark shadow stalking the mountains of Rainwood, Arizona. There's no one here who will take him away and harm him.

There's only me. His great love. His destruction.

He gets out of the car when he sees Moody and me descending the stairs. His arms are open to me, and I sink into him. Sweat and desert dust and the cologne of his body wash. I will never forget the smell of him. I know I'll never find it in this world again.

"How are you feeling?" he murmurs against my ear.

I squeeze my arms around him gratefully. "Better."

We're here in this moment, the three of us, even though he doesn't know about our baby. I close my eyes, let the love overtake me, painful in its intensity.

It is with great care that he draws away. He opens the passenger-side door for me, and I climb in. I lick my thumb and wipe away a smudge of my blood that's caked on the console.

"I've changed my mind; I think you should kill him now," Moody tells me from the back seat. I glare at her through the mirror, and there's a playful gleam in her eye. "I'll strangle him with the seat belt while he's driving us. It'll be fun."

She's trying to get a reaction from me, and it's no matter that I don't respond because she can read me well enough. When she laughs, I almost lunge into the back to take out a chunk of her hair, but then Edison climbs into the driver's seat. Moody smiles and says, "Finally, I get to spend some time with the mysterious Edison my sister is always talking about."

Edison is good at small talk. He chats with Moody about the monsoon season, and Moody, in turn, tells him all about Lisa's husband. It turns out he's a lawyer in San Francisco and he's passionate about the pressing social and economic state of the nation.

Moody has a wild imagination. She can make the most mundane of details come alive. Wherever I was in foster care over the years, when she mailed her journals to me in a manila envelope, it was as precious as receiving a copy of a favorite book.

While they talk, I'm thinking about Dara's money in the trunk. I can't get it now, because Moody will see and then she'll want us to take it, claim a mechanic must have stolen it when Dara asks me. But no—the money should go back to Dara. When I have the car back, I'll return it to her. With Tim gone, she won't need to hide it anymore, but she'll have to be careful about making any large deposits.

When we pull into the parking lot for the mechanic, Moody sees the car, its hood scrunched from where I slammed into the mile-marker sign. "Jesus, Sis," she says, forgetting, in her shock, to use my fake name. She recovers quickly and says, "Jade, you're lucky you had a seat belt on."

In the waiting room, Moody and I sit on a bench while Edison finesses the mechanic at the front desk. It's clear that he knows him and he's been here before.

Moody watches him. She studies the profile of his face as he laughs and raps the corner of his credit card against the faux-marble counter. Her green eyes take on that fullness I've only ever seen when she's luring in her own kills. When she's fantasizing.

What is she seeing in her head right now? What story is she concocting about Edison—*my* Edison?

I jab my elbow into her ribs so hard she gasps.

In response, she hooks her arm around mine and rests her head on my shoulder. To anyone who passes by, we're just a set of twins. One of us bruised and bandaged, the other trying to comfort her. But her nails dig into my wrist, sending stabs of pain up my arm. She brings her lips close to my ear and whispers, "Careful that you don't fall too far, sister."

I wrest away from her, and there's bewilderment in her eyes. But Edison turns to face us, and her dark expression morphs into a sweet smile the moment his gaze touches her.

"They can have the parts here tomorrow, and be done in three or four days," he says.

"How much?" I ask.

"It's taken care of," he says.

Moody is still smiling when she says, "That's way too generous. We're going to have to think of some way we can repay you."

Montana loved my sister madly, but it was a selfish love. The deep and reckless kind—all motorcycle engines and frantic lust. If she'd crashed her car, he would have told her to just leave it. He would have hoisted her up onto the hood and made love to her in the plumes of smoke. And Moody would have wanted it that way.

But deep within, I've always suspected that my sister longs for someone who could repair the things that break in her life. She looks at Edison and he ignites some deep need for stability she's afraid to admit to.

My nails are digging into her wrist. *Fuck off,* I'm saying. *He is mine.* My sisters will have me for the rest of their lives, and Edison is only a single bright star in my sky. I love Moody, but if I have to, I'll fight her for that small bit of brightness while it lasts.

I don't say any of this because I don't have to. She can hear it plain as day.

22

IN THE TWO WEEKS FOLLOWING TIM'S ABSENCE, I BAL-
ance my attention between Dara and Edison. My bruises are nearly
gone two weeks after the accident. The body has an amazing way of
stitching itself back together. My stamina springs back, but even so,
the discovery of the trucker's body has soured things. Edison is
nervous.

My sisters are too smart to succumb to paranoia; they don't
run any internet searches for the news, waiting instead for whatever
broadcasts play on television. They're ready to flee at a moment's
notice, and they want a full report of everything Edison and I talk
about.

I'm not entirely truthful. I tell them that nobody at church has
mentioned the trucker's murder since the prayer vigil, when in truth
I've sat through two different sermons about God calling his children
home and us not having the capacity to understand why.

On a night when it's impossible to fall asleep, I'm not sure whether it's the guilt that keeps me awake, or the worry that my sisters may be right. Edison sleeps with his chest against my back, his arm hooked around my bent knee. He smells like summer and the honey I bought for his coffee.

His breath rustles the small hairs at the base of my ponytail. Is every moment I spend with him putting my sisters at risk? Am I betraying them just by being here? My fingers are woven between his, his right arm and mine stretched out over the edge of the mattress. He has the most beautiful veins, bright and sloping like lines in a map. I imagine covering that arm with dirt and there's a twinge in my stomach.

There's a loud *ding* that makes me flinch. Edison grumbles, and his grasp around my knee tightens. On the bedside table, the screen of his phone lights up.

"Jade?" Edison says.

"Go back to sleep," I whisper. I don't move, and eventually his breathing goes even again.

Once I'm sure he's out, I reach for the phone, quickly dimming the brightness of the screen. There's a text from a hidden number. An emoji of a clock.

Moody and Iris reminding me that my little dream can't last forever.

DARA IS BACK TO smoking her cigarettes on the balcony, but most of the day, she takes Tim's car and she drives off. To collect her thoughts, to shop, to park in the middle of the desert wilderness and scream—I don't know.

On Sunday, I take her with me to church.

She sits with Liam, the would-be neurologist, and when I look over my shoulder through the first chorus of "Amazing Grace," she's smiling at a paper crane he's folded out of the weekly prayer sheet. There's a grief in her eyes, and sometimes it weakens only to come back with a force.

Today, she looks effervescent. Her hair is curled and she's wearing mascara that accentuates her long and heavy lashes. But the grief is a black hole within her, and her smiles don't reach her eyes.

Some days are better than others. She's becoming a bit paranoid. She swears that someone broke into her house and pawed through her laundry. She says a hand towel is missing. I wish I could convince her that it's her own mind, her guilt toying with her emotions. After disposing of Iris's first boyfriend, all three of us bolted wide awake whenever we heard an ambulance wailing past the apartment. Yesterday, Dara was positive there was a wiretap on her phone and she mangled it in the garbage disposal.

She wanted to call a plumber, and I explained that it would look bad. People don't mangle their phones in the garbage disposal for no good reason, and even if it takes a year for Tim's family to report him missing, that plumber will be called to testify. It took three hours for me to dismantle the entire disposal unit and shake out the broken bits of glass and metal.

When the service is over, Edison tells me he wants to try a new diner that's opening up. But I check in with Dara before we leave. She's standing alone by the snack table, considering the pastries that have been cut into squares and staked with toothpicks.

"Do you want to come with Edison and me?" I ask her. "Bring Liam. Might be fun."

"No," she says, canting her head and then deciding to fill a paper cup with coffee. "I'm going home. I promised my brother we could FaceTime before he goes to bed." She sucks the cream and coffee off the wooden stirrer, and there's a bit of her usual spark when she looks at me. *Come back to us, Dara,* I think. *Life can be so beautiful for someone like you.*

"You know, I never really pegged you for the hallelujah type," she says.

"Busted. Total heathen," I say. "I'm just here for the stale pastries."

"And the men." She nods to Edison, who's standing in the doorway talking to Jeannie. Sunlight brightens the outline of his golden brown curls, the fine hairs on his arms, making him something holy.

"Especially that," I say.

"Take good care of him," she says, her voice strained with an impending onslaught of tears. "He's a good one. I can tell."

I wrap an arm around her back. Gentle, always gentle. I lead her into the bathroom and I close both of us in the stall. She doesn't find this strange.

"Do I need to worry about you?" I whisper.

She stares at me for a long second before she lowers her gaze to the ground.

I tip her chin with my finger, and she resists looking at me as her eyes fill with tears.

Fuck.

"Look at my eyes," I tell her, and she flinches at the snarl in my voice, but she does as I tell her. "It's over," I say. "Do you understand me?" In this moment, I'm Sissy, not Jade. Not the sweet neighbor who gossips with her on the porch over glasses of strawberry Arbor Mist. I'm the menacing force who dismembered her husband and disposed of his pieces, and I need her to hear me.

Dara's wide dark eyes explore mine, and there's curiosity behind all the tears and mourning. The intensity of it flares brightly across her features, and I think that she can see the truth in me.

She grits her teeth and nods.

"I will help you," I say, and brush her tears away gently with my thumbs. "But you have to let me."

"I already told you, I'm not going to call the—" I put my hand over her mouth before she can say the word. *Police.* Even though we're alone in here, if there's one thing I've learned about these small towns, it's that the walls have ears.

Now she stares at me, breathing hard, both of us crammed together in this small space. She sees—I know she does—that I am not what I seem when I'm out in the world. I'm something much deeper that she's only just scratched the surface of. Rather than being scared of me, she's curious.

I'm the one who cleans the messes, Dara. Because the ones who make them always find me.

When I climb into Edison's car, he leans across the console to kiss me slow. His hand curls under my chin, thumb sweeping across my throat, making my blood go hot.

He's so careful with me since the accident. He offers to drive us everywhere. He brings tea to me in bed and kisses me in places that drive me wild. We're still tentative with *love*, that colossal word. But even though it's rarely said, it's always felt.

I watch the way the sunlight and shadows play with his skin as he drives. He catches me staring and reaches out for my hand.

"I should change the air filters," he says.

"I've always wanted to learn how to do that," I say. A lie. I've never given air filters a thought in my life, but now suddenly I need to learn this ordinary thing. Ten years from now, when I'm picking out air filters, I'll think of him.

"It's not horribly exciting, but I'll show you." A little laugh in his voice. But then his face turns serious and he eases on the gas.

I follow his gaze and see what he does: Sadie pacing across the desert dirt with her fists balled at her sides, her head down. Her light hair gleams like hot chrome in the sun.

Sadie looks up when Edison pulls alongside her, and now that we're close, I can see the tears streaming down her pink cheeks. "Sades, what is it?" Edison's voice is the measured calm of a parent treating a swelling bee sting. "What happened?"

"Nothing," she sobs, and swipes her arm across her nose. It comes away slick with snot and tears.

"Come on, get in," Edison says.

She shakes her head. "I want to be alone."

Alone, Edison can't abide. Not out here, a mile from the nearest building. It would be all too easy for someone to pull over and grab her. Ever since the trucker went missing, the news in this tiny town has been all about the fear factor in their evening ratings. Lock up your children, be wary of hitchhikers, carry pepper spray. All good advice, but it shouldn't take a missing person's case to remind us.

Sadie starts walking again, ignoring Edison as he calls after her. He puts the car in reverse to follow her, but I gently take his wrist. I have consoled my sisters enough times to know what a broken heart looks like. "Let me see what I can do," I tell him. "Wait here."

"Jade." He grabs my hand so I won't get out of the car. "Is this about that boy from her school?"

Even he could see that Sadie's tears are those of someone whose heart has just been broken. He's never mentioned the boy who cozies up to Sadie as they emerge from the school, but he's noticed. In his own quiet, protective way. What else does he notice?

I'll have to be careful about my response. He restrains himself around Sheila's killer. Sheila is dead, and he knows that no act of vengeance would bring her back. But Sadie is alive. He can still protect her, and I know that he would kill someone to do it.

He would come to me in the middle of the night, smeared with desert dirt and blood. I would make sure he got away with it.

"I'm sure it's nothing serious," I tell him, watching his response. He glances at Sadie in the mirror, making sure she's safe as she storms down the dusty road.

"You don't think—you don't think he did something to her."

He can barely get the words out, and it stabs at me to hear the pain in his voice, to see the uncertainty in his eyes. What is wrong with me? Why am I so protective of a man I'll only have to kill?

"I'm sure it's nothing like that," I say, and with those words, I let the image of Edison coming to me smeared with dirt and blood dissolve. We aren't Bonnie and Clyde. We can't be. There's only me, one-third of a murderous trio of sisters, and him, a man who will be buried in the early hours of January first, while New Year's fireworks light the black desert sky.

Sadie looks over her shoulder when she hears my car door slam shut, and the confusion on her face makes her stand still. I'm part of a package deal to her, something that she's grudgingly accepted as an extension of Edison. This is the first time I've ever sought her out alone.

When I stand before her, she lets out another sniffle and stares at me, that bewilderment turning to curiosity.

She's walking in the direction opposite her father's house. There's nothing ahead of her but the town's paltry strip mall with the ice-cream truck parked outside the thrift store, both of which are closed on Sunday. She doesn't have a destination, then. Heartbroken, sweating from the heat, she just wants to disappear in the barren wilderness. Maybe she's hoping whoever took the trucker will take her too, I think. Edison and her own father have been warning her for weeks not to go out alone, even in broad daylight.

She's too young yet to understand how loved she is. Her mother is gone, and the loss magnifies every bitter thing she feels. Grief has a way of shrinking away the good things, putting them in the periphery until they're just the vague outlines of shadows. Her father may be a miserable stick-in-the-mud, but he cherishes her, the one precious thing in his life. Edison lies awake nights worrying about her.

If Sadie's corpse were found on the mountainside pecked clean by hawks, it would break those men in a way that cannot ever be repaired. It would tear the fabric of Rainwood itself in two, and all the melted wax from the candlelight vigils couldn't hope to repair it.

I cannot possibly tell her this. The words would be wasted. She can't fathom it. So I say, "What's his name?"

There's a meanness to her stare, but it isn't directed at me. It's because that boy's name has just been conjured in her mind and she has to hear it again. "Chris," she mumbles. "He's on the lacrosse team."

"Well, then, fuck Chris," I say. "I never liked him."

She snorts out a laugh. She turns to Edison, who's doing a bad job of acting like he isn't watching us through the rearview mirror. "Will you tell him?" she asks.

"Not if you don't want me to," I say.

Her shoulders heave with a sigh. "He's fourteen," she says. "He's going to be a freshman. His parents went to a retreat in Flagstaff, and he wanted me to come over."

I have been a teenage girl and I know where this is going, but I don't let on. I don't tell her that she's only thirteen, which is far, far too young. Whatever she did or didn't do, it's already happened, and there's no point in me scolding her. She doesn't have a woman in her life to listen, and this is an opportunity to reach her that may never come to me again.

When she realizes no reprimand is coming, she goes on. "He said he wanted to be my first. But . . . I don't know. He put his hand up my shirt and I panicked. I locked myself in the bathroom and started crying, and he—" Her voice cracks, a fresh well of tears making her mouth and nose wet. "He said I was a little baby and he never wanted to see me again. He said, 'That's what I get for dating a middle schooler.'"

"Did this just happen?" I ask.

She nods, shuddering as she cries.

"Okay, it's okay," I tell her. When I open my arms, I'm not sure if she'll spurn my efforts, but she crushes herself against me, her arms tight around my back.

Something strange floods me. Sympathy. Worry. A ghost of a life that I could have had. This is how I would console my own daughter, if I could let her come into this world, if I didn't have to leave her behind with her father's ghost.

Her tears soak my church dress. I put my hand against her hair, which has been made hot by the sun. "You're going to dehydrate yourself." I say the words tenderly, the way that a mother would. The way I always wished that someone could do for me when I was as small. "Come on. Let's get you in the air-conditioning. We'll get some lunch before we take you home."

She nods, takes a step back.

"Sound good?" I say.

Her nose is running. "Yeah."

Edison can't read lips, because if he knew what Sadie had just confided in me, we'd be speeding over to that little punk's house to do something that would probably get Edison arrested. He keeps his violent side hidden, but I know it's there. He parks outside late at night and watches the man who killed his wife, his fists clenched, his mind alight with fury. If he knew what that boy tried to do to Sheila's little girl, if someone did to me what I did to that missing trucker, his quiet love would break into a tremendous rage.

The thought electrifies me, and I wish we were alone.

By the time we get to the diner, Sadie has pulled herself together. The AC has dried away her sweat and tears, and she says she could go for a cheeseburger. "Anything you want, kid," Edison says.

His loss will hit her far deeper than a sweaty high school crush ever could. I'm mending her heart only so that I'll break it again. This is what I'm thinking as we file in through the front door, a bell chiming our arrival. We're a little family today. A mom, a dad, and an ethereal blond child who looks too pure and holy to belong to either one of us, as though she were gifted by the divine.

Sadie stands close to me as we wait to be seated. We read the daily specials on the chalkboard above the cash register. I feel a painful want to tell her my little secret, since she shared hers with me. I've looked up where all the clinics are, and there's one an hour away, but when I leave the house I find myself driving past the on-ramp. I talk to the little thing. I tell it what I am and ask it why it chose me, of all things, to use as a portal into this world. Doesn't it know how fucked it would be with me as a mother?

But I can't tell Sadie. I can never tell Sadie. I can't even tell my sisters; if I would swallow my pride and come to them, they would give me the strength I need to follow through. That's why I haven't. I just need a little more time before I'm ready to let go.

Sometime after our food has arrived, Sadie goes to the bathroom. Edison reaches across the table and takes my hand. "She really has a hard time opening up to people," he says. "I don't know what magic you worked out there."

"She's a sweet kid," I say. "Really, really sweet."

I'll take care of her when he's gone. The thought stabs at me, and I think of Iris curled in her bed in the dark after each kill. I think of Moody's anger when she relives her fights with Montana. I will feel the gaping wound like what they felt, because it's my turn. This is the price of loving my sisters, and of being loved by them.

They're all that I have. They're the only ones who will never break my heart. I will remind myself over and over, until the world ends, or until it feels like enough.

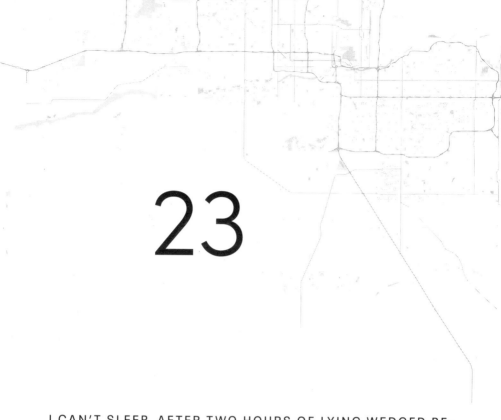

23

I CAN'T SLEEP. AFTER TWO HOURS OF LYING WEDGED BE-
tween Moody and the wall, listening to the rasp of my sisters' breathing, I climb out of bed.

The TV is on in the living room, and without Dara's music coming
through the wall, it feels strange. More invasive somehow, like the
actors on the screen know that we're using their voices to cover up our
secrets.

I make a mug of chamomile tea and cradle it as I curl up on the
ugly recliner. It's two weeks into September. Three and a half months
before I'm in Edison's bed for the last time. I've given a lot of thought
to how it will go, how I can make him say all the things I want to hear,
but it doesn't feel like enough.

There's the creak of footsteps coming down the stairs, and then
Iris emerges in her oversize Lilith Fair T-shirt, which she fished out

of the bargain bin at Goodwill back in Iowa. She saunters to the couch and then flops onto the cushions and stares me down.

Iris can smell a secret the way a jungle cat smells blood.

When I don't relent, she says, "It might help to talk about it."

To what end, Iris? So you can pin me to the ground and call me weak? I take another sip of my tea. I'll have to give her something. She's already suspicious.

Iris was smart not to ask me a direct question. She knows that I'll avoid it in order to maintain control over the direction of the conversation. What she brings in brute strength and ruthlessness, I apply to the art of manipulation.

I know what she wants. She's looking for me to mention Edison so that she can convince me it's time to kill him and leave. Abandon my romantic burial and do what's practical. What's clean. That's what Iris would do. She's cold and she's calculating, and that indifference brings its own sort of poetry to her kills.

Every kill but her first one, that is.

"Why won't you talk about that night with your first kill?" I ask her.

"Where the hell did that come from?" she says. I've rattled her and that makes me smug. She thought she was going to have the upper hand.

"Did you really want to do it?" I ask. "You never talk about him."

I don't have to tell her who I mean. She knows. Her eyes flit to the screen, the gray-blue glow making her eerie and elegant. *Do you regret it? Do you dream of what your life together would have been?* I don't ask, because I know the answer, and if Iris is honest with herself, she knows it too. He was never going to leave his wife. She was just a passing fancy, a pretty young thing he could have on the side. He would have already thrown her away by now, or she would have gotten exasperated and left him. Keyed his car, stuffed a potato in his tailpipe, found someone else she didn't love half as much.

Finally, Iris says, "Your situation is nothing like that."

Situation. Is that what Edison is? Like a parking ticket, or outstanding student loan debt.

"How would you know?" I say.

She shakes her head, makes a bitter sound. We both watch the meaningless faces on the screen.

"You're more like me than you realize, you know," Iris says.

I look at her, but she's smiling into the glow of the television. "You don't want to do it," she says.

There's a sick feeling in my stomach, and I try to melt it away with another sip of tea, but it's been building for weeks now. I have been so careful to hide this very thought from my sisters. I've answered their questions; I've even told them that I plan to do it on New Year's Eve. We've decided that Iris will be the alibi, attending a party two towns over, while Moody will be parked outside, waiting for the signal to help me with the cleanup.

But it hasn't been enough to deceive Iris, who has a way of seeing right through me, even though Moody is the one I confide in.

Iris is older somehow. She says little about her time in foster homes when Moody and I were placed together, and I still don't know all the things she's seen. I wonder often if this is what having a mother would be like—someone who is always a step ahead, someone who tries desperately to stop me from making her mistakes.

"I want to do it," I say.

"I hope you learn to lie better than that when you're in prison because you fucked it up," she says.

"I'm the reason *you're* not in prison." I regret it the instant I say the words, but a dam has been opened and I can't stop myself. "You couldn't take it that he broke your heart. You cry about him all these years later like he was your one shot at happiness, but he wasn't, Iris. He was a piece of shit. You think he was going to marry you? Hell, you think you were even the only one?"

Fire in her eyes, she clenches her jaw.

"Millions of people get their hearts broken every day, but you had to kill him. Violently. And I had to wipe the blood off of the walls, then pick up your broken pieces. So if you don't like the way I'm handling things now that it's my turn, then maybe you shouldn't have dragged all of us down into your own personal hell."

I've said them. The words that have been trapped so deep inside me that I've never heard them myself before now. But they feel familiar, like the chorus of an old lullaby.

Iris isn't rattled. Just as easily as she can read my emotions, she can hide her own. Patient enough to knit a scarf, cool enough to kill a man in under three minutes and never look back. "Watch it, Sissy," she says. "Moody and I are all you have. It's a really dark world out there."

I have never been strong enough for Iris. All my life, she's been holding me at knifepoint, twisting my arm behind my back, pinning me in the dirt when there's no one to hear me scream. Be stronger. Be faster. Be colder. The world will kill you, destroy you, if you aren't.

"I'm not the one putting us in danger," I say. "That text you and Moody sent to his phone was real cute, Iris. Do you even understand how stupid that was?"

"We used a burner." She waves her hand dismissively.

"Don't underestimate the cops just because this is a small town in the middle of nowhere," I snap. "A clock isn't exactly genius levels of cryptic."

Iris gets up. She walks across the room and crouches in front of me until her face is all I can see, identical to mine and yet entirely her own. "It was just a reminder," she says. "He isn't worth the risk. He isn't worth ruining everything for."

"I know that."

My eldest sister is taciturn until suddenly she isn't, and all the anger and sharpness she carries come out in bursts. I try not to be mad at her. Something is hurting Iris, though I can't figure out exactly what. I'd never have expected her to be jealous of the time I'm spending with Edison. She didn't envy Moody when she pursued her own lovers, even as recently as Montana. Delighted in it, in fact. Asked Moody about how she would do it, where they would be. She drove me to the burial site, belting out the words to "Livin' la Vida Loca" along with the radio while his pieces were stacked in three coolers in the trunk.

There's no reason that Edison should be any different. If anything, she should be relieved that I've finally settled on a mark and she doesn't have to pick up my slack like the last time.

She takes the mug from my hands, sets it on the end table so that there's nothing between us, not even a little piece of ceramic. She sees all the moments with Edison that I've hoarded for myself. His hands on my hips; the taste of him in my mouth; the things we whisper when we can't sleep; his hand on my shoulder as he walks past while I sit on the floor and teach Sadie to play the guitar.

"Moody goes up and down like a light switch," she says. "But I could always count on you to see ten moves ahead, Sis. I know you can see how dangerous this is."

My heart is beating faster, but I don't let her see. I meet her gaze, unflinching. Just this once, Iris is wrong. With Edison, I *can't* see ten moves ahead. I have no idea what he's done to me or why I can't let go of him. As much as Iris's bluntness has wounded me, I know that she's right. My sisters are all that I have, and they've sacrificed everything for me. They've killed their lovers so that we can always remain together, three identical ropes in a braid. If they found themselves in my predicament, they would do what needed to be done.

When we were children, Iris used to tell me that she could read my thoughts even when we were miles apart. I tested it by thinking about bubble gum, a new bike, how badly I wanted a pit bull that was loyal only to me. I could never be certain, but in this moment, I am.

She sees past every silly wish I've ever made, right through the heart of me, to the thing I want and that I would never dare to say.

AFTER A WEEK OF delaying the inevitable, I find myself staring up at the ceiling. It's early, and my sisters are still asleep. Although we aged out of the system nearly a decade ago, there's some part of Moody that's never forgotten how scared she is of being alone; she sleeps with an arm coiled around mine, her forehead pressed against my shoulder, the condensation from her warm, shallow breaths dampening my skin.

Maybe I don't have to tell them about the baby. That's what I'm thinking as the sky begins to lighten outside. I can make the drive to Planned Parenthood and be back before lunch, tell them I stopped by Edison's place and reeled him into bed so he'd have a reason to think of me at work all day.

I look at the crown of Moody's rumpled hair. Beside her, Iris sleeps with her back to us, so still and silent it's almost like she's dead. If childhood in foster care taught me to be observant and Moody to be assertive, it taught Iris to be invisible. You don't know she's nearby unless she wants you to, and you don't know she's dangerous until she's already cutting off your air.

My hand slips under the hem of my shirt and presses against my stomach. All I feel is the slope of my belly button. My baby is stealthy and clever; I haven't felt my body change, not even nausea, but I know it's in there. If I let the time pass, it will grow fingers and eyelashes and a beating heart. Wait a little longer, and it will grow desires and dreams. Maybe these things have already been decided. Maybe it is already going to be good at math, or hate the metallic tang of citrus fruits the way that I do. Maybe those vocal cords will form and already be able to carry a tune.

But with a serial killer for a mother, what kind of life would it have? Nothing good.

It has to be this way.

Moody shifts in her sleep, and I kiss the top of her head. There's no room for me to build a new family; the three of us have fought so hard for the family we already have.

I slip out of bed, silent like Iris. I don't bother changing out of the tank top and cotton shorts I fell asleep in as I pace for the car; if I linger, I won't go through with it.

"This isn't your baby, Sissy," I tell the reflection of my tired eyes in the rearview mirror as I start the ignition. "It's Jade's, and Jade isn't real."

The radio is off, and all I hear is the thrum of the concrete beneath the tires and my own ragged breathing. It gets louder as I approach the on-ramp for the highway, until my chest is so tight I can't breathe and my vision starts to tunnel.

At the last second, I swerve off the on-ramp and back onto the road. I curse at myself, and anger and frustration fill me, but I can breathe again. I can see how clear the line where the desert meets the sky is.

It's only after I turn onto Edison's street that I realize I've been heading here. Early riser that he is, he'll be awake by now. We would be a family of early risers. The baby would get me up at dawn, and I'd sit nursing it at the kitchen table, my boob hanging out of my shirt while Edison poured the coffee. I'd hum, and the baby would gurgle and sigh as it swallowed my milk, and Edison would watch us with love in his eyes.

Stop it.

The driveway is empty when I pull up to his house, but the front door is open. Sadie peers out through the screen door. Her face changes when she sees me. Is that a smile?

"Hi," she chirps as I step out into the waxing morning heat. "Looking for Edison? He had to run an errand. He'll be back in an hour."

Most stores won't be open until eight thirty. He must have found an AA meeting, but he hasn't told Sadie about his one-night relapse. He doesn't want to worry her.

I almost don't recognize this Sadie; she's upbeat, a far cry from the shy and withdrawn girl she was just a few days ago. "The power's been out at my house since last night, so my dad said I could come here to use the Wi-Fi. I have an assignment due tomorrow," she says. "Are you staying until he gets back?"

No, I'm not staying. I need to get back into my car. Crank the AC, slam down on the gas pedal. I should be halfway to Planned Parenthood by now.

"Yeah," I say. "I'll stay."

"Good." She's already turning back into the house. "I have a surprise for you."

I'm already surprised enough by her enthusiasm. Is this how quickly trust is formed? Weeks ago, she was cautious, even contemptuous, and now she greets me like we're friends. I had anticipated Sadie to be a long-term project. I didn't need her to like me—only to trust me. That way, when Edison is dead, she'll be my ally.

I'm hit by the cool air inside Edison's house. The smell of him everywhere.

Sadie has taken over the coffee table. Her iPad, phone, and books are scattered there. Her violin case is resting against the couch. The portrait of an overachieving only child. She stoops to retrieve her violin, and I've never seen her eyes so bright.

She wields the bow and doesn't make a production of using the rosin or testing the strings. She dives immediately into a song, like the song has been waiting for her; like it's an old friend.

I recognize the opening chords to Metallica's "Nothing Else Matters" immediately. It's Moody's favorite. She loves how long and slow it is, how James Hetfield rasps some words and cries out others in what Moody calls a fit of desperation. I have heard this song a hundred times throbbing softly from Moody's headphones as she rested her head against my shoulder on long bus rides, or slept wedged beside me in our group homes. When I hear it, all I think about is her. How glazed her eyes get when it comes on on a store radio and takes her by surprise. How I can see the thoughts filling up her mind, and how I've always wondered what she sees or why it means so much to her.

Now Sadie only hums in tune to the words. There's a studious look on her face as she tries to remember all the beats. She's told me that her father made her take up an instrument as an extracurricular and that's the only reason she plays, but she has an ear for music.

As she plays on, I wonder why Sadie chose this song. Maybe she wanted to impress me with a classic, as a way for us to bond and to show me that she's letting me in. The thought is so endearing that I decide not to tell her she's missed the mark. I wasn't even born when this was released. Not that I would expect her to know something like that. Even though I was born at the tail end of the 1990s, to her it's all last century. Jade is older and more worldly. Less like a friend to her and more like a mother figure.

She only plays for about a minute, and then she stops with an embarrassed grin. "That's as far as I got," she says. "But when you told me it was your favorite, I went online to see if I could learn."

My body goes cold. Sadie is still talking, but I can't hear the words over the rushing of blood in my ears. "When?" I manage to blurt out, my voice hoarse.

I've interrupted whatever Sadie was saying, and she looks confused.

"When did I tell you that was my favorite song?" I press. *Be calm,* I tell myself. I have to be Jade right now, not Sissy, and Jade would have nothing to be alarmed about. Because Jade doesn't have serial killers for sisters.

"Last night." There's an apprehensive squeak in Sadie's voice. "When we went to that ice-cream truck."

Last night, Moody and Iris demanded that I stay at home and rest. They told me I looked pale and that they were worried I was pushing myself too hard after the car crash. I'd felt perfectly fine, but I'd wondered if the pregnancy was starting to make itself known, and I didn't want to arouse suspicion.

But Moody had gone out, returning hours later with a bag of groceries, singing to herself as she put them away. Singing her favorite song, the one Sadie has just performed.

It's not just anger that fills me now, but helplessness. Moody didn't hurt Sadie. Instead, she proved her point.

I walk over to the open door and push it closed. Sadie winces at the sound. "You shouldn't leave this door open, you know," I tell her. "You're just as bad as Edison. Anyone can just march right in here."

"Okay." Sadie's voice is small. She's retreating back into her shyness. If ever there was a time for me to act like Jade, this is it. I should tell her I'm sorry for acting so hysterical and tell her that the song was beautiful. I should make small talk about music and school and ask her how things are going with that boy who broke her heart. I should. But when I turn around to face her again, when I grasp her shoulders, Sadie is looking into the eyes of the real me.

"There are dangerous people out there," I tell her. "A man was murdered, and they still haven't found who did it. Do you hear me?"

Sadie nods, the violin still clasped in one hand, the bow in the other.

"I want you to be more careful," I say. "A lot more careful." I reach into my pocket and draw out the box cutter from the collection that my sisters and I use for protection. "Carry this," I say.

Sadie's eyes widen. The murder doesn't worry her at all. It's just something that happened to a stranger on the news. "I can't bring something like that to school," she says, making no move to take it. "I'll get suspended."

Gently, I take the bow from her hand and replace it with the retracted blade. I close her fingers around it. "Not if they don't know you're carrying it," I say.

I meet her eyes, and I hope she understands. I'll never be able to protect my own child, but I can do this much for Sadie. I can help to keep her safe.

24

I DON'T CONFRONT MOODY ABOUT WHAT SHE'S DONE, and I don't ask Iris how much she knew about it. There would be no point; the message was loud and clear. Moody might not know what my secrets are, but she knows that I'm keeping them. Jade isn't real, and no matter how hard I pretend, I'll never become her. I'll never be able to run away with Edison and our baby and have our little life together.

Either I get rid of this baby now, or I wait until I start to show and my sisters will make me do it. They won't let me hand it off to a nice family or leave it in a stroller the way that we were left, because this baby has Edison's DNA and mine, and even if it takes decades, this will come back to haunt us. I am harvesting living, breathing evidence of our crimes.

The only real friend I have in this town is Dara. I'm going to tell her about the pregnancy. I'll tell her that Edison isn't the one I intend to spend the rest of my life with—a half-truth—and she won't judge me. She'll drive with me to the clinic and tell me that I'm making the right decision. After, she'll drive us anywhere I want. To see a movie or to wander around until we find a food truck that looks promising.

It will make her feel better to help me with my own problem, rather than wallow in her grief. I want to believe she's getting better now that Tim is gone. She's young, smart, beautiful, and she should get out of this town. By the time we part ways, I want her to be ready to stand on her own. But there are moments when she retreats into herself. She disappears for long hours of the night, and I lie awake, waiting for the headlights of her car to steal in through the blinds when she returns. She stares off into the distance. She flinches and won't meet anyone's eyes.

This will pass, I tell myself. Dara isn't like me, and I can almost envy her for that. She can look at someone as awful as Tim and still see the possibility for redemption. Something worth saving. It was only for one short, frenzied moment that she saw the monster within him. After years of enduring his rage, she understood that only one of them would survive that night. She made the right choice. But it scares her.

It's time to take a new approach. If I can't convince Dara that killing Tim was her only option, I'll distract her. She can't go back now and save him, and it will help her to channel that compassion into something else.

If I start to cry, she'll know what to do. And I may cry, I realize. But for now, I swallow all of it down. *One moment at a time, Sissy.* I count every slat in the porch that connects my front door to Dara's. I take a deep breath and then I knock. There's no answer. Her car is still in its parking space and the curtains are drawn. I wait a few seconds and then knock again. When I try the doorknob, it's locked.

"Dara?"

The dread is immediate, and all I can think is that she's thrown her future away so quickly. I admire Dara's heart, but it's a danger to her. The human conscience is a liar. It grants compassion to those who don't deserve it, and no matter how much Tim has hurt her, some piece of Dara still wants to believe she should have shown him mercy. Mercy he wouldn't have shown her. I run down the stairs and around the back of her unit to the sliding glass door of her laundry room. It opens when I tug on the handle, and I barely have the cognizance to close it behind me.

I picture her pacing back and forth in the bedroom, staring at the neatly made bed. The blue cotton comforter with little yellow flowers on it and the matching pillow shams. The catalog-perfect life she tried to build with a man who overpromised. I picture her holding the phone, waiting for her hands to stop shaking so that she can dial the number that will connect her to the police department. She just needs a few minutes to stand here among all her pretty things and say goodbye to the life she'll never have.

"Dara!"

I reach the living room, and something about the silence stops me. A three-wick candle burns low in its jar, nearing the end of its life, the glass blackened by the flame. The kitchen is clean, one cigarette butt rumpled in the ashtray on the coffee table. A blanket is neatly folded on the couch; she's told me that she hasn't been able to sleep in their bed since it happened. After we disposed of his body, she fluffed the pillows and made sure the comforter was even, and she only walks by to get to the bathroom.

I have heard this particular silence before, and I understand that something has changed.

"Dara?" My voice is soft now. The bottom step creaks as I ascend the stairs. With each passing breath, I'm sure. This is the silence of Iris's dead lover. Of Moody's first kill. The blood on the tiles and the wood grain.

My legs are moving too slowly. My ears pulse with the rush of air and blood and dread. When I reach the landing, the bedroom door is open, and I can see the flicker of candlelight on the bathroom wall.

"Dara?"

Her silence is its own answer. I know, somehow, that she's here. That if I'd come earlier, if I hadn't slept for so long, today would be very different. Dara and I would be in her car, speeding down the interstate as I tried to steel myself for what I was about to do. She would be singing along to the radio, and I would see glimpses of the real Dara in her spirit. The girl I know is still in there, under all the guilt and sorrow. The girl who still has a thousand tomorrows left to squander.

I see her even before I've stepped onto the tiles. I hear something—a breath—hers? Mine?

She's slumped against the rim of the tub, chin-deep in the water. Her eyes are half-open, dark, and as empty as they are full. I bridge the space between us before I realize I've moved, and her body is so heavy, so uncooperative, as I pull at her. She slides over the edge of the tub and onto the floor with a heavy sound like an overripe fruit falling off the vine.

She's wearing a green version of the pajama set she wore the night she killed Tim. A tank top that's plastered to her stomach, shorts that are bunched against the seam where her thighs meet her torso.

There's no blood. That's my first thought. No bruises. I lay her flat on her back and I take her face in my hands. Cold, but not stiff. She's still in there. I can bring her back to me.

The world is shaking. Someone is crying, murmuring uselessly, even though it's just us in here. I bring my mouth to hers and I force air down her throat, over and again, until finally I taste the metallic tang of vomit. It's all over her chest, floating misty in the water.

You didn't. You wouldn't.

The empty bottle has rolled under the sink, and I catch the translucent orange gleaming in the candlelight, winking at me. The cap is gone, not a single fentanyl pill left.

I scream. It comes out as I press my palms into her chest, trying to coax her heart into beating even though I know it's been too long. She's too cold, too still. It's not my loss that makes me so desperate to save her, but all of hers. Liam, gentle and warm, who might love her. Cigarette smoke wafting up into the night. Sunlight in her hair as she speeds across the Arizona state border to start over somewhere new. Meeting her little brother at the airport, his hug nearly bowling her over. *Don't leave us, Dara. Don't you dare go out like this. I won't let you.*

Her body jolts under my efforts the way that a rag doll would, and I don't know how long I try before I stop. I can hear the finality of it. Not a single breath, or a sob, but just the small sound of water leaking around the drain plug.

THE AMBULANCE ARRIVES WITHOUT a siren, all its lights flashing. I stand in the parking lot, watching them carry the gurney down the stairs. They didn't even try to save her. They knew, just like I knew. The only difference is that I was stupid enough to hope.

Moody wraps her arms around me, her skin sticky in the late-morning heat. Neighbors peek out from their blinds or stand on their porches and pretend they're outside to read or to talk on the phone or to catch some of the sunlight.

"Oh, love," Moody whispers. "She wasn't strong enough to live with it. She wasn't like us."

Don't you think I know that, Moody? I wrest myself out of her grasp, and I can feel that I've hurt her, but I don't care. The paramedics are taking their time loading the gurney into the ambulance, and they talk in low voices about something to do with how ungodly hot it is. The doors slam shut. There's one blip, the start of a siren, and then the rumble of the engine as they drive off.

I look up the stairs. They've left her door wide open, all the cool air escaping.

I have to close it, I think. I have to lock it so that nobody comes in and disturbs her things. But my legs won't move. She wasn't like us. That was why I loved her.

There was a note, typed up and printed, in the sink, its edges warped with water. She confessed to what she had done to Tim and what he'd done to her. She said that she still loved him. She said that she was sorry to her mother and to her brother and to Tim's family.

It will be her word against his; their families will argue. Dara had been so good at hiding the bruises at her throat, the broken fingers, the sprained wrist. I think I was the only one who ever saw.

"Sis—"

I'm already climbing the stairs with such force that the boards shudder under my weight. Iris is coming into the living room when I step inside, and I come at her so fast that she doesn't have time to brace. She falls back and her head bounces against the staircase.

"You!" I cry. She grabs for me, but I snare her wrists, pinning them, forcing my knee into her stomach. It's a move she's made on me a dozen times. I have never hated her—never hated anything—this much.

I'm distantly aware of the door closing behind me and Moody coming after me. She peels me away from Iris, and I jab my elbow into her ribs. She doubles but doesn't let go. "You killed her," I shout at Iris, who is wiping the blood from her mouth.

"Sissy." Moody's voice is placating, and in this moment, I hate her too. I hate both of them and this life they've created for all of us. I hate that I'm so much like them, and nothing at all like Dara, who I thought was stronger. Who I thought I could save.

Moody is still holding my arms when I slump forward. She comes with me as I fall into a pile on the ground, screaming, my weakness laid bare. I tried for so long to hide my friendship with Dara from my sisters. I tried to hide what she really meant to me, beneath the act, just as I do with Colin.

Iris comes toward me, and I expect her to hit me, but she only puts her arms around me. She and Moody hold me until I stop hitting at them. They shush me, kiss my cheeks, wipe at my tears with their bare hands.

I sob. "Which one of you was it?"

"Sissy." Moody holds my chin so that I'll look into her eyes. "Sweetheart, Dara killed herself."

"That's a lie," I spit out.

"It's the truth." Moody knows that she's the only one who can reach me. For all our fighting, she has never lied to me. She's trusted me with pages and pages of journal entries when we were children. Every dark fantasy, every vulnerable thought. Every kiss. Her first time with her high school boyfriend, the one who broke her heart. She told me about the rags she stuffed into his tailpipe to try and kill him. She fell into my arms and cried for him.

I have seen Moody at her ugliest, and I know what she's capable of. But I also know how much she loves me. Enough to tell the truth.

She sees the change in my expression, and she frowns sympathetically. "You tried to save her, Sis, but she didn't want it."

"No." I understand that I'm being unreasonable. *This is grief*, I think. *This is what will happen to me when Edison is dead.* It terrifies me that I could be so unlike my sisters in this moment. So weak.

Iris runs her fingers through my hair, pushing so much love into the gesture that it breaks me anew. "She wasn't strong enough."

But she was. I was sure that she was. How could I have been so wrong?

I never even told her my real name.

I see myself with Dara as she speeds over the state line, both of us singing, an open bag of gummy bears in the cup holder and melting in the sun. Somewhere unreachable, that car is still going, disappearing into a horizon I will never reach. I can't follow her. Dara has made her choice, and she's left me here alone to deal with mine.

25

TWO DAYS PASS BEFORE I DECIDE TO SEE EDISON. IT'S AN act of restraint not to answer his texts asking how I'm doing. He knows Dara was a friend, and the fact that he doesn't ask questions about what happened only deepens my love for him. But I say nothing, not even to tell him I don't want to talk about it.

When I finally pull my shit together and pick up my phone to call Edison, Moody puts her hand over mine, stilling me. It's late morning, and Iris is in the shower belting out a Drowning Pool song as she lathers her hair. *Let the bodies hit the floor / Let the bodies hit the floor.*

"I want to make sure you're okay," Moody says.

I know she doesn't mean Dara. There's been an unspoken agreement that Dara is behind me. She was only ever supposed to be a tool in my plan, and if I formed an attachment to her, that's my own fault. She should have been nothing to me. Barely a friend, and certainly not a sister. It is only in some very distant, dark, small place within me that Jade is grieving for her. And Jade isn't real. She's not even a ghost.

"I'm fine," I say.

Moody nods to the phone in my hand. "Are you sure you're ready to talk to him?"

"It's been two days. Any longer and it will start to look suspicious," I say. "He might come over to check on me." Beneath the sweet, caring Edison who always texts to be sure I got home safely, there's an undercurrent. A fierce, protective man who would break down the door to save me if he thought I was in danger.

If it were me in the bathtub, if I'd tried to take my own life the way that Dara did, he would have ripped me from the water, shoved his finger down my throat to make me gag the pills back up. Grabbed me by my shoulders and shaken me and demanded to know what I was thinking. Don't I know how stupid that was? Don't I realize he would die if he lost me?

Dara deserved to be loved like that. She deserved to have someone who could have saved her.

Moody sweeps the hair from my forehead, and she smiles. The sunlight steals across her face, making her angelic. But I know her. I'm not some man she's seducing; she can't hide who she is from me. "You know I trust you with all of our lives, yeah?" she says. "I didn't want to ask you this in front of Iris. You know how she gets." Her sober tone forces me to meet her eyes, dread churning in my stomach. "Are you sure you're keeping Edison alive because it's what's best for us, and not because you want more time to play with him?"

I hate it when my sisters say his name. As though he's a part of their world, as though they're in on his love for me.

The selfishness of this thought startles me, but I don't look away. I keep my gaze steady. Pulse even. Breaths calm.

"The plan is the best way to avoid suspicion," I tell her.

Edison's corded arms around me. My skin rising with bumps when he kisses the back of my neck in his sleep. The churning of his blood and the beating of his heart when I press my ear to his chest.

"I don't care about him," I say. "I'm doing it for us."

The grace fades from Moody's expression, and all I can see are her wild green eyes. Unreadable. Cold. Deadly. A perfect mirror of my own.

She tries to read my mind, and I lock her out. I don't want her to see what Edison means to me. I don't want her to see that I'm lying.

26

EDISON UNDERSTANDS MY ABSENCE COMPLETELY. WHEN I call him, he doesn't try to coax my feelings out or offer platitudes. "What can I do for you?" he asks. I tell him that I just want to forget for a few minutes. Not Dara, but everything. He knows a place, he says.

Loss, Edison understands. The soul-deep pain that stuns you to your core and makes the whole world feel like poison. He will always mourn Sheila, not because he lost a wife, but because he's lost a lifetime of tomorrows that will never come to pass.

When he picks me up, he doesn't ask if I want to talk about it. He doesn't say that we need to go to church on Sunday to remind ourselves that God has a plan for all of us. He doesn't say this because he isn't like them—the purest of our congregation, the steadfast believers. Edison dresses in a suit on Sundays and he sings the hymns, and he fixes the sound equipment when the microphone isn't working or the squealing interference splits everyone's eardrums.

But beneath all that, he's beautifully flawed. He knows the power of his vices. He's been to the bottom of his bottles. He understands that goodness is more of an image and less of a human characteristic.

We don't talk about Dara or Tim or the body that was found. But Edison weaves his fingers through mine as he drives, and I feel the worry in his muscles. Rainwood was peaceful only a few weeks ago, and some dark cloud has shadowed the blue desert sky. He's scared that it will take me, and he has no idea that I'm the one who's brought it.

I'm unsettled by how guilty this makes me feel. I'm ashamed at myself for keeping so many secrets from my sisters—my fantasies about having a life with Edison and my anger that Moody killed a man who should be at home with his family, because his only crime was helping me with a tire that wasn't flat. But none of this compares to the hatred I feel for myself because I couldn't save Dara. I scoured the blood and I told her what to do. But I should have held her when she broke down and cried. I should have been more patient.

Stop it, Sissy. Dara made her choice. She's gone, and I have my sisters to protect. Family always comes first. If I get soft and make a mistake, they're the ones who will suffer.

Edison and I are halfway up the hiking trail when the rain clouds start to form.

"It's supposed to be clear today," Edison grouses, waving his phone with the weather app pulled up.

"We can wait it out." I take his hand, reeling him toward an alcove in the mountainside. It's just wide enough to shield us before the sky erupts and a deluge pours down. The ground turns to mud that splashes up on my new hiking sneakers. I don't know why, but it makes me laugh.

Edison sticks his arm out so the water will pool in his palm, and I watch the way the water drips down him in frantic rivers. I want to touch him the way the rain does, disappearing in his sleeves, finding every crease in his hands.

I grasp his shirt, pull him to me. He spins me so that my back is against the mountainside, grabs me under one knee so that my leg is hooked around his waist. His mouth is open, breaths shallow. When we draw back from our kiss, I see a sleepy haze in his eyes that I've come to know as intimately as the flutters in my own chest.

I grin and hang my arms over his shoulders; he presses his forehead to mine. His hand, slick with rain, traces the side of my face, the hollow of my throat. All it takes is the barest touch for him to transform me into this desperate thing. I want him right here, in the rain, in the vastness of this desert I've come to love almost as much as I love him. The sunset is shining through the downpour, making the world a strange color like we're trapped in the flash of a camera, illuminating all these things I want to take with me but know I can't.

There's beauty in our numbered days. This can't last, so I'll give him all that's in me.

His hand reaches under my shirt, fingers spread across my belly. He starts to move it toward my breasts the way he always does, but I hold it there. "Leave it," I say. "I like the way it feels there." In answer, he presses into my skin, and it sends wild roiling waves through me.

He nudges my forehead with his. "Hey." He wants to know if I'm really here with him, rather than lost in my thoughts about Dara. Thoughts about my heart that shouldn't be broken, because when I came here, I knew that I was leaving with exactly what I had when I arrived: two sisters, a pile of fake IDs, and no evidence of the mess I made while I was here.

We're so close I can taste his skin on the air between us. I grab his wrist and bring his hand to my throat. Something charges in him when he presses forward to kiss me.

"I just want you," I whisper, and kiss behind his ear, making him groan. *Make me forget. Please make me forget.*

I gasp when I feel him push into me. My back is pressed against the rock; my leg hooks around his hip. His fingers clench against my throat with so much force I can scarcely breathe, but then he looks at me and his eyes are soft.

"Is this okay?" he asks. I nod, coil my arms around his shoulders to bring him closer to me.

Beyond our little alcove, the rain floods the world. All I can hear is the rasp of his breathing and the water washing everything away.

"Jade," he says. I've come to like my fake name, now that he's brought so much life to it. I slide my hands under his shirt and I feel his breath hitch when my fingers dig into his skin. He's rough and careful all at once, a hand pushing into my stomach, as though he knows what I'm hiding there just under his palm, as though he's protecting us because we belong to him.

"Come with me." It's a command, his voice a growl. I feel the wickedness of the smile he coaxes out of me, and then my head lolls back. He can read my body by now, and he covers my mouth when I scream, catching the sound the way that I caught his that first time.

I feel him shudder against me, over and again. He buries his head in the curve of my throat, gasping.

"You drive me insane," he murmurs. All wildness and force moments earlier, and now helpless in my arms. I was his then, and he's mine now. All mine. I kiss him and I inhale the smell of the rain, heady with a strange perfume that only the desert can make. It's the madness of this moment that makes me brave—him inside me, the air around me. We are two figures lost in time, and very soon the rain will end, and our time together to follow.

"Edison?"

"Mm?" He raises his head now, and his thumb sweeps across my cheek. I shudder.

I search him. In this moment, I need to know if there's some part of him—however small—who could love the real me. Not Jade.

I press our foreheads together and his eyes close when I kiss him. My mouth lingers beside his and I breathe him. This man who, to the world, is just another churchgoer. A stranger in a diner. A car passing by on a stretch of open road.

But he's shown me what's inside, the darkness that frightens him even as he holds it like the precious thing that it is. He thinks of the driver who killed his wife and the quiet rage that never stops turning in his heart. If I'm meant to murder him for love, he would murder for vengeance.

Soon he'll be gone, and I have to know if we're more alike than he may realize. If his darkness is a mirror match for mine. If he thinks of me at all the way I think of him.

"If you had to kill me, how would you do it?" I ask the question in a whisper with my eyes still closed from our last kiss.

He stills. His hand stops toying with a piece of hair that's fallen over my shoulder. The whole world goes silent, and I can't hear our breathing or even the rain anymore.

I wake from my lust, too late to have stopped myself from asking such a stupid thing. I've just ruined everything. *He loves Jade, not you. Never you.* And now I've lost even that. When he looks at me, he sees the darkness that's been churning behind my eyes as long as he's known me. Longer than that. He sees the ugliness that Dara saw the night I cleaned her mess with that practical efficiency. He sees the monster that only my sisters could love.

I open my mouth to—what? Apologize? It's too late for that.

He eases back, and my body feels cold where he's left me. I close my eyes to the sound of him zipping his jeans, buckling his belt. I've done it. I've lost him. He's going to step out into the rain and leave me here.

I flinch when his fingers weave through mine, and for an unguarded second I meet him with surprise. His expression is unreadable, and he raises our picnic blanket over my head like a shawl. It was supposed to be a clear, mellow night. We were going to lie out under the stars. Spending the night out here was my idea. I wanted a peaceful memory of us all alone. I wanted to forget the feel of Dara's body in my hands. The sight of her arm falling slack over the edge of the gurney before they wrapped her in the sheet.

"Come on," he says. "I want to show you something."

Confused, I follow him down the hiking trail. We move at a brisk pace, and he doesn't seem to mind that he's getting drenched. He stops at a ledge that overlooks the desert wilderness. Brush and boulders stretch out into the horizon. In the gloom it's especially beautiful, like we're standing in the heart of the storm itself. We're part of the intrinsic beating pulse of the universe itself.

Edison lifts the blanket so that it's wrapped around both of us. I feel the warmth of his skin as he moves his face close to mine. "See that lake out there?" he says. In the storm, it's black as ink, faintly gray around the edges as though it's alight.

"Yes," I say.

"Here's how I'll kill you." The timbre of his voice shudders through me. "I'll bring you someplace like that, where there's no one around. I'll hold you under until I feel you go still."

The rain patters against the dirt. It falls in the hollow spaces between the branches, and it splashes in the puddles that it makes in the hollows of the rocks.

When I look at him, there's a playful gleam in his brown eyes. The light in them winks when he looks at me. "Then I'd reel you out," he says. "Breathe air into your lungs. Bring you back to me. I don't want you to die—only to know that I'm the one in control."

I picture it. The power struggle. I wouldn't make it easy for him. I'd claw at him and bite. I'd pinch the soft flesh behind his knees so that he would let me go, and then I'd climb onto his shoulders and pin him down.

For the second time today, an irrepressible smile rises on my lips. He's had this thought before. Saving me the way that he did that night I ran my car off the road. I felt it in his arms then, a need to protect me, to be the reason that I'm breathing. This lake wasn't visible from where we stood when I asked my question. He saw it and already had the thought. How many times has he rescued me in that imagination of his? How many times has he brought me to the edge only to reel me back?

I take his face in my hands and rise on tiptoe to kiss him, and I say, "You really think you're the one in control?"

I am not Jade in this moment. I'm me. Really me, all my darkness and ugliness laid bare, and he loves me.

"No," he confesses. His fingers dig into my hips, coaxing a gasp out of me. "You have me. I'd burn this whole world down if you asked me to."

Oh fuck. The things he can do to my heart. I grab his collar and pull him into a kiss. "I don't want the whole world to burn," I murmur against his lips. "Only us."

His phone rings. The loud chime pierces through the sound of the rain, but we ignore it, and eventually it stops. It starts again only a second later, and Edison's brows draw with the early makings of concern. It's a Saturday and his entire job site is closed. Nobody would be calling him to pick up a shift. His father has only called once in the time I've known him, and he would have just left a voicemail.

Edison fumbles in his pocket, and I don't get a chance to see the name on the screen before he answers. "Hello? No—I—all right, calm down."

I adjust the blanket to protect his phone from getting wet. Edison presses his finger into his ear to block out the sound of the rain.

"I can be home in twenty minutes. Sadie knows where I keep the spare key. I'm sure—yes—" He pauses, and I catch a note of the worried voice in the speaker. "I'm sure that she's fine."

When he hangs up, I already know that our little moment together is ended. "Sadie got into a fight with her dad this morning and stormed off."

"Are you sure she'd go to your house?"

"She's done it before," he says. He looks pensive, but not alarmed. "Come on." He takes my hand and we sprint down the hiking trail, getting drenched in the process.

Lightning bolt has proven to be an apt nickname for Edison's stepdaughter. She'll disappear for long stretches of time, but when she returns it's with brightness and theatrics. The quintessential thirteen-year-old.

We drive in silence as the sunset melts, and the approaching evening is made darker by the clouds.

"This isn't healthy for her," Edison says, breaking me out of my thoughts. "All this going back and forth between her dad and me."

I rub gentle circles on his biceps to let him know I'm here and that I'm listening. But I don't ask questions or interrupt him, because I want to hear his unbridled thoughts. The closer we get to New Year's Eve, the more studiously I collect every precious moment with him.

"Maybe I should be better about discouraging her from coming around," Edison goes on. "She's going to be in high school next year. It's time she makes some friends and puts herself out there. Stops being so shy." Even as he says the words, I know he doesn't believe them. He's willing to relinquish Sadie to her father even as it breaks his heart, because he thinks it's healthier for her.

Sadie is thirteen to Edison's twenty-nine years. His late wife came to him with a ready-made family. And as Sadie gets closer to high school her dilemmas and heartaches will only magnify. But still, when he could just as easily foist her off onto her own father, Edison tries to fill the empty space left by her mother's death. He picks up when she calls; he worries about where she is and if she's safe whenever he watches the evening news.

He goes quiet as we turn onto his street.

"You'd make a great dad," I say. He smiles at the road ahead, but he doesn't correct me and say that he already has a daughter in Sadie. For all his love, he knows that she doesn't belong to him. He knows that she will eventually have to stop coming to him at times like these.

There aren't any lights on inside the house when we pull into the driveway. Edison is the first to the door, and I'm a step behind him. When he tries to turn the knob and realizes it's locked, for the first time since the hiking trail, I see the worry starting to ebb into his features.

"Here." I unlock the door and push it open.

Even before we've crossed the welcome mat, I know the house is empty. It's too quiet, and Sadie is always orbited by her own cloud of noise. Muffled music blaring from her headphones, shows she's streaming on her iPad, the *clack-clack-clack* as she sends infinite texts.

"Sades?" Edison's muddy shoes squeak against the hardwood. He goes down the hall, knocks on the bathroom door, checks the guest room.

I cross the kitchen and open the sliding door that leads to the backyard. Edison said there was a spare key. If Sadie came by while we weren't here, she might have taken it, stayed for a while, maybe grabbed some money from the change jar to buy herself something at the gas station. This would have to mean she left before the rain clouds formed. She's waiting for the rain to let up before she comes back.

Edison isn't one for lawn ornaments. There are no potted plants or semiconvincing fake rocks. Apart from a capsized patio umbrella, there's nothing but the glazed ceramic toad with a chip in its left eye that looks like the reflection of light. Edison is lucky he lives in a safe neighborhood. I've never seen anyone so blatantly lax about home security.

The key is there where Edison left it, and judging by the outline it leaves on the concrete when I pick it up, it hasn't been moved in a long time. Sadie hasn't been here.

I don't know anything about her friends. Edison says she's shy, but she must have someone. She's always texting when her phone is out. She may have reconciled with her boyfriend, the pushy freshman. I don't know how I'll tell Edison about him. Sadie will hate me and I need her to trust me. I'll need her when it's time for an alibi. But telling Edison something that leads to Sadie's safe discovery—in the arms of her idiot boyfriend—will deepen his endearment to me.

"Jade?" he calls from somewhere in the house.

"The key's still here," I tell him. This will only worry him, but it's for the best, I think. This is one for Sadie's father. Let him go snooping through her things and find some clue that leads him to the boy's house. Sadie's father will drag her out of there by the arm, positively apoplectic, and be the bad guy while Edison remains her knight in shining armor.

Edison turns on the patio light, filling the yard with its feeble orange glow. He's in the kitchen now, pacing as he calls Sadie and listens to her outgoing message. Her phone is off; it doesn't even ring.

I should go in and console him. I've been thirteen and angry enough to run away from my foster placements and group homes. I always came back alive. Edison doesn't know the real story of my life, but I can channel this into something fictional. *One day, my parents were arguing and I ran away . . .*

But the story comes to an end even before I can finish the thought, because my eye has caught something just beyond the reach of the patio light. The fence is locked from the inside, latched by a small black bar. Just below that, in a shallow puddle and filling with rain, is a single neon pink Converse.

I MAKE MYSELF SCARCE before the police arrive. I tell Edison I'm going to take a drive around the block and look for her, and he hands his keys over without question.

I don't want to leave him. His broad frame is sunken, shoulders hunched, and he looks so small standing in the doorway. He watches me as I back out of the driveway. He's holding the phone to his ear and there's a bewildered look in his eyes as he talks to the police. It's happened. It's finally happened. How many times has he told her it isn't safe for her to be out there alone? Doesn't she know a man went missing?

A teenage girl might run off without her phone or her umbrella, but she needs her shoes. Especially in this downpour. Even Edison could see what must have happened. The front door was locked and she was scaling the fence to get to the spare key. Her left shoe, loosely laced and tied, made it over. The rest of her didn't.

There wasn't a drop of blood or a tuft of pulled hair. There were no frantic smeared footprints in the dirt, which tells me that whatever happened was done before the rain started. I know that I won't find her pacing this suburban grid, bemoaning her overbearing father and wearing one shoe. She could be anywhere by now.

But still, I drive to all the places she might be as I turn this mystery over in my head. There are two gas stations in walking distance. One she would have passed on her way to Edison's, the other she only would have gone to if she'd kept walking. The cashiers at both haven't seen her. I hold up my phone with the picture I took of her scrunched against Edison in the diner booth, a bright green silly straw between her lips, and I make them really look. Still no.

I'm parked beside the gas pump with the rain drumming on the roof, and I pull out my phone and search for the freshman high school lacrosse team. It takes a bit of scrolling to find an article that's of use to me, dated four months ago. I scroll through the article about the team's latest win until I find the name Chris. There's only one student on the team with that name. *Chris Byrne stands off with his opponent in the final . . .*

I'm on Whitepages looking up the address of the only Byrne in this zip code. The information is behind a paywall, but the map below it is all I need. A red dot rests on the intersection of West and State roads. I turn the key in the ignition.

Little girls don't disappear into thin air, especially not in a place like Rainwood, where the last reported murder had been in 2001. Before the murder in June, the last cold case was a teenage boy who vanished in 2005. Drugs may have played a factor, his friends said. He probably wandered off into the desert, got lost, and died of exposure.

I find Chris Byrne's house. His parents are loaded. It's a two-story modular with stone facing and a wraparound porch. There are a Mercedes and a Jeep parked beside each other in the white driveway with their mirrors inches apart like two lovers holding hands. The motion lights illuminate one by one as I pass.

Chris's mother comes to the door with the relaxed, pleasant expression of someone who is used to having unannounced visitors. She doesn't even waver when she sees me, wearing a tank top and muddy sneakers, looking like a drowned rat.

"Yes?" she says. "How can I help you?"

"Your son goes to school with my boyfriend's stepdaughter," I say, realizing too late how convoluted all the labels are. I don't care. "Sadie. I was wondering if she's here."

My heart is beating fast, suddenly. Over the woman's shoulder, I can see the light from the dining room and hear the clatter of silverware. It's dinnertime. The entire family is here, and they've been settled in for a while.

"Chris," the woman calls, still maintaining her calm. Why shouldn't she? It isn't her daughter who's disappeared.

The boy from Sadie's summer school appears in the doorway to the dining room. Two younger boys with his same curly hair and slender physique peer out curiously behind him.

"Have you seen your friend Sadie?" the woman asks him.

His expression goes from blank to startled. "Sadie's missing?" His voice is surprisingly deep for his age, but he says the words quietly.

I watch him closely. I look for any sign that he's hiding something. But all I see is the same sudden helplessness I saw on Edison when I left him.

All the Byrnes can do is take Edison's number and promise to call if they see her. Chris is still standing at the threshold when I leave, and the angst on his face kicks up a level of fear that surprises me. He is already thinking the worst.

I thought he had her. She called him and said she was locked out of Edison's house and she didn't want to go home. He rode by on his bike and found her trying to scale the fence and teased her for not being able to make it over. She lost her shoe and he told her to just leave it; he wasn't going to wait all day. She went with him because her young and foolish heart was willing to forgive him. She sat up on the handlebars and together they pedaled off into the sunset just as the first rain clouds started to form.

I realize that this had been my hope. This was it, and I don't know where else she could be.

Or I don't want to believe it. Not yet.

I can't go back to Edison's house. There will be police everywhere. They'll want to ask me questions. They'll also want to know my name. They might run my fake ID.

"Fuck," I whisper. "*Fuck.*"

By now, Sadie could be anywhere. In the trunk of a car speeding toward Utah. Handcuffed to the radiator of a basement thirty miles away. Buried in a mountainside or laughing in a friend's bedroom as they both eat ice cream out of the carton.

I think about how small she is. Ninety pounds at most soaking wet. Sadie wouldn't look at herself in the mirror and see what a predator does. Her emotions are larger than life, her joy and sadness big enough to fill all the empty desert space. But she can't possibly know what lurks out there in broad daylight. The types of people who look for someone exactly like her.

She is to someone what Edison is to me.

It isn't just for Edison that I want to find her, I realize. It isn't just that I want to rescue her and bring her home like an offering at the altar of our love. But it should stop at that. Everything I do in this place should be for him, to deepen our love and to sweeten our final moment. Sadie was only ever supposed to be a tool to utilize, and I shouldn't worry for her. I shouldn't have this desperate, sick feeling about what must be happening to her, how scared she must be, how she's hoping that someone will come for her.

If she's still alive, Sadie has learned something that even I didn't know when I was her age. It isn't just the ones who walk down alleyways at night. It can be the woman pushing a baby stroller in the grocery store, or the man in the three-piece suit waiting for the crosswalk signal to turn. All it takes is someone with an insatiable need, and by the time such a person has chosen you, it's already over.

27

THE MORNING NEWS SHOWS SADIE'S FACEBOOK PROFILE photo. She's wearing a ten-gallon hat, laughing maniacally as someone snaps the photo in the dressing room of the school theater. They show this one even though, from an identification standpoint, it isn't the clearest picture. The dim lighting adds a false strawberry sheen to her yellow hair, and you can see that her eyes are light, but not necessarily blue.

They show it because it captures Sadie for what she represents: a carefree young girl with her life laid out before her. Someone's daughter—maybe even yours.

The church community is more practical. They've taken Sadie's junior high photo—bright lighting, her heart-shaped face in full focus, her gold star-stud earrings visible—and printed three hundred laminated copies. Volunteers are stapling them to telephone poles and every trash can in the parks. This is their contribution to Edison, although it's been six months since he's brought Sadie along to Sunday services, because her father is not exactly president of Jesus's fan club.

Edison hasn't slept. I returned to him last night after a solid six hours of searching. I don't tell him that I tore open the bags of every dumpster downtown. As the rain let up, I pulled over at every ditch, parted a path through every dense bit of shrubbery I could find. Not a single blond hair to be found.

If Sadie is dead, whoever had her was either very smart about hiding her, or very lucky.

Edison has taken a more hopeful approach, calling her friends. Next he called the hospitals and the walk-in clinics just in case an unidentified patient came in after being hit by a car.

Now he sits on the couch beside me as the laughing photo of Sadie is shown for the third time. He knows that if she was safe, she would have turned up by now, and his mind is opening to the uglier possibilities. I can see the change reach his face. He's too pale. His eyes are glossed over. First Sheila, and now Sheila's only child. An entire legacy slipped through his fingers in a year's time.

Sadie's loss should be a gift to me. Edison is malleable, desperate, and I'm all that he has. This couldn't have worked out better for my plan. I should be soothing his pain with my touch, distracting him with sex, telling him that I'm here, that he still has me. If I do this, slowly, his grief will fracture its bones and take a new shape. He'll need me more than ever. I'll be his only light. His oxygen, his purpose.

But when I look at him, it's as though his pain is mine. I can't breathe, the sadness is so crushing.

"Edison, love," I say against his ear. "You should sleep."

He looks at me, startled, like he forgot I've been here for hours. "I can't sleep." His voice is congested, even though he hasn't been crying.

"Let's lie down, then," I say. I smooth my palm over his short curls. "You can't help her unless you take care of yourself."

I stand and pull him to his feet before he can argue. I lead him to the bed and make him lie down. I tug the muddy sneakers from his feet and then sit on the edge beside him. The second I touch his face, he falls apart. All those hours of keeping the dark thoughts at bay have finally burst through his defenses. He sees the things that I began to fear last night. Sadie tortured. Sadie dead. Sadie irrecoverably changed even if we get her back.

He curls up, his long legs drawn, his big hands grasping at my shirt. He buries his face against my stomach and lets out a howl that lances through me.

I gather him to me and I cradle his head in my lap. I listen as he murmurs the words *I promised her* over and over again. The night he went to the coroner's office to identify his wife, they offered him the option of doing it through a closed-circuit television, but he refused. He wanted to go to her. When they peeled back the sheet, by then her skin must have turned waxy and begun to discolor, but he still would have seen the beautiful thing in his wedding photos. Now he tells me that he cupped her cheek. She was so cold. He promised that he would still treat Sadie like a daughter. He would do everything he could.

"You still are," I tell him, rubbing circles along the muscles of his back. "You are doing everything."

"Jade," he murmurs. That name I've used to make him love me. That lie I've given him. He calls for that girl, and I wish that I could be her. I wish that I could stay here in this little town, in this house he's restored, in this bed where we've given ourselves to each other. I wish I could give him decades of breakfasts in bed, and hikes through the Arizona mountains, wild kisses in the rain. My hands in his when we're old and spent.

I wish I could give him this baby. I wish I could tell him that it's there, right beside his head.

Be strong, I tell myself. But I'm not. His pain threatens to undo me. Edison is meant to be a flash of headlights on a dark road speeding by. A moment's fancy. I am not meant to love him more than my sisters.

I press my lips together, afraid of what I will say if I open my mouth again.

My sisters are everything to me. They would dive into a riptide to save me from drowning. They would kneel on the tracks to free my trapped foot with a train hurtling toward us. They live for me and they would die for me, and we made a promise to one another. No lasting loves, only the shared pain of killing our men before they can change us.

After a while, Edison's sobs turn to quiet breathing. He's fallen asleep.

One at a time, I uncurl his fingers that are still grasping my shirt, and once I'm free, I kneel beside him so that our faces are level.

"I'm sorry, love," I whisper, and I kiss his slackened lips. "I can't choose you."

28

WHILE EDISON SLEEPS, I PACE THE LENGTH OF THE HOUSE.
The dusty clock ticks on in the kitchen, and desert insects sing as the
rain subsides.

I hold the burner phone in both hands, cradling it and looking for
any reason not to send the text I've typed out for my sisters: What did
you do?

Sadie is gone, in this quiet town that was safe before we got here.

I wait until the sun begins to rise before I delete what I've typed
and simply ask for one of my sisters to pick me up so I can come home
and shower. I'll have an opportunity to observe them this way. I'll be
able to tell if they've slept and if anything has changed. My sisters are
cunning, but they make mistakes. They're sloppy. That's why they
need me.

Sure thing, sister dearest, is the reply. I can tell it was sent by
Moody. I can practically hear the playful glee in the words.

Iris pulls into the driveway fifteen minutes later. "Good morning, sunshine," she says as I climb into the passenger seat. "How's your Prince Charming holding up?"

There are bags under her eyes. Her hair is drawn into a ponytail, and I can see that she's slicked it down with water. She's covering up the small fringes of hair that frame her face when she's been sweating from doing something labor-intensive. The pale blue nail polish on her left index finger is chipped, and it looks like she's tried to scrape her nail beds clean with a thumbtack.

There's a long strip of gauze running from her wrist to her elbow, pinned down with medical tape. The blood has seeped through and stained it brown. And even before Iris says a word, I know that she's behind whatever happened to Sadie. I know that Sadie used the box cutter I gave her to fight back, and that she lost.

Iris notices me watching her. The green in her eyes shifts, and I see what her victims see the moment before she goes in for the kill. Her sweetness disappears quick when something sets her off.

"A child goes missing in a small town, she's not out somewhere catching butterflies," I say. My sister and I circle each other in the bloody water like sharks in the womb. "There hasn't been a single murder or missing person for years in this town, and we show up and there are two."

"Three," Iris corrects. "You're forgetting the stunt your friend pulled."

I don't let on how much it hurts to be reminded of Dara. Iris is testing me to see how I'll react, and this outrages me anew. The time to grieve Dara is over; my sisters gave me two days. Two days of letting me cry and blame everything under the sun—them, myself, even Dara. And if it hurts, it's my own fault for loving her when I knew I couldn't keep her.

I don't take the bait. Iris, the queen of clean breaks, would be disappointed that I've been so messy with my heart since we've come here. Even now, she drives at exactly the speed limit, hands at ten and two, unaffected by all that we've done. "What did you do?" I ask. "Edison's stepdaughter wasn't part of the plan."

"No?" Iris's tone is dulcet. "Then I'm sure she'll turn up."

"It was you," I say. I didn't want to believe it. Last night, I turned this entire town upside down looking for that little girl. I held Edison as he cried. I waited, hoping that she would mysteriously appear like bits of glittering sea glass. I even hoped that, if the worst had happened, there was another serial killer roaming the streets. Anything but this.

"We don't kill anyone without discussing it. Isn't that the rule?" I don't let my voice betray a single thing. I speak to my sister as though we're going over the rules of a simple board game, but inside I'm alight with rage. If Iris hurt that girl—the stepdaughter Edison is at home crying for—I don't want to think about what I'll do.

Iris slams the brakes and we both lurch violently forward. There's nobody on the road, but even if there were, I don't think it would matter to Iris. She's the center of the universe when she's riled up enough about something.

"Sissy, you are on dangerous ground. Tell me that you understand."

All four doors lock with a loud click.

"Iris." I'm not sure whether I'm warning her or trying to save myself.

"Think carefully about the next words that come out of your mouth, little sister," she says. "Moody and I are the only ones who will protect you. You think that boyfriend of yours wouldn't go to the police if he knew what you are?" A car comes up behind us and wails

283

angrily on the horn. Iris doesn't take her eyes off of me. After a few seconds, the car peels off with a loud squeal, horn blaring anew. "He doesn't love you, Sissy. He doesn't know you. He's never even heard of you."

She's right. He doesn't know the nickname my sisters call me—the very one I call myself in my own head. He doesn't even know the legal name that's on my birth certificate—the one I sign on bank statements and tax forms. He doesn't know about the child I was, the nightmares I've clawed through, the messes I've cleaned. He doesn't know one thought in my head.

He fell in love with Jade. Uncomplicated, clean, churchgoing Jade, who would make a great wife and mother someday. There have been hints at a darker side. That day in the church when he tasted me, his fantasy about the lake. But still, I know these are innocent games to him, that he would never harm a hair on my head. That the real me would frighten him.

"I know," I say, because I want Iris to stop looking at me in that way I've always hated. She can see the real me, and in this moment, I hate that person.

"Sissy." She touches my cheek, giving me a taste of that motherly approval I'm secretly desperate for. "You think I don't want this life for you? I do. But it isn't us. It just isn't."

I nod, and then I force my thoughts to turn numb the way that I learned to do when I was small, when there was no use working myself up because there was nobody to console me.

"Just tell me if she's alive," I say.

There's a candlelight vigil at eight o'clock, and Edison will need me. He's not strong enough yet. His sobriety is on the line, and I'm the only one who can make sure he doesn't ruin everything he's worked for. I want him present with me at the end, not drowning in

Jack and weeping over Sadie's grave. I want the memories I keep of him to be strong and whole.

"You know what you need? A nice walk," Iris says. She resumes driving. "We'll get some fresh air into your lungs. Give you some time to think."

"Iris." I put a lifetime into those words. It's as close as I've ever come to begging with her.

She smiles, bright enough to make up for the absent sun on this dreary overcast day. "We're going to take a walk, Sissy."

Only after she says this do I realize that I've missed a critical detail. She's not wearing Lisa's wedding band. She would never make a mistake like that. Iris is smart and deliberate, and if she didn't leave the house as Lisa, it's because she already planned to take me someplace where we wouldn't be seen.

The thing inside me seems to know that we're in danger. A wave of nausea overwhelms me, and Iris says nothing when I roll down the window. She doesn't even slow down as I hang over the frame and vomit onto the street that speeds below us.

I don't ask Iris where we're going. I don't plead. I have been in the back seat as she's led her kills to their destinations enough times to know that it will do no good. I'm not one of the men she's loved. I want to believe that she won't harm me, but for the first time in my life, I'm not sure.

"Dara?" I make myself ask.

"Dara killed herself."

"Bullshit, Iris."

"I know you don't want to hear it, but she didn't have the stomach for what she did," Iris says. "You could clean the blood, but you couldn't fix what was broken in her head."

Iris didn't know Dara the way that I did. The Dara I remember was strong. She stands tall in my memory, defiant. She withstood everything Tim dealt her, and when she at last realized the danger she was in, she plunged a knife into his chest.

But Iris's words give me pause. I cannot remember a time when my sisters have ever lied to me. I have seen my sisters at their ugliest. I've picked up their broken pieces, just as they've done for me. And Iris is right—Dara did turn fragile at times. It took only the slightest reminder of Tim for her eyes to fill with tears. Guilt for killing such a vile man, I couldn't relate to. All I could do was remind her that she was strong. Sit with her as she downed cup after cup of black coffee and held her cigarette in trembling fingers.

Believing that Dara took her own life means admitting that I failed to stop her.

Iris senses my grief, even though I haven't said a word. She can just feel it, the way I've felt hers since we've come here. She picks up the bottle of water that's sitting mostly empty in the cup holder and hands it to me. "You'll feel better if you drink something," she says, in that placating way that makes me remember she loves me.

The water is lukewarm, the plastic heated from being in the sun, but it's better than nothing. For thirty minutes, neither of us speaks. I know we've left Rainwood when I no longer recognize the horizon. Storm clouds roil overhead, and very faintly a voice in the radio sings "Dream a Little Dream of Me" . . .

Iris pulls over at a stretch of barren wilderness that leads to a mountain trail.

"It's going to rain," I tell her. I don't know why I expect this to change anything, as though we can turn around and go home if the weather is bad, and she won't show me whatever she's dragged me out here to see.

"Good. The weather will be cool." She unlocks the doors and gets out.

We passed a gas station two miles back and there's been no sign of civilization since. My legs feel rubbery when I step out onto the pavement, and then Iris takes my hand. "Come on," she says. "There's something I want to show you."

"You've been here?" I ask. If I can keep her talking, eventually her tone will give something away. If she's overly chirpy, I'm in trouble. But while she's this unreadably calm, it could mean anything.

"I needed something to do," she says. A drop of rain lands on my nose. We reach the base of the trail and I hesitate. If I scream, nobody will hear me. If I run, Iris will be faster. She always is. I have a box cutter in my pocket, beside Jade's phone. I can't reach for it now or Iris will see that I'm carrying it.

I only stop for a second, but it's enough to make Iris's eyes flash. I start walking again, and together we move along the jagged rocks and brambles. She puts her hand on the small of my back and it takes effort not to flinch. "Do you remember when I had meningitis? When we were nine."

Elaine got a call from our social worker. I'd never heard the word before in my life, but I was worried for Iris nonetheless. Elaine wouldn't let me visit her because the hospital was three hours away and it was the start of the school week.

"Moody ran away from her group home to visit me," Iris says. "It was after hours when she got there, but she made herself cry and the nurse said she'd let us have five minutes."

I've never heard this story. Iris barely spoke about her time at the hospital, said she didn't remember it. I didn't know that Moody was ever there at all.

"I was really sick," Iris goes on. She takes a broad step over a jutting rock in the trail. "I could barely speak, but Moody laid down on the bed next to me and said it would be okay. She sang 'Beverly Hills' by Weezer, and when I fell asleep, I had a dream that we were walking through Hollywood Boulevard. I got better after that. She holds us together, Sissy. More than you realize."

"Iris." I stop walking. She's five paces ahead before she realizes and turns around. "Cut the bullshit, okay?" My voice is soft, not angry. "What is this about?"

She smiles, and it's a distracted, wistful smile, like my words have endeared me to her.

"I adore you, Sissy," she says. "But I don't trust you. Neither does Moody. You've kept too many secrets."

"How can you say that?" My head feels light, and I think I may be sick again. I lean against a boulder and focus on breathing. "I've cleaned up every mess you've ever made."

"But you haven't made your own mess," she says.

"Is this about the last time?" I ask her. "I told you. He didn't feel right."

"It's about this time," she says. "I don't think you're going to do it. You have three more months to go, and I think you're going to try and keep him."

I think of Edison writhing under me as I stop him from drawing a breath. His still body lying flat on the kitchen tiles as I undress him and fold him so his limbs will stiffen that way. Rolling the industrial trash bag into the dirt and covering it up.

It's been weeks since I've let myself think of it, and now I realize it's because I hate the woman who will do this thing to him. When that woman puts her hands around Edison's throat, I want to lunge for her. I want to kill her, not Edison.

Too late, I let the hesitation cross my face and Iris sees it. The sadness in her eyes is almost enough to knock me over.

"That isn't true," I say. It's a weak lie, but I say it with conviction.

"Then why haven't you gotten rid of his baby?" she says.

There it is. "How long have you known?"

She doesn't answer. I don't know why she's brought me here. I don't understand. But I know that something is waiting for me at the top of this trail, and that it's something bad.

Iris takes my hand in the same impenetrable grasp as when we were five and the social worker was prying us apart. She starts marching up the mountainside and I stagger after her.

As we round the corner, the rain picks up and the sky goes deep gray. There's something bright in all the gloom. Crumpled in an alcove, a yellow-and-white dress, splattered with mud, being worn by a teenage girl with pure terror in her eyes.

"Sadie!" I run for her, throwing Iris off me. My sister doesn't try to stop me.

Sadie crawls away from me, pressing her back against the rocks and whimpering hysterically against the cloth gag tied over her mouth. Her hands are bound before her with strips of cloth expertly tied. Iris is still where I left her, not visible from Sadie's line of sight, and that's when I realize Sadie has no idea there's more than one of us. Whatever Iris has done to her, she did it as Jade.

"Sadie." Her name is all I can think to say in my shock. I kneel down before her and peel the gag out of her mouth. It falls limply down her neck. "Sadie, it's all right. I won't hurt you."

"Are you sure about that?"

When I look up, Moody is standing over me, Iris at her side. They're wearing identical white T-shirts and shorts. Sadie looks at them and then at me, her breath coming in panicked gasps.

She's seen all three of us now. No one who sees all three of us when we're on a hunt lives to tell the tale.

I stand to face my sisters. "What is this?"

"A test," Moody says. There's a .22-caliber revolver in her hand, black with a silver barrel. "More like a gift, really." She takes my hand and lays the gun flat in my palm. I've never seen it before, but I know that it must have belonged to Montana, collector that he was.

"We weren't supposed to take trophies," I say. "Your rule, remember?"

"New rule," she says. "To call it even, you can have something that belongs to the girl. Her earrings, maybe."

Sadie has gone deathly silent, her teary eyes fixed on me.

I keep my finger away from the trigger and aim the barrel at the ground. I've always hated guns. They're too easy to trace. Serial numbers, bullet types, fingerprints. A body will decompose, but a gun will survive being submerged at sea or buried in the deepest grave. "I'm not going to kill her, Moody."

Iris is eerily quiet now. She fixes me with her unreadable gaze, letting Moody take the lead for once.

"There's one bullet in the chamber," Moody says, in that same soothing whisper she used when she was lulling me to sleep in our group home. "Kill her. And then bury her, and go back to your boyfriend and take him to the candlelight vigil."

Sadie is hearing all this, and I know that something has just happened that can't be undone. I always thought that the price for betraying my sisters would be that they would lock me out of our little trio and leave me behind. But instead, they've come up with a test so brilliant that I didn't see it coming. If I let Sadie go, my sisters and I will all go to prison for the rest of our lives. Sadie will tell the police what we've done and what she overheard just now. Our identities will be discovered. Our photos plastered all over the news until the families of the victims we've left behind see and recognize us. Life sentence upon life sentence, or death penalty. The three of us will fall together.

Or I can kill her. An innocent child who was never meant to be more than a tool to help me get what I want. Her life will be the price for the rest of my days with Edison. As he sobs in my arms, as he hangs missing person photos, I'll hold him with the hands I used to kill her.

"Jade?" Sadie murmurs. She's stopped crying now, her fear too overwhelming for her body to know what to do with it. I don't look at her. I look at the gun.

Only now that I feel the weight of it in my hands do I realize what my sisters already know. I was never going to kill Edison. I can wait in the car while Iris strangles her lover with a bra. I can clean the blood Moody smears all over the tiles. But it's not because I want to. It's because I love my sisters.

"We talked about it after you left, and we decided this approach was best," Moody says. She means that she wants us to take the serial killer angle. Sadie, Edison, and the man in the truck all found dead on a hiking trail.

"Sissy. It's time to kill for us." She talks in a soft voice even as she says these awful things. That's the way it's always been. Moody showering me with love so that I'll scour the blood and bury the bodies she makes. Moody soothing Iris, kissing her cheek, working her up when it's Iris's turn to kill. It's Moody who keeps us together. It's Moody who keeps me from being free.

"No," I say. A word I realize has been trapped inside me for years.

"You were right," Moody tells Iris. "She is just like you."

I stare back at them, confused. It wasn't long ago that Iris told me that very thing, and I still haven't been able to work out what she meant. Even now, my sisters don't let me in on their secret.

There's heartbreak in Moody's eyes, and she reaches for the gun but I step back, keeping it away from her. I fire the shot into the wilderness, and then I pull the trigger again, but Moody was telling the truth; there was only one bullet. There was only one opportunity for me to redeem myself to my sisters, and I've thrown it away.

"You shouldn't have done that," Moody says, sadness in her voice. Not for Sadie, but for me, and for what she knows this is doing to my heart. "A bullet would have been more humane than what we'll have to do to her now."

I grab Moody by the shoulders and throw her down the shallow embankment off the trail. She stumbles through five feet of brush, screaming with outrage.

I don't realize I'm going to speak until suddenly I'm howling. "Tell me what you did to her!" I don't mean Sadie, and she knows it.

Moody tries to claw her way up the embankment and I kick at her. She grabs my ankle and pulls me down with her, both of us tumbling through the weeds and grasping at each other, growling like tigers in the wild. I get her on her back and she stares up at me, panting, her eyes gone dark.

"Tell me." Spit flies out from between my bared teeth. "Tell me the truth."

"She was weak," Moody says. "You were too blind to see it, but I followed her one night when she went on one of her drives. Do you know where she went? To the police station, Sissy. She got out of the car and paced up and down the sidewalk."

"She wouldn't have gone in." My own words feel far away. There's a hairline fracture in my heart threatening to spread and shatter all of me to pieces.

Some of Moody's edge fades away, and she says, "She was going to do it eventually."

"You . . ." I can't find the rest of the words, though I'm sure that they would be ugly. Violent. Hateful. Some part of me has always known, the way that my sisters knew about my doubts with Edison and the baby growing inside me. There's a sameness to us, even in times like this when I hate it, when I hate my sisters so much that I wish I could drain all the blood I have in common with them and become someone new.

I read the coroner's report. Dara died of a fentanyl overdose. There were no suspicious bruises, no signs of foul play.

"How?" My voice is cracked, hoarse. With everything laid bare, I know Moody will tell me the truth. When it comes to her kills, at least, she does.

"She had already taken one when I went over there," Moody says. Her voice is barely a whisper because she doesn't want Sadie to hear. "She was half-asleep on the couch, and she looked at me and she said, 'You're not Jade, are you? You're Lisa.'"

The thought hurts and warms me at the same time. Dara knew me well enough to recognize me, even in her haze. I don't move, don't say a word, because I know that this is the only chance I'll get to hear the truth.

"She asked why I was there," Moody goes on. "I told her that I was going to make it stop hurting. I drew her a bath, and she climbed in, just like she was getting into bed. I fed her the pills, and I was gentle, Sissy. I stroked her hair and I told her that it would be over soon. I think she understood."

I can see it too clearly. Dara, pliable and heartsick, trusting Moody because she had a kind face that looked like mine, and because she said nice words, and because she was something sweet after so much violence.

I won't let myself cry. I won't let Moody see. But it's no matter—she already does. "Sissy," she says in that honeyed voice she must have used on Dara, "it was for the best."

The scream starts deep within my chest and explodes out of me. Only then does Iris intervene, prying me away before I can do something to Moody that I'll regret, something that can't be undone. She's my sister; some small whispering voice reminds me that there's nothing more important than this. But the louder voice comes out of me as a rabid cry, and I see the briefest moment of shock in Moody's eyes, not because she thinks I'll hurt her, but because she can see how much she's hurt me. More than she thought was possible, because I cared for Dara—someone who wasn't family, someone who should have been nothing—more than should have been possible.

If Moody can break my trust, then I can break hers too. I tear away from Iris and run for Sadie and press my phone into her hands. I work frantically at the knots around her ankles. She kicks and writhes, trying to help me.

"Run and call the police," I tell her. She stares back at me, wild, breathing hard, wondering why I would help her and if she can trust me. "Go!" I tell her, and she snaps out of it and scrambles to her feet.

Iris only watches, and I think I can hear her let out a sniffle, but I don't have time to look at her. I don't have time to think about the consequences for what I'm about to do. Sadie's left foot comes loose just as Moody grabs at her. But Sadie is surprisingly quick.

I grab Moody's legs and she falls, hard, on her stomach.

"You don't know what you've done!" she roars, and there's so much frustration in the words, like I've just set all our lives on fire. Maybe I have, but only because she forced my hand.

"Yes." I climb onto her back, pinning her arms. "Yes, I do."

Iris grasps at my shirt, trying to pry me off of Moody, but I dig into Moody's wrists with my nails, unrelenting.

Iris lets go, and then moments later, the cloth that was binding Sadie's ankles is around my throat, tighter and tighter in Iris's fists until I can't get any air. She's played this game with me before, but it's different this time. I've never felt this much desperation, this much anger. She hauls me to my feet, and I'm only distantly aware of Moody scrambling out from under me and then taking off after Sadie as the thunder booms and the rain turns riotous.

I grasp helplessly at the cloth, trying to ease it up even an inch, even just enough to draw the littlest breath. I know that this too is futile. I've seen my sister at work. Men twice my size haven't been able to fight her off. She kills her victims from behind and it only occurs to me now that she does this so she won't have to see their faces, their shocked, gaping eyes staring back at her through the veil of death. Reconciling with the aftermath is my job, but who will come to clean her mess if she kills me now?

Iris. The sky is getting dark. My arms have gone numb, and I reach feebly at my throat before my hands fall like deadweight. I don't blame her for hating me because I let Sadie go, but I could never have believed I'd be one of her victims. The strongest sister, the bravest, the one who raised hell to teach us how to survive.

She lets go of me and I collapse to my knees. I hear my ragged gasps before I feel the burn of air stabbing its way back into my lungs. Dizzy, vision tunneling, I claw at the mud.

Iris drops to her hands and knees beside me. She peels back the curtain of my hair so she can see me.

"You don't want to kill him," she says. It's not a question. "Tell me the truth."

"No," I cough, my voice raspy. "I don't want to kill him."

The words are such a relief to say out loud. All the images of Edison decomposing beneath an Arizona suburb dissolve like water going down a drain.

Iris takes my face in her hands. I flinch, but she's gentle. "I tried to spare you from having to kill him," she says.

"That's why you wanted us to leave," I say, finally understanding. "When you saw our kill on the news."

Her thumb brushes the curve of my cheek. She gives me a wistful smile, and there's so much love in it. "You shouldn't be with us," she says. "You should run off to someplace where Moods and I can't ruin your shot at happiness."

She wasn't going to kill me, and she didn't make a move to stop me as I freed Sadie and handed her my phone. She didn't betray me. She betrayed Moody.

I don't have time to ask her why. I start running down the trail after Moody; if she hasn't caught up to Sadie, there's still time to stop her. The rain obscures my vision, and I slide on the wet ground, but I keep fumbling my way down the mountainside, screaming Moody's name.

For what feels like an hour, I stumble through the brush, my voice raw, vision compromised, wet hair clinging to my face. I'm lost. "Moody!"

I know I've somehow made my way to the bottom of the trail when I see the police lights flashing. This is also how I know that Sadie managed to escape.

Someone grabs my arm, reeling me back behind the giant shrub at the mouth of the trail. I turn and am immediately face-to-face with Iris.

"Moody got away," she tells me. "The police aren't going to find any of us if we're smart. We can split up."

"And then what, Iris?" I ask. I'm so tired. My legs ache. My head is fuzzy from lack of sleep. I've spent all night searching for a missing girl, and all morning trying to save that same girl from my sisters. To know that Iris and Moody would do this has changed something in me—something that I know can never be fixed. I never thought that my sisters would test my loyalty, but that's what they've been doing all my life, isn't it?

I couldn't love Elaine because being adopted into a new family would betray the family that I had with them. I couldn't call Colin my brother because he wasn't my blood but they were. I couldn't tell them about this baby because there's no room for it in our trio, just like there's no room for Edison. There's no room for anyone or anything but them.

"Run if you want," I tell her. I don't want to kill Edison. I don't want to be any of the names on our pile of unused IDs. "I love you so much, sister. But I'm done."

When I step into the flashing lights, I know that this marks a seam in the map of my life. I'll never be able to go back to the moment before this decision.

I don't know what will await me. Aiding and abetting. Accessory after the fact. Unlawful imprisonment. Desecration of multiple corpses. Once my photo is on the news, I may even be blamed for murders my sisters committed; with both of them on the run and unable to testify, the county sheriff will need a witch to burn for his bid at reelection. Whether the murders were committed by me or one of my identical sisters, I'm the warm body they'll have, and I'll do just fine.

Sadie is wrapped in a blanket in the back of a cruiser, talking to an officer who leans against the open door. She's safe. She'll go back into the waiting arms of her father. Edison will be so, so happy. That little brat who broke her heart will be grateful too, and maybe he'll treat her better—not that she should give him the chance.

I'll never see Edison again. The thought is too big for me to stop and consider now, but I know that the decision has already been made. If I ran with my sisters, he would hear the story from Sadie and piece the rest together on the news. And if I turn myself in, he won't want to visit me. He'll hate me either way. He'll still love Jade for a while, mourn her—not me—until she fades away and he finds a worthy woman to love.

A floodlight blinds me; a muffled voice shouts through a megaphone for me to put my hands up, and I do.

I don't know where Moody and Iris have gone. They could be crouched behind the shrub to my left, or halfway across the desert by now. They may have split up and will use their burner phones to plan their rendezvous in New Mexico.

I may never see them again. Another thought I'm not strong enough to face just yet.

And then I'm not alone. I know my sisters by more than just sight. I know the way their footsteps fall, the way they breathe, smell, approach. That's how I know Iris is the one to grab my arm and try to pull me back into the wilderness with her. It took all my strength to leave her, but it turns out she isn't strong enough to let me go.

Another shouted command. "Put your fucking hands up!" But she doesn't. She thinks she can evade them the way that we always have.

"Iris," I hiss.

"Don't turn yourself in!" she cries. Her voice is trembling. All of her is. "You're going to ruin your life, and you're the only good one, you idiot!"

But it's too late, and I don't get a chance to say this to my sister before the first shot is fired.

One second, Iris is beside me. The next, she's lying at my feet.

It is as though someone has reached into my chest and ripped the breath right out of me.

I'm frozen. The entire world gone still. There is nothing beyond this blinding glow of the police light, and the rain, and Iris's blood spilling out onto the dirt. My breath hitches, coming in shallow gasps, and my hands are still up over my head.

When the scream comes, it's my voice, but I'm not the one who made the sound.

Moody comes running out of the shadow of a giant boulder in the distance.

"Hands up!" the same voice shouts, and the fact that she listens is enough to make me believe there is a God. I'm grateful to whatever entity has compelled my stubborn sister to listen, because I can't lose her too.

Over the squall I think I hear Iris make a sound. I can't be sure if she moved, or if it's just the flashing lights playing tricks with her shadow.

I'm too numb, too startled, too drained, to do anything but oblige when someone handcuffs my wrists behind my back and pushes me forward.

"She's innocent!" Moody is screaming from where she stands, someone else pinning her wrists. She'll say anything to stop them from shooting me, now that she's seen what they did to Iris. "She didn't have anything to do with it!" She's still shouting as the officer pushes her into the back of a cruiser. She's begging him to let me go, to check Iris for a pulse. She's saying, over and over, that this is all her fault.

We're locked into the backs of separate cars, and we both watch, helpless, as an ambulance speeds up onto the grass and the paramedics sprint over to Iris. I don't know where she was shot. I don't know if she's alive. I don't know if she can hear Moody—but I do. As my car starts to pull away from the scene, I press myself against the glass and I see Moody's red and teary face looking back at me. We're five years old again, being ripped away—this time for good.

29

I DON'T TALK WHEN I'M BROUGHT TO THE INTERROGATION room. Not even to ask for an attorney. I ignore them when they ask me if I'd like something to drink, something to eat—even though I feel like I'm about to pass out. This pregnancy has ruined my stamina, and maybe if I told them that I was pregnant, they would have to bring in a nurse to make sure I'm okay. But I sit in silence, staring at the wall, until the interrogating officer finally gives up on me and says, "Take her back to holding."

Then, and only then, do I say, "I want my phone call."

I'm brought to the sheriff's office. He leans back in his swivel chair and lifts the corded phone off of the receiver. "Number," he says.

"Five-five-nine—"

"Out of area's going to be a collect call," he says. "You sure your person will pick up?" I nod. I give him the rest of the number and he hands me the receiver. The recording asks me to say my name clearly so that it can patch me through. And then it connects.

I haven't called him since I was with my sisters in Montana. I told him I was in Niagara Falls. I said it was beautiful and that I'd send him a postcard. I never did. Now he answers on the first ring with a sleepy "Hello?"

"Colin." My voice cracks. "It's me."

"Hey." He's awake now. I hear a rustle. "Where are you? I thought the operator said you were calling from jail."

He calls me by my name and I recoil at the sound of it, feeling exposed. I've always hated it. It's meaningless, issued to me by a faceless state employee because my mother didn't think to give me one. But Colin says it with so much affection, because it's the name of the troubled little foster child who helped him put worms in his brother's shoes and told him scary stories as we huddled under a blanket fort in the living room.

"I don't have long to talk." I swallow my grief so that he won't hear how upset I am. "I'm in La Paz County."

"Where the fuck is that?"

"Arizona. Listen to me. I need that lawyer, the one who helped you the last time." I hope he knows what I'm talking about, because I don't want to list his bevy of possession charges in front of the sheriff.

"Is this because of your sisters?" he asks. "I told you. I told you they were going to get you arrested or killed. The three of you are like a goddamn coven when you're together."

I close my eyes, tears squeezing out. "Please," I say.

"Yeah." He says this like it should have been obvious to me. "The lawyer's my next call. I'm on the first flight out there, okay? Don't say anything. Don't even tell them if you've got to take a dump."

I nod, even though he can't see me. It's all that I can manage.

"It's going to be all right," he says. "Whatever it is, it can't be worse than the shit you've dragged me out of. We'll fix it."

I DON'T KNOW HOW much time passes. Minutes. Hours. I curl up on the metal bench in the holding cell and drift in and out of a fitful sleep. Voices all around me, metal doors slamming, a loud cackle like a vengeful ghost.

Was it only this morning that I held Edison for the last time? He came undone in my arms, and I was the only one who could soothe him. Now I dream that he's here. He walks right through the metal bars and kneels before me. *They told me what you did,* he whispers. *I forgive you. I still love you.*

His face is blurry. No matter how I try to focus on him, he evades me.

I need to get to my sister, I tell him. *She was bleeding.*

Edison doesn't answer me, and when I reach out to touch him, he dissolves into nothing.

"West," a voice bellows, and I wake with a start. West is my last name, because my sisters and I were found at a rest stop on the west end of State Route 99. There's a lieutenant shuffling a key into the door and then sliding it open. "Get up," he tells me. "Your charges were dropped. You're free to go."

30

THE WEST TRIPLETS IN AN UNDATED PHOTO.

At the top of the article is one of the only pictures of my sisters and me together. We're eighteen, arm in arm and smiling in a blurry photo that a reporter has taken off Elaine's Facebook profile. It's our high school graduation and Elaine hosted a party in her backyard, even though she never fostered my sisters and didn't especially like them. They were bad influences, she would tell me. But she took my letters for them to the post office. She handed me the phone when they called, because in her own way Elaine loved me despite my efforts to shut her out.

Below that photo, my mug shot and Moody's. I look dazed, my eyes fixed straight ahead. I don't even remember having it taken, processing was such a blur. But Moody stares at the camera in defiance, jaw clenched, eyes red with old tears.

From the article, I learn that Moody has admitted to the kidnapping of a Rainwood teen, whose identity is being withheld due to her age. Iris was taken to a hospital and her condition is unknown. All three of us were famous for being abandoned at a rest stop in 1999.

The article goes on to say that I was cleared of any wrongdoing. Sadie told the police that I was the one who saved her. And whatever Moody said in her own confession must have corroborated it.

Both my sisters are staring down the barrel of life imprisonment when they go to trial. And even then, this is the best-case scenario. There's no mention of all the bodies that have gone missing in our wake. No one has discovered the fake names. Prior to our processing, our records were clean. I scoured every crime scene and made sure there wasn't a single fingerprint to enter into the database.

But it's only a matter of time. Our photos will make the national news. Someone will recognize us, call the police because we were dating their cousin's aunt's brother, or a neighbor, or a friend.

It's over. Those were the words Moody said to me on our first day here, right after she knocked out the trucker with a tire iron. They killed him to protect our secret, and it's all going to come out anyway. It was always going to, I realize now. All those years of blood and of rage and of bodies had to float up to the surface sometime.

Over.

In the silence of the empty apartment, I've had plenty of time to think about Edison's murder. I would have climbed on top of him in the heat of passion. I would have looked into his eyes and seen the vulnerable, wild love he shows me only when we're alone.

And I wouldn't have been able to do it.

I love my sisters. I would walk into a fire for them. I have cleaned all their messes. But when I was finally tested, I discovered that I wouldn't kill for them. That I have never wanted to do anything but protect them, even as it slowly killed any promise of finding happiness for myself.

When Colin's flight touches down, he takes a cab to my apartment and finds me curled up on the couch. I'm spent from hours of sobbing. For my sisters. For Edison. For all those years of living a lie, and the violent, bloody relief of letting those false identities go.

Colin comes to me the way that I always did for him: without judgment, without anger. As a friend—no, a brother. He kneels beside the couch and peels the blanket away from my face. "You're looking rough, kiddo," he says, and I snort with an unexpected laugh.

"I'm so fucking glad to see you," I tell him.

"Been a while, hasn't it?" he says. "I read the news on the plane. Kidnapping doesn't really sound like your idea of a hobby."

Even though his tone is light, I catch his meaning. He flew all this way to help me, and he can't do that unless I tell him what's going on. So much of our friendship has depended on not asking too many questions. I didn't ask where he'd been all night when he snuck back into the house at three o'clock in the morning. He didn't ask me why I needed so many fake IDs, or why I never told him where I was going when I left the state for a year at a time.

I brew two cups of tea before I settle in to tell him the story. "Sorry. It's all we have," I say. "There's no coffee."

"I quit coffee," he says. "Caffeine was making me too jumpy. I'm trying to cleanse." He says it with a flourish, like he's trying to make me laugh.

"I'm proud of you," I say. "At least one of us is holding it together."

"What are you doing in this dump?" When he talks, he calls me by the name I never use; the one I left behind when my sisters and I first fled California. Every time I hear that name, I replay some lost image from my past. Being shouted at by someone in a group home. Writing it on my drawings with red crayon. Hearing it murmured by my first boyfriend just before he kissed me. There was a time when I felt some connection to it, but now it's like a ghost. "Where have you been on and off for the past six years?"

In this moment, I wish that my foster brother wasn't in recovery and I wasn't pregnant, because this would be so much easier if we were both drunk.

I start with Iris's boyfriend. The skewer in the back, the pieces of his body still submerged in the San Joaquin. Our pact I made with my sisters, only I call them by the names he's familiar with. I tell him about the mark I couldn't kill, and so Iris did it for me. The gallons of peroxide. The fake identities.

Last, I tell him about Edison. The way I tried to be like my sisters, only to realize that all that passion and that painful longing were love. Just plain love.

Colin sits like a statue through all of it, not betraying even a flinch. His mug is empty by the time I'm through, and my own tea has gone cold in my hands.

He looks down at his mug and then at me. "Why didn't you call me?" he says. "That first time, with the guidance counselor boyfriend. I would have helped."

"You would have called the police," I say.

"No," he says. "I would have gotten you out of there."

A fierce protectiveness rises in me at the thought. I belong with them.

Even though I don't say this, Colin sees the change in my expression. His tone shifts, like I'm the little foster child I was when we met. "You have never been like them. You tried, and you're still trying. But you're just not."

"You don't know them like I do," I say. "They're my family. They would do anything for me."

"That theory is about to be tested," Colin says. "They're both in hot water right now, and they could strike a plea deal if they throw you under the bus and help police solve those cold cases you cleaned up for them."

I want to argue that my sisters won't do this, but I can't be certain. Before this morning, I wouldn't have ever thought my sisters would kidnap an innocent child just to test my loyalty. I wouldn't have thought I would fail, or that I'd still feel so certain I'd made the right decision—even as one of them sits in jail and the other in the hospital.

"You won't tell your attorney about any of this, right?" I ask.

"Of course not," Colin says. "He's waiting for my call. He'll fly out whenever you say the word."

"I need to talk to my sisters before I do anything," I say. I called the hospital the second I was released from jail; they handed me my burner phone in a brown paper bag, and it was the only one I had after giving Sadie my smartphone. All the nurse could tell me was that a patient with my sister's name had been admitted, and if I wanted to know more I would have to speak to the doctor in person. I asked three different times if she was alive, if she was *sure*, until she finally lost patience and hung up.

Colin doesn't say anything, but I can feel his exasperation. He takes the mug from my hands and brings it to the kitchen sink. He can't understand this feeling—no matter what my sisters have done, they're a part of me. If they had run off to New Mexico, or Iowa, or Canada, two sharp identical pieces of my own self would be missing.

The car that my sisters and I were sharing is gone, likely evidence in the ongoing investigation. I'm not worried about it. They won't find anything damning. Covering our tracks is what I do.

Once I was sure the police were done combing Dara's apartment, I snuck into the laundry room. I put her money in the front pocket of a hoodie with the name of her brother's college on it. I know that he'll find it when her family comes to collect her things, and she would want him to have it.

Colin says he'll help with anything I need. He arranges for a rental car to be dropped off, and he uses his own credit card and refuses the cash I offer him in exchange. He calls me by that name, and after enough times, the name stops feeling strange to me. Less of an invasion, more of an old friend returning to my memory.

"You could come back to California." He broaches the suggestion without force, like he's merely suggesting we go to the movies. "Mom has been trying to find you. I didn't tell her you're here. She's afraid you're dead." The thought of Elaine typing my legal name into a search engine, reading police logs and obituaries looking for me, tugs at a piece of my heart I pretend not to have. The part that has always longed to be somebody's daughter.

I stare at my lap and will myself not to break down. Colin doesn't press the issue. Exhaustion finally overpowers me, and my foster brother doesn't wake me when I fall asleep mid-conversation on the couch.

When I open my eyes again, it's morning and the sun is beaming in through the window. I realize I've never seen what this room looks like in the daylight because we've always kept the curtains closed. But now the yellow light casts a certain cheer over the hideous outdated furniture and fixtures. It's nice—I think—to let the light in.

I shower, dress, make myself eat something. This place feels too quiet, even with Colin rattling around in the empty space.

When I grab the car keys, he says, "I can't talk you out of going to see her, can I?"

Although we look nothing alike and we've never shared a womb, Colin knows me well. That's part of why I've avoided him so much in the past six years, ever since Iris killed her boyfriend and our ritual began.

"No," I say, because however the world might judge us for it, my sisters and I will always come back to one another.

"They could have gotten away, you know," I tell him. "They would be safe and free right now, but they came back for me."

"Hey." He bridges the space between us in two steps. "Your sisters aren't free because they kidnapped someone and told you to kill her. They belong in jail. You *are* free because you wouldn't do it."

Colin frowns at me, and in his expression, I see the truth that he's trying to drive home. I know, logically, that this is true. But the arguments rise in me anyway. *You don't know them. You don't understand. My sisters need me. I need them.*

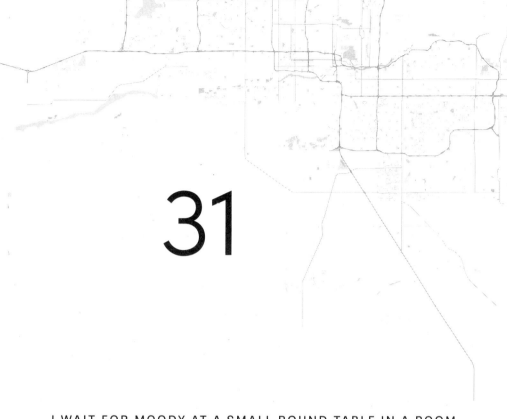

31

I WAIT FOR MOODY AT A SMALL ROUND TABLE IN A ROOM with concrete walls. There are several tables all around me, waiting for inmates and their visitors to occupy them, but for now I'm the only one here.

The door opens and Moody is escorted in, her ankles and wrists cuffed. But even in the restraints, there's a confidence in her stride, her chin cocked, eyes bright. There's an angry bruise purpling her left cheek, and her knuckles are swollen.

"Nice job lying low," I tell her.

She sits across from me. "Oh, please," she says, after the guards have moved to stand by the door, away from us. "You can't take anyone's shit in here. Otherwise you'll get knocked around."

I can't hide my anger. "I'm trying to get you out of here," I say. "I've got an attorney who's willing to meet with you, but not if you get time added to your sentence by starting fights."

Her fingers twitch, and I think she's going to reach out and take my hand. But then she remembers the handcuffs, and the guards watching us from ten feet away. "Sis." Her voice is so soft I can barely hear it. The playful gleam in her eye disappears, and she turns sober. "I'm never getting out of here."

"The kidnapping charge will be bad," I tell her. It's the truth and it's good that she knows it. "But there's a chance—"

"I'm not talking about that," she says. "I'm talking about the other things."

I start to speak, but before I can open my mouth, she glares daggers, warning me to stay silent. The words die on my tongue. *I protected us. Even when our photos make the national news, there's no DNA. There's not even motive. Only coincidence. People go missing every day.*

But Moody was right to silence me, because as I play the words in my head, I realize they're only a form of denial. Even if I cleaned every drop of blood, even if I secured our alibis, circumstantial evidence has put people away for far less than what we've done.

"They know about the guidance counselor," Moody says, not using the man's name. I don't know if she even remembers it. I do. I remember everything. "His wife saw our mug shot. She knew about the affair."

Iris is my next stop, just as soon as the hospital visiting hours begin. I think of her, lying helpless, God only knows in what condition. She's fighting for her life, and if she makes it, she'll only end up spending it in prison.

A new determination rises in me. I can protect Iris the way that I always have. It will be harder this time, but that just means I'll need to be more clever. "What do you need me to do?"

Moody smiles. It's a sweet smile, and it only lasts a moment before her guard goes back up. "How could I have ever doubted your loyalty?" she asks. "You really would follow us right into the depths of hell."

I want to remind her that she and Iris will always have me. I'll always love them, always protect them, even if they had tried to kill me up on that hiking trail rather than Sadie.

But before I can say any of this, Moody says, "I told them it was me."

A loud throbbing fills my ears, and I realize that it is the sound of my own heart thudding hard and slow in its shock. I think I whisper the word "Why?" *Why the hell would you do that, Moody? Why would you give up already? Why would you take the fall for a crime that wasn't even yours?*

She is looking at my face, staring at me as though I'm the most treasured thing in the world. "Because it's the truth," she tells me. "Because I was jealous. That bastard was ruining Iris's life, and I wanted him dead."

"Stop that," I say. "Iris wouldn't want you to take the fall for her."

Moody doesn't answer right away. She listens to my breathing, which has started to come on a little faster. She waits for me to understand, and then she says, "You know that you're my favorite, Sissy. I'm telling you the truth."

"You didn't," I rasp.

"I wanted us to stay together." There's a crack in her voice. And in this moment of vulnerability, I see the Moody who's been lost to me since we were children. The frightened little girl who was forced to live with strangers when all she wanted were her sisters. "That's all I've ever wanted," she says. "And now I'm the reason we can't."

"Yes, we can," I tell her, ferocity steeling me. I can fix this. I always find a way. I reach across the table and take her hand. A guard takes a step closer, gruffly tells us there's no touching. A snarl begins in my throat, but Moody pulls out of my grasp. She doesn't want me to incur their wrath.

She squares her shoulders. "Get yourself out of here. Don't fuck this up. Iris is facing a lot of charges and she may be screwed no matter what we try to do, but you still have a chance."

If more victims' families come forward to say their friend or their relative dated one of us before he disappeared, they'll have no way of knowing which one of us it was. If Moody takes the blame, they'll believe her. But back in Fresno, it was a poorly kept secret that Iris was sleeping with her guidance counselor. Ironically, the one murder Iris may be accused of is the one she didn't commit.

"Ten minutes. Time's up, Amelia," the guard says. Moody flinches at the use of her real name; hatred flashes in her eyes. It brings her back to a time she would rather leave behind for dead. But neither of us moves. My stunned eyes meet hers that are full of heartbreak, and defiance, and unflinching truth.

She stands only when the guards haul her from the chair. I watch her shuffle in her chains.

"Don't bother writing. I won't read a word," she calls over her shoulder. "Have a nice life, Sis." To the guards listening, it will seem like a brush-off. But we both know what the words mean. She's taking accountability for the path she led us down. She held us captive for all these years, and she can't undo it; she can't even save Iris. But I'm the only one of us who broke the rules and refused to kill my victim. I still have a chance, she said. But only if she lets me go.

32

I DRIVE FOR THE HOSPITAL, DAZED.

The night Iris called me after her lover's death, she was hysterical. She didn't tell me what happened, but when I stepped into the apartment, I could smell the blood. I could feel the weight of the terrible thing that had happened.

Iris couldn't look at him. She was curled up in the hallway with her back to the wall, blood all over her hands and shaking.

Moody had rage in her eyes, and she only softened when Iris ran to the bathroom and started throwing up. While I dealt with the body, Moody drew Iris a bath. She sat on the edge of the tub and talked softly to her and made sure every last drop of blood was scrubbed off her skin.

Iris was despondent, nearly catatonic, until we made her snap out of it when it was time to dispose of her lover's remains. In that moment, she had looked so powerful, I'd thought. She had made a tremendous and terrible decision.

But now I look back and I see the frightened nineteen-year-old girl she was. I see the grief that I missed in the heat of the moment back then. And I see new meaning to the wrath in Moody's eyes. Moody was an impulsive teenage girl made angry after a lifetime of watching her sisters being hurt and suffering. She was tired of being powerless. She was tired of what the world had done to us. All those broken hearts. She had no tolerance for this man who had Iris wrapped around his finger.

We were only children—how could we have ever believed we were more than that?

It was Moody. It was always Moody, held captive by her anger. Her resentment for the world beyond our little trio. Her desperation to keep us together. Now she's alone, and this is too big. I can't save her.

By the time I make it to the hospital, visiting hours have just begun. A nurse tells me that Iris just came out of a lengthy surgery the night before, and she's fragile.

This is not a word I ever thought I would hear used to describe Iris. She stands the tallest and proudest of us all. She's the most tenacious. But now everything is starting to come to me in a new light. She would attack us, challenge us, demand that we fight back. If we broke free of her grasp, she rewarded us with pride. If we couldn't, she let us go and she demanded that we be stronger next time. Begged us.

She never talked about that night with her first lover, no matter how many times I asked. She never talked about so much of her life when she was being kept away from us.

Iris is being charged with her role in the kidnapping. Sadie—now in the protective custody of her father—has already expressed willingness to testify against her whenever there's a trial. Sadie also told the police that I was the one who set her free, that I had nothing to do with the abduction. I read all this in an article on my phone, and I do my best to prepare myself as the nurse leads me to my sister's room. But seeing Iris's wrist and ankles cuffed to the bed still tears at me.

Kidnapping can carry a life sentence, and I don't know what Colin's attorney can do for her when he gets here. All I know is that I'll stay here as long as it takes. I'll help her any way that I can, even though we're out of places to hide.

The bullet shattered her skull. It was a seven-hour surgery to remove the fragments, and the nurse tells me that she regained consciousness for a few minutes this morning, which is encouraging. When I take her hand, her skin is pale against my own. When I squeeze, she doesn't respond in kind.

I bring my face close to hers and whisper, "Iris, I'm here."

They shaved the hair from the left side of her head, and in its place is a row of angry-looking stitches.

She lets out a small moan and then her eyes open. Dull, cloudy green, almost glowing in the fluorescent light. I don't realize how much I've missed her until I see the recognition come to her as she looks at me.

"Hey." I brush my fingertips against her face.

"Fuckers . . . broke my skull," she rasps. Her voice is strained, her mouth chapped from hours of intubation.

"Yeah." I laugh, hoping she won't sense that I'm trying not to cry. "But they're going to fix it."

She closes her eyes for a long moment, and her body deflates with an exhausted sigh. "Moody?" she asks.

"Moody told me the truth," I say. She's white as a ghost, and I rub warmth into her cheeks with my thumbs. "That idiot confessed to everything."

I don't have to explain what I mean; Iris knows. When she's well again, I'll ask her why she took the fall for her first lover's murder. Why she let me go on believing she was the one who started us on this path. But for now, all that matters is that she's here with me. She's the one sister that I can still protect.

"I was so—so mad at her," Iris says. "She did it so we could be together." She snorts. Look how that turned out.

Moody killed Iris's lover. When I found Iris that night, her sobs weren't of guilt or shock, but of true grief. The kind I feel when I think of losing Edison.

"Don't hurt him," Iris says, reading my thoughts. "You'd never forgive yourself." She jabs her finger against my heart. *You're more like me than you realize*, she told me only a few days ago.

I'm shocked by how liberating the words are, as though she's just handed me a key. "I was afraid to tell you," I say, my voice strained. "About Edison. I thought you'd call me weak."

Her throat rattles when she lets out a feeble laugh. "Nothing takes more strength than loving someone. Especially for us."

"Why did you go along with it?" I ask. "Why did you kill the others?"

She closes her eyes, and I think she's falling asleep, but then I see a tear squeeze out from behind her lashes and roll down her cheek. "Because Moody was willing to kill for me. She loved me that much. I wanted to show that I loved both of you too."

She can barely stay awake, but she fights it. I try not to let on how scared I am. I need to be strong for her. But the gentle tone and motherly touch were always Moody's talent. Moody is impulsive and reckless when she's out in the world, but with Iris and me she has always been practiced. Cunning and manipulative under her gentleness. But this morning, she finally let us go, and that's how I know her love was never an act—even if so many other things were.

"Sis—"

"Rest," I say, pleading. "I can't save her, Iris, so you have to get well. It looks bad for you legally, but I can fix this."

"Moody was scared that you'd run off with him and we'd lose you," Iris says. "But I told her that would never happen because you love us way more than you should."

What would have happened once I decided to let Edison live? I would have spent one final night with him and tiptoed out while he slept. I'd have retreated to my sisters in shame, begged them to forgive me. I would make it up to them, vow to clean all their messes until we're in our nineties, do anything they asked. Anything but kill the man I love.

Iris is right. I would have abandoned Edison, not them.

Iris sees the conflict in my face and she curls her fingers around mine. "It's time to stop cleaning our messes, Sissy. Let go. You're too good for us."

Tears, traitorous and heavy, fill my eyes. Iris never spoke of the horrors she endured in her group homes and foster placements, but as the years went on, I saw the hardness that she cultivated just so that she'd survive. She pushed Moody and me to be strong, to be ruthless, so that nobody could ever hurt us. It was the only way she could protect us.

I still remember the child she was. I remember all the times she saved my life just by loving me. "You're good too," I say.

"No." She says this with her familiar stubborn certainty. "Maybe once. But not anymore."

I don't have words for how much I need her, and so I say nothing when she squeezes my hand. I'm not going to fly out of Arizona and leave her and Moody here, no matter what they say. If Colin's attorney can't keep Iris out of prison, I'll find her a better one. I'll deplete our life savings if I have to.

But I've never had to say a word around Iris. She fixes me with her usual scrutiny, and she can read every thought in my head. She can see the future that I'm laying out for us. A fresh start. Someplace we've never been, with four full seasons. Lush white blizzards in the winter and bright colors in the fall. When the baby comes, she can help me raise it, the start of a brand-new trio. We'll be better people this time, like who we might have been if we'd had a better start. Iris smiles at me, and it fills her weary eyes up with life again.

Then her hand goes slack in mine, and her head lolls to one side. "Iris?" I hear the alarm in my voice before my panic reaches the rest of me. Her eyes fix, pupils dilated, and even before she shudders, I know that something is wrong. I'm already screaming for the nurses by the time the beeping on the heart monitor turns frantic.

When the first nurse rushes into the room, she tries to pry my hand out of Iris's, but I don't let go. Not Iris. She's the only one I have left.

"Iris, please." I say the words too softly for anyone to hear, but I will them into her. I beg her to hear, to fight her way back to me. Her eyes roll up, revealing a glazed white. Her lashes flutter and her shaking turns violent. The veins in her neck bulge. Her skin turns an angry, strained red, like her lovers when she tightened the garrote. She makes a choked sound, a pitched whine that she would never make if she were conscious because it sounds too much like a plea.

The human body is intricate and complicated. There are a thousand things that can go wrong after a surgery. A blood clot the size of a grain of rice could travel to the brain, the lungs, the heart. Distantly,

I'm aware that there are more hands prying me away. I hold on the way I did when we were small; I fight the way that she did that awful first time we were torn apart. She bit, scratched, kicked like a child possessed, because she loved us. "Samantha!" The nurses call her by the name she abandoned years ago. "Come on, Samantha," and "Stay with us, Sam."

I don't struggle anymore when they shove me into the hallway. I don't cry out for her, because I know that she can feel me just as surely as I feel her in this moment, all fight and chaos. With my back against the wall, I can still see her through the open door. Iris, the most powerful, the strongest of us all. Her wrist is cuffed to the metal railing of the bed, and her body jolts from their efforts to bring her back. The monitor screams, and the sound turns long and flat and unchanging. Her muscles go limp. Her skin is pale like the sharp glint of a blade in the moonlight.

They're trying valiantly to bring her back, but I feel how futile it is. There's a pull as a third of my heart is ripped away. All of her life flashes through me—angry and beautiful and full of hope; what was, what could have been—fast and bright like a train through a tunnel.

"Stay," I sob. "Please stay."

But she doesn't, and for the first time in my life, I know what it is to be alone.

33

FOR DAYS, IT HURTS TO BREATHE. I SHUT MYSELF IN THE bedroom, arguing when Colin tries to make me eat, barely dragging myself into the shower.

Moody refused my visit even after the chaplain told her about Iris, and of all the things she's done, this is the one I can't forgive. I stood outside the jail, screaming at her even though she couldn't hear me. I called her a coward, a traitor, a terrible sister, and then no sister at all. I said that I wish she had died instead, and in that moment, I meant it. The guards dragged me away when I started crying. They left me on the sidewalk outside the chain-link fence, blubbering helplessly like a lost little child. When I came back to our rented condo and saw Iris's unfinished knitting project in the basket by the couch, my knees buckled.

I think of everything Moody cost me. Things I gave up willingly to try to fill the bottomless well of her sorrow, her jealousy. When I was a child, I had a chance at happiness with my foster family, but I fought them. I said cruel things I didn't mean to Elaine. I snuck out at night, flunked classes I could have passed in my sleep. I made her hate me so that she would give me up and I wouldn't carry the guilt of living in a nice house while my sisters bounced like pinballs from one nightmare to the next.

"She isn't your mother," Moody told me. We were six years old, crouched in the tall grass that surrounded the pond in Elaine's yard. "That makes her bad."

Iris sat between us, gently stroking the papery wings of a dead moth she'd found in the dirt. Bits of it flaked onto her fingers, and as she watched it fall apart, she grew angry and her face went red. She plucked the wings off, leaving only a husk of a body, exposing how small and insignificant the thing really was.

"Say it," Moody told me. "Say that Elaine is bad."

"She's bad," I said. "I hate her."

But my hatred wasn't for my foster mother. It was for whatever force had decided I could see my sisters for only a handful of hours every few weeks. I hated the moth for being broken. I hated my bedroom for having only one bed. I hated our real parents for not loving us. I didn't want to hurt Elaine. I didn't want to hurt anyone, but I was horrible to her anyway. I did it so that Elaine wouldn't want me. And then, I thought, Moody, Iris, and I could be together. Even if we were only united in our misery, it was something.

In the end, all of it was for nothing.

Colin stays, even though I tell him he should go back and that my mess isn't something he should have to clean up. He tells me, "How many times did you wash the puke out of my sheets? Who called 911 when I ODed?" and then he finds something to do, like vacuum or brew us some tea. He calls me by my real name, not Sissy. There are only two people in this world who called me Sissy, and they never will again.

Colin is something familiar and comforting, even as I try to reject him. I don't know who I am without Moody and Iris, and it perplexes me that I can still stand upright at all, that I'm expected to find my way alone. I don't want this.

Edison doesn't call, not that I would answer even if he did. He and Dara were the only ones who had that number, and without them my phone is little more than a paperweight. I let the battery die.

A week after Iris's death, I see Moody for five seconds on a livestream on my laptop as I lie in bed. *New murder charges in the case of a Rainwood woman accused of kidnapping.* She's handcuffed as she stands in the courtroom for her arraignment, her bruise faded now. Her jaw is clenched. The judge asks her how she pleads to the charges of murdering the man whose remains were recently found on a closed-off hiking trail. Through the camera lens I see what the rest of the world does: a remorseless killer. A kidnapper. A woman who is never going to be free.

She pleads guilty. She knows details not released to the public—that his teeth were shattered and what he was wearing. She says that she and Iris acted together and that I had nothing to do with it. As though I was some imbecile who didn't know she was living with two serial killers.

Colin sees the same broadcast on the TV downstairs, but when he comes to check on me, I pretend I'm asleep. He fits a blanket around me and leaves a sandwich on the nightstand. He doesn't say anything, but he presses his hand against my shoulder before he leaves. I'm not alone, he's telling me. You don't have to share a womb with someone to love them like a sibling.

We'll have to get out of this town. It's small, and the media has already begun to descend. But he hasn't pushed me. I know that if I had let my sisters see how much my foster brother means to me, he would have ended up like Dara. I've known this since even before that first kill. I knew something awful would happen if any of us tried to have a family outside of our trio.

I listen to him moving about downstairs, and I can see the lines and shadows of a life I could have had. A prettier life. A free one. But in this moment, for all the ugliness and destruction they've wrought, I only want my sisters.

Take the freedom, you idiot. The voice belongs to Iris, and to Moody, and to me. *Better late than never.*

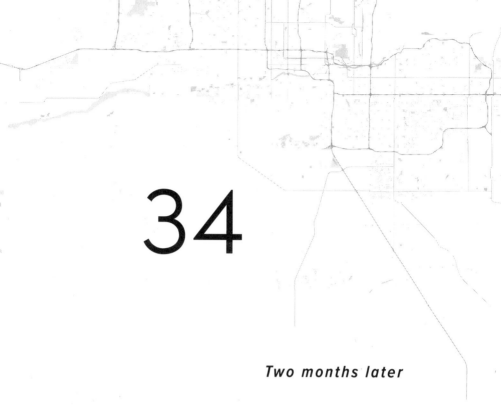

34

TRUE TO HER WORD, MOODY WILL HAVE NOTHING TO DO with me. My letters are returned, torn open and stamped by the jail staff, with no indication that she has read them. I sent my latest letter a week ago, the ink dark and bleeding from the force with which I pressed the pen into the paper. It was one sentence long:

> *At least help me decide where to scatter her ashes, you selfish bitch.*

But Moody's silence says more than any words could. Iris is dead, and she blames herself. If she hadn't tried so hard to control us, maybe Iris would be off making terrible love decisions out there with another man Moody and I both hated. Maybe she would be a dentist, a famous singer, a chef. Maybe she would have robbed a bank and gotten herself killed anyway. The torment is in all the things we'll never know.

But my life, Moody can predict: if she stays out of it, I'll get to have one. So, when my letters come, they stab her through the soul. She sees my name there on the concrete floor of her cell and it reminds her of everything that's ruined between us—everything that could have been. It hurts her so much it steals her breath. This is the cross she will bear for the rest of her life, and her only redemption is to let me go.

Maybe that's why I send them, knowing they'll go unread. Because this pain will never go away, and I want to make sure she feels it too.

When we were together, I could hear my sisters in my head so clearly, narrating my conscience, telling me what to do, their will so tangled up in my own that I never knew which ideas were mine. The clarity in their absence brings little solace now. I stare at my own face in the mirror and I don't see a fake identity. I don't see one-third of a whole. There's a stranger I'm still learning, and the only messes left to clean up are my own.

I left Rainwood the day after I saw Moody's arraignment, got into the rental car with Colin and drove two hours away from anyone who might recognize me. The media was relentless for days. The famous West Triplets took a dark path. They forgot about us for all those brutal years when we were left to the foster system, but now that we were entertaining again, they brought in some TV psychologists to speculate where it all went wrong.

But just as quickly as the hype came, it disappeared. I knew it would. My sisters and I were babies when we first became the subject of the limelight, but there's always a more exciting story around the corner. A toddler who falls down a well, a set of quintuplets born to a couple who thought they were infertile, a little boy who flatlined and swears he met God.

I return to Rainwood on a Sunday evening, when I know all the upstanding members of polite society will be home for the night. Edison's car is already here, parked on the shoulder near the ten-mile marker, and empty. When I called him last night after nearly two months of silence, I wasn't sure what he would do. He picked up on the first ring even though I called him from a blocked number, and even before I heard his voice, I knew he'd been waiting for me.

I see him when I park my rental car in front of his. He's high up on the dirt path that leads to the new housing development. Standing on his would-be grave.

He turns when he hears the car door open and stands with one hand shielding his eyes from the brightly setting sun. From here, I can see his guarded expression, the way his lips press together when he sees my stomach. Four months, a half-moon in my pale blue shirt. I didn't tell him about this part. But he doesn't speak as I make my way toward him.

We stand arm's length apart, and I can hardly believe he's real and that he was crazy enough to meet me after everything I confessed to him last night.

His hand hovers over my stomach, some magnetic pull, an instinct that overtakes him before he remembers himself and draws back.

"Everything you told me last night, and you didn't think to mention this?" There's no anger in his voice. He's learned how to protect his emotions, giving just enough to let me know he's in there, but not so much I can read him as easily as I once could.

This is a skill learned while we've been apart. He was dragged into the media spotlight too; a news van camped outside his house, he told me during our call. Took photos through his blinds. Every time he jogged from the door to his car, a coat over his face, someone asked him to speak up about the accusations against his girlfriend, who had gone MIA.

"I was afraid you'd feel like you had to come if I told you about her," I say, bringing a hand to my stomach.

"Her?" At that, something within him cracks. A bit of light coming through the veneer.

I nod. I only first went to a doctor last week when I thought the media scrutiny was gone and I'd found someone who wouldn't have seen me on the news, or remembered me if she had. "There's her heartbeat," the doctor said, changing the trajectory of my entire life without even looking up from the screen. "Nice and strong."

"She's mine?" Edison's voice is dazed, and I can see that he wants to touch me, wants to touch the place where our baby's heart is beating.

"Only if you want her to be," I say.

"Of course I want—" Edison starts, but cuts himself off. He remembers that I'm not Jade. That the woman in his bed all those times was a stranger. But not entirely. There's some part of me he recognizes. Some part of me that he has always loved and still does.

The housing development is much further along than I remember. The support beams for most of the houses have gone up, sharp skeletons against the setting sun.

Now Edison stands before me and I focus on a bright blue vein in his throat. It recedes into the abyss of him, and I want to reach out and trace it. I want to feel his heart thudding against my fingers.

I look at him and he stares back at me, both of us wary. But the strangeness between us isn't unpleasant, and for the first time I think he sees the real me. Not Jade. My face and name have been all over the news, and he's heard what the reporters have to say about my sisters. I'm the mysterious one who has been cleared of all charges, who has never been implicated in a single crime. Moody has begged the media to leave me alone, screaming from the courthouse steps at the journalists and cameras that she and Iris did everything.

It's true that I'm not a killer. I couldn't even do it for my sisters. If I had been able to, Sadie would be buried in a hillside and Iris and Moody would still be here with me. I replay that day over and over in my head, but I make the same decision every time. I can't stop Iris and Moody from making theirs.

But I'm not as innocent as Moody tells them. I have hidden their crimes, watched in silence as their victims struggled and slowly died with their eyes pleading with me. I have destroyed evidence. I have been a half dozen different girls in a half dozen cities, and I wish I could say I was haunted by the things I covered up, but I did it because I loved my sisters. I would burn this world down to nothing if it would save them.

I called Edison because I had to confess to someone. I needed someone to know the real me, even if I'm still learning who that is. Moody and Iris would have been livid that I was telling him these things; they would have said that I was throwing my chance away. But the more I ignore their voices in my head, the more I start to hear my own.

I told him the whole ugly truth of our serendipitous meeting in the church that first day. The thoughts lurking in my head when I sang "Ave Maria" for him. I told him my real name. I told him why we'd come. The fantasies. The burial site. The revelation that I couldn't do it, and that it still terrified me to be so different from my sisters even now.

He was silent through all of it. He could have hung up, I thought, and called the police. Driven to my new apartment and shot me through the window. Told me he never wanted to hear my godforsaken voice again. I wouldn't have blamed him.

There was a long pause through the line, and I could hear him breathing. I could feel all the space and stars and cell towers between us. Then, in a quiet voice, he said, "Show me where you were going to bury me."

We're both standing over the spot now. He looks down at my stomach, and then at me. "When would you have done it?"

"New Year's Day."

"How?"

"In bed, I think." I meet his gaze when I say it. We're both tentative, but some undercurrent churns within our silence.

"Why here?" he asks.

"I thought it was pretty." I nod past his shoulder to where the cacti and brush are silhouetted against the fading golds and emerging blues of night. "Peaceful."

He turns around to see the desert beyond the development, and I think he sees what I do in all that vastness.

"You're pretty fucked up," he says.

"Yeah." I touch his hand, and he doesn't pull away. He doesn't flinch. When he looks at me, I wonder if there will be revulsion, or fear, or anger. But instead I see the beginnings of a smile.

"I wouldn't have been able to do it, you know."

"I wouldn't be here if I thought you would," he says.

When he reaches out and touches the curve of my cheek, I don't dare move. I don't breathe, afraid that he'll dissolve to ash the way he has a dozen times in my dreams since I last saw him.

"It's nice to meet you," he says. "Really meet you."

"You aren't afraid I'm like them?" I say. Although I know I'm still on fragile ground with him, I have to be sure.

"You could have killed her." He means Sadie. "No one would have found out. You would have been able to get away with all of it, but you saved her." His thumb traces my lip and then moves to tuck the hair behind my ear. "You saved me."

When I look at Edison now, I don't see the man who entered the diner that day. There is no sinister love that ends in destruction, and a new picture starts to form:

To the world outside, we'll be like everyone else. We'll dress up on Sundays and we'll go to church. I can offer voice lessons online. He can repair anything that breaks. When our daughter comes, he'll worry about her with the same tortured love he's shown for Sadie. He'll say the girls in his life will be the death of him, but he'll do anything to make us happy. We'll live in a modest house in a peaceful suburb. But sometimes, he'll look at me from across a crowded party and wink. I'll bite the cherry off the tip of my toothpick. Inside us both, there will linger an edge that comes out only when we're alone. A full, dark desire in his brown eyes. A razor-thin sharpness to my smile. His hand tightening at my throat, my nails digging into his shoulder. I'll tell him all the ways I could have killed him between our kisses. We'll tally up all the people who've wronged us and whisper the ways we could get away with it if we really wanted to. He'll tell me that we're so lucky to have found each other.

There's no promise that this will come to pass, but in this moment, all that matters is that he's here and he's alive. It's the best place to start.

For now, there is only a future as blank and clean as the Arizona desert sky, and the daughter we made beneath its stars. There is only Edison, and me, Emily.

Acknowledgments

This story is the light at the end of a very long and very dark tunnel. The nature of being a writer is to live every moment waiting to be visited by that first sentence that changes everything. The moments before and between those sparks are ugly. You wonder if you'll ever get there. By saying this, I hope I can convey how deep my gratitude is to those who saw me at my worst, who read pages and pages of shitty drafts, talked me through years of downward spirals, and held me up when I had nothing to offer in return. The ones who believed in me when I thought I'd never get there. I'll never know what I did to deserve the love of these humans, but I can tell you this story wouldn't be here without them, and neither would I.

Thanks infinitely to my massive extended family. But especially to my parents, who never tried to make me be something I'm not, and who told me to go for it whenever I talked about my dreams.

Huge, huge thanks to Aprilynne Pike: You're hilarious and wise, and you've seriously read All My Things. Christine Munger: You've also read All My Things since college, when we lived on waffle fries and your burned CDs, and for this I'm hugely grateful; hopefully I'm better at writing than I am at making microwave macaroni and cheese. C. J. Redwine: Thank you for spending hours upon hours on the phone listening to all my ideas and offering such warmth and wisdom. Also, thanks for calling me at midnight to tell me I'm a genius. I'm not, but it felt nice to hear it.

Beth Revis: Thank you for being one of the first friends I made in this big, wide industry over a decade ago, and for all the love and humor and coffee you bring. You came into my life at the time when I most needed a friend. Thank you for knowing all my stories—the ones I've written and the ones I've lived.

Harry Lam, who has been reading my stories since we were in ninth grade: You're my Person. Thank you for being there. For loving me. For knowing me.

Sabaa Tahir: Where would I ever be without your wisdom and advice? Mewling sadly atop a pile of candy wrappers in a dumpster behind a Walgreens, for sure. Friends like you come along once every thousand lifetimes, and even then, only if one is very lucky.

The world's largest gratitude to my agent, Barbara Poelle, who has been on this publishing Tilt-A-Whirl with me since 2008 and still hasn't kicked me off for some reason. I still don't know how I lucked out this much, but I continue to be grateful.

Jen Monroe! I couldn't have asked for a better editor if I were given a magic wand and told to dream one up myself. Thank you for believing in this story and grabbing it up before any other editor had a chance to read it. Your energy and creativity are what made this story what it is.

Thank you to the ENTIRE team at Berkley—those I've met and

those I haven't—for taking a chance on this story and working so damn hard to bring it to readers in the best way possible.

Thank you to everyone who has shown me any bit of kindness, love, patience, or time. These acts are gems. Thank you to the readers who found me during my time in children's publishing and followed me this far; you've done more for my heart than I can ever say.